FLOOD OF DESIRE

When the knock on the door finally came, Patricia was standing on the landing halfway up the staircase where the stairway took a bend. She leaned heavily on the dark mahogany banister and looked as alluring as she knew how. Not only did she have on the sultry wrapper and gown, but she had purposely left the wrapper open, tied only at the waist, to reveal the daringly low cut of the gown underneath.

"Come in."

Cole thought it was strange that she had not greeted him at the door, but then decided she must not be ready just yet. His eyes went immediately to the vision of the remarkable beauty that stood before him. He blinked. She was definitely there and dressed in what had to be the most enticing outfit he had ever seen.

Patricia had not counted on the reaction her own body was going to have upon seeing him again. An urgency to touch this man had flared inside her. Why not punish him further! She slowly walked toward him, and when she stood directly in front of him she reached out and ran a gentle finger across the crisp texture of his shirt. She was dismayed to discover that in doing so, she had kindled intense desires of her own. Desires that made her wonder what it would be like to make love to this man, right here, right now . . .

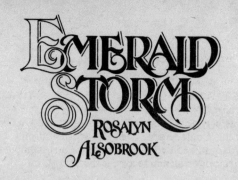

EMERALD STORM
Rosalyn Alsobrook

ZEBRA BOOKS
KENSINGTON PUBLISHING CORP.

ZEBRA BOOKS

are published by

Kensington Publishing Corp.
475 Park Avenue South
New York, NY 10016

First printing: August 1986

Printed in the United States of America

This book is lovingly dedicated to my husband, Bobby, for all the love and support a woman could ever want.

Author's Note

Although *Emerald Storm* is purely a work of fiction and the major characters exist solely in my imagination and do not fully represent anyone actually living at that time, the events involving the Johnstown flood of 1889 are presented as accurately and honestly as possible according to the extensive research I have done into the terrible disaster and the incidents that led up to it.

Special Thanks

I would like to express a special thank-you to all the following people and institutions: To Dad, for keeping back copies of *The American Heritage* in his personal library which is where the initial spark for this story came from; To Mom, for letting Dad keep all those old copies despite their growing lack of space for books; To The Upshur County Library, for acquiring a copy of *The Johnstown Flood* by David G. McCullough from the Dallas Library system and letting me devour it for three weeks; To Margaret McClelland, for loaning me her personal copy of *History of the Johnstown Flood* by Willis F. Johnson, which was written just months after the disaster happened; To The Johnstown Flood Museum Association, for sending me a brochure that had the most detailed map of all my resources; To my Granddaddy Harry Rutledge who also kept old books and had an old copy of *The Johnstown Horror* by James H. Walker, which was also written just months after the flood occurred; To Jean Haught and Patricia Rae Walls, for their expert input; To Catherine Creel and all my other writer friends who kept encouraging me and helped me face an early deadline; To Becki Reid, Shane Jackson, and Ruth Cohen, for answering some of the strange questions that occurred at the oddest times through the course of this book; To Editor Hilari Cohen, for choosing this book over all the others; To my sons, Andy and Tony, for waiting as patiently as they know how for Mother to finish "just one more little paragraph."

DRAWING OF FLOOD ROUTE

North Fork Little Conemaugh

South Fork

Lake Conemaugh

South Fork River

Mineral Point

Viaduct

Conemaugh

Little River

East Conemaugh

Woodvale

Johnstown

Stony Creek

Kernville

Cambria City

Morrellville

Conemaugh River

Prologue

June 2, 1889

Low rumblings of distant thunder threatened to unleash yet another merciless downpour onto the already rain-soaked Allegheny mountain area. The deep rolling cadence haunted the dreary gray heavens with its baleful discord—like the sardonic laughter of an elusive demon who lurked nearby hoping to feast upon the misery and heartache it had bestowed on so many.

Weary to the point of exhaustion, a tall young man made his way to the crest of Prospect Hill. Ragged and worn, he fought the slippery mud of the rain-drenched hillside. An unseasonably cold wind spat haughtily in his face and his mud-soaked clothing hung heavy on his back, but he was near his destination. He could not stop now. With unlagging determination, he pressed on.

For nearly two days the young man had struggled against the swollen rivers and fought his way around heavy landslides and dangerous washouts in a desperate effort to reach Johnstown and make sure that his beloved wife was safe. Every muscle in his body protested each movement he made, but he had to find her. He had to keep going. Sinking at times in mud drifts to his knees, he continued on until he reached the crest of Prospect Hill and was finally able to see Johnstown below, or what little was left of it.

Appropriately, the rain fell again only moments after he

had gotten that first glimpse of the morbid destruction—
Johnstown. The sight was far worse than he had anticipated.
Staring down in horror at the hideous valley below, his
stomach knotted and sent a blistering bile up to his throat. A
putrid stench of decay and ruin railed his senses, causing him
to gasp for breath. Tears filled his hollowed eyes and his
worn and bleeding hands trembled as he looked down upon
the death and desolation with a despair that gripped his very
soul.

Throughout the valley before him was a vast sea of mire
and twisted wreckage. Telegraph poles, giant pieces of
machinery, chunks of houses, bent rails, shredded trees, torn
carriages, crushed railroad equipment, countless household
items, and mangled corpses of both humans and animals
were strewn everywhere. The two fawn-colored rivers that
usually flowed in from the surrounding Alleghenies and
formed the Conemaugh River at the lower end of Johnstown
were now a sickening gray black in color and the filth-filled
water had collected to form a small encrusted lake at the west
end of town. Hundreds of people moved about the ruin,
searching through the large heaps of wreckage and mud.
Huge piles of the debris burned in scattered locations, but
the largest fire was near the old Stone Bridge at the far end of
town.

The smoke was too thick for him to discern just what was
burning at the bridge, but it was massive whatever it was.
Towers of black, gray, and white smoke rose and blended
high in the air, despite the continuing downpour of chilling
rain. Beyond this huge bridge where the Cambria Iron
Works usually whirred with activity lay the corpse of a
ravaged iron mill with its huge smokestacks toppled over, its
equipment crushed, and one of the largest buildings little
more than a pile of brick and rubble.

It was a heartbreaking sight. Entire streets had been
obliterated; whole buildings swept away by the angry wall of
water. Few buildings remained along the valley floor. From
the distance of Prospect Hill, he could see that the Methodist
Church and the B & O depot still stood where they always
had, as did Alma Hall, the Union Street School, the Adams

14

Street School, and the Presbyterian Church. Even a few houses had withstood the onslaught of water but even so they all showed signs of severe damage.

Gone were the breweries, saloons, hotels, library, opera house, and the night school. Gone was the park where he had proposed to his dear Kate and gone was the roller rink where they had spent many a happy hour. Also gone was the gaily painted trolley where he had stolen his first kiss from her and she had pretended such outrage.

How many times had they been warned? For years people had been told the dam was faulty but no one had listened to such prophecies of doom. Even he had scoffed at the idea. No one had wanted to believe it was possible, and now nearly all of Johnstown was destroyed. Where once stood a thriving city of over ten thousand there now lay a ravished wasteland, torn and shredded beyond belief. That it was even the same place was hard to comprehend.

No. This had to be some sort of ghoulish nightmare. Surely he would wake at any moment to discover he was still aboard the Chicago Limited bound for Johnstown. He would then be met at the station by his beautiful young wife and once again he would hold her in his arms and gaze down into her adoring blue eyes. Then the two of them would board the very next train back to Philadelphia just as they had planned, together again at last. Everything would finally be as it should be.

A sharp blast of cold air peppered with enormous raindrops stung his tired, unshaven face. Nature's brutal slap brought him from his straying thoughts and made him bitterly aware that the destruction that lay before him was indeed reality. There would be no waking from this particular nightmare. He would have to see it through. A violent shudder overtook him as he moved down the muddy incline toward what once had been his home. Dread hung deep inside him like a heavy weight. Would he find his beloved Kate still alive?

Chapter One

Late September, 1888

Everyone at the charity picnic waited patiently for the loud rumble of the passing train to fade. With the main lines of both the B & O and the Pennsylvania Railroads coming within a few blocks of the lovely tree-dappled town park, such noisy interruptions were expected. The shrill whistle of the locomotives and the ever-jangling sound of the railroad cars as they clattered their way along the tracks were little more than everyday nuisances to the people of Johnstown. After all, the coal trains that rolled in and out of the city were as much a part of their lives as the Cambria Iron Company and Gautier Wire Works. Johnstown would not be the thriving, progressive city it was without the noisy railroad and the clanking mills.

"Who'll start the bidding at fifty cents?" Dr. Harrison Rutledge called out as soon as he felt he could be heard over the noisy rumbling. At age thirty-one, Harrison was one of Johnstown's youngest surgeons. He was also one of its finest.

With accidents such a common occurrence at the mills, Johnstown needed good surgeons and Harrison had been brought in by special effort of the Cambria Iron Company only a few years prior, almost before the ink on his surgical diploma had dried. He had graduated medical school with extremely high marks and already had managed to impress

17

the hospital's administration enough to be appointed to head the entire surgery department. One of the first things he had chosen to do as head of surgery was to upgrade the antiquated equipment and immediately had started searching for the funds to do just that.

This picnic was one of Harrison's fund-raising ideas. That's why he had gladly accepted the duties of auctioneer. Carefully, he held up a food-ladened basket so the throng of people scattered across the lawn of the huge park could see what it was they would be bidding on, and shouted with a huge smile, "And remember, the money goes to Johnstown's hospital, so let's be generous."

The basket belonged to Marie Rosenthal, who now stood on the platform beside Harrison with her back turned to the crowd so that she could not watch the bidding. At Harrison's request, she had already described the delicious contents and because she was eighteen, pretty, and unmarried, the bidding was brisk.

"Sold!" Harrison called out once the bidding had stopped. "To the handsome young gent in the dark blue shirt with the red kerchief, for three dollars and fifty cents. Come claim your prize, son," he said, grinning, giving the young man a noticeable wink that brought laughter from everyone and a blush to the young man's neck—the three-fifty he had just bid could have gotten him that silver-cased watch he had been keeping his eye on, but a chance to have lunch with a girl as pretty as Marie was too much to resist.

"Let's keep this thing moving right along," Harrison shouted. Although the train was gone, he still had to keep his voice loud so the people near the fountain could hear over the water's gentle splashing. He was impressed with the number of people that had turned out for the event. Why, there were people here from Johnstown, the neighboring suburb of Woodvale, and even East Conemaugh, which was several miles upriver. He supposed the lovely weather had something to do with the good turnout. It was unseasonably warm for Pennsylvania this time of year, almost *too* warm. The September sun shone brilliantly down from a beautiful cobalt blue sky high above the burly mountainside and added to the gaiety of everyone who had come to spend the day at the park.

It was certainly a morning for colorful parasols and ornamental fans. As Harrison looked out over the gathering from his position on an elevated wooden platform especially built for this occasion, it was like looking out over a moving field of colorful flowers. And despite a gentle breeze curling down the deep river gorge from altitudes higher up, which prevented the day from becoming too unbearable, several of the women were busily working their fans, mostly to their advantage.

Harrison smiled to himself. With such a good turnout, it was possible the Johnstown Hospital would make enough from this auction to get the better grade of lighting needed in the surgery rooms and maybe also buy a piece or two of new equipment. He realized whatever they grossed today would just be a start toward getting all the improvements they needed, but at least it was a start in the right direction.

"As you can see, we have quite a number of picnic lunches here to bid away today," he went on to say, indicating the long, heavy mahogany table overflowing with baskets and fancy food boxes. Reaching behind him while smiling out at the vast assembly of faces, Harrison lifted another large wicker basket. Quickly, he read the name neatly scrawled on its tag. Smiling when he recognized the name, he turned and called Patricia Morgan's name. While she made her way to the platform steps from a gathering of the women who had so graciously donated lunches to this worthy cause, Harrison patted his stomach and began, "Fellows, you are in for a real treat if you get your hands on this one. Being this young lady's brother-in-law, I know from experience how good her cooking is."

Pulling back the bright yellow linen cloth, Harrison peeked inside and described some of the delicious treats he saw. "Looks like we have something a little different than the fried chicken we have been seeing so much of. Looks like we have ham, fresh bread, a vegetable salad of some sort, pickles, and there is a whole apple pie in here." Taking a deep whiff, he sighed loudly, "And does it ever smell good. If it

19

wasn't against the rules, I would bid on this one myself and risk my own Jeanne's anger in doing so."

Patricia rolled her emerald eyes heavenward and shook her head in exasperation, causing her long ebony curls to shimmer in the bright sunlight. She knew that Harrison was overdoing it a touch and tried to keep from laughing as he continued his ravings. "And not only do you get to feast on all this wonderful food, just take a look at the woman you will have keeping you company. A man couldn't ask for better. And as soon as Patricia has turned around, we will get the bidding under way. Again, let's start with fifty cents, and remember there is no limit and an opening five-dollar bid would be well appreciated by the hospital."

Knowing that William Speck would be the one bidding on her basket, Patricia spotted him in the crowd and gave him a meaningful look so that he would understand that she expected him to offer a decent bid, whether anyone bid against him or not. She did not want all that good food and hard work to go for a mere fifty cents. After all, she had her pride.

Lifting her long turquoise Venetian skirt by the silk trim that ran its length, she quickly turned around and let her eyes focus absently on the open windows along the upper floor of the post office across the street. Although she knew the offices to the Johnstown *Tribune* were located there, the fact did not register on her mind. Her attention was centered on what was going on behind her. Carefully, she listened for William's bid, knowing that if he bid too low, he just might be eating his meal alone.

"Do I have an opening bid for fifty cents?" she heard Harrison ask in order to officially start the bidding.

"I bid ten dollars," William's lofty voice shouted out.

A contented smile curved her lips. That was the best bid so far today. She would be able to leave the platform with her head held high. Really, she never had much to worry about. William was not about to let the woman he believed to be his intended be disgraced. He had his own pride to consider and ever since his promotion to second vice president of the First National Bank, quite a noted accomplishment for a man of twenty-eight, William had taken great care of his pride and social status.

"A ten-dollar bid!" Harrison said happily. From the corner of her eye, Patricia could see the broad smile beaming on her brother-in-law's face. It was obvious the high bid had delighted him. Maybe this would set the prices higher in the bidding to follow.

Although Harrison knew exactly why William had made the generous bid, he added with a chuckle, "Looks like William here likes ham and apple pie. There wouldn't happen to be a higher bid out there, would there? I have a ten-dollar bid here near the front, will anyone bid higher?"

"Twenty dollars," she heard another voice call out from the distance. Patricia's green eyes grew wide. She did not recognize the man's voice and was perplexed. Who would bid such an outrageous price for her basket? Why, for twenty dollars one could buy an entire parlor suite and leave enough to purchase the curtains.

"Did you say twenty dollars?" Harrison asked, his voice filled with the awe of such a bid. Patricia looked over at her brother-in-law again and saw his mouth gape open slightly and his dark eyes widen with surprise. She could also tell by the way he hesitated that the size of the bid had made him a little nervous.

"Yes! Twenty dollars is exactly what I bid! And I think an afternoon spent in the company of that lovely young lady will make it twenty dollars well spent," the unfamiliar voice went on to say.

A low murmur swept the crowd. This man was offering twenty dollars to be with William Speck's beautiful fiancée. Even though William and Patricia had never formally announced their engagement, after two years of being continually in each other's company, everyone knew it was just a matter of time until they did—everyone except the tall, handsome young man standing near a massive red oak at the back of the crowd. Although many of the onlookers had seen the man around Johnstown for years now and knew he was connected somehow to Cambria Iron Works, few really knew his name, which was not unusual in a valley of thirty

21

thousand people, but that was about to change.

Patricia had been able to hear the distinguished voice more clearly that last time, but she still did not recognize it. The voice was a complete mystery. It was deep and silky smooth, yet extremely masculine. The golden sound of it caused her skin to tingle along the base of her neck and made her extremely curious to see what sort of face went with it. She was eager to turn around and take a peek at him, but knew the rules forbade it. Even though she usually gave in to sudden impulse, she was determined to remain standing with her back to everyone until the bidding was over. If she turned around, her sisters and her friends would have a good reason to tease her about her impetuousness and they already did enough of that. It took all the determination she had to resist the temptation.

"I have a bid of twenty dollars," Harrison said as he ran his hand through his thinning black hair, his brown eyes still wide with anticipation. Lines formed high above his arched brows when his gaze met William's narrow face. Judging by the stern expression he found there, the situation did not sit too well with his friend. But then why would it?

"I bid twenty-five dollars!" William shouted angrily over his shoulder so that whoever had bid against him could hear the warning in his voice. He had been very willing to pay ten dollars for Patricia's basket, but twenty-five dollars was a bit steep and, if this was someone's notion of a joke, he did not see the humor in it.

"Thirty dollars!" came the response before Harrison could even comment on William's bid.

The crowd fell silent as they waited to hear what William would have to say about that. The only sounds they heard were those of the water babbling softly in the fountain, the chattering birds in the many treetops overhead, and the faint clanging of the machinery at the iron mills in the far distance.

"Thirty-five dollars and not a penny more!" William yelled, craning his neck. He wanted to see just who was making such exorbitant bids against him, but being only five-foot-ten, he was unable to see over the many taller men standing behind him. That irritated him more. The muscles

22

in his narrow face grew rigid and his thin fingers curled into tight fists at his sides.

"Forty dollars!" came the response.

William ran his splayed fingers through his cropped brown hair, furious with whoever kept bidding against him. He grumbled to himself a moment, then jerked his chin up and shouted out obstinately, "I bid one hundred dollars."

The crowd gasped then fell silent as again everyone awaited the response. Heads turned and necks stretched. Everyone wanted to see what sort of expression was on the man's face. Was he as angry as William was? Apparently not. The man gave a light shrug of his broad shoulders as a slow smile spread across his handsome face that caused his light blue eyes to sparkle and long narrow indentations to carve into his lean muscular cheeks. Many of the ladies noticed how charming his smile was and wished it had been their basket he had bid on. Everyone continued to look at him speculatively. They now wondered what he was going to do about William's hundred-dollar bid.

"Enjoy your meal" was the man's response and laughter filled the park.

Patricia cringed, knowing how that laughter was going to affect William, but even so, she could not seem to keep an impish little grin from taking over her own lovely face. She dared not turn around now. William would be furious with her. That thought seemed to make her ridiculous smile stretch even further. Poor William.

"Does anyone out there want to top that last bid of one hundred dollars?" Harrison asked, his own lips twitching. He was struggling valiantly to keep his expression straight and not join in the laughter. "No? Then the basket goes to William Speck for one hundred dollars!"

Still bewildered over who the voice belonged to, Patricia did not wait for Harrison's permission to turn around. Drawing in her naughty little smile which she knew would only offend William and putting a disinterested expression in its place, she immediately spun around and scanned the crowd. She hoped to discover the man that belonged to that incredible voice. Quickly, she searched the faces, all smiling

23

but none revealing the answer for her. She looked to William in hopes he might be staring at the man, but William's eyes were on his wallet while he searched its contents for the money to pay for her basket. Curse it all. Whose voice was that? Which one was he? Patricia was determined to find out before the day was over.

It was hours before the last basket was finally auctioned off and, as Patricia had expected, hers brought the highest bid by far. While she and William chose a place for their lunch under a spreading red oak, the bravest of her friends stopped by and commented on the remarkable price her basket had brought. William, having decided to make the best of it, immediately agreed with everyone that the amount was indeed quite remarkable. He then explained what a worthy cause the money was to be used for and behaved as if he had intended to bid a hundred dollars all along. But when he tried to pull that same story on her sister, Jeanne, it fell on skeptical ears. She knew William well enough to know how he hated to part with his money. William had ambitious plans for his future and money figured heavily into it. He already had a promising career and with it dreams of living in one of the finer brick homes on Main or Walnut Street with a beautiful wife like Patricia by his side. He fully intended to fulfill his father's dream and become one of the most prominent citizens of Johnstown—if not the richest.

For the rest of the day, the mystery of the unknown voice plagued Patricia. Every time a stranger glanced her way, she wondered, *Is he the one?* But each time, she decided for one reason or another that he was not. Whoever owned that extraordinary voice was going to be exceptional. He just had to be.

Later that evening, after all the festivities had come to an end, Patricia feigned a headache and asked William to take her on to her father's house to rest. Actually, the only ache she really had was caused by her nagging curiosity. She was still determined to find out who that voice belonged to, but did not dare ask questions of anyone while William was beside her and he had not left her side once all afternoon.

Shortly after they arrived at her father's house, William

decided to join Clayton Mackey in his study for a spot of brandy and a brisk conversation on the world's economy. Anxious to be alone with her thoughts, Patricia politely excused herself and went to lie down in her old bedroom on the second floor.

Even though she had moved out of the house years ago, her room remained just as she had left it and she still used the room whenever she visited her father and needed a bit of privacy. It would always be her room. It would forever hold the rosewood bed with the whitework spread and matching white curtains she had chosen when she was just fourteen years old. The walls would always be pale yellow and the brass and ceramic appointments around the room would never change—that is, unless she wanted to change them.

Patricia knew her father secretly wished she would move back in with him and her sister, but she also knew that day would never come. She enjoyed her freedom too much. It may have broken her heart when Robert died only two months after they were married, but at least the short marriage had left her with the means to be independent. She could pretty well live her life the way she wanted. She was no longer considered a maiden and could dispense with all the silly proprieties that went with maidenhood. She had her own house and at the time of Robert's death had had her own horse and carriage. But she had sold both the horse and carriage almost immediately, not truly needing either, and after she had convinced her father to let her help him with his bookwork at his main brewery, she also had a means of supporting herself.

Although she loved this old house, having spent much of her girlhood within its red brick walls, Patricia would never return to it permanently. Nor did she plan to accept any of William's marriage proposals any time in the near future. She knew if she ever married again, she would be forced to give up some of her freedom and she was not anywhere near being ready to do that. She was not sure she ever would be. Her freedom had become too precious to her. She was perfectly content with her life-style the way it was.

Once Patricia had topped the carpeted stairs and had

25

started down the narrow corridor where a dark red stencil design that underlined the high sculptured ceilings always drew her attention, she found herself unable to resist stopping at her youngest sister's door. But because it was closed, as was almost always the case, she rapped lightly on the dark mahogany frame and waited patiently for Catherine to respond.

"Who is it?" Catherine's soft, girlish voice called out.

"Patricia," she answered. She tried to keep her voice low enough so that she would not be heard downstairs and yet could still be heard through the heavy wooden door.

There was a light rustle of paper from inside before Patricia finally heard her sister tell her to come in.

"What took you so long?" Patricia asked as soon as she had closed the door behind her. She stepped over to the elaborate brass bed and sank down into its soft depths facing Catherine, who sat several feet away at a small writing desk near the window. While waiting for Catherine's reply, Patricia took in a deep appreciative breath. She loved the way her youngest sister's room always smelled. It was a mixture of wood, furniture oils, and the lovely floral scent of Catherine herself.

"Nothing," Catherine answered, shaking her head and displaying her usual round-eyed innocence. Absently, she reached for a tendril of her curly brown hair and began twisting it around her finger.

Patricia cocked her head sideways and gave her youngest sister a skeptical look. Her pretty little sister was hiding something, why else would she be seated facing her desk like that when the lid was closed? What had she been writing? Patricia's curiosity grew but she decided not to press. Catherine had a right to her privacy, and besides, she had more pressing matters to discuss.

"Were you at the picnic when my basket went on auction?" she asked, leading up to her question casually. She did not want Catherine reading anything ridiculous or out of the way into any questions about the man's identity she might have, giving the answers more importance than they deserved. It was merely natural curiosity and nothing more.

26

Who wouldn't be curious?

A gentle knock at the door interrupted Catherine before she could reply. Patricia sighed, exasperated, and hoped it was not William. She had honestly had enough of that man for the day, especially the way he kept boasting about how greatly he had contributed to the hospital when everyone knew he had never intended more than a ten-dollar bid.

"Come in," Catherine called out to whomever had knocked. Patricia frowned at how quickly Catherine had responded to the knock this time and wondered again what her sister had been doing when she had knocked earlier. Unlike then, Catherine did not bother with questions of identity this time. What was sweet little Catherine hiding from her oldest sister now?

The door eased open and in popped Jeanne's perfectly coiffed head. "So there you are. Father told me you had a headache and had gone to your room to lie down, but when I went to see about you, you were not to be found. And judging by the perfectly smoothed coverlet on your bed, you hadn't even bothered to lie down at all. What is going on?"

"Nothing." Patricia tried to sound very nonchalant, flicking her hand casually in the air. "I just wanted to stop by and chat with Catherine." Of the two sisters, Jeanne was the most likely to try to read things into her questions. Jeanne had a very active imagination and had a tendency to leap to the wrong conclusions. "I haven't had a chance to visit with her lately."

"Because you try to work yourself to death at the brewery," Jeanne cautioned. Knowing from experience that Catherine preferred her door closed, although she never really understood why, Jeanne quietly pushed it shut before joining Patricia on the bed. Carefully, she removed her black velvet hat and gave her head a gentle shake, sighing heavily from exhaustion. The movement loosened the chestnut-colored curls that were piled high on top of her head, but did not make them fall.

While lightly examining the tiny blue taffetine rosettes with her fingertip, Jeanne turned to Patricia and eyed her older sister critically. "Maybe you should be lying down. A

27

headache can be the first symptom of something serious. Harrison will be up to check on you as soon as he has pooled enough strength to climb those stairs. That auction certainly took its toll on him. When he wasn't performing as the auctioneer, he was helping take money at the claiming table. But he said to tell you he would be up very shortly to see about your headache."

Although she had never truly felt better in all her twenty-five years, Patricia pulled herself further up onto the bed and stretched out across it, lying on her side with her head propped up on her folded arm. Having chosen to wear her long ebony hair combed high back upon her head, allowing it to flow freely down her back in long loose curls, it now fell across her arm and onto the covers in long shimmering waves. She did not particularly care if she was tousling her hair or if she was wrinkling her plaited skirt and fitted jacket. She was comfortable.

"There is no need to have Harrison come up at all. I am already feeling better. I think I simply had a little too much sun and excitement is all," she said and smiled inwardly as she realized that the only thing ill about her was that excuse.

"Excitement?" Jeanne's hazel eyes danced with delight. "I mean to say you had a little too much excitement. I only wish that man had bid again. I think William would have fainted dead away. What if the man had called out 'two-hundred?' We just might be preparing to bury poor William at this very moment."

"What excitement? What bid? What are you talking about?" Catherine demanded, her blue eyes sparkling with anticipation. "If something happened to cause William concern, you know I want to know all about it."

"Didn't you hear it when you arrived at the picnic?" Jeanne replied, delighted she was going to get to tell the story once more. "I thought it was all anyone was talking about."

"I didn't go," Catherine said simply, then took a deep breath and waited for the response.

"You didn't go?" Jeanne's smile faded to an impatient frown. "I thought we had convinced you to go. What made you change your mind?"

"I never got my food basket ready, and besides, you know I don't like to socialize like that."

Patricia and Jeanne exchanged a disappointed look. Although neither had seen Catherine at the picnic, they had both assumed she had gone. She had promised she would. It worried them that their youngest sister still refused to go anywhere where she would be thrown together with men. Was she ever going to get over Franklin? Here she was twenty years old, pretty as a spring flower, and not a single man in her life.

"Well, my sweet sister, you should have attended," Jeanne informed her, wagging her finger as she spoke. "You missed the bidding on Patricia's basket."

"Did it go well?"

"Did it ever," Jeanne said. Her enthusiasm returned. "Someone started bidding against William for the basket and caused him to keep bidding more and more. Our dear William was so angry about it that by the time the bidding had reached forty dollars, he reared back and shouted a bid of a hundred dollars. A hundred dollars! Can you imagine?" She cackled with glee.

"And what did the bidder do then?" Catherine asked eagerly.

"The bidder called out for him to enjoy his meal. Those were his exact words, 'enjoy your meal,' as if anyone could enjoy a meal he had paid a hundred dollars for. Why, one could furnish a whole house with that kind of money." Jeanne shook her head and let a fiendish smile play at her lips. "I was only a few feet away from William. You should have seen how angry he became after the man had told him to enjoy his meal. He turned scarlet. Everyone was laughing. It was too funny not to. Even Harrison had a hard time of it. Being up on the platform at the time and in front of everyone, he tried not to laugh, but I could see it in his eyes. You just should have been there."

Catherine started to giggle, which caused Jeanne to giggle, too. Soon Patricia joined in and the three of them laughed until tears filled their eyes and they could barely catch their breaths.

"And you should have seen the forlorn look on poor William's face when he opened his wallet and started counting out a hundred dollars," Jeanne added between gales of laughter. "You would think they were taking away that shiny new nameplate he is so fond of or that fancy ring of his by the long look he had on his face."

Again the girls burst out laughing. Patricia knew she should not be laughing with them, but could not seem to help herself. It was so funny.

When the three of them had finally regained some of their composure, Patricia decided to try to see if Jeanne had seen this mystery bidder and if she perhaps knew his name. Dabbing at the tears that still clung to her long lashes, she asked, "Did you happen to take a look at the man who bid against William? I wonder why he did it? What did he look like?"

"No," Jeanne replied, still sucking in deep breaths in order to halt her persistent laughter. She opened her handbag and searched the contents for a kerchief so that she could dab away the moisture that had gathered at the corners of her eyes. She had laughed so hard even her nose had started to run. She sniffed lightly as she added, "No, but I wish I had. I would love to know who it was."

"Didn't anyone mention his name?"

"No, no one I talked to seemed to know his name. He is from around here, though. Rebecca Rocque told me she's seen him around before, but could not remember where. She seemed to think he was quite handsome."

"Yes, but then look at that bear she is married to," Catherine said with another giggle, her blue eyes glistening. "He is as hairy as a monkey."

"Come to think of it, he does remind one of a big monkey, a big ape monkey," Jeanne chuckled and it set the three into fits again.

Patricia had not laughed so hard in years and felt silly for laughing so hard now. She really should be defending William and poor Mrs. Rocque's hairy husband, but she just could not. All she could do was hold her middle and hope someday the giggles would subside and she could breathe again.

Later, after William had taken her home and she had bid him good night, Patricia's thoughts again went to the voice that had so thoroughly enchanted her earlier. As she slipped into a tub of soothing hot water, she closed her eyes and imagined what his face might look like, still certain he had to be extremely handsome. Shivers ran along her spine, contradicting the warmth that surrounded her, and caused tiny bumps to form under her skin as she thought of what sort of man he might be.

Earlier, at supper, she had hoped to casually extract certain information about the man from her brother-in-law, but was very disappointed to learn that although Harrison had indeed gotten a look at him and had felt the man's face was vaguely familiar to him, he had no idea who he was. And Patricia had felt too afraid of what everyone might think to press him for a description, especially with William sitting right there beside her. Besides, she doubted Harrison would have told her much. After all William was one of his friends and he wouldn't have wanted to say anything that would make his friend feel uncomfortable. Harrison was too kind for that.

While the warmth of the water gently seeped into her, relaxing her fully, Patricia started to doze, wondering who she could ask next. Maybe someone from one of her father's breweries had seen him and could tell her all about him. She just had to know who her mystery man was. A smile formed on her delicate lips as she thought of what it would be like to meet this man and have him whisk her away into the wondrous realm of fantasy and fairy tales.

Chapter Two

Patricia's gaze scanned the intricate pattern of the apricot-colored wallpaper that lined the walls in her small office but her thoughts were elsewhere. Two weeks had passed since the hospital's charity picnic and, although the auction had been a grand success and had brought in over a thousand dollars of needed funds, Patricia's quest to find out who that intriguing voice belonged to had met with utter failure. But even so, she had not been able to stop wondering about him.

Her thoughts of the voice plagued her at the strangest of times. She wished she knew why a man she did not even know had bid so elaborately for her basket. Was it a grudge of some sort against William? Or could it be the man had been that interested in being with her? Or did he just happen to have a strong hankering for ham? Maybe he had been so stricken by her glorious beauty that he had been unable to help himself.

"Hardly," she responded aloud to that last thought with heavy sarcasm, knowing that although she was fairly attractive to men, she could not claim to be overwhelmingly beautiful. Her nose was too small for one thing and her eyes were far too large. Besides, if he had truly been interested in her, he would have made himself known to her by now and she was no closer to knowing the man's identity this day than she had been two weeks ago.

Wishing she could keep her concentration on her work instead of these fleeting thoughts of a man she did not even know, Patricia scowled down at the long columns of figures and started to add them for the fifth time. Maybe this time the totals would balance and she could move on to something else. Although she was usually extremely efficient when it came to her work, she had already spent two hours doing what should have been a mere twenty-minute job.

Before she could finish re-adding the first column to see if her mistake lay there, she noticed voices, men's voices. Usually she could ignore the sounds from the other offices, but not today. Today even the rain beating lightly against her window disturbed her. She looked up from her large oak desk, perturbed to find her door open, then back down at the long page of figures. Pulling her resolve together, she tried once more to push the distractions aside and fully concentrate on her work, but to her dismay, she kept finding herself paying more attention to the voices than to the numbers in her columns and that irritated her more.

"Iris?" she called out, hoping to avoid getting up. She tapped the hard lead of her pencil against the paper while she waited for a response. "Iris, will you please come close my door?" When there was no answer, Patricia knew the secretary must be away from her desk, probably on an errand for her father.

"Looks like I'll have to close that door myself," she muttered with a heavy breath. Annoyed by the interruption, she slammed her pencil down and shoved her desk chair back, letting the legs rake across the wooden floor in sharp protest. Being unable to make her totals for last month balance had already put her in a foul mood. Now this. It annoyed her even more to glance at the handsomely carved Jeffrey clock on top of her file cabinets and see how late it was getting to be—already well past three o'clock and she had so hoped to be able to go home early this afternoon before William had a chance to stop by the brewery. The way her work was mounting on her desk, she felt she would be lucky if she ever saw home again.

Having recognized one of the voices that had disturbed her as being her father's, Patricia paused a moment with her hand on the door and glanced toward his office, curious to see whom he might be talking to in such a brusque manner. Had poor old Mr. Haught been caught napping at his job again? Or had Mr. Minter been sampling again? But, no, the other voice was out of place here. It certainly was not Mr. Haught's craggy voice nor was it Mr. Minter's low guttural muttering, yet it was familiar. Then, as she gripped the door to close it, her green eyes flew open wide. Suddenly she realized why the other voice sounded so familiar to her, so awfully familiar. It was deep and silky smooth despite the intense emotion being powered through it and it transmitted tiny shivers to every part of her. There could be only one voice like it.

"It's him!" she gasped breathlessly, her hand flying to her throat. "It has to be."

Excitement sped through her as she stepped out into the reception area and listened more carefully, closing her eyes a moment in order to do so. There was no doubt about it now. What was he doing here? Her curiosity had the best of her—she had to have a glimpse of him. She had to find out what he looked like and who he was.

With her heart throbbing wildly against her chest, she cautiously stepped closer to her father's opened door and found she could see a young man, maybe a few years older than she, standing and facing her father's desk. He waved his hands slightly to emphasize whatever it was he was saying. His authoritative stature matched the hardy sound of his voice perfectly. He was not facing her at the moment, but she could already see that he was tall, manly, and very broad across the shoulders. His tailor must have had quite a time of it trying to make that stylish tan-colored coat fit those broad shoulders so well. It could not have been an easy task. Nor could his barber have an easy task of it either. The man's dark hair was extremely thick and slightly wavy, giving it a fullness any woman would be jealous to have. It was also a bit longer than most men usually wore their hair and, despite the fact that it lay combed and well kept, its length and fullness gave him a rather roguish look.

Patricia could hardly wait to see the face that went with that wonderfully rich voice and such a sturdy, rugged build.

Was he as incredibly handsome as his voice was masculine? Yes, he just had to be. Burning with anticipation, she boldly edged ever closer to her father's office in order to have a better look at the man and see if she might be able to hear exactly what it was he and her father were saying to each other. She felt very much like a silly schoolgirl sneaking up on the door the way she was, but she could not seem to stop herself. She had to know more.

Inside her father's richly furnished office, the two men were on the verge of an argument. Cole Gifford had come to see Clayton Mackey in hopes of getting the man to sign his petition, but just like all the others he had approached that day, Clayton Mackey was being totally apathetic to his cause.

"I don't think you understand just how dangerous the situation is," Cole said, his voice full of the frustration that the tense muscles in his lean jaw had already revealed. Why was it no one cared enough to do something about that dam? "Consider the size of the lake. It stretches back almost three miles and is over a mile wide in places. Granted, the shoreline is shallow, but that lake is over a hundred feet deep through the middle. That is a lot of water and that dam is just not going to hold it much longer and here we are just fourteen miles downriver. Doesn't that worry you?"

"If that dam is so unreliable, how has it held Lake Conemaugh back all these decades?" Clayton slumped back in his sturdy high-backed desk chair and stared up at this haughty young stranger. He really did not have time for such nonsense, especially not this late in the day.

"I would say it is nothing more than pure luck," Cole retorted, running his hand through his thick hair in a disgruntled gesture. "And as you should recall, that dam has failed once before. We were just lucky that the break was minor and the lake was down at the time."

"That was back when no one was taking care of it," Clayton quickly pointed out.

"And what makes you think it is being taken care of now? Almost from the day it was so carelessly rebuilt by the present owners, which was nearly ten years ago, it has been constantly deteriorating. It now sags in the middle and the face of it leaks in several places. It needs to be fully repaired and updated. There are not even any discharge pipes to allow anyone to lower the level of the water if the need arises. They did away with them all when they remodeled the dam. I know. I have surveyed it myself. It desperately needs a major overhaul and the owners don't seem to care. I have tried several times to talk to them about it but they keep putting me off. They even put off Cambria Iron Works. Back when Daniel Morrell was still alive and president of Cambria Iron, he and the company generously offered to help pay for the repairs. The Cambria officials were smart enough to realize the company's safety was at stake."

"And why wasn't it repaired then?"

"Because the owners felt it was adequate enough and did not want to bother with the mess," Cole told him then shook his head in disbelief. It irritated him that the owners cared so little.

"And they were probably right. That dam is one of the largest of its kind in America." Clayton wished this young man would simply accept the fact that he had refused to sign and leave it at that. His patience in this matter had worn thin.

"But it is falling apart." The exasperation Cole felt made it impossible for him to stand still. He began to pace about in front of Clayton's desk, oddly aware his footsteps made very little sound in the rich blue carpet that lay in the center of the room. "And unless we can get the government to step in and help us, that dam is going to break and that entire lake is going to come down on us."

"Even if what you say had some merit, I still cannot sign your petition. Look, it is important that I not become involved in this matter. The hunting club that owns that dam does business with my breweries," Clayton said, waving his arm to indicate his plush surroundings. Although he had other business interests, his breweries were his greatest source of income and the hunting club was one of his best customers, especially in the summer season when the luxurious lodge and the outlying cottages were filled to capacity with its elite members. "What if they were to find out I had signed that thing? It very well could cost me their business. I don't need that kind of loss." Forcing a courteous smile, he added, "Business before pleasure, you know."

Cole could not believe he was hearing any of this. How could anyone be so narrow-minded? "Pleasure has nothing to do with this, sir. It is your safety that's at stake. Aren't you at all concerned with the safety and the welfare of your family, your friends, of this whole city? Where will your business be when that dam finally gives way?" Clayton opened his mouth to reply but before he could actually voice his opinion, Cole blurted, "I'll tell you where your precious business will be. Several miles downstream. That's where!" Cole's anger finally got the best of him.

"I think you are exaggerating just a little," Clayton replied, sitting up and leaning heavily on the polished surface of his massive desk. It was easy to see by the glint in his pale blue eyes that he was just as angry as Cole.

"And what if I am not exaggerating? Can you afford to take that chance?"

"I think so," Clayton said with a sarcastic nod. Then deciding he had put up with this young man long enough, he purposefully reached for a file that lay on his desk and opened it. Without further word to Cole, he slipped on his reading glasses and started to look over the papers before him with mock interest, obviously dismissing Cole from his presence. As far as he was concerned, this matter was closed.

Appalled that the man was putting his business with the hunting club before the safety of Johnstown, Cole stood staring down at Clayton Mackey angrily. "Listen, Mackey, it's not as if I'm asking for money or even much of your time. No amount of business can be worth the risk you are taking by not getting involved with this. Besides, all I am asking for is your signature on a petition."

"And I can't give it," Clayton said simply, his face lean and rigid as he looked up into the angry dark blue eyes of this young man again. "It is as simple as that."

Cole stared down at him with disgust. He had run out of arguments. What did one say to a man who did not listen to reason? How could he get it across to him that the danger

38

was real and getting worse by the day?

"Look, Gifford, I know you seem to think that dam offers Johnstown a great threat, but I honestly don't believe it does. I saw that dam myself last summer when I was a guest at the lake. It looked just fine to me. Our buggy passed right over it on the way to the club's hotel and it seemed like solid ground. I didn't see any big sag in the middle or any leaks along the face. That dam has held up well enough for over forty years and I see no reason why it should not hold for forty more. Besides, even if that dam did burst, so what? By the time the water reaches Johnstown, it will be all spread out and should only cause the river to rise a few feet, five at the most."

"And where did you get a notion like that?"

"I heard it from reliable sources," Clayton commented, narrowing his pale eyes as if daring this young man to dispute him further. Actually, he could not remember just where he had heard it originally, but it seemed to be a common consensus of those who should know.

"Sir, your sources are not as reliable as you think."

"They are reliable enough," Clayton growled and slammed his fist down on the hard surface of his desk with such a force that it caused several locks of his thinning gray hair to fall forward across his forehead. Huge veins the same color as his pale blue eyes protruded in his neck. He'd had just about enough of this intrusion and of this young man's impudence.

Cole realized Clayton was no closer to changing his mind now than he had been when they had started this inane conversation. Cursing inwardly, Cole decided to give up. It was impossible to make a blind mule see, especially a stubborn old blind mule like this one. Jamming his petition back into its heavy folder, he reached for his satchel and stalked away in a fit of frustration. This was the third such confrontation he had suffered through today. No one would listen to him. No one wanted to accept the fact that there was a true danger out there and even those who did believe the dam was in risky shape were unwilling to become involved in any way. How could they act so unconcerned with so very much at stake?

Shoving the folder inside the satchel as he stormed toward the door, he became aware of a beautiful young woman standing in the doorway watching them. He glanced her way as he brushed past her and suddenly realized who the young woman was. She was that same woman from the picnic. The same one he had been trying to find out about for the past two weeks. Having stood so far back in the crowd that day, he had not been able to hear her name. A friend had told him he thought her last name was Morgan or Morrey, but he had no idea of her first name or any notion of where she might live. Now, suddenly, here she was, the vision of beauty that had haunted his dreams for so many nights. What was she doing here?

He frowned when he realized she had obviously been listening to their conversation. Feeling every muscle in him tighten, he wondered how long she had stood there and if she was secretly amused by his foolhardy attempts at the impossible. He supposed she was and that made him angrier still.

Holding his head erect with as much dignity as he could muster under the circumstances, he tried not to look toward her again. Quickly, he strode past and headed for the front door. He wanted to hurry and get as far away as he could from this place. He greatly preferred the dreary, wet afternoon to this stifling, overly furnished office, and would definitely prefer a raging ice storm to the cool, penetrating look he had seen coming from those huge green eyes. He must have made quite an impression on her today.

"Mr. Gifford?" Patricia called out to him when he reached for the door. She had caught the name her father had called him earlier but it had taken her a moment to find voice enough to use it. Once she had seen just how handsome the man really was, her breath had literally left her. He had not only measured up to her high expectations, he had far surpassed them. He was the most stunning man she had ever beheld—handsome and virile. She guessed him to be about thirty years old, maybe younger, and had immediately decided she liked him, despite his obvious temper, or maybe because of it.

Still seething with frustration, Cole turned around and responded to his name in a barely controlled voice, "Yes, what is it?" He watched as she took several steps in his direction before bothering with a reply.

"I'll sign your petition," she said impulsively.

Although it was not the signature he had hoped for—after all, a woman's signature did not hold as much weight as a man's—Cole was not about to refuse. She *was* a part of the population, a very beautiful part at that. His anger quickly melted and he stepped toward her, puzzled. Reopening his satchel, he reached inside and pulled the heavy folder back out. He immediately started surveying the room for a flat surface to set the petition on so that she could sign. He hurried over to the vacated desk where Mackey's secretary had been when he first arrived. Quickly, he grabbed up a pen, not wanting to give her a chance to change her mind.

"I appreciate this," he told her, watching as she bent over and scrawled her name at the bottom of the list. His deep blue eyes glistened with delight while he took in her slender but shapely frame and the regal way she held her head as she signed. She was just as beautiful as he had remembered her. Although her long dark hair was pinned up in some sort of bun at the back of her head and her attire was far less than feminine, more businesslike, she was still just as beautiful and alluring as she had been at the picnic. How he wished he had carried more money with him that day.

"And I appreciate the effort you're making to try to force those people to repair that dam," she told him with a sincere smile. "I was with my father when he visited the lake last summer and saw for myself the condition of that dam. Although I was not aware of the sag you spoke of in the middle, I am almost certain you are right about the leaks. There was a patch where the vegetation along the face of the dam was much greener and thicker than anywhere else. That can only mean that heavy moisture was seeping through. Although the leak may be minor now, it will merely erode and grow worse unless it is repaired. Your petition may be just the thing to help get those repairs done."

Cole could not believe it—a kindred spirit. He stared

down into the deep sea of green of her eyes and fought an overwhelming urge to kiss her—not just because she was so extremely beautiful, but because she believed. She had seen the dam for herself and *believed*. After butting heads with so many of the town's most prestigious businessmen, it was pure joy to find someone with enough sense to know that there was a definite threat.

After her words had time to fully soak in, the slight look of awe on his face twisted into a curious frown and he questioned something she had just said. "Your father?"

"Clayton Mackey," she clarified for him while indicating the office he had just stormed out of.

"Clayton Mackey is your father?" he asked with a grin. It amused Cole to no end that this beautiful young woman had the audacity to ask to sign something her father had so adamantly refused to even look at. She was a woman of true spirit. Those were hard to find. He glanced toward Clayton's office and wondered if the man was even aware of what was happening out here, but decided he probably had no idea. After all, they were on the far side of the reception area and not at all in view of the man. Still, she was taking quite a chance by risking her own father's ire.

"Yes, Clayton Mackey is indeed my father," she said, timidly tilting her head, wondering why he kept staring down at her and grinning. It occurred to her that she was rarely shy around anyone, usually far from it, so why was she feeling so shy now? Was it because he was just as handsome as she had hoped he would be? Now that he was in the same room with her, she could see every detail of his face—the slender crescent-shaped dimples that carved into his lean cheeks, the deep shining blue of his eyes, and the long dark lashes that outlined them. The shape of his clean-shaven face revealed his solid strength as did the shape of his nose, which was straight with a slight flare at the nostrils. His generous lips stretched into an easy smile and it occurred to her that those lips would feel wondrous against her own. She had never felt such an urge to kiss a man.

Not wanting to pursue such inappropriate thoughts any further, at least not while he was scrutinizing her as closely as he was, she pulled her gaze free of his and looked back down at the short list of names on the petition. Picking it up, she started to hand it back to him. "How long have you been at this?"

"Trying to get signatures? Over three weeks now, but I can only work on this at nights and on my days off."

"On your days off? Where do you work?"

"I am an engineer with Cambria Iron," he said simply, not wanting to boast that he was now the chief engineer of the company. Although he had not come to Cambria Iron until 1884, he had quickly managed to make a name for himself within the company. He'd had a lot to do with Cambria's decision to convert to natural gas in the fall of '86 and had even helped oversee the installation procedures. Then when John Fulton had moved up to take over Daniel Morrell's place after Mr. Morrell's illness and eventual death in 1885, Cole had been promoted to take over the vacated position of chief engineer. It was an accomplishment he was proud of, but did not tend to brag about.

"I only have a few days off a month and have spent most of those trying to persuade people to sign the petition, but as you can see, I have only managed to get sixteen signatures thus far. No one seems to want to have their names involved in this. It is either that or they honestly don't believe the dam offers any true threat."

"That's a shame. You would think they would want to do something about it."

"I agree. I don't understand everyone's lack of concern. It's as if they believe that by ignoring it, the problem will simply go away."

"Maybe you haven't approached the right people yet. I know my sisters could be convinced to sign. As you have already seen, not all Mackeys hold my father's opinions." Patricia smiled inwardly at that thought, knowing how Catherine would leap at the chance to sign something she knew her father had so adamantly refused. "And I imagine my brother-in-law could also be persuaded to sign. He has been known to listen to reason and, being a doctor, he is already deeply concerned with everyone's safety and well being. You probably remember him—he was the auctioneer at the picnic."

So! She did know he was the one from the picnic. Since she had held her back to the audience the whole time, Cole had wondered if she had any inkling that he had been the bidder. For some reason, it pleased him immensely to discover she knew he was the one. Either she had recognized his voice or had done some investigating of her own. Either way, it meant that he had made an impression on her.

As he took the papers from her, Cole's spirits started to lift. Maybe there was hope for this petition after all, and with that hope came other hopes. He looked longingly down at the beauty that stood before him so deep in her thoughts and realized he still had a strong urge to kiss that sweet mouth of hers. He wondered what her reaction would be if he did just that and decided she would probably slap him soundly across his cheek. A lazy grin tugged at his mouth as he realized it would be worth it and it took all the control he had not to carry out the thought.

"And I have a couple of cousins who live in Woodvale that would probably sign. After all, Woodvale would be hit even before Johnstown," she went on to say, aware that he continued to stare down at her with an intensity that caused tiny shivers to form along her neck. Her shoulders twitched in reaction.

"And how about your husband?" he asked. He knew he was not being very subtle, but was too curious to care. It had not yet occurred to him to simply look at her signature and see if she had signed her maiden name, Mackey, or some other name, even though he had thought of checking her left hand. But to his dismay she now held both of her hands clasped behind her, which prevented him from seeing if she wore a wedding band or not.

"My husband is dead," she said softly, her smile fading. "He has been dead for several years."

"I am sorry," he said, feeling uneasy about having asked, knowing from experience how painful such a loss could be. "I had no idea."

"Of course you didn't," she replied lightly. "I am surprised you even knew that I'd been married at all." Pulling her hands forward, she gazed at them. "After all, I don't wear the ring anymore."

He was curious to know why that was, but did not dare ask. Instead he changed the subject back to the petition and wondered how he should approach the subject of dinner. He definitely wanted to know this lovely woman a little better. Why, it just occurred to him that he didn't even know her name. "So you think your sisters would be interested in signing this? I certainly would appreciate it. As you can see, I have quite a way to go if I am to impress the federal government enough to get them to intervene in this matter."

"The federal government?" she asked, impressed that he would carry it that far.

"I've already tried to make the local and state governments listen, but it seems those people of the hunting club pull too much weight in this area. I guess money does buy power. So the next logical step is to travel to Washington with this, but I don't dare go without a lot of names on that petition backing me and professional reports from reliable sources detailing the serious condition of the dam. Because that dam is privately owned, I will have to fully convince them that it holds a threat to the lives and property of others. With any luck, I will be able to present my case sometime this summer and by this time next year, the South Fork Fishing and Hunting Club will be repairing that faulty dam. But then again, the way things have been going this week, I may never have enough signatures and without them, I'm afraid that I won't have much impact."

"If there is any way I can help you, just let me know," she offered in earnest, looking up into his eyes again and trying not to become lost in their crystal blue depths. Now that he was no longer angry, his eyes had turned to the most incredible shade of azure.

"Have dinner with me," he suggested quickly, surprising himself as much as her. He had hoped to weave the dinner invitation smoothly into the conversation, but was too eager to wait any longer.

"But I just met you. In fact, I don't even know your first

name," she told him, feeling an odd sort of panic at his sudden invitation. She had a notion this man could upset her serene little world in a hurry. In fact, he already had. Nothing had been the same since the first moment she heard his voice. Her heart spun a wild course at the mere thought of being with him. It had been a long time since she had felt such a reaction to a man. Even William, with all his courtliness and exquisite manners, had not set her blood to surging through her this way. It was almost frightening.

"My name is Cole—Cole Gifford," he said, and offered her his hand as if they had just been formally introduced. "Pleased to meet you. And your name?"

"Patricia Morgan," she replied cautiously, staring at the hand a moment, wondering if she should accept the handshake or simply ignore it. She felt almost afraid to touch him. But for some reason, she chose to accept it and slowly lifted her hand to meet his. As she expected, his handshake was firm and warm and lingered a bit longer than it had to. The tiny waves of excitement that stemmed from where he had touched her were uncalled for. She thought it was a ridiculous reaction for a woman of her age; after all she was no silly schoolgirl. She was twenty-five years old for heaven's sake. And here she was with gooseflesh from the mere touch of a total stranger. It simply did not make sense to her. Nor had the way she had been so fully absorbed in foolish little fantasies ever since she had first heard his golden voice at the picnic.

"So now that we've been properly introduced, will you agree to have dinner with me? Tonight."

"Unescorted?" That thought both terrified and intrigued her.

"Of course not," he said, although he had hoped so. Quickly, he searched his mind for someone who might be willing to join them on such short notice. "My sister will be accompanying us."

Patricia fully intended to say no, sister or not. After all, getting involved with this man could only cause trouble for her and she was not at all certain she was emotionally ready for a relationship with a man like Cole Gifford. He was far different from the men she was used to. Besides, she had all of that work to finish and she had never been one to shirk her duties. But despite all the many arguments she provided for herself, when Patricia finally answered him, the word "no" came out sounding remarkably like the word "yes." Then it dawned on her that she had indeed agreed to dine out with this man—a man she had just met—a man who set fire racing through her. Why did she have to be so implusive?

She cringed at the thought of how William and her father were going to react to this bit of news. They would be furious with her. But then her dire expression slowly gave way to a slightly mischievous smile when she realized how truly little she cared. Let them be angry. At least her sisters would be delighted by such an unexpected turn. Her eyes glistened the deep color of jade. Yes, this was definitely going to stir things up at the Mackey house, and for some strange reason that thought delighted her immensely.

Chapter Three

Patricia's booted foot clicked sharply against the walkway as she hurried along Main Street. She had managed to leave the brewery early without having to answer any inquires her father might have about her plans for the evening. Smiling to herself, she remembered how she had immediately shoved her work aside, her totals still not in balance. Suddenly, finishing her work had not seemed nearly as important to her. She had merely leaned into her father's office and told him she was heading home, then left quickly, giving him very little opportunity to reply at all.

Luckily, she had caught him deep in concentration and had received only a simple nod and an "all right, dear" in response. Had he called her back into his office and asked, she wouldn't have lied. She would have told him exactly what her plans were and he would have been furious with her. He had such high hopes that one day she would finally agree to marry William. He saw William as the son he never had and would not care for this particular turn of events in the least.

Turning two blocks before she normally would, Patricia avoided crossing in front of the First National Bank, where William might look up from his desk and notice her. He was also going to be furious with her. She cringed again at the thought of what he would have to say about her plans for the evening, but with any luck William and her father would not know a thing until it was too late. Maybe she would be truly lucky and they would not find out at all, although she doubted it. The way talk spread through Johnstown, they would both undoubtedly know by tomorrow. Running her tongue over her lips in nervous apprehension, she knew she would have to deal with both of them later and deal with them she would. Right now, though, her thoughts were on getting home as quickly as possible in order to have plenty of time to prepare for the evening. Cole had said he would call for her around seven and she certainly wanted to be ready and looking her very best.

As she made her way along the streets of the business district, she nodded to familiar faces. At this hour, the boarded sidewalks were thronged with late afternoon shoppers, food peddlers, flower women, newsboys, beggars, and businessmen. On the narrow stone street beside her, buggies, carriages, carts, and wagons all fought for passage. Horses whinnied and hurried under their drivers' stern commands while dogs occasionally gave chase. As usual, Johnstown was bustling with activity.

The early afternoon rain had brought cooler temperatures with it and had left tiny puddles for her to avoid, but had washed away the smoke that sometimes drifted in from the iron mill to the northwest. It had left the cool October air smelling brisk and clean. Patricia breathed deeply the rich city scents.

There was a certain mixture of smells that was common to Johnstown. Horses, restaurants, breweries, tanneries, the iron mill, fall flowers, the huge trees that shaded the narrow streets and shrouded the surrounding Allegheny mountains, and especially the swift-moving river that flowed right through the middle of the business district; all were much a part of Johnstown and all contributed to the delightful way the city smelled. Patricia loved the smell. She loved the city and she loved the vast mixture of people that was its lifeblood.

Like Pittsburgh, which lay seventy-five miles to the west, Johnstown was a steel center. Blast furnaces lit up the sky at night and carloads of coal rumbled past on the main line of the Pennsylvania Railroad that ran alongside the Little

Conemaugh River. There was a constant clanking and whistling that went virtually unnoticed by the townfolks.

Two main rivers came down out of the surrounding mountaintops and joined at Johnstown—Stony Creek, which flowed in from the south, and the Little Conemaugh, which dropped down the mountains from the east. Together, they formed the Conemaugh River and flowed windingly westward toward Pittsburgh. The fawn-colored rivers added greatly to the vast beauty of the area and were a delight for area fishermen because they were usually filled with trout, pickerel, and bass.

Except for the days when it rained heavily, Patricia liked walking to and from work. She enjoyed being outdoors and feeling the fresh air against her delicate skin, and she was especially fond of walking along the river that came within a block of her father's brewery. Living in a nearby neighborhood enabled her to make the trip to and from work easily in fifteen minutes. The only time she accepted a ride with her father in his canopied carriage or his Portland cutter was when it was raining very hard or if it had snowed and the snow was too deep to walk through comfortably.

Turning once she had reached Mockingbird Street, Patricia caught sight of her small house and hurried her steps along. Just like most of the houses in this neighborhood, hers was wood-framed and painted in pastel colors pleasing to the eye. She had chosen light gray for her house and had trimmed it in bold white. The waist-high woodplanked fence was also painted white. Although her yard paled in comparison to her next-door neighbor's with its elaborate gardens, she had dark green holly bushes growing in the front beds, trimmed to even heights, and mountain laurel at either side of the house. There were still a few white petunias and a bright pink geranium blooming in her flowerbox and a big fern sitting in a pot on the banister around her porch.

During the summer months, Patricia paid Jack Hester, a young boy from the next street, to tend her plants and keep the grass cropped short, but it was not a huge chore for the boy since her yard was small. In fact, he also kept the yards of six of her neighbors, who had equally small yards, as well as the tiny patch in front of the Catholic church just down the street.

Johnstown and the neighboring communities had really started to grow over the past decade and because of the lack of space to spread out, having been built in a deep valley bed the way it was, the houses were packed closely together. The steep hills surrounding the city kept its boundaries limited. Even in the more elegant neighborhoods where the statelier brick homes were built, space was a problem. Everyone's yard was relatively small and streets usually narrow.

Upon entering the house, Patricia pulled off her black wool cape and draped it over a wooden clothes tree that stood near the front door. Dropping her handbag onto a table nearby, she called out for Duchess and was met at the top of the stairs by the fluffy white cat and escorted to her bedroom—one of the only two rooms that was upstairs.

Patricia's bedroom was spacious, but not as elegant as what she had been accustomed to as a girl. The pale yellow wallpaper was not as elaborate nor the furniture as intricately carved, although definitely sturdy and durable, and the rugs were not nearly as thick. The curtains she had hung at the two windows viewing Mockingbird Street were made of a serviceable linen instead of the taffeta and lace she had known as a child. She saw no reason to have such elegance in her bedroom when her sisters were the only other people to ever see it.

Knowing Patricia was headed for her armoire as was her custom, Duchess hurried in front of her mistress and waited near the armoire door, hoping to be noticed and eventually petted. But to the cat's dismay, Patricia was in too much of a hurry to pay attention to her furry little friend. Duchess tried rubbing gently on her mistress's skirt, but still did not get the attention she desired. When none of her usual tricks had worked, she sat back on her haunches and contemplated what she should try next. It was not usually this hard to get attention.

Cole had told Patricia they would be eating at the Hulbert House, Johnstown's new four-storied brick hotel, and she was too concerned with looking her very best for the occasion to notice Duchess. Although she had never been there before, she had heard the restaurant was one of the finest around. She could hardly wait. But it was more than a chance to dine at the elegant Hulbert House that caused her such giddy anticipation. It was a pair of uncanny blue eyes and a set of deep narrow dimples that set her heart to racing.

Of all the times for her buttons to become so stubborn. She tried her best to hurry but her fingers fumbled with each and every one. Finally, when she had undone her heavy woolen skirt and her delicate Sicilian blouse, she quickly discarded them both in a nearby chair then sat down right on top of them in her haste to remove her contrary boots and her stockings.

Hurriedly, she reached inside the armoire and pulled out a mint-colored percale wrapper and slipped it on over her skimpy camisole and underskirt. She ignored the loud protest of the cat when she turned away and padded barefoot down the stairs to the bathroom that had just recently been added on at the back of the house. It was a thoroughly modern facility with two faucets leading to her bathtub. Because of the wonder of natural gas heaters, she had all the hot water she needed to fill her tall roll-rimmed, footed enamel tub. To relax in a hot bath was one of her true pleasures. But she would not have time to relish this bath. She had to hurry.

Searching the cabinets, she located her floral scented soap and placed it in the soap cup beside the tub. She took a quick, but thorough bath. She patted herself dry with a thick towel then applied a light coating of talcum to her soft, velvety skin to help keep her feeling fresh through the course of the evening. Next she slipped her wrapper back over her creamy white shoulders and hurried upstairs to dress, tying the sash into place as she went.

The only drawback Patricia had ever found to living alone was having to fasten her own clothing, especially if the garment had several stays or ties in the back. She was working frantically with just such an awkwardly placed tie at the very middle of her back when there came a knock at her front door.

"No," she gasped. Quickly, her eyes sought the small gilt clock on the narrow mantel of her upstairs fireplace. She was relieved to find it was not yet six o'clock and knew she should still have at least an hour before Cole arrived. It had to be someone else at her door. Looking heavenward, she pleaded aloud, "Please, let it be anyone but Cole." Then as an afterthought struck her, she adjusted her plea accordingly, "Or my father." She still was not ready to face her father with her plans.

Or William either for that matter.

After having glanced out of the window and finding no carriage awaiting that might have given her a clue as to who was at her door, Patricia hurriedly descended the stairs in a rustle of petticoats and taffeta. But before she could get all the way down the stairs, the door started to open and she knew that it was either Catherine or Jeanne. Remembering that difficult tie she had been struggling with, she was pleased by the disruption.

Jeanne had stopped by in hopes that Patricia would be free for a quick supper at the Silver Moon. She had been out shopping with several friends and had let her excursion run a little late, but because it was Harrison's night to stay late at the hospital, she was in no real hurry to be home anyway. Whatever Ruby had prepared for her supper could wait until another day.

"Sorry, but I have plans," Patricia told her. Glancing down at her lovely emerald green taffeta dress with a darker green velvet trim, she added, "As you can see, I am already getting ready."

"William must be carrying you someplace special to-night," Jeanne remarked, nodding at her older sister's elegant attire with approval. "I'm surprised he can afford to take you out at all." Despite herself, a fiendish smile drew across her wide mouth at the thought. William must have suffered quite a blow to his finances with that hundred-dollar purchase he had made. It was still the talk of the town, only the more facts that came out about it the more interesting the situation became. Such a juicy piece of gossip she had learned just that very day. "Where to? Dinner and

54

the opera?"

"I—I am not going out with William tonight," Patricia said, not volunteering any more details, but knowing Jeanne's curiosity would make her demand more information. Her younger sister would not rest easy until she knew just exactly who was calling and where they were going. It was simply Jeanne's nature to want to know everything.

"You are not going out with William?" Jeanne's hazel eyes widened with interest then narrowed again with sudden suspicion. "Is Father taking you out?" It was not really like him to want to dine out during the middle of the week. But if he had such plans, she was certainly going to have herself invited too.

"No," she answered simply, stifling the smile that pressed against her lips. She could see her sister's curiosity growing by the moment and drew such pleasure from tormenting Jeanne with her own impatience. Whatever information dear Jeanne was to come by, she would come by it very slowly. It was a game they had played even as children.

"So, it is not William who is taking you out and it is not Father," Jeanne recounted under her breath, tapping a perfectly manicured fingertip to her lower lip as if that might help her to concentrate better. "But it is a man, am I right?"

"Most definitely a man." She beamed. Cole was the most manly man she had ever known. Just thinking about him sent shivers of awareness down her spine. She felt he had to be the most handsome and most interesting man she had ever met. And that voice . . . he could melt butter with that magnificent voice of his.

Unable to stand it any longer, Jeanne grabbed her sister by her shoulders and shook her gently. "Do not do this to me. Don't be so mysterious about everything. Tell me who it is."

"If you would just be kind enough to help me finish with this dress, I just might feel inclined to give you a hint," she said, and presented her back so that Jeanne could do just that.

"Okay, there, done. Now tell me, who is calling for you?"

"Do you remember the man who bid against William for my basket?"

"I didn't get to see him, but yes I remember," Jeanne said cautiously, her cheeks beginning to pale. The excitement quickly drained from her face and was replaced with deep concern. "You are not going out with him, are you?"

"Yes," she said, blushing slightly and not even knowing why.

"But he's married!"

Patricia stared at Jeanne. The sudden statement had jolted her to her very bones, causing her pert mouth to fall wide open. "What?"

"He is married!"

"How do you know? You told me you didn't even know who he was," Patricia argued, feeling her heart sink.

"During lunch today the subject came up and Lola Bellmont told me all about him. His name is Ben Butler and he works for Cambria Iron. And not only is he married, but Lola says he has two young children as well. And according to rumor this is not the first time he has dallied."

A strangled gasp forced its way through Patricia's lips. This was too much of a shock for her. She had to sit down before her knees gave way and the nearest accommodation was the stairs. With a stricken look, she sank down on the third step and let what her sister had just told her sink in.

"But he told me his name was Cole Gifford," she said, still not ready to believe.

"You don't think he would use his real name, do you? If you knew that, you could discover he was married," Jeanne put in quickly. "Besides that, if you knew his real name, you might mention him in passing to someone he knows and that could certainly lead to a delicate situation at home."

"But his sister," she continued to search for reasons not to believe. "He said his sister would be joining us for the evening. If he is married like you say, why would he let his sister join us?"

"And I will wager that his first order of business when he arrives will be to make excuses as to why his sister will not be able to join you after all," Jeanne said with a firm nod. "He will be extremely apologetic of course."

Patricia looked up into Jeanne's concerned face and knew

that what she was telling her was the truth. Anger began to race through her veins at the thought of the man having lied to her. And what an elaborate liar he was. What extraordinary lengths he had gone to. "How dare he!"

"What are you going to do about it?" Jeanne wanted to know. She knew her sister well enough to know that Patricia was indeed going to do something. She was not the sort to let such as this pass idly by and be forgotten. Not Patricia.

"I don't know yet, but I'm certainly not going to go out with him," she said, shaking her head sharply. Her green eyes narrowed while her brain started to present ideas, none of which were truly good enough. This cad deserved something terrible and it had to be something he would remember for a long, long time. "Maybe I should find out who his wife is and let her know just what sort of a man she's married to. That would fix his wagon." But no, she imagined the poor woman had enough heartache in her life, being tied down to such a monster. Whatever she did had to be more direct than that. It had to be something done to him.

As she sat drumming her fingers impatiently on the hard surface of the step beside her, a devilish idea started to form. Her green eyes sparkled with mischief. "Help me get out of this dress and into something more appropriate."

"Like what?" Jeanne asked. Curiosity seized her. She wanted to know whatever it was Patricia was up to. Even if it was something she did not approve of, she still wanted to know about it.

"Like that black satin nightgown and the matching wrapper that I bought when we were in New York last year," she said with a slow smile. When she had bought the outlandish outfit, it had been on a whim. She and her sisters had been in one of their sillier moods and all three of them had gone into a little shop that specialized in fancy things to wear in the boudoir. Each of them had come out with something tantalizing to wear and had felt wondrously wicked for having bought them.

"You are joking," Jeanne said, laughing lightly at the absurdity of the idea. Then, upon catching a glimpse of the determination in her sister's dark green eyes, she asked hesitantly, "You are joking, aren't you?"

"Not at all. It's obvious that the man is interested in only one thing from me. So why not let him think he is going to get just what he wants? Why not dangle the carrot before his nose and tease him a little before jerking it away? It will serve him right."

"But aren't you taking a big chance? What if he becomes so angry that he decides to take what he wants anyway?"

"That is exactly why you are going to stay and be in the next room listening."

"But what if he tells someone?"

"Who would he tell? His wife?" Patricia asked and noticed an evil little glimmer creeping into Jeanne's eyes as she listened attentively to the entire scheme.

Despite her uneasiness about the plan and her voiced objections, Jeanne was secretly delighted that she was going to get to stay and be in on it. The more she heard, the less inclined she was to try and talk her sister out of it. With the two of them conspiring together on this, they could really do this up right and no one would ever know what they had done except for the wicked man himself. They hurried to get ready.

Just minutes before seven, Jeanne positioned herself inside the tiny closet beneath the stairs. Leaving the door open just enough to allow her to see the man enter, she gently stroked Duchess in an effort to keep the cat lying contentedly in her lap and out of Patricia's way. Jeanne was giddy with anticipation yet scared to death as they waited for Mr. Butler's knock. But despite her fear of what might go wrong, she was bursting with admiration for her sister for having the audacity to do such a thing.

Jeanne had always been deeply proud of the boldness her older sister possessed. Patricia had always done things her own way. She was outspoken, independent, and beautiful. If she had been born a boy, there was no doubt in Jeanne's mind that Patricia would have set Johnstown on its ear. She would have been quite a driving force of power, someone to be reckoned with—a lot like their father. Jeanne admired that but at the same time had to admit she was a little jealous.

58

Boldness was a trait she did not often possess.

Patricia, on the other hand, was seething with justifiable anger and very eager to deal with this horrid man. Had he thought she was an easy mark because she was a widow? There were so many stories around about how eager widows grow to be, having tasted the fruits of married life. Those stories simply were not true, but evidently this man believed them. She wondered how often he sought out lonely women to meet his lust-driven desires, tempting them with his elegant charm and undeniable good looks. Well, this was one time he was going to wish he hadn't.

When the knock finally came, she was standing on the landing halfway up the staircase where the stairway took a bend. She leaned heavily on the dark mahogany banister and looked as alluring as she knew how. Not only did she have on the sultry-looking gown and wrapper, she had purposely left the wrapper open, tied only at the waist, to reveal the daringly low cut of the garment beneath. She had brushed her long ebony hair until it shone with glimmering highlights and had decided not to bind it in any way. She had let it cascade freely down her back and had carefully draped several silky tresses forward across her shoulder, where it shaped a soft curve around one nearly exposed breast. The only lighting in the room came from a candelabra on a table near the foot of the stairs when she called out to him.

"Come in."

Cole thought it was strange that she had not greeted him at the door, but then decided she must not be ready just yet. He tested the door and found that it was not locked and quickly entered. When he stepped inside, his thoughts were on how she was going to react when she learned that his sister would not be joining them for dinner after all. Would she refuse to go out with him because of it?

His eyes went immediately to the lone candelabra before they swept upward to take in the remarkable beauty that stood before him. He blinked. Then, he took in a second glance. She was definitely there and dressed in what had to be the most enticing outfit he had ever seen. He stared at her, suddenly speechless.

"I have been waiting for you," she said softly, in the most seductive voice she could muster. She felt certain satisfaction in the way his eyes boldly took in every inch of her exposed flesh, exposed flesh he undoubtedly wanted to touch, but would never have a chance to. She leaned slightly forward so that he might have a better view of what he would soon be denied.

"Y—you have?" he asked, perplexed. Never in his wildest dreams had he experienced anything like this. His pulse pounded through him with such a force that his breathing grew ragged and irregular. Had it occurred to him to try to swallow, he would have found it impossible.

"I hope you don't mind. I have decided not to go out after all," she told him while giving him an impish pout. "But you can stay and visit for a while if you would like, that is if your sister won't mind your being a little late. I know she is expecting us to be there in just a few minutes."

"My sister was not going to be able to join us anyway," he said in a breathless voice.

Aha, just as Jeanne had guessed! No sister. Patricia smiled. "Wonderful, then you can stay and keep me company. I get so *lonely* sometimes."

Cole did not know what to say. Of course he was going to stay and take full advantage of whatever it was she had on her mind, but he could not for the life of him put his thoughts into words. He simply stood, gaping at her sultry beauty. Then when she started down the stairs toward him, he felt his blood coursing hot trails through him and his knees growing a little weak. The same thought kept recurring to him— *never in my wildest dreams.*

"Why don't you take off your coat and make yourself comfortable?" she asked, offering him a generous smile as she gave him a coy little wink. Reaching for the tiny silken tie that held her wrapper to her waist, she slowly and seductively began to undo it, letting the garment fall completely open when she was through.

Take that, she thought vehemently, though her eyes still offered no sign of the anger that boiled within her. The enticing garment beneath was now in full view of him and

60

undoubtedly he liked what he saw. His eyes had grown dark with desire and kept roaming freely over her. The shining black gown dipped very low, almost to her navel in front and was embroidered with tiny pink rosettes and the inner swell of her bosom beckoned him, hinting of the wondrous treasures that lay beneath the soft fabric. Treasures Cole was ready to explore.

Jerking at his sleeves, Cole was out of his coat in an instant. He tossed it haphazardly toward the clothes tree and did not bother to pick it up when it missed its target by a good three feet. With an eagerness he could barely control, he headed toward her, but when he came within a few feet of her, she began to step away, keeping just out of his reach. Stopping, confused, he ran a hand through his thick dark hair while he tried to figure out why she had backed away. But when she reached up and ran her fingertip along her soft exposed flesh then looked upward, he realized she was beckoning him to follow. She was leading him upstairs, to her bedroom no doubt. He still found it hard to believe that this was happening, but he was not about to question any of it. At least not now.

Afraid she might let her presence be known, Jeanne had to press both of her hands over her mouth to keep the gasp that was welling inside her from escaping her lips. Knowing the intended outcome, she could barely keep to her seat as she watched the proceedings through the tiny crack. She had underestimated her sister. Patricia was far more daring than she had ever thought.

"Please, take off your vest and shirt so that I can see what a strong and muscular man you are," Patricia went on to say as she slowly backed up the stairs and continued to trail her finger over her flesh in a maddeningly seductive gesture.

Cole had no intention of refusing her and his hands went immediately to the large round buttons of his vest then to the tiny buttons on his pale blue shirt. Adeptly, he undid them all and pulled his shirttail out so that his shirt gaped open for her. Patricia had not counted on the reaction her body was going to have upon seeing the wide mass of curling brown hair that grew in soft patterns across his strong, muscled

61

chest, narrowing to a tiny trail of darker hair that ran downward and disappeared beneath his waistband. An urgency to touch this man flared inside her. Why not punish him further? Slowly she reached out and ran a gentle finger across the crisp texture, but was dismayed to discover that in doing so, she had kindled intense desires of her own. Desires that made her wonder what it would be like to . . . No! Desperately she pushed such thoughts from her mind. How could she even consider making love to a man such as this? Desperately she tried to get her heartbeat back under control.

Patricia's touch had set Cole on fire and he eagerly reached out for her, wanting to explore the many feminine curves and hollows that the flimsy gown revealed, but was thwarted in his move when she turned and quickly disappeared into one of the two doors at the top of the stairs.

Following closely behind, he found himself in her bedroom. A finely knitted pale yellow bedcover had been folded back and crisp white sheets beckoned them. No electric lights burned. A lone candle glowed in an elaborate silver stick on the small table at her bedside, letting a soft island of light fall upon the bed. The soft glow wavered in the gentle evening breeze that drifted in from the open window nearby.

"Let me have your vest and shirt and I will lay them over the chair," she told him and held out her hand. Almost before she had spoken, they had been removed and were in her grasp. It pleased her that he was so eager. "Now, please, take off your trousers and I will see that they are draped over the chair too."

"Take them off for me," he said with a seductive growl and stepped toward her.

Patricia had not counted on that. Suddenly, she became very nervous. She looked out into the dark hallway to be sure Jeanne had followed them upstairs like she was supposed to. Upon seeing her sister's shadowy figure at the top of the stairs, she decided that if she wanted to see this through, she would have to undo his trousers for him.

Her hand trembled slightly when she reached for the clasp

that held his waistband together. Her fingers burned where they came into contact with his warm flesh. Suddenly, it became very difficult for her to swallow. It was not until she glanced up into the darkened hallway and saw the startled look on Jeanne's face that she was able to regain control of her wavering emotions and see this for what it was—a way of getting even with this man for trying to trick her with lies and deception.

As she undid the pants and began tugging at them, her eyes, with a will all their own, dipped down and took a quick peek at his flat stomach and noted that beneath his fitted underclothing he was fully aroused. Embarrassed that she had actually looked, she glanced hurriedly away, feeling a hot blush creep up her neck. As she pulled the pants down over his lean hips, she turned her eyes toward the door and noticed that Jeanne had suddenly disappeared.

"There now," he said, smiling when she had both his shirt and his pants in her hands. He stood before her in just his underwear and socks, having already discarded his shoes himself. "Now it is your turn to undress."

When he stepped forward and his deep blue eyes grew even darker with his desire, she dropped the seductive look and her anger showed through. "No. I don't think your wife would really want me to."

"My wife?"

"Yes, Mr. Butler, your wife!" she said triumphantly. "I doubt very seriously that she would enjoy hearing that I had undressed for you. In fact, I honestly feel you should be worried about getting your own clothes back on. I don't think she would be at all pleased with your current state of undress," she spat at him, then stepped over to the window and threw his clothes just as far into the night as she could. With angry tears forming in her eyes, she shrieked, "And you can very well do your dressing outside. Get out of my house, Mr. Butler!"

Cole looked at her with a quiet fury burning in his steel blue eyes. Not quite understanding what was happening but well aware that his clothes had just gone out the window, he flexed his jaw muscle and wondered what he should do about this odd predicament. There was a tiny white edge forming along his drawn lips.

"And don't you dare take another step toward me, because my sister just happens to be in the next room and . . ." Suddenly she was not so sure that her sister's presence alone would be of much help against a man as powerful as this Mr. Butler was should he truly want to do her harm. "And she has a gun." Then calling out in a loud voice, she asked, "Don't you, Jeanne? Don't you have a gun—a *big* gun?" Sensing the danger emanating from him, she was having belated thoughts about all of this. She now fully regretted having taken such a thoughtlessly drastic course of action in her quest for vengeance. Why did she have to be so blasted impulsive? Her father had always said it would be the death of her and here she was about to oblige him by proving him right.

"Yes" came the muffled voice from the direction of the door. "A big gun."

Cole turned and stared into the darkness in exasperation, but saw no one. What the hell was happening here? Were they planning to rob him? If so, he hated to think what their reaction was going to be when they discovered they had just tossed his money out with his pants.

"I said get out of my house, Mr. Butler!" she repeated, her voice climbing until it strained at the very top of her cords. Every fiber in her was taut with anticipation as she waited to see if he would obey, but she refused to let her fear show.

"Why do you keep calling me Butler?" he asked. There were so many questions he wanted answered, but that one seemed as good a place to start as any.

"Because I happen to know that you are really Ben Butler and that you are married and even have two children. How dare you try to woo my affections when you are already married!"

"And where did you ever get the idea that I am Ben?" he asked, his brow dipping low. There was no look of guilt or even anger in his eyes now, just confusion, and that worried Patricia.

"My sister told me all about you," she said. Suddenly she

felt less sure about all of this. Was he denying he was Ben? Why would he bother to continue with the lie at this point? Could it be because he had not lied at all? Oh, heavens! What if this man was not and never had been Ben Butler? What if he actually was Cole Gifford? Her blood felt as if it had turned to ice and her stomach began to tighten in alarm.

"Your sister told you that I was really Ben Butler?" he asked, and a smile started to twitch at the corners of his mouth. "Why would she do something like that?"

"Aren't you?" she asked in a weak voice. Her defiant tone was gone and in its place was pure horror and mortification. Jerking her wrapper closed and folding her arms securely around herself, she started edging her way toward the bed, her eye on the pale yellow cover.

"Not the last time I looked," he told her, and his smile stretched the full width of his lips, causing his magnificent dimples to deepen. "No, the last time I looked I was still Cole Gifford. Besides, Ben is much shorter than I am and he is not nearly as handsome." Oh, how he was enjoying this. "Hey, sister dear, what ever made you think I was Ben Butler?" he called out and turned his eyes toward the door to wait for an answer.

There was no response, only the pattering of footsteps as they hurried down the stairs.

"Jeanne?" Patricia called out, her eyes flying wide open with horror. "Jeanne, you come back here. You come back here this minute."

The next sound heard was that of a hastily closed front door.

Chapter Four

"I think my sister and I may have made a terrible mistake," Patricia said in a weak voice as her heart hammered violently against her chest. She glanced only briefly at Cole then let her eyes dart away. Looking into those glittering blue eyes was too discomfitting at the moment. Her stomach coiled tighter and tighter with cold dread. She had never felt such impending doom. No longer in control of her own situation, she had little idea of what was going to happen next and was afraid to contemplate the possibilities. First thing to do, though, was cover herself. The seductive outfit she wore was an open reminder of what she had tried to do. Glancing again at the nearby bedcover, she forced a wavering smile to her lips and took another tentative step toward the bed. "We really did believe you were Ben Butler."

"Did you?" he asked in that low sultry voice of his and started toward her. There was a devil of a smile on his face that sent blood-chilling panic racing through her. It left little doubt of his evil intentions. "Yes, that was some mistake you made. Care to make another one?"

"Mr. Gifford, please try and understand. What we did to you, we did thinking you were a married man just out to . . . to . . ." She paused as she tried to find a delicate way to word it. ". . . to have his way with me."

"You were close. I may not be married, but I would love to have my way with you." He shrugged lightly. His roguish smile deepened.

Patricia's green eyes grew wide when she realized he was already coming toward her. Making a mad grab for the cover, she tried to yank it off the bed, but the contrary thing clung to the mattress. It refused to let go. Frantic, she jerked at the stubborn cover again until it finally began to come loose, but Cole was too close.

Frightened by the seductive glint in his eye, she abandoned the cover and scrambled across the mattress, hoping to put a little distance and the huge poster bed between them. She was unaware that her wrapper had come loose in the process until she noticed where his silvery gaze lingered. With a sharp intake of air, she reached for the edges and jerked them together again then tugged the sash tighter. This time she tied it in a secure knot, hoping to make it hold better.

"I really am sorry for all this," she stammered nervously and wondered what she would do next to get this situation back under control. There must be something she could say to explain it better. Again, she tried to offer him an apologetic smile, but it wilted immediately when she realized he was coming right over the bed after her. "I—I, uh, I really *am* sorry."

"I don't doubt that," he chuckled mischievously and continued to move ever so slowly toward her, his gaze never leaving hers.

The menacing expression on Cole's face sent hot chills down her back and caused her skin to prickle into gooseflesh. Without taking time to study her direction, Patricia backed away from him. Her fear was growing by the second. When she passed a small wooden chair, she reached over and swung it in front of her in a pitiful attempt to set up a blockade, and continued to back away. There was still several feet between them and she wanted to keep it that way.

"If you would just step out of the room for a moment and give me a chance to get dressed, I'll gladly go outside and get your clothes for you."

"I'll bet you would." He smiled and never paused in his slow pursuit of her. He was like a lithe wild animal stalking its prey. His bared shoulders allowed her to view each movement of his sleek muscles as he came ever closer. She tried her best to ignore his near nakedness, but was finding it impossible to do. With a flick of his foot, he sent the chair sailing out of his way. She jumped with a start at the sound of it clattering against the far wall. "But I'm not really concerned about my clothes at the moment. I'm more concerned with your clothes."

He decided a little turnabout was called for and felt no guilt for what he was about to do. It was no worse than what she had intended for him. Besides, he was enjoying her plight too much to end it just yet. His blue eyes sparkled with delight when he realized she was unknowingly headed into a corner from which there would be no escape. He could hardly wait to see how she would respond to that.

"Mr. Gifford, please try to understand," she pleaded with him and took another step backward. When she saw that her pleas went unnoticed, she next decided to try making demands. It was time for a change in strategy, time to take charge. "Don't you dare take another step in my direction, Mr. Gifford! I want you out of my room right now."

Demands certainly didn't work. He continued to approach her. He never paused, never even flinched.

"Mr. Gifford, I—I am going to scream if you take another step," she warned, trying to swallow so she could take a deep breath without strangling on her own fear. She could sense that her doom was near. Her heart pounded with such a fierceness that she was afraid it might explode inside her.

"Oh, come on now, Mr. Gifford sounds so formal. Please, call me Cole," he told her in a mellow voice. Slowly, he took that next step, his gaze never leaving hers as he studied every emotion revealed in her huge green eyes.

"I mean what I say. I'm going to scream."

"But why? This was all your idea. I thought it was what you wanted."

Mortified, she began to stammer. "That was when I thought you were Ben Butler."

"Oh, you wanted to seduce me only if I was Ben and married," he said and lowered his brow as if trying to understand.

69

"No! I never intended to go through with anything. I just wanted to teach him a lesson I thought he deserved . . . or would have if he had been you," she said with exasperation. She wondered why it had to be so complicated to explain. It all had made perfect sense to her until she had tried to put it into words. "I never intended to let anything really happen. I had already taken my scheme as far as I was going to."

Her attempts to defend her bold actions with futile explanations distracted her just long enough. Before she could think again about screaming for help, he was upon her.

"You should never start anything you don't intend to see through to the finish," he told her in a voice that was husky with desire. Boldly, he took the step that forced her back against the cold hard surface of the wall. He was just inches away from her. If she screamed now, he could easily stop her.

Nowhere were their bodies touching, yet Patricia could feel his warmth. The gentle heat radiated through her body, and as the warmth spread, so did a strange new sort of panic. Her fate was clear. Everything inside her spun with such a force it was hard to remain standing. Her knees grew weak yet her body, still sensing the danger, felt ready to defend whatever was to come, and somewhere deep within her was an eagerness to do battle with this man. Win or lose, the skirmish was going to be a dandy.

Patricia had never known such emotional confusion. The more she tried to determine just what she felt the more confused she became. What exactly did she feel? She was prepared to fight him off with every ounce of strength she had, yet at the same time she wanted to reach out and feel the smoothness of the beautiful mass of dark curling hair that ran in soft patterns across his muscular chest. Why this unexpected urge to touch the man, to feel the strength in his arms, the tautness of his skin? This sudden awareness of him made her more afraid than ever.

Trapped in her own horrible web, Patricia's mind frantically fought for a means of escape. She had to get away from him if for nothing more than her sanity's sake. Her eyes darted about. There were two ways out of the room, the open

70

window and the door. The window was the closest. Using the wall for leverage, she shoved him with all her might and made a lunge for the window, but only got a few feet before his hand had a firm grip on her arm. She felt herself being spun around and gently shoved backward. Suddenly he had her sprawled on her back across the bed and was hovering over her. His silvery blue eyes sparkled as he smiled victoriously down at her. The weight of his body on hers prevented her from escaping, yet did nothing to stop her from trying to slap that insidious smile from his devilishly handsome face. But before she could effectively land a blow, he had her wrists secured in his grips and pinned to the bed, one on either side of her head. She was furious. She tried to kick him, but couldn't. She was trapped. He had her.

"Quite a predicament you have managed to get yourself into here," he said as he smiled seductively at her. From this angle, she became absurdly aware of how long and dark his eyelashes were. Never had she seen such attractive lashes on a man.

Aware of her distraction, Cole slowly lowered his face to hers and let the tip of his nose caress her rigid jawline. His touch seemed to sear her skin with a tingling burn. Anger flared and she jerked her head to the side in defiance. Narrow dimples formed in his cheeks as he chuckled at how clearly his nearness disturbed her. When he had come closer, he had seen much more than anger flaring in her dark green eyes. There was so much passion of every kind bottled inside her that it was almost frightening to behold.

Turning her head back to stare up at him, she thrust her proud chin upward and glowered directly into his contented face. Her dark hair had spread out in a splendid array around her and a deep rose color had risen in her cheeks, making her appear even more enticing. Although she was still fighting other emotions, she quickly gave her anger its full reign. Her lips tightened against the tips of her even rows of white teeth when finally she spoke. "Go ahead."

"What?"

"Go ahead. Take me, if that's what you really want. I can't stop you."

Cole's broad smile fell into an open gape. His eyes studied her beautiful face a moment then dipped briefly to the provocative view the low cut of her outfit provided. Her breasts swelled proudly against the straining black material, making him very aware of the pleasures that were barely hidden from his view. It was interesting to consider. She was certainly tempting enough and she really could be his for the taking, for no court in the country would convict him under the circumstances. Suddenly he threw his head back and roared with laughter. When he looked back at her surprised and furious expression, he bent down and kissed the tip of her regal nose, which flared in response. "You amaze me, Patricia Morgan. You truly do."

Her anger fused with humiliation and grew until it burned a black hole deep within her. In a voice heavy with sarcasm, she narrowed her eyes and said, "I'm delighted that you find me so entertaining."

"There's no denying you would be a special treat. But I'm not about to try to take you, as you so blatantly put it. Hell, I probably wouldn't know what to do with you if I did. You are like no woman I've ever known."

Slowly, letting go of her wrists, Cole rose until he was only kneeling over her. His magnificent body towered above her, still drawing her attention, while he explained. "I never intended to see this through any more than you did. I couldn't resist playing it out."

"You saw this as a game?" she demanded, not knowing which she felt more—relief or resentment. He had played her for a fool, but she was well aware he could have played her for much worse. Angrily, she curled her lips into a mock smile. "I certainly hope you enjoyed yourself. I do like to keep my company entertained. I would truly hate to know that you were bored with me."

"I doubt you could ever bore me," he replied earnestly. "By the way, although I love that outfit, I really think you ought to change before we go out on the street."

"Out?" she asked, confused.

"To eat," he said, shrugging offhandedly as he eased himself off her bed. "I don't know about you, but I'm

72

starving. All of this activity has done wonders for my appetite. The sooner we can get dressed and out of here, the sooner I can satisfy this complaining stomach of mine. I think an extra large portion of roasted beef and braised potatoes should solve the problem. What about you?"

"I'm not exactly hungry," she muttered in astonishment. Where did the man get such audacity? Did he honestly think she would still go out with him?

"You will be once you get a whiff of their sumptuous roasted beef. The Hulbert House has the best I've ever tasted, that is next to my own mother's, but Virginia's a little far to travel just to satisfy my need for a good roasted beef, don't you think?"

"Your mother lives in Virginia?" she asked, pushing her anger aside for the moment. At last she was learning something about the man who had remained such a mystery to her until now.

"In a little community near Manassas. They have a small farm there. It isn't much, but they are happy with it. My sister and I go back every Christmas to visit. It's a nice place."

"So you really do have a sister?"

"Why would you question that? Do I look like someone who wouldn't have a sister?" He tried to look offended.

"No, I just thought you had made up the part about your sister going along with us," she said meekly. "But that was when I thought you were Ben Butler."

"That's understandable," he said with a serious nod. "Ben doesn't have a sister. At least none that I know of. But he does have a brother," he grinned, knowing she did not care if Ben had forty brothers and a pet mule. "You'd probably like his brother. Nice fellow. Come to think of it. You'll probably like my sister. She's not a bit like me."

Starting to smile despite every effort not to, Patricia nodded. "Then I'm sure I will like her."

Pretending not to notice Patricia's intended insult, Cole continued. "Although we won't be seeing Sis tonight, she is more than eager to meet you. She was impressed with the way you signed that petition and went against what you knew your own father would want in order to do what you believed was right. Actually, she's a lot like you. She always has had a tendency to do things her own way. It used to send our mother into fits. But we can talk about all this later. I really am hungry. I'll go on down and see if I can retrieve all my clothes without alerting the neighbors to my, ah, state of undress while you change into something a lot less . . . distracting. I'll wait for you downstairs. Try to hurry." Before she could voice an opinion either way, he had gathered both of his shoes and was headed down the stairs in his stocking feet.

"Harrison, please hurry," Jeanne urged anxiously while she knotted her hands in her lap. Absently, she pushed a damp curl off her forehead and stared ahead into the night's looming shadows. Perspiration had not only formed along her brow and neck but had dampened her underclothing until her chemise clung to her like a second skin. Having walked to Patricia's house, she'd had to run all seven blocks to the hospital in order to find her husband as quick as she could and was not used to running such long distances. She knew they needed a man's help and right away but had been afraid to summon the authorities, not after what all they had done to the man. So she had gone for Harrison and hoped he would not ask too many questions.

"I am hurrying. If I drive this horse any faster, I could cause an accident," Harrison called to her. Even though she was sitting right beside him, he had to shout to be heard over the clattering wheels of his new Stanhope. He was pushing the horse as fast as he dared. The lightweight buggy may have been built for such speed, but the narrow, cobblestone streets of lower Johnstown made traveling in excesses very dangerous. "How serious is she?"

"Very serious," Jeanne replied, unable to look her husband in the eye. She kept her face diverted to the street ahead. Just how serious she would not know until they got there.

Despite the fall of night, the bright electric lights that

burned at every corner would enable Harrison to glimpse the guilt that surely had to be visible on her face. She dared not look in his direction. The only thing she had told Harrison was that Patricia needed him right away. She had not bothered to give him any details. She hadn't had to. Her hysterical state had been enough to set him in motion.

Jeanne was glad to see that her husband had thought to bring his medical valise. There was no telling what-all that man had done to her poor sister. When she had heard the anger in his voice, it had sent ice-cold shivers right through her. She had realized right then that the two of them would be no match for the man. She knew she had to go for help. She only hoped they would arrive before the man could do his worst, but if they didn't, she knew Harrison would be able to do whatever needed to be done to take care of her medical needs and do it discreetly. No one outside the three of them need ever know.

There was another reason Jeanne was so glad to see Harrison's medical valise beside him. Harrison always kept a small derringer in one of the side pockets for use in handling drunken brawlers. Even those injured enough to need a doctor's attention sometimes had a tendency to want to continue to be rowdy. Once, several months ago, Harrison was severely beaten by a man he had gone to tend and then had been tossed unceremoniously into the Little Conemaugh River. Ever since that night, he always carried what he called his persuader. He never paid a call down on Washington Street without it.

"Whoa, Rebel," Harrison called out to the horse as he pulled back on the heavy leather straps. Without waiting for the buggy to come to a complete stop, he jumped to the ground and hurried around to help Jeanne down on the other side, but discovered she had already climbed out on her own and was headed for the front door. She wasted no time. Grabbing his bag, he quickly followed her.

Just before Jeanne reached the steps that led to the front porch, she stopped sharply. Harrison had not anticipated the stop and bumped right into her, nearly dropping his valise in the process. He cursed and gently rubbed his nose,

75

which had come into abrupt contact with the back of her hard head. As if she did not notice him at all, she spun to stare out into the yard with a look of horror in her hazel eyes.

"What's wrong?" he asked, alarmed. Quickly he scanned the shadows for whatever had startled his wife. The only movement he detected was a shadow crossing a neighbor's curtained window and there seemed nothing menacing in that.

"They're gone," she gasped, then turned to hurry inside. The clothes that had been strewn across the yard were gone. The man had already done whatever he had intended to do and had left.

"Who's gone?" Harrison asked and dashed up the steps in order to keep up with his frantic wife. Jeanne muttered to herself while she hurriedly fumbled with the door. Harrison was beginning to worry about his dear wife's sanity and nearly jumped clear off the planked floor when she suddenly let out a bloodcurdling scream that literally raised the hairs on his back.

Harrison was not the only one Jeanne's scream had startled so completely. Standing just inside the door, Cole had almost strangled himself with his own tie. He made a strange sort of gasping sound as his fingers quickly dug to loosen the narrow black strap from his throat.

"What the . . ." Harrison muttered and shoved his wife aside in time to see a man standing before a mirror yanking his tie off as if it was a snake that had bitten him. "Who are you?"

"Who are you?" Cole returned, his eyes wide from such an unexpected invasion. Although he was certain he had never seen the woman before, the man was oddly familiar.

Suddenly Jeanne felt weak and started to swoon. Alerted by her soft moan, Harrison forgot about the man for the moment and grabbed for his wife before she collapsed. Seeing the predicament, Cole quickly helped the man get the woman over to the stairs, where they gently set her on the third step and began patting her hands and cheeks to keep her from fainting further. To their relief and her dismay, she remained conscious even though all color had left her face.

When Harrison saw that Jeanne was going to be all right, he straightened and faced Cole. "I am Dr. Harrison Rutledge, Patricia Morgan's brother-in-law," he said in a way of explanation. No longer did he need to ask about the man's identity. Suddenly, he had remembered. This was the same man that had bid against William at the charity picnic. Frowning, he wondered what the man was doing here alone in his shirt-sleeves with his tie undone. Before Cole could return the introduction, Harrison's brown eyes glanced around the room in search for a sign of his missing sister-in-law. His frown deepened when he finally had to ask, "Where is Patricia?"

"She's upstairs," Cole told him, gesturing toward the ceiling with his head. "In her room."

Not bothering to ask further questions, Harrison bounded up the stairs, taking them two at a time. Something was not right about this. With reason for alarm, he called out his sister-in-law's name as he rounded the top of the stairs.

Realizing it would do no good to try to stop the concerned doctor, Cole turned his attention to the pale woman still seated on the stairs before him in a huge puddle of gray skirts. It was obvious she was trying her best not to look at him.

"I gather you're Patricia's sister, Jeanne?" he asked with a broad smile that brought his dimples to the surface. Now that he had addressed her, she *had* to look up at him. Extending his hand in a formal greeting, he bowed toward her. "I've been looking forward to meeting you, although for some reason I feel we already know each other."

Instantly, Jeanne was to her feet and on her way up the stairs, just a few steps behind her husband. Cole stared after her with a huge grin. She never missed a step. Her sudden recovery was indeed remarkable.

Chapter Five

Patricia was aware of the smile on her face even before she caught a glimpse of herself in the huge beveled mirror that hung just above her dresser. When she thought back over what had happened, she realized that Cole had never intended her any true harm and discovered she was truly amused by what he had done. She knew she would have retaliated in much the same way had she found herself in a similar situation. In that one way, they were much alike. Nothing tasted as sweet as a little justifiable revenge, especially if no one would be truly hurt by it. After all, the whole reason she had started this whole affair was because she thought she would be getting even with a man named Ben Butler. It was nice though that the man turned out to really be Cole Gifford.

Cole Gifford. Bold and impulsive, Patricia thought as her smile broadened appreciatively. She certainly liked those traits in a man. Yet at times those very traits exasperated her when she found them in her own father, but then she possessed them, too, and although they were far from being ladylike traits, she was proud of them. She rarely made an attempt to hide her bolder nature despite her many reprimands. Minnie Hess, bless her caring heart, often proclaimed Patricia would never have another husband as long as she behaved the way she did—headstrong as a bull—always doing whatever it was she had a mind to do. With a slight laugh, Patricia knew that her father's housekeeper was

79

probably right. No man wanted a wife who behaved in such a way, but that was just another reason to display her willfulness proudly.

After Robert had died and left her with her independence, Patricia had never again felt the need to be any other man's wife so why bother conforming? She liked being in charge of her own life and never again wanted to be emotionally bound to any man. Once had been enough. She had allowed herself to become completely dependent on Robert both physically and emotionally. That had been a disastrous mistake. The pain proved to be too severe when that dependence and their deep bond had been destroyed. When Robert died, she felt a little of herself die with him. It took her almost a year to adjust to the loss and get charge of her life again. It was not until afterward that she realized she never should have let such control leave her hands in the first place, even for Robert.

No, love and marriage were not for her. She was too smart to get caught in that sort of involvement again. She would not set herself up for another emotional tragedy or a life of bending to someone else's every whim. The price of marriage was far too dear, the pain of losing someone far too severe.

Awkwardly twisting her arms behind her, Patricia worked to reach that same contrary tie that she had been working with earlier when Jeanne had stopped by. She tried to push all thought of Robert from her mind. There was still too much heartache in remembering. Suddenly, she heard a loud scream come from downstairs. It was enough to raise goosebumps on the dead. Even though temporarily startled by the noise, Patricia's smile grew wide. She knew that scream anywhere.

So my departed sister has returned, she mused. Poor Jeanne. She must have thought Cole would be gone by now. Laughing slightly, Patricia wondered what sort of retaliation Cole would have for her dear gossiping sister. She hurried to finish dressing so she could find out.

Patricia just finished with the last fastener of her emerald green dress when she heard loud footsteps coming up the stairs. They were too heavy to be Jeanne's. Her sister was on the plump side, but would never make such a heavy sound on the stairs. She worried that it was Cole coming to tell her that her sister had fainted—she had that tendency in times of duress—until she heard Harrison's voice calling out her name.

Noticing the wispy black garment still lying on the floor, she made a quick grab for it and was able to stuff it under her pillow right before the knock sounded on her door.

"Just a minute," she called out. Hurriedly, she tugged on the bedcovers in hopes of hiding the fact that there had been a tussle there earlier. *Such incriminating evidence,* she thought with a wicked smile, knowing that if it was Jeanne coming in she would have left it the way it was or maybe even made it look worse.

"Patricia? Are you all right?" Harrison called through the door, his voice raised with concern. He knocked again impatiently. "Patricia?"

"Yes, I'm coming," she called out, then heard someone mumble and the door start to open. Jeanne must be with him. Running her hand once more over the cover in hopes of smoothing at least one more wrinkle, she realized it still looked too much out of kilter and decided to sit on it and give it a reason for being rumpled. She spun and was just coming down with a hard bounce when Jeanne entered.

"Are you decent?" Jeanne asked, her eyes huge with nervous curiosity over what she might discover inside this room.

"Depends on what you mean by decent," she said with a sad tilt of her head, knowing that Jeanne was going to worry over that remark for quite some time.

"Harrison wants to come in," Jeanne said quietly and clasped her hands together as if offering a silent prayer. "I told him how you were, ah, not feeling too well. He's here to check on you."

"Yes, may I come in?" Harrison asked, leaning his head through the doorway. After receiving her nod of approval, he stepped inside and walked over to stand beside her. His dark eyes scanned the room and missed nothing. He saw the chair lying on its side near the far wall. He observed how unkempt the bed appeared and even noticed a scrap of something black and satiny sticking out from under her pillow. He also noticed that despite the room being well lit by a brightly glowing gas light, there was a candle burning on the table beside the bed and had been burning for quite some time. He wondered about it all and why his wife had been so adamant in getting him here so quickly when Patricia appeared to be in perfect health. But he felt it was not his place to question. He was here as a doctor. He would perform as a doctor.

"Jeanne wanted me to come by and check on you. What seems to be the matter? She never did say."

"Hiccups," Patricia said quickly, not taking time to consider any other possibilities.

"Hiccups?" Harrison and Jeanne responded together. Harrison noted that his wife had been just as surprised by that answer as he had.

"Yes, hiccups," Patricia repeated firmly. She tried not to chuckle at her sister's paling face—any paler and someone was going to mistake her for a ghost. No doubt Jeanne had hoped she would be a bit more creative than hiccups, but on such short notice, hiccups would just have to do. "I have a terrible case of the hiccups and I need to get rid of them as qui—quickly as possible." She had thrown in a fake hiccup for good measure. "I am supposed to go out to dinner with a friend of mine. You probably met him downstairs. His name is Cole Gifford. He wants to take me to dinner at the Hulbert House, but I came down with these blasted hic—hiccups. You simply must help me get rid of them. I'd be too embarrassed to let him hear me making such horrible noises. Why, he'd think I swallowed a frog or something!"

Harrison had to admit his sister-in-law sounded convincing, but then she always did when trying to cover up for something Jeanne had done and Harrison had an odd feeling that whatever had happened here tonight, his own dear wife was responsible. Gazing intently at how she fidgeted nearby, he was certain of it. Jeanne never was one to mask her emotions very well and there was guilt clearly evident on her pallid features and in the way she seemed so abnormally interested in her own short, perfectly rounded fingernails.

"Does William know you are planning an evening out with this Cole Gifford fellow?" Harrison asked casually while he took his hat off and laid it on the night table. Quietly, he opened his large black medical valise and started to search through its contents.

"Not that I know of," Patricia told him, irritated that Harrison had mentioned William's name at all. She knew everyone was going to side with "poor William" once her evening with Cole was made known. Everyone that is but her sisters. She knew Jeanne and Catherine would love to see William become the odd man out. "Cole did not ask me until late this afternoon and I haven't seen William since then to let him know. And I certainly saw no reason to make a special trip by the bank just to tell him. Besides, I didn't have the time."

"I see," Harrison said in that exasperating way of his. He always used it whenever he truly did see—too much and too clearly. "And couldn't you have telephoned him? Your father's brewery does have a telephone now, doesn't it?"

"When it works," she muttered. "I guess I just didn't think about the telephone. After all, we've only had it a couple of weeks."

"So William has no idea of your plans. But I suppose your father knows," he went on to say while he picked up small bottles of medicine, examined the labels, and then put them back when they did not suit his purpose.

"No," Patricia said, raising a brow in defiance. "Father was very busy at his desk when I stopped by to tell him I was leaving. I didn't want to disturb his work."

"I see," Harrison said. Again. "And have you known this Cole Gifford very long?"

"For a while," she answered carefully.

"I see." By now Patricia had no doubt that he did see. Harrison was no fool. She was just glad he was not going to give her some sort of lecture. Instead, he continued to search through his valise for whatever medicine he might have for hiccups.

The silence that followed was so unnerving, Patricia

finally asked, "So, are you going to be able to get ri—rid of my hiccups?"

"I have just the thing for them. Works every time."

A cure for hiccups? Patricia had never heard of one. Of course she knew there were old wives' remedies that sometimes worked but she had never heard of a sure cure. He had her full attention when he finally pulled out a bottle and nodded satisfactorily at it.

"Here it is. One spoonful of this and your hiccups will be gone. I guarantee it," he said, then began searching his bag for the spoon he carried. While he unwrapped the spoon from the linen cloth he kept it in, he went on to say, "You may want to hold your nose while I give it to you. I know how you hate to take medicine."

Obligingly, Patricia pinched her nose as tightly as she dared and waited for him to administer the medicine. He was right. She hated to take medicine. Always had. But she had to see this through. When she noticed Harrison drawing the filled spoon toward her lips, she closed her eyes and waited until she felt the cold object against her tongue. Wrinkling her face, she forced her mouth shut around it. She swallowed as Harrison slowly slipped the spoon back through her lips. Then she waited a few seconds before letting go of her nose. When she did, she couldn't help but sputter and twist her face into a tight grimace. "What was that?"

"Cod liver oil," he replied in a mild voice.

"Cod liver oil cures the hiccups?" she asked, rubbing her tongue against her upper teeth in an effort to scrape the foul-tasting medicine off. It was no use. Her mouth was coated in the fishy taste.

"You are not hiccuping, are you?" he answered smoothly. Outwardly, he was somber. His face revealed nothing of the laughter he felt inside.

"No . . . no, I'm not," she had to admit. Eyeing him warily, she waited, as if checking to see if she was really cured of her make-believe hiccups.

After a moment, Harrison smiled in satisfaction. "Yes, I do believe your hiccups are gone. You're cured."

"And I owe you a chess game," she mumbled, knowing it

was going to be the next thing he mentioned. That was the only price he ever extracted from her for any doctoring he did for her.

"Payment due next Sunday, right after dinner at your father's house." He smiled and pushed the cork back into the bottle. Bending over his valise, he made certain everything was in order before strapping it shut. As he lifted the heavy leather satchel, he reached for his hat and carefully placed it on his head.

With a pleasant smile, he turned to Jeanne and took her by the arm. "I really need to get on back to the hospital now. I still have two more patients to see. You two can visit each other some other time. Besides, Patricia's young man is waiting below." He paused only a moment before adding, "Surely he's dressed by now." He felt Jeanne's arm stiffen in his grasp and wondered again what her part had been in whatever had gone on here. Although he would not presume to judge his sister-in-law, he was curious to know what she had been up to, yet was not really certain he wanted to know.

The Hulbert House was all it was reputed to be. The parlors were furnished in the richest upholstered furniture and thick heavy drapes hung on every window. Majestic carpets lay on the parlor-room floors and in the huge dining area. The floors in the hallways were highly polished wood with narrow carpets running up the centers. The wallpaper and appointments blended with the color of the carpets perfectly. In the entryway was a blue and white marble floor and on it stood some of the largest, most exotic plants Patricia had ever seen. To her amazement, the building even had an elevator like the ones she had ridden in New York. It was the closest to elegance Johnstown had ever known. Only the Washington Street Opera House came close. Patricia was delighted and vowed to come here more often. Silently, she hoped many of those visits would be made with Cole as her escort.

In the fifteen minutes it had taken them to stroll the four blocks to Clinton Street, Patricia and Cole had had a chance to get better acquainted and she had finally come to relax in his company. She was delighted by his wonderful sense of humor and his quick responses to her endless questions. He was much more interesting than William could ever hope to be and Cole's topics of conversation were far more varied. He did not drone on and on about the nation's economy or about the way local politics were being handled nor did he brag endlessly about what wonderful things he planned to do with his career. Cole rarely talked about himself at all, but he was not opposed to answering personal questions. He was open and honest and loved to laugh. The more they talked the more Patricia found what she had suspected would happen from the beginning. She liked Cole—liked him a lot.

It was not until their steaming plates of roasted beef, braised potatoes, and baked corn had been served that their conversation finally slowed, but not for long. Patricia finished with her meal first, having received much smaller portions, and took advantage of it by using the time to study her companion better. In the soft light of the dining area, he was incredibly handsome and when his silvery blue eyes came up to meet hers, she sensed for the first time that he was somehow vulnerable. He was not at all the demanding devil with a staunch will of iron that he had been earlier. He was different. Before, his exterior had seemed solid, impossible to penetrate, yet now she sensed that he was a profoundly caring person and capable of being hurt deeply. She would hate to ever be responsible for hurting such a man. She would be careful never to put herself in the sort of position where she might end up hurting him.

"I see you agree with me," Cole said suddenly, startling her. Although she had realized he was looking at her, she had not expected him to speak.

"In what way?" she asked as she watched him place his last bite of beef into his mouth. There was something tantalizing in the way his lips seemed to caress his food as he chewed it that totally distracted her. Although she felt she probably did agree with whatever he was referring to, she hadn't a clue to what it might be. Had she been so deep in thought that she had completely missed something he had said?

"Judging by your empty plate, it appears you agreed with me about the beef. Delicious, wasn't it?"

"Oh, that. Yes, I'll admit you were absolutely right about the food here. It was exquisite. But don't let it go to your head. I'd hate to think I had done something to feed that monstrous ego of yours," she said, laughing.

Cole tried to look offended but burst out laughing. Even when she insulted him, it felt like a compliment. "So would you care for dessert?"

"No, I'm too full as it is." She patted her stomach soundly as if to demonstrate just how full she really was before realizing how unladylike the gesture was. She usually did things like that to vex William but now wished she was more aware of social etiquette. She did not want Cole to think her vulgar.

"I am, too, but I was hoping to find something to prolong this evening. I'm just not ready to walk you back home yet. That is unless you are planning to invite me in, and maybe put that little black gown back on and pretend I'm Ben Butler again," he suggested with an ominous wiggle of his forehead.

Patricia raised a brow in warning.

"No?" he asked innocently. Then seeing the other brow raise threateningly, he shrugged. "It was just a thought. How about a stroll down by the river instead?"

"Are you to be trusted?"

"Are you?" he asked, grinning.

She threw him a cocky smile and agreed to try to behave herself if he would.

As they made their way toward the river that ran through what locals called "the flats," Patricia began to grow cold. Although her dress had a long full skirt that was layers thick, as were the sleeves that went all the way to her wrists, the crisp autumn night air was penetrating right through the material. She tried not to let Cole notice she was cold for fear he might change his mind about the walk and see her home instead. She was no more ready to see this evening end than he was.

"How long have you lived in Johnstown?" he asked and

87

stepped closer in. Although they were not actually touching, she could feel his nearness as they walked and it warmed her enough that she forgot all about the chilling night air. Her attention was now drawn to how remarkably tall he was. He had to be at least six-foot-two, broad at the shoulder, and lean at the hip. For some reason his build reminded her of a lumberjack. He just appeared to be the outdoor type. It seemed odd to her that his job was one that probably required many hours indoors behind a desk.

"I've lived here as long as I can remember," she answered. "I was about four years old when we moved here. Catherine wasn't even born yet. In fact, Mother was not quite aware she was with child when we made the move to Johnstown."

"So you have two sisters," he commented, as if trying to memorize every detail about her. "Any brothers?"

"No, just my two sisters. How about you? Do you have any brothers?"

"No, thank goodness. Having a sister is bad enough," he said, laughing. Upon seeing her shocked look, he explained. "Once you meet her you'll understand. But I must admit, Faye has certainly made life interesting. There's never a dull moment when she's around."

The more candid remarks Cole had to make about his sister the more interested Patricia was in meeting her. Surely this sister was not the hellion Cole pretended her to be, but in a way Patricia hoped that she was. Already she liked her. "How long have you and your sister lived around here?"

"I've lived here about five years. Sis has lived here almost three. And despite all I have to say about her, we are pretty close and always have been. So it just seemed natural that when it came time for her to strike out on her own, she chose to come to Johnstown and be near her dear, sweet, lovable brother." He batted his eyes coquettishly at the compliments he had just handed himself and got the intended response. Patricia's laughter filled the night air and the dark skies seemed to brighten with more than the sputtering arc lights and the distant glow of the Cambria Iron Works.

"Maybe her reasons run deeper than you realize. She might have come here just to get even for all the horrible

88

things you probably did to her when you two were children," she put in quickly.

"That's a thought to consider." He laughed, then fell silent while he reflected on her comment. It could be. It just could be.

While they walked on toward the river they were barely aware of the common noises of the city. In the distance was the constant clanging of the iron mill and the faded chugging of a coal train. An occasional horse's whinny or a dog's enthusiastic bark broke the monotonous sounds of hooves clopping and carriages rattling as they passed on their way to their varied destinations. Even the laughter coming from a nearby saloon was lost on them both.

When Cole and Patricia finally neared the river, the many sounds were drowned out by those of the rushing water. The river was moving swifter than usual, churning wildly in its determination to hurry along. They both realized it was due to the heavy rain they had gotten earlier that afternoon. The watershed from further up in the mountains was still feeding into the Little Conemaugh River and keeping it alive with activity. The loud noise of the rushing water made conversation too difficult so they continued to walk in silence for a while, glancing occasionally into each other's eyes. No words were really necessary.

After a few blocks, Cole reached out and took Patricia's arm in pretense of directing her away from the riverside. But once she had taken his direction and they were headed along a street that would eventually intersect with Mockingbird, he did not let go like she had assumed he would. His hand continued to rest gently at her elbow and she did not bother to pull away from him, not even when she saw Sam Neely's carriage approach in the other direction.

Sam worked at the First National Bank with William and would no doubt be quick to inform his close friend of what he was about to see, but Patricia did not care. She was not going to deny herself the wondrous pleasure of Cole's gentle touch. When Sam passed them, his mouth opened slightly in recognition just like she had expected. Smiling, she nodded a polite greeting in his direction. He nodded briefly in return, then pretended to be unconcerned with the fact that her companion had not been William when he returned his attention to the road.

"Friend?" Cole asked, having noticed the exchange.

"A friend of a friend," she said, wondering how short-lived that friendship was going to be once Sam had told William exactly what he had seen. She did not especially like the thought of losing William's friendship, but at the moment it did not seem very important.

All too soon, they reached Mockingbird Street. When they turned toward Patricia's house, less than a block away, the pace along the stone walkway slowed considerably. The closer they got to her front steps, the slower they moved, until they hardly made any progress at all.

"I want to thank you for that wonderful dinner," she said, hoping to strike up a conversation that would cause him to linger a moment longer. "I have been wanting to see what the Hulbert House was like ever since it opened. Do you eat there often?"

"Often enough. I hate my own cooking," he admitted offhandedly. "Every now and then Sis cooks a meal for me, but she tends to stuff me with vegetables. She got that from my mother. Those two have a passion for vegetables. Can you cook?"

"I'm a fair cook," she admitted. She had to be. Unless she had an escort, she either took her meals at home or at her father's.

"Mind if I invite myself to a home-cooked meal?" When she did not immediately answer, he added, "If you're afraid of being alone with me, I can bring my sister."

"I guess that would be all right," she hesitated, wondering what she would prepare for them. It would have to be varied. Meat and potatoes for him and lots of vegetables for her. She would want several days to prepare. "What about Sunday?" She would gladly give up her usual Sunday dinner at her father's for this.

"No, Sis can't come Sunday. How about Saturday?"

"Saturday's fine." She shrugged, glad she had never formally agreed to dinner with William. "Would seven

90

o'clock be all right for both of you?"

"Great. Then we could still have time to ride over to the park and listen to the music for a while. Sis loves the Saturday night concerts in the park. I'll ask her tomorrow and make sure she can come so we'll have time to make other plans if she can't."

Other plans? That made it sound like he wanted to be with her Saturday night no matter what. The thought of that thrilled her. Suddenly, she wondered what she should wear. That alone amazed her. Although she usually took pride in her appearance, she rarely worried with it days in advance like many women seemed prone to do. Jeanne had always been the sort to plan her outfits weeks in advance, while Patricia usually waited until the day before, giving herself just enough time to be sure the outfit was clean and any wrinkles pressed out.

Noticing Patricia was deep in thought about something, Cole waited before finally starting to say good-bye. "It is late. I guess I should be going."

Brought abruptly out of her musings, Patricia tried to think of something that would make him stay, if only a moment longer. "I wonder what time it is."

"I suppose it's after ten o'clock by now."

"It can't possibly be that late." She frowned.

Taking out his pocket watch, he flipped the casing open and held it up to the dim rays of light the nearest street lamp offered. "I'm afraid it is. It's already ten-thirty. I would apologize for having kept you out so late but it'd be the same as lying because I'm not at all sorry to have taken up so much of your time. I thoroughly enjoyed it."

"I enjoyed it too," she said quietly. Suddenly she felt shy and that was not at all like her. "It was nice."

They both knew they were purposely drawing out their good-bye and neither cared if it was being artfully done or not. They just wanted to grab as many seconds together as they could.

"Would you mind terribly if I kissed you good night?" he asked, amazed as she was with the forwardness of his question. Usually if he wanted a kiss, he simply took it, but he realized he did not want to take a kiss from Patricia. He wanted her to willingly allow him to have it.

"I wouldn't mind at all." She smiled and tilted her forehead to receive his kiss. She closed her eyes in order to enjoy the touch of his lips to its fullest.

But Cole had a different sort of kiss in mind. Slowly, he lowered his lips to hers. At first her eyes flew open with surprise, then gently closed again as a warm tide of delightful sensations flooded her. She offered no protest when he pulled her closer and pressed her soft body firmly against his sturdy frame. Instead she slowly raised her arms to encircle his neck and reveled in the tantalizing sensations his gentle kiss offered her.

Immediately, the kiss deepened. The feel of his lips fiercely caressing hers and of her breasts firmly pressed against his muscular chest sent a need coursing through the very core of her. This need was so strong and so basic that it startled her. She felt suddenly threatened by the intensity of her own feelings. A silent alarm sounded and she quickly pulled away.

"That was some good-night kiss," she gasped. Her senses still reeled and her heart pounded hard against her chest. It had been quite some time since a mere kiss or a man's touch had affected her like that and it scared her. She liked Cole and had wanted to be kissed, but now she regretted it. Emotions had flared inside her that she had thought long dead and really had preferred they stay that way. She would not have to even worry about being hurt again if she could only keep herself away from any vulnerable sort of relationships.

"I agree," he said, struggling for a breath. "I knew it was going to be good, but I had no idea it would be that good."

Patricia did not know exactly how to respond to that. It was the sort of compliment she knew she should reprimand him for, but didn't. Instead, she simply thrust out her hand and smiled timidly. "Good night."

Sensing her reluctance to discuss the kiss further, he accepted her hand and gave it a brief squeeze. The time was not right. Yet. "Good night. I'll see you Saturday."

As he turned and walked away, she felt an odd desire to call him back. She had disappointed him by pulling away like she had, but she had been too afraid to continue. He had aroused too many deeply seeded emotions far too quickly. As she touched her lips where a languid warmth still lingered, she realized she would have to be more careful in the future or chance actually falling in love with him, and that would never do.

"Well? Did you get a good look around the place?" Captain Reid asked when he stepped out onto the porch and watched while the new residential engineer came up the boardwalk toward the main clubhouse with his dark gray cassimere trousers wet to the knee. He had wanted to show the boy around himself but the lad had insisted on going out alone, and being busy with that broken pier the way he was at the time, it had really been best for them both.

"Yes, I find it quite impressive," James Seale said in earnest. He had spent the past five hours walking all the way around the lake and exploring his new domain. He had expected the place to be elegant, knowing the sort of people that summered here, but still he was in awe at just how magnificent Lake Conemaugh really was.

"Think you'll like your new job with the fishing and hunting club then?" the captain wanted to know.

"Definitely. I'm going to love it here," James replied with a smile. He had always been partial to the outdoors, especially the mountains, and this job would put him right out in the middle of nature at its finest. And as long as the resort was in its off season, he would practically have the whole place to himself. He looked forward to it.

He had begun to have his doubts, though, during that two-mile dusty ride from South Fork in which the driver of the wagon had managed to hit every rock and washout along the dusty road. The farmhouses they passed along the way were neat but simple, and the quality of life not what he had expected. For a moment, he had started to wish he had stayed in Pittsburgh. It was not until they had reached the

93

dam itself that his expectations began to be met. The lake was extraordinarily beautiful, its glassy surface coming within just a few feet of the top of the dam. And because the dam was an earthen one and was covered with wild grasses, bushes, saplings, and loose rocks, there was hardly any indication that the lake was man-made. It looked as if it belonged, truly belonged, in its natural wooded surroundings.

"Have you gotten settled into your rooms?" the captain asked, pulling up a sturdy bentwood rocker and easing his large frame into its wickerwork seat with a slight groan of relief. It had been a long day and now that it was near its end, he was ready to relax and enjoy. He was glad to have company other than Cody Cook, the one hired hand that stayed on at the clubhouse during the winter months. Cody was even younger than James. The boy couldn't be a day over twenty and not much in the way of a conversationalist.

"Yes, the driver helped me unload all my belongings and I'm all settled in upstairs. In fact, I was finished unpacking even before it stopped raining. My, but that cloudburst came up suddenlike. It was really something. Must have rained an inch." He reached down and pulled the clinging wet pant legs away from his skin. "Mind if I sit with you a while?"

"No, please, join me." Waving a hand, he indicated the nearest of the many rockers and lounging chairs that lined the wide front porch. In the summer these seats would be taken by men and women in their dapper new clothes passing the lazy summer days with idle chit-chat.

"I love this time of day," the captain mused. "It's so peaceful. The sky starts to turn colors and the night creatures tune up for their evening of revelry."

"How long have you been caretaker?"

"More years than I want to count. That's my farm over there," he said, and pointed to the land just beyond the eastern shore. Hayfields, still green from the unusually late warm weather, were surrounded by neat split-rail fences and higher up on a ridge was a large orchard where the leaves were multicolored with their vivid signs of autumn. And off to the left, glittering through the trees, was a large angler

94

farmhouse. Nestled in a dense wooded area like it was, the evening shadows caused an early dusk to fall over it, and a light already glowed brightly in the windows.

"You don't live here at the clubhouse?" James asked. He had assumed the man did, since he was the caretaker.

"No, I wanted a little place of my own. But I'm near enough that I can be here in a matter of minutes whenever there is trouble. After all, I'm just a short boatride away."

James did not blame him one bit. He would love to have a home near a place like this. He wished he owned one of those cottages he had passed during his walk, although he thought the word cottage understated their size. There were sixteen of them, most were at least three stories tall, with high ceilings, long windows, and fancy railed porches along the front. And every one of them was much larger than the house he had grown up in as a child. What it must be like to have one of those cottages to come to each summer! He would like to be rich like that someday. He would especially like a house similar to the Lippincott cottage. With its two sweeping front porches, one set right on top of the other, and its fancy jigsaw trim, it reminded James of a Mississippi riverboat. How he wished he could see the inside.

"I guess you are ready to get started planning the new plumbing system," the captain said, interrupting the young man's thoughts again.

"Yes, that is part of my new job," he said, then grinned sheepishly. "But I must admit, I'd rather spend my days on the lake enjoying these wonderful surroundings."

"I know what you mean. I feel that way, too. Tell you what, why don't you set up a work place on one of the piers. Up under the awning of one of the boathouses. Then you could draw up your plans and be outdoors enjoying the lake at the same time."

"That sounds good to me. At least as long as the weather holds out. Once winter sets in, I'll be more willing to stay inside and work by a window."

The two men sat in silence watching a squirrel ease up to the water's edge and take a drink. Knowing it was in no danger from the men up at the clubhouse, it stayed to play with a stick that had floated to the edge of the lake, until a large fish surfaced near the shore and made a tiny splash, scaring the squirrel back into hiding. Both men laughed at how quickly the little animal had shimmied up the nearest hickory and disappeared from sight.

"And when I get through with the plumbing, I might see what I can do about that dam," James said, continuing along the same line of thought. "And the bridge over that little spillway could use a few reinforcements too."

"The bridge maybe, but there isn't anything wrong with the dam," the captain replied quickly, his response defensive. "Whatever makes you think there's something wrong with the dam?"

"When I got to the end of the lake, I decided to leave the main path and look around at the bottom of the dam. I noticed several large leaks. If they aren't patched pretty soon, they could become serious."

"Oh, those. No, son, those aren't leaks. There's a big spring at the base of the dam. That's not leaks."

"I don't know. These are pretty high up to be caused by a spring," James went on. He was almost certain the water was coming from leaks through the bottom of the dam wall.

"Take my advice. Don't go stirring up trouble with that nonsense about leaks. That dam's as sturdy as the day it was built. It doesn't need any repairing. It wouldn't be worth the mess it would cause and think of the fish we would lose. We got that lake well stocked with the finest trout, bass, and pickerel anywhere. That's why we got those steel screens across the spillway, so those fish can't get out. Besides, that dam's been inspected by several of our members who know about such things and they all agree that it is just fine the way it is. And even now, it continues to get inspected at least twice a year. No, there's no problem with the dam."

James frowned; his eyes narrowed thoughtfully. There was no sense arguing about it. It was obviously a sore subject with the captain. He would just have to keep an eye on those leaks himself. If they got any worse, he would simply approach the president of the South Fork Fishing and Hunting Club himself. They could always make the repairs during the next off season. They could start right after everyone had left at the end of summer. That way the mess would not really inconvenience anyone other than the locals. With enough men on the job, they could have the dam repaired and serviceable again by the following summer. And with the rainfall this place got in the springtime, it would not take long at all for the lake to be back at its regular level. They could even save some of the fish by transferring them to a huge holding tank of some sort. He might go ahead and start drawing up a few preliminary plans before next summer to show just how he would do the repairs. Then maybe he could get an okay to start the work by next fall. It was well worth a try.

Chapter Six

Patricia was tired of waiting for the explosion. She already had spent most of the day wondering when someone was going to telephone or come by and tell her father all about her evening out with Cole. But rather than wait for the inevitable, she finally decided she might as well be the one to tell him. It would be better to simply go ahead and get it over with. Reaching for her water glass, she took a long determined sip, then rose from her chair to go do just that—tell her father about Cole.

As she stepped out of her office, she happened to glance toward the front window and noticed William headed for the brewery's front door and, judging by the rigidness of his jaw and his purposeful stride, he knew. . . .

She had two choices. She could stay where she was and face the rantings she knew were to come, or she could turn and duck back into her office and hope he never found her. Deciding she needed another drink of water anyway, she quickly returned to her desk and sat down. Even as she waited for the sound of the front door, she knew she was merely postponing the outcome, but if the moment of truth had arrived for her and William, she felt better facing it in the privacy of her own office.

Taking tiny sips until the water glass was empty, she sat facing the door and waited. Her nerves drew taut while her mind anticipated what he might say to her, the insinuations he was certain to make. In all honesty, she knew he had a reason to be angry. After all, he did consider her his girl despite her staunchest objections—and so did most of his friends. He would no doubt feel as if he had been cheated out of something he had always considered his. With vanity the depth of William's, she knew he was having a hard time dealing with the talk her evening with Cole had no doubt started. She would try to remain calm and soothe his ruffled feathers. Though he was not well known for listening to reason when upset, she would do her best to explain. If she could get William to understand, maybe she would be able to get her father to understand as well.

To her dismay, William did not come to her door as she had expected. He had no plans whatsoever of stopping by for any sort of explanation before running to tell her father. Instead, he barely threw her a sideways glance while he marched straight into her father's office with his chin thrust forward and his shoulders back. It was a familiar stance for William whenever he felt he had been insulted and obviously that was exactly how he felt now. It was only a few seconds before she heard her father's booming voice summon her. "Patricia Anne!"

"Tattletale," Patricia thought venomously as she tried to take one last sip from her dry glass. Quietly, she rose from her desk chair and took the time to smooth the larger wrinkles from her plaid skirt and adjusted her shirred waistline before heading into her father's office with an angry scowl. She wondered exactly what William had said and how badly incriminating it was. With William's talent for exaggerating, there was no way for her to even try to guess.

"Where were you last night?" her father demanded of her even before she had reached his desk. He lifted his fingertips and adjusted his glasses in order to focus clearly on her guilt. He frowned when he found her not to have conscience enough to even look mildly guilty or dutifully ashamed. There was absolutely no remorse on her face at all.

As Patricia considered the abrupt question, she thought about asking at what particular time he might be referring to, but decided nitpicking would just make matters worse. "I had dinner at the Hulbert House."

"Alone?" William asked accusingly, his thin nostrils flared with anger as he spoke. He was leaning insolently against her father's massive oak desk with his arms folded across his chest. Patricia felt a childish urge to kick his legs out from under him and had known William long enough to remember a time when she might have done just that.

"Of course not alone. I had dinner with a friend," she retorted defensively. Sometimes William could be so aggravating.

"And does this friend have a name?" he went on to ask.

"Of course. Everyone has a name. His is Cole Gifford," she shot back, narrowing her eyes to let him know just how angry she had become.

When she narrowed her eyes like that, eliminating the whites around the vivid green, she looked remarkably like a cat ready to strike. William shuddered inwardly at the thought.

"Who is this Cole Gifford?" This time it was her father who questioned her. Slowly, she diverted her gaze from William's to meet his. "That name sounds very familiar to me."

"It should. He was in here yesterday trying to get you to sign a petition concerned with repairs at the Lake Conemaugh dam."

"Him? You allowed that arrogant . . . you allowed him to pay call on you? How do you even know the man?"

"We introduced ourselves after I asked to sign his petition." The anger grew in her father's pale blue eyes and she added defiantly, "I felt one of us should." She tried not to flinch as she waited for the tirade she knew would follow the impudence of that last remark.

"You *what?*" He was furious with her all right. That telltale vein stood out in his neck and a tiny white line formed around his drawn lips. "You *asked* to sign that petition? Don't you know that those people who own the dam are some of our best customers? Don't you realize what you have risked by signing that blasted petition?"

"And don't you realize the risk we'll be taking if that dam

101

is not repaired? We are in serious danger and it grows worse with each year that passes."

"What are you two talking about? What petition?" William wanted to know, and pushed himself away from Clayton's desk in order to turn and face the man. He had not heard of any petition that dealt with the Lake Conemaugh dam and since some of those men had generous accounts at his bank, he wanted to know about it.

Clayton quickly explained about the visit Cole had paid him the day before and about the petition the man had asked him to sign. William was clearly disturbed. "Why don't people let that old chestnut go? We've both seen that dam. There's nothing really wrong with it. And those people that own it help out the economy around here by supplying jobs for the locals in the summer and by buying a lot of their summer supplies from area merchants. We don't need to chance making them angry with us by nagging them about their dam."

"Don't tell me, tell her," Clayton spouted, gesturing toward Patricia. "She's the one that obviously agrees with the man."

"Enough that she was willing to have dinner with him," William added with a heavy intake of air. Crossing his arms again in a judgmental fashion, he leaned back against the desk and glowered at her.

Patricia had wondered when they were finally going to realize that they had been sidetracked from their original topic of concern.

"What I don't understand is how she could agree to go out with a man she just met, especially when she is supposed to be engaged to me. Makes you wonder about her morals, doesn't it?"

"I've tried my best to raise her right," Clayton said with a disgusted shake of his head.

"Wait a minute," she interrupted, tired of being talked about as if she was not even there. She took a step toward William and leveled a determined finger just inches from his thin, aristocratic nose. "I have never once told you I intend to marry you. You can't stand there and pretend that I have.

In fact, I've turned you down more times than I can count. In no way am I committed to you nor have I ever been."

"But you have continued to go out with me and accept my advances," he pointed out. "We have been seeing each other steadily for two years now. Neither of us has been out with anyone else in all that time. That's the same as a commitment."

"Just because I enjoy your company *most* of the time and have allowed you to kiss my forehead or hold my hand on occasion does not mean I want to marry you. I've told you and told you that I don't ever plan to marry again—not you or anyone. Look, I like you and I like Cole, but I don't intend to marry either one of you. Marriage no longer appeals to me at all. Why can't you get that simple idea into that thick brain of yours?"

"Patricia!" her father reprimanded her. "Watch that tone of voice, young lady."

"Cole? You call him by his given name already?" William sputtered, unaware he had interrupted Clayton.

"Yes, Mr. Speck, I do," she replied pointedly.

"Patricia, I'm warning you," her father inserted.

"I'm sorry, Father," she sighed with resignation. "I don't want to argue with either one of you. I just want to be free to run my own life the way I want. So I went out with Cole Gifford last night and had a wonderful time. So what? It is my life and I am going to make my own decisions as to what I do with it. I would appreciate it if you two would simply accept that." Turning back to William, she spoke in a restrained voice. "Try not to take this so personally. I still like you as much as I ever did. It's just that I like Cole Gifford, too, and you may as well know that I already have plans to see him again Saturday night. He and his sister are coming over to my house for dinner."

Patricia and William both jumped at the unexpected sound of Clayton's fist crashing down on the hard surface of his desk when he shouted, "I will not allow you to continue to see this Cole Gifford. The man's a troublemaker. I'll not have my own daughter out gallivanting around with the likes of a man like that."

"And what do you plan to do to stop me?" she wanted to know, whirling to face him again. "Restrict me to my room? That will be hard to do since I have a house of my own. Or maybe you plan to have him run out of town like you did Franklin? Yes, I know more about that than you realize and I have a feeling Cole is not the type to cower down to your threats, whatever they might be. I may not know exactly what you did to get rid of Catherine's fellow, but I do know you were responsible for his sudden disappearance and I seriously doubt it would work on Cole Gifford. I just wish you would finally realize that I am a grown woman and have been for quite some time now. I'm not your little girl anymore."

Realizing Clayton was about to say something he would regret later, William quickly put in, "That's all right Clayton, let her see this Cole Gifford a few times. She'll tire of his company soon enough."

William firmly believed that. His ego was such that he honestly believed that she or any woman would be a fool to choose another man over him—after all he was good-looking and a man of growing prestige in Johnstown and there was no doubt he would someday be as rich as any man in the town. He saw it as just a matter of time until she came to her senses and quit seeing the man. Then she would be his property once more. He was certain this was just a temporary rebellion of Patricia's. It just seemed to be in her nature to want to rebel against something every now and then and she would feel it was to his credit not to have interfered. And in an afterthought he knew that if she did not tire of this Cole Gifford quickly enough, he would simply persuade the man to find other things to do with his time. Every man had a price. Every man had a weakness. He would just have to find out what Cole Gifford's weaknesses were.

"Maybe so." She shrugged agreeably. She knew it was the same as lying but was tired of arguing. She might decide to stop seeing Cole for other reasons, but she doubted she would ever actually grow tired of a man like Cole Gifford.

Clayton sat studying William's face as if trying to read the young man's thoughts. He knew William well enough to know his young friend was planning something. William was not the type to give an inch unless he thought he could gain a mile in doing so.

"We are still going to the play Friday night, aren't we?" William asked, turning so that Patricia could not see the knowing wink he had for Clayton. Now Clayton was certain William had already planned his strategy and relaxed a little.

"Yes, of course," she replied. Although she was not looking as forward to the evening as she once had, she had told him she would go and did not plan to back out on that promise now. Besides, going out with William on Friday would help pacify her father until she could decide exactly how to handle him on this. Despite his ornery ways, he was her father and she did love him dearly. She just wished he would let her lead her own life without meddling in it.

When Friday night came, Patricia dutifully got dressed in an elaborate dress the color of vintage burgundy with a high neck and small white collar edged in brown lace that matched the narrow white sash at her waist and the tiny white cuffs at her wrists. The bodice fit snugly to the waist, then a full skirt flowed out in wide folds until it fell gracefully to the floor. She had decided to wear her hair pulled back away from her face, which showed the delicate widow's peak at her forehead. Held in place by two silver combs, she allowed the length of her dark hair to dangle in long curls down her back. When she appraised herself in the mirror, she felt beautiful. She wished Cole could see her, but it was William's voice that heaped lavish praises on her that night.

Throughout the evening, despite William's strong attentiveness, Patricia found her eyes straying to the people around her, hoping by some miracle Cole might be there. Not that she wanted him to see her with William, she simply wanted to be able to look at him. She would be content with just a glimpse of his strong handsome face. But he was not around and none of the faces at the opera house that night could even compare. She felt oddly disappointed, listless,

105

ready for the night to end.

Later that evening, when William finally walked her to her door, her thoughts were already on all the preparations she needed to make for her dinner guests the following night. She was hardly aware of the man beside her, which turned out to be to her disadvantage, for when she leaned forward to allow him his perfunctory kiss on her forehead, he pulled her to him and kissed her squarely on the mouth.

Surprised and dismayed, she tried to pull herself free of his grasp, but found his grip tightened with each movement she made. He continued to press his lips against hers in what had to be the most lifeless kiss she had ever had to endure. Although she had never truly felt aroused by William's sophistication and well-bred good looks, she had never dreamed his kiss would be so dull. It was nothing more than a hard pressure against her mouth, almost painful.

"Good night, sweetheart," he cooed, obviously pleased with himself. No doubt he thought by her stunned expression that she had enjoyed it.

"Good night, William," she replied, absently stretching her lips forward in an attempt to bring feeling back to them. He had pressed her lips so hard against her teeth that they had grown numb. But William mistakenly took her protruding lips as an invitation for more. Smiling to himself, he quickly obliged.

The second kiss dragged out even longer than the first one had and Patricia finally had to shove him away in order to catch a needed breath. Thinking he had left her breathless with desire, William reached out and tapped her lips lightly in what he felt was a most intimate gesture, turned, and swaggered proudly back to his awaiting carriage.

Little did he know he had numbed her lips so effectively that she had not even felt his finger. Nor did she really feel the back of her hand as she wiped the moisture he had left on the corner of her mouth. But by the time she entered the house and had securely locked the door behind her, she was able to feel the smile that slowly grew from the thought of how much William had to learn about the art of kissing and how Cole could very well be the one to demonstrate for him. Cole was certainly a true master in his own right.

The inane smile lingered on Patricia's face far into the night, for even as she drifted off to sleep, she found she could think of nothing more than Cole Gifford, that notorious sister of his, and their upcoming evening together.

Chapter Seven

"Ah, Miss Mackey, I kinda thought you might be coming around here soon," Jeb Sobey said with a slight wrinkle of his upper nose. Ever since the postmaster had gotten new glasses, he was having a time of it keeping them where he wanted them.

"Then you do have a letter for me?" Catherine asked, her blue eyes bright with hope. She glanced around the post office to be sure there was no one near enough to see her get the letter. Except for a small boy who had come in just to enjoy the new bentwood bench near the front door, they were alone.

"Yessum, came on yesterday's morning train as a matter of fact," he told her, then leaned back so he could see under the counter where he kept any mail marked general delivery. Once he had spotted her letter, he bent forward again and retrieved it for her. "I was sorta expecting to see you sometime yesterday afternoon. You usually have an uncanny knack for knowing when you got one of these letters."

"I tried to get by, but I had to work late. With two women having quit last week, the hospital is short of helpers these days," she explained eagerly, her eyes on the letter as he held it out for her. Her heart raced with its usual excitement when she timidly reached out her slender hand and accepted it.

"I thought about bringing it by your house on the way home yesterday, but I was afraid your father might be home," he told her with a warm smile. Although he had

109

never actually been told that these letters of hers were secret, he was no idiot. He knew that they were and he had gladly kept her secret all these years. He would hate to do anything that might hurt this pretty little lady whose eyes lit up with such joy every time he had a letter for her stamped from New York State. Besides, it was none of his concern what was in the letters or where they came from. His job was to get the letter to the addressee and nothing more.

"I'm glad you didn't. He was home all right and has he ever been in a foul mood these days," Catherine confided, leaning forward even though she knew they were now alone. It was just her private nature that made her do so.

"Speaking of your father, you'd better hide that. Here he comes," Jeb said and nodded toward the front windows. Suddenly he reached for his main drawer and yanked it open. About that time the little bells over the door jangled but Jeb did not look up. Poking around in the drawer for another moment, he looked back up and said in an overly loud voice, "No ma'am, I seem to be fresh out of postcards. Sorry, I couldn't help you. Check back next week. Probably around Tuesday."

Catherine's initial flaring of panic gave way to relief. Her friend had provided her with a logical excuse for being there. With her back still to her father, she carefully stuffed the letter she dared not let him see inside her pale yellow cotton blouse while Jeb politely looked elsewhere. She hoped the material was bulky enough to hide the outline of the envelope. Inhaling a strengthening breath, she turned to leave. "Oh, Father, what are you doing here?"

"Miss Cook went home early and I have some papers to send out that have got to get off today," he said, his brow raised with surprise at having run into his youngest daughter. Except to go to that blasted hospital three days a week, or to the library occasionally, Catherine rarely left her rooms. He was pleased to see her out. It was about time she started to get over that damn stubborn streak of hers. After all, it had been three years now and his patience had stretched about as far as it could go. And if she was finally getting over it, he wondered if she was ready for any new gentlemen callers yet. "What are you doing here?"

"I've been feeling guilty for not writing to Cousin Karen. We haven't corresponded in months and we used to be so close. But I really don't feel up to writing her a whole letter. I never can think of enough to say, so I thought I'd see if Mr. Sobey might have some postcards. But he doesn't, so I may have to go ahead and try to write her a whole letter after all." Nervously, she reached up and played idly with a tiny brown curl that had come loose just behind her ear.

Clayton had too many other things on his mind to stand there and talk with Catherine about postcards or her younger cousin, Karen Taylor. He needed to get back to the brewery. He could talk with her later. Hoping to hurry her along, he muttered his usual, "That's nice, dear." Lifting his large envelope, he shoved it toward Jeb and reached into his pocket for his money. "You really should write her a long letter anyway." It would give her something to do besides brood endlessly. Then to Jeb, he pointed at the address and said, "I need to get this to there as quickly as possible."

Seeing she was dismissed, Catherine turned and threw Mr. Sobey an appreciative glance, then hurried outside with her special letter pressed very near her heart. Usually, she carried his letters across the street to the park and read them there—under the shade of one of the huge red oaks in the summer or on one of the stone benches placed in the sunshine during the winter. But with her father still nearby, she decided to carry it back to her bedroom before reading it. Anxious to see what he had to say, knowing it was almost time for the good news, she caught herself almost running down the walk with a bright smile beaming on her lovely face, unaware of the many faces that turned to catch sight of her beauty.

Only moments after she had securely closed her door behind her, she reached inside her blouse and pulled out the small rumpled envelope. Gingerly, she ran her fingertip over her name written boldly in his very own handwriting then turned it over and began to pull the flap loose. Wanting to prolong this moment of ecstasy as long as she could, she first made herself comfortable on her bed, then eased the paper

111

out and neatly unfolded it. She pressed the paper to her face for a moment as if to soak in his very touch and breathed deeply in hopes of finding his scent lingering there. How dreadfully she wanted to see him. She could bear their parting no longer. Tears of joy filled her blue eyes as she began to read; his first words were a declaration of his undying love for her and how their torment of waiting was soon to be ended.

Patricia brushed her hair back into a lovely array of dark curls and carefully wove a satin ribbon of gold through it. Having spent most of the day getting the meal and table ready, she had not left herself much time to get dressed. She had hurriedly bathed with scented soap and slipped into the special dress she had chosen to wear, made of beige lawn, heavily trimmed in white lace. Even the long sleeves were adorned with wide bands of lace from the elbow all the way down to the cuff. Having taken just enough time to pinch her cheeks and press her lips together to add color to her face, she scurried downstairs for one last look at the table before they arrived.

Gently, she reached out to adjust one of the redware dinner plates that seemed to be a little too far from the table's edge and pulled in the large etched water glass. The flatware had to be moved down just a little as well. Once she felt she had the setting properly positioned, she stepped back and eyed the table once more. The linen and lace tablecloth she had chosen was not extremely elegant, but was far nicer than the woolen cloth she usually used. And the centerpiece was not one of sterling silver like she had been accustomed to as a child, but she felt the small gathering basket full of fragrant flowers added a nice touch just the same. She felt proud of her table and hoped Cole and his sister would notice just how nice it looked.

Apprehensively, Patricia circled the table. Her insides were fluttering. She was anxious to be with Cole again, not having seen him since their evening at the Hulbert House, but she was also eager to meet that sister of his. She hoped to make a good first impression for she dearly wanted his sister to like her. She wanted to fit into Cole's life well enough that they could remain friends for a long time. She adored his company and wanted to share more of it.

At precisely seven o'clock came the knock on her door. With her heart thudding nervously, she took a deep breath and went to answer it. Just before she put her hand on the handle, she gave her beige sleeve a brisk swipe and then lifted the skirt in order to fluff it out to a better fullness. She felt as giddy as a schoolgirl.

When she swung the door open, her eyes came to rest on Cole's handsome face. His broad frame filled the doorway and she could not help but notice how stunning he looked, dressed in a dark blue three-piece suit. The deep color seemed to bring out the sparkling highlights in his pale blue eyes. She wished she could stand there and stare at him forever. He was that handsome, but then remembering the sister she was to meet, she broke her trance and glanced around curiously for the missing guest.

"Hello," he finally said, giving her a dazzling smile that warmed her to her toes.

"Hello." She smiled back, wondering what it would be like to reach out and touch those long narrow dimples of his. "Didn't your sister come?"

"Yes, she's coming up the steps now," he informed her, then stepped aside so she could see while he started the formal introduction. "Patricia Morgan, girl of my dreams, I'd like for you to meet my dear sister, Faye Gifford."

As her gaze fell on the beautiful young woman slowly climbing the steps, her mouth fell open with stunned amazement. "That's your sister?"

Grinning from ear to ear, he spoke proudly while he held an arm out to the woman who was still fighting her heavy black skirt in an effort to make it up that last step without tripping. "Yes, this is my sister—the sister. She's known as Sister Mary down at St. John's. But she's still Faye to me."

Aware that her mouth gaped open, but unable to do anything to pull it shut, Patricia held out her hand in greeting. "Very pleased to meet you. But he never told me

113

you were a . . . a . . ."

"Nun?" she supplied cheerfully. When she came to stand beside her brother, she gracefully accepted Patricia's hand in a warm clasp. "He never does. He just loves to surprise people with my chosen way."

"It's just that I keep forgetting," he said innocently. Tapping his temple lightly with his fingertip as if trying to jar his senses, he added, "I seem to find it hard to forget the adventurous little imp you were as a child. I still see that mischievous little girl in braids that loved to don boys' britches and climb trees."

"He loves to tease me," she confided to Patricia before she turned and punched her elbow sharply into her brother's side. "Now behave yourself before I do something you'll be deeply sorry for."

"Yes, sister dear." He grinned, clutching his side in pretended agony. "Whatever you say."

"He may be strong and demanding, but he can be handled," Faye said with a coy wink as she brushed past Patricia. "You just have to know how."

"Hey, I resent that," Cole said, following his sister inside and closing the door for them.

"And well you should," she said agreeably. "But don't press your luck. Any man who lets his sister get away with all you have let me get away with through the years shouldn't be standing around arguing with a nun. He should be atoning to God for such sins."

"And well I might," he said, trying to sound serious. "I should ask that he forgive me for not taking you over my knee years ago and teaching you a little respect for your brother."

Patricia was still too overwhelmed to say much. With only a word or two of direction, she invited them both into the parlor to sit. She cringed at the thought of the tall cut glass wine decanter she had placed out earlier. She wondered what Cole's sister the sister was going to think of her for having such a beverage in her home. Although she very rarely drank wine herself, she had thought it the hospitable thing to have it to offer her guests. She could strangle Cole for not having

114

warned her about his sister.

"Please make yourself at home while I go into the kitchen and check on the brisket," she said while she edged her way toward the wine decanter in hopes of removing it before it was noticed. She wished she could remember Catholic views on drinking wine. But knowing Catholics did not partake of meat on Fridays, she was certainly glad that today was Saturday.

"What a lovely home you have," Faye said as she glanced around the room. "I especially like that lovely clock. Chippendale, isn't it?" Upon seeing Patricia's nod, she went on. "And aren't these wing chairs Chippendale too? My but you certainly do have good taste."

"Thank you," Patricia responded with a smile, noting that Faye's wandering gaze was coming dangerously close to the decanter. She took another step and casually lifted the container of wine from the table.

"Oh, wine, mind if I have a glass now? I am dry as a bone. I was rather rushed by a certain pushy brother who was afraid we were going to be late in arriving."

"You would like a glass of wine?" she asked, feeling relief flood her. So nuns did drink wine. Wonderful.

"A small glass if you don't mind," Faye responded with a smile. When she smiled, dimples formed that looked very much like Cole's. Patricia wondered if her hair was the same deep color of brown. With the wimple of her headdress she wore coming so low on her forehead, she was unable to really tell but judging by her dark eyebrows, it probably was.

"I'll pour," Cole said, feeling the two had forgotten he was even in the room. "You go check on that brisket. The delicious smell of it is spurring my appetite. I'm ready to eat."

"Oh, you are always ready to eat," Faye imparted. Turning to Patricia, she confided, "Mother used to worry that he was hollow inside."

Cole grunted in response. "I don't remember you turning down any meals."

"I imagine not," she admitted with a nod.

By the end of the meal, Patricia had fully adjusted to the

fact that Faye was a nun. She had gotten over the initial discomfort she had felt and found Faye was a lot of fun to be around. Her sense of humor was just as sharp and witty as her brother's, though it was not always pointed in the same direction. She often gave heaven an apologetic glance for some of the things Cole had to say, but never did she openly find fault with his comments.

When it came time to leave the table, Faye insisted on helping clear away the dishes. After pushing back her heavy black sleeves, she gathered up an armload then turned to find her way into the kitchen.

"So, what do you think of Sis?" Cole wanted to know once his sister was out of the room.

"I like her."

"Isn't she everything I said she was?"

"And more," Patricia said meaningfully. "Why didn't you warn me she was a nun?"

"And chance you putting on pretenses with her? No, I wanted her to meet the real you. I wanted her to understand why I like you so much."

"Oh? And do you like me?"

"More than I should."

Patricia smiled. Something warm inside her stirred to life. Although she did not want any deep involvement with him or any man, she did so want him to like her.

"And do you by any chance like me?" he asked, not about to let this subject be dropped just yet.

"Despite my better judgment." She laughed, knowing he was expecting an open assessment of her feelings and hoping for better.

"Thanks," he replied in a flat voice. "You really know how to boost my confidence."

"Sir, I doubt your confidence needs boosting," she said, laughing.

Faye walked back in at that moment and agreed. "No, the last thing he needs is to have his confidence boosted."

"That's right. Gang up on me," he pouted playfully. "Just for that, I'm not going to help clear the table. You two will find me in the parlor when you are ready to go to the park. I

116

just hope your attitudes will have changed by then." Having said that, he rose from his chair and left with his chin held high.

"Sensitive, isn't he?" Faye laughed and reached for more dishes.

"Very. Tell me, how have you tolerated a brother like Cole for so many years?" Patricia wanted to know, laughing right along with Faye.

"He's the cross I have to bear," she said with a shrug as she turned to carry another load into the kitchen.

"Faye, uh, Sister Mary, you really don't have to do that. You are a guest."

Faye turned and smiled. "To my close friends not associated with the church, I'm Faye, not Sister Mary. And since I do want us to be close friends, that is what you should call me. As for the dishes, I don't care if I am a guest. I enjoy helping." Having established that, she went on into the kitchen.

Soon they had not only cleared the dishes, but had washed them, also at Faye's insistence. Only the huge roaster pan was left soaking in soapy water for scrubbing the next day. By the time they entered the parlor they found Cole sitting comfortably on the upholstered sofa with a plump hand pillow propped between his shoulder and the tall winged arm.

"I hope you made yourself comfortable," Faye said with a raised brow upon finding her brother so.

"Very," he said, slowly rising. "Are you two finally ready to go?"

Having learned her lesson from the other evening, Patricia took the time to get her cloak before leaving. Seeing the good judgment in such a decision, Faye had Cole stop by the church to get her cloak too. It took only a minute and Patricia waited for them in the carriage. While they were gone, she quietly reflected on how much fun she was having. She couldn't remember having laughed so much in years. Soon Cole and Faye returned and they were back on their way to the park. It was not long before they could hear the first strains of music drift along the crisp autumn night air.

"Invigorating, isn't it?" Faye said, breathing deeply the cool air and turning an ear toward the music.

"Yes, it is," Patricia replied, but realized it was just as invigorating for her to be sitting next to Cole. With the three of them on the same seat, they were forced to sit extremely close. She was very much aware that his thigh was pressed gently against her own and with each jolt of the carriage, his shoulder came into contact with hers.

Every touch between them seemed to intensify whatever it was she was feeling. Without meaning to, she remembered just how those shoulders had looked, bare of clothing and gleaming in the soft candlelight. His body was splendid, what she had seen of it. She wondered what he would look like with absolutely nothing on. She felt a sudden stab of conscience knowing she had considered such a thing while sitting next to a nun. Even though she realized Faye had no way of knowing her thoughts, she found herself smiling apologetically. Luckily, Faye was too engrossed with the music to notice.

When they reached the park they discovered all the benches taken. Undaunted, Faye walked over to where several of the town's youths were sitting on the lawn and knelt there beside them. Smiling and nodding her head with the beat of the music, she was unaware when Cole laid his coat on the ground for Patricia and the two of them joined her.

Despite the chill of the autumn night, the three of them thoroughly enjoyed themselves. The music was kept light and lively and occasionally a couple would be unable to bear sitting still and would start to dance. It was great fun. All too soon, though, it was ten o'clock and time for the band to quit. The men allowed themselves to be cajoled into one last number and promised to return the following Saturday, weather permitting.

"La-ta-da-ta-da," Faye sang, echoing the chorus of that final song as they made their way through the dispersing crowd to Cole's carriage. The lively tune came out in a frosty mist as she waltzed along her way.

Soon Patricia had joined her and before they were far on their way down the street in the carriage, Cole too was singing along. When they pulled to a stop in front of the church, they sat long enough to finish the song.

"It certainly was a joy to meet you," Faye said, reaching over and patting Patricia's hands when it came time for her to climb down. Patricia was amazed at how warm Faye's bare hands felt against hers. "And everything Cole has said about you has proved to be true."

"Is that good?" she asked warily.

Laughing, Faye nodded. "Yes, that is very good. It's not often Cole finds something worthy to say about any woman. He's determined to remain a widower you know. Maybe you are just the one to change all that."

Patricia didn't know what to say to such a remark. It stunned her to learn Cole was a widower. She could not remember his having mentioned being married before. Even so, she had no intentions of marrying him herself just to change that status. But she decided not to bother with explanations at this particular moment and simply offered a noncommittal smile.

"That's enough of that," Cole warned as he hopped down and circled behind the carriage in order to help his sister down. Looking apologetically at Patricia, he shook his head. "She's a hopeless matchmaker."

"Not hopeless," Faye corrected him. "Hopeful. Always hopeful."

The two of them continued to argue the point while Cole walked Faye to the side door. Once they had reached the tiny veranda, they both turned to look toward the carriage and then Cole burst out laughing. He patted his sister on the head and turned to leave, still chuckling. Patricia found this sudden outburst unnerving and looked down to see what they could have found in her to be so funny. It made her uncomfortable.

"What seems to be so funny?" she asked when he had climbed in and given the reins a slight flick.

"My sister. She seems to think I need coaching in what to

119

do at a pretty lady's doorstep. She thinks a tiny kiss to the forehead might be in order if handled discreetly. She never ceases to meddle in my affairs."

"And what do you think?"

"About my sister's meddling?"

"No, about what is in order at my doorstep."

"Let's just say I have my own ideas and it won't be a tiny kiss to the forehead, I assure you." His white teeth gleamed in the bright glow of the street light as they passed beneath it.

Intrigued by that remark, Patricia could not help but smile back. Did he intend to kiss her soundly on the mouth again? She might not want a serious involvement with him, but she decided she did not really mind if he kissed her. Besides, she enjoyed the way he kissed far too much to want to deny herself such pleasure. She would just have to be careful not to let the kiss get out of hand.

As the carriage neared her house, she felt an odd tightening in her chest and a fierce thundering of her heart that was unfamiliar. Just knowing a kiss could be coming excited her far more than it should. She remained silent for the remainder of the trip while she anticipated the tantalizing touch of his lips on hers. She had already decided to act properly coy about it, but would not deny him his kiss.

"I hope you have forgiven me," Cole said while walking with her to the porch. He looked at her and noticed how the street light glimmered off her dark hair. He wanted to reach in and take the pins from it and let it fall below her shoulders as he had seen it before.

"Forgiven you? What for?" She had no idea what he was talking about.

"For not having told you about my sister—the sister."

"Oh, that. Yes, Cole, you are forgiven."

"And I hope you will forgive me for something else," he went on to say.

"Now what for?"

"For this," he growled and crushed her firmly against him. He wasted no time in claiming her lips in a passion-filled kiss that immediately overwhelmed her. Her gasp of surprise was lost in the sweet depths of his mouth as was the gentle sigh that followed. She had never felt anything so wondrous. His sudden possession of her mouth was just as warm and masterful as she had remembered and caused her heart to soar to the heavens. Hands that had pressed against his chest in an initial protest relaxed as his lips worked their passionate wonders on hers. Soon her hands, seemingly with a will of their own, eased upward to encircle his strong neck and her arms rested comfortably on his shoulders. She moaned aloud her pleasure as his fingertips became entwined in the soft thickness of his hair. "So much for being coy," she thought as her hands roamed freely down his back. Eagerly, she returned his kiss with shameless abandon.

His kiss was like no other. It sent hot shafts of pure delight circling through her in a fiery turmoil, entering every fiber of her being, consuming her, possessing her. Never had she felt such need coursing through her depths. A stab of guilt tormented her when she realized even Robert's kiss had never aroused her quite like this—the passions had not been of the same caliber, but then she had been so very young. Now, older, she found herself lost in a turbulent sea of emotions, some of them vaguely familiar but so many of them totally new. It made it hard for her to think. It made her not want to think at all.

She felt herself trembling when his hands moved from the small of her back around to ease inside her opened cloak. Slowly a hand made its way to her rib cage, then up to gently cup the underside of her breast. Despite the clothing between them, she could feel his touch burning her skin and knew she should pull away. Her inner alarm sounded, but she chose to ignore it. Instead, she responded by timidly sliding one of her hands beneath his coat in like exploration. She marveled in the feel of his strong muscular back and firm, powerful shoulders beneath the thin fabric of his shirt. For the moment she simply wanted to enjoy whatever pleasures Cole had to offer. She did not want to worry about the heartaches the future might bring.

The kiss deepened. Starved for a taste of her, Cole slipped

the tip of his tongue through her parted lips and gently urged them to part further. Gently, he glided over the velvety edges. She responded in kind. He could not remember ever having tasted such sweetness nor having craved a woman so deeply. Desire for her pounded through him but he knew he had to be careful. He did not want to frighten her and chance losing her before he could even make her his. Suddenly, it occurred to him that was exactly what he wanted. He wanted to make her his. Not just for a night, but forever. Such a revelation stunned him.

Although Patricia had anticipated being the one to pull away from the kiss, she found that she could not. It wasn't because he had overpowered her in any physical manner. She simply did not want to. She had fallen prey to the lunacy of passion and wanted more of whatever he had to give her. Her common sense completely abandoned her and her womanly desires quickly took over. It was Cole who finally broke the kiss.

"It's getting late," he said in a gruff tone. He was having a difficult time catching his breath. His chest heaved with his every attempt. "I should be going."

Patricia felt confused as she watched Cole hurry back to the carriage and climb in. Hurriedly, he brought it to motion with a brisk slap of the reins. Why was he in such a hurry to get on his way? she wondered. Was it because she had been too bold? Why had she not been the one to pull away like she should have? How foolish she had been. She knew better than to allow herself to become so carried away. What had become of her resolve not to become seriously involved anyway. It was wrong. It was all so wrong.

Patricia knew she needed to do some serious thinking and sort through what had just happened. If she could not come to an understanding of her own emotions where Cole was concerned, she would need to take drastic measures. Maybe she should not see him anymore or at least not until she could get better control over her desires. If she didn't get such control, she was headed for another heartache and she just could not go through that again. Her heart still bore scars from having loved Robert so deeply. If she was to come to love Cole and lose him too, she would not be able to bear it. No, she must keep her firm resolve. It would simply be much safer for her not to fall in love with Cole at all. But why was that so hard for her to remember whenever he was around?

Chapter Eight

Cole was unable to sleep. The harder he tried, the more he tossed and turned until his bed was a jumble of twisted sheets and quilts. He had not been ready for the powerful feelings Patricia had aroused in him. It was more than the natural urge a man got when he was attracted to a beautiful woman. It far surpassed that; otherwise he never would have pulled away from her like he had. He would have let nature take its course. But the importance of what he felt had been too great. What worried him the most was that he was dangerously close to falling in love with her. He had not expected that nor had he thought he would ever again want to claim another woman for his own.

Marriage or even falling in love with Patricia simply did not fit into his future plans at all. But what was he to do about it? What he felt for her was already a part of him. There was no way to change that.

Finally, he gave up on the chance of ever falling asleep, untangled himself from the sheets, and climbed out of bed. Without giving his actions much thought, he walked into the kitchen and made himself a small pot of coffee. While it brewed, he searched the pantry for something to eat. For some unknown reason, nibbling always seemed to help him concentrate and his brain was not going to let him be until he had sifted through his feelings for her and had come to a decision as to just what he should do about them. If he allowed his emotions full rein, he would find himself spending all his spare time with Patricia. After all, that was when he was happiest. He would never be able to complete the petition on time and it was very important he did. It was as if his sense of dedication was somehow threatened by these new feelings for Patricia.

It worried him. His convictions could fall idly by the wayside. Yet, if he didn't spend a little time with her and explore what it was he felt for her, he would always be thinking about her, wondering what might have been, and never be able to get anything done. It was quite a predicament. One he should never have allowed himself to get in. Not at this time anyway. If only he had not met Patricia until after he had completed his mission and seen the Conemaugh dam finally made safe and Johnstown no longer under the threat of a dangerous washout.

He had to keep his priorities straight. But what were his priorities? Rubbing his stubbled chin as he slumped down into one of the high-backed wooden chairs, he was no longer certain. Was there a way he could find a balance between the two? He doubted it. Ever since he had met Patricia he had spent almost every spare moment either with her, thoroughly enjoying himself, or wistfully thinking about the next time he would be with her. Since that day in her father's office, he had not obtained as much as one more signature on the petition. In the past few days, he hadn't even tried to get anyone to sign it.

Sitting forward with his elbows planted on the table, he buried his face in his open hands and brooded over his situation. His thoughts slowly drifted back to Vella. Despite the eight years that had passed, he could still clearly visualize her lovely young face and her gentle manner. They may have only been married a year when she died, but she had been a good wife and had done much to enrich his life. He felt an odd sort of loyalty to her memory, always had, and a strong sense of remorse in knowing he was coming to care as much for someone else, someone so completely different. He had never thought he could care that way again. When Vella had died trying to give birth to their son, he had sworn he would never be able to love another. It was bewildering now to

126

discover that he could.

As the sky turned misty pink with the first faint indications of morning, Cole had not come to any clear understandings. His only conclusion for the night of lost sleep was that he needed to be careful and take things slowly. He must not lose sight of his goals concerning the dam, but he could not risk his chance for happiness should Patricia happen to have a true place in his future. He would have to find a balance and not allow one to interfere with the other.

With a shake of his weary head, he poured the last sip of stale coffee down his throat and headed for his bedroom to see if sleep was yet possible. He still had an hour before time to get ready for work at the iron mill and an hour was better than nothing.

"Father, I'm through with today's work, I'm going home a little early," Patricia said cheerfully when she leaned into Clayton's office. Even though he had yet to forgive her or make even as much as an attempt to be civil toward her, usually choosing to completely ignore her instead, Patricia tried to act as if nothing had happened. She still announced when she was coming or going from work and she had even attended the regular family dinner on Sunday just like she always did. So did William.

It had been an awkward situation, having William on one side of her and her father on the other and neither speaking to her, but she had endured it without complaint. Besides, her thoughts had been on Cole most of the time anyway. She had never before been so prone to daydreaming.

"Patricia, come in a minute," Clayton said with a broad smile. When he noticed how she hesitated near the door he politely added, "Please."

She eyed him suspiciously before she decided to go ahead and enter his office like he asked. The friendly tone in his voice had sparked her curiosity. She had to find out why the sudden change in attitude. Was he beginning to soften and forgive? This quickly?

"Patricia, I want you to meet someone." Shoving his chair

back across the carpeted floor, her father stood and gestured with a deep wave of his arm to a man sitting in one of the three black leather chairs across from his desk. As she came closer, the man stood and turned around to greet her. When she saw his face she was surprised. He was much younger than she had expected. For some reason, maybe it was his six-foot stature or the manner in which he carried himself, she had thought he would be older than herself. Instead he appeared to be several years younger; she guessed him to be around twenty-two or twenty-three. Freckles he had developed in his youth had just started to fade. But he was a handsome young man with dark curling hair and huge eyes that held a coloring hard to distinguish. At first, his eyes had looked green like her own, but as she got closer she was able to see heavy traces of blue and gold in them—a whole kaleidoscope of color.

"Tall, dark, and handsome," she thought with an inward smile as she waited to be introduced.

"Patricia, this is Anthony Alani. He recently moved here from Altoona and wants to buy that property I own over on Franklin Street," Clayton said with a beaming smile. "He's just gotten settled into a house and now wants to build an office building here in Johnstown. He needs a place of his own for his practice. He's a lawyer. And that location would be great for a lawyer's office."

"But weren't you planning to put another rooming house on that land?" she asked, wondering how he had been so easily swayed.

"True. I was thinking about another rooming house, but I can always build it on that property over on Bedford," Clayton told her uneasily. "It doesn't necessarily have to be on Franklin Street. A rooming house is going to do well in this town no matter where it is located."

Patricia eyed him warily. He had made such a big ordeal out of his plans to build a rooming house right next to the other one and join the two with a manager's apartment and a small garden area to be shared by both. He had already had the plans drawn and had approached several builders. Why this sudden eagerness to sell? This Mr. Alani must have offered him much more than the land was worth.

"Well, if you do buy the land, I hope you will do well, Mr. Alani," she finally said, extending her hand. Instead of the polite squeeze she had anticipated, the young man grasped her hand firmly and shook it much as he would a man's. Patricia smiled. She liked that.

"Don't call me Mr. Alani. Please. Call me Tony. All my friends call me Tony," he told her. His smiling eyes indicated he was sincere. "You will let me count you as one of my friends, won't you?"

"I'd be very pleased to be one of your friends." Patricia's smile widened. He was certainly personable. Maybe the young man had used this undeniable charm to convince her father to sell him the land. But she doubted it. Clayton's business sense was too strong. "And since we are friends, I should like for you to call me Patricia."

"It's getting late," Clayton interrupted while he glanced purposefully at his silver pocket watch. He easily grew tired of such pleasantries. Carefully, he tucked the watch back into his vest pocket and frowned. "But I'd really like to get our business settled as quickly as possible. I hate to leave things hanging. The sooner we can talk out the details of the sale, the quicker you will be able to start building." His face then lit up and he waved his finger in the air profoundly. "I know, why don't you come on home with me and have supper at my house. My housekeeper is the best cook around these parts and loves to show off her cooking to newcomers. We could then discuss this afterward in my study."

"Won't your wife mind?" he asked, looking doubtful at such a sudden invitation. It was almost five o'clock. He knew his mother would be beside herself should his father decide to bring company home for dinner at the last minute this way. And if he himself had a wife, he would never be so presumptuous as to invite last-minute guests like this. "Maybe you should call her and make sure."

"My wife died years ago and I assure you that Minnie is used to my sudden whims." He laughed reassuringly. "And as of yet, we don't have a telephone at the house. The telephone company is new. So far, they are servicing mostly

129

businesses. Only a few houses have had telephones installed. So you see, I couldn't call if I wanted to."

Patricia wondered when this change in Minnie had come about. This was Tuesday, toward the middle of the week, and the last time her father had brought company home unannounced in the middle of the week, Minnie had dropped things for days on end. Dropping things and letting them break or dent was Minnie's usual form of protest. True, she rarely complained aloud, to her father that is, but the dishes and utensils could be counted on for doing the talking for her. She wondered how many glasses tonight's unannounced guest was going to cost her father. It would depend on Minnie's mood and how much food she already had planned.

"Patricia dear, since you were leaving out of here anyway, why don't you head on over to the house and warn Minnie there will be extra places to set. Of course I'll want you to stay for supper too and since William's bank will be handling the transfer, maybe we should call and invite him too."

Patricia had been all for staying, mainly to help Minnie prepare the table for a guest, until she heard William's name. For some reason, she just was not up to sitting through another meal listening to William expound upon the upswing in the economy and how it was going to help Johnstown become much more prosperous. Although she was not against prosperity, she had taken about all of that she could stand last Sunday.

"I'm sorry, Father, but I already have important plans for this evening," she said and wondered if reading that novel she had started the night before counted as truly important. She decided when compared to an evening with William, it did.

"With Cole Gifford?" Clayton asked, his tone suddenly brusque. His pale blue eyes narrowed and his face hardened noticeably while he waited for her response.

"No, my plans have nothing to do with Cole," she assured him, wishing they did. She also wished there had not been such animosity in her father's voice when he spoke Cole's name. She had hoped he would start to mellow some by now.

"Good. I'm glad of that." His rounded shoulders visibly relaxed while he continued. "But I'm sure whatever your plans are they can be changed. I really would like for you to join us." His smile had made a miraculous reappearance when he reached out to pat her lightly on her shoulder. "See if you can't rearrange your plans and join us tonight."

Patricia did not answer immediately. She wondered if this was a maneuver to get her and William together for the evening. Was he really even planning to sell his land or was he leading this man on just to be able to have them all together at his house? She hoped not. Although she thought better of it, she finally agreed to go on and tell Minnie of the guests and stay for the meal, but warned him she would need to leave early. She did not intend to stay for any after-dinner conversations if William was going to be there. The man seemed to interest her less and less these days.

Just over an hour later, Patricia had cautiously delivered her message and was helping Catherine set the table in the dining room while Minnie grumbled in and about the kitchen. Neither woman wanted to step foot inside Minnie's domain while she was in such a mood, but they had both wanted to help in some way and had decided a joint effort was called for if the table was to look its company best.

"I really think Father could have given her a little more notice," Catherine said in a flat tone while she carefully searched the glassware for dust spots. "Why does that man have to be so inconsiderate? Sometimes I wonder if he even has a heart."

"Oh, he has a heart all right. I hear it beating every time someone mentions money," Patricia said with a chuckle, glad that there was no longer any bitterness in her youngest sister's voice when they spoke of their father. Catherine had been bitter for far too long. It was good she could finally speak of him, however disparagingly, without the bitterness or the hatred spilling from her. She was a far cry from having forgiven him, but at least the hurt was mending. Catherine was finally headed in the right direction and maybe someday she would be able to forgive him.

Feeling a little guilty for her quick remark about their

131

father, Patricia tried to look as serious as she could when she decided to apologize. "I'm sorry. I didn't really mean to say that about Father."

"Yes, you did," Catherine said and grinned. She had fully agreed with the blunt assessment of their father.

"Such wicked daughters we are," Patricia said and grinned too. Stepping back to admire their handiwork with the table thus far, she tapped a finger to her chin and carefully considered how it looked. "Wouldn't Mother's porcelain be better than the glazed mochaware? After all, we are using the silver appointments and the lace tablecloth."

"Is the man that important?" Catherine asked. They rarely used their mother's porcelain. Usually it was reserved for the more special family holidays.

"Well, he did appear to be the type who would be used to finer things. His clothes were expensive and stylish and his manners were very sophisticated. I think he might feel more at home with the porcelain."

"Whatever you say." She shrugged and began to gather up the blue and white mocha plates in order to replace them with their mother's white porcelain with delicate silver inlays. Patricia was usually a good judge of these things. Besides, Minnie was less apt to break their mother's fine porcelain as she would the mochaware. Minnie knew the porcelain could not be easily replaced.

"Besides, it never hurts to impress a handsome young man like Anthony Alani—I mean Tony. The man doesn't waste time. He has already insisted I call him Tony," Patricia said as she pulled a chair over to the hutch so she would be able to get the porcelain plates down without having to strain herself on her tiptoes.

"Handsome, is he?" Catherine wanted to know. A smile tugged at her lips. "But don't you have enough to worry about with that Mr. Gifford you have been seeing? Between his attentions and William's, I would think your hands would already be too full. I don't see how you could have much time for this Mr. Alani."

Patricia laughed. "I wasn't exactly thinking about him for myself. He's too young for me anyway. But I was thinking how he would be just about the right age for you." She watched closely for Catherine's reaction. "And you could do much worse than to find yourself interested in a handsome young lawyer with his own house and evidently the means of purchasing land on Franklin Street and building his own office building there. Rich and good-looking. That is a hard combination to beat."

"And is your Cole Gifford rich?" Catherine wanted to know.

"Not exactly. Oh, I don't think he's poor by any means, but no, I can't claim that he is particularly rich either. I really haven't seen his house to know for certain, but no, I don't think he's rich." She paused to realize what Catherine was doing. She would have to be careful or Catherine was going to have her contradicting herself about the importance of a man's wealth. "But Cole is very handsome. So handsome that it makes up for his not being rich."

"When do I get to meet this handsome man of yours?" she asked, accepting the plates as Patricia handed them down to her, hoping she had effectively changed the direction of the conversation before having to hear the "you don't socialize enough" speech she knew her sister was headed for. Besides, she was in no mood to have to offend either one of her matchmaking sisters again nor did s ɛ wish to risk starting another argument.

"Soon, I hope. I would like for you to meet him. I know you are going to like him. He's a lot of fun."

"Anything is better than William," Catherine stated bluntly. "I don't know what Father seems to see in that man."

"A little of himself I think," Patricia said and her smile faded while she thought about that. It was true. The two of them were a lot alike, maybe too much. She wondered if that was one reason she had never wanted to marry William.

"Maybe Father should stop trying to push him off on you and marry the man himself," Catherine mused aloud then laughed at the thought, her blue eyes glistening at having made such a wicked remark.

"Oh, well, it could be worse."

"How's that?"

"Father could be trying to push him off on you," Patricia said and her impish smile returned, letting Catherine know she was just teasing.

"I agree. That would be much worse," Catherine said. Her eyes grew wide with the repulsion such a thought caused. But aware that Patricia had made the remark in fun, she pushed the disgusting idea from her head and started handing the plates back to her sister one at a time.

"Maybe Father will grow tired of my constant refusals to marry William and really will try to turn William's attention toward you. Father would still be getting him as a son-in-law," Patricia suggested lightly, not ready to drop her teasing.

"Bite your tongue," Catherine quipped. That would certainly make these last few months unbearable. They were going to be hard enough to get through. Having William at her heel would make them pure torture.

The stamping of several pairs of feet on the front porch promptly followed by the sound of the front door as it opened brought their conversation to an abrupt end. After they quickly placed the last few plates where they belonged, the two gave their skirts and jackets last minute adjustments and hurried into the front salon to greet their guests.

When Patricia entered first and noticed that Tony's back was to them, she turned to watch her sister's reaction. She wanted to see Catherine's expression the moment Tony turned around. She wondered if Catherine would be as affected by his handsome looks as she had been. It would be a hopeful sign if she was.

"Catherine." Clayton called her name as soon as he had spotted his youngest daughter entering the room. He was glad to see that she had put on one of her nicer outfits and had set her hair up in a lovely array of golden curls. Now he felt certain Tony was going to be impressed. "I want you to meet someone."

At that moment Tony turned around and smiled down at Catherine, and just as Patricia had hoped, Catherine's blue eyes grew wide with wonder. Undoubtedly, her youngest sister found him to be just as attractive as she had. Patricia was pleased. There was truly hope for Catherine yet.

"Catherine, this is Anthony Alani, but he keeps insisting everyone call him Tony," Clayton said, equally aware of what Catherine's reaction had been. A slow smile spread over his face that gave him a look of total contentment. He too had been hoping Catherine and Tony would like each other. The moment he had met Tony, he had been impressed with the young man and immediately had thought of Catherine and how her attitude had recently shown signs of change. This young man was not only from one of the most prominent families in Altoona, he was well educated and would be the perfect match for her. Clayton just hoped she would prove to be more receptive to Tony than she had been to the young men he had brought around in the past.

"Pleased to meet you," Catherine said in a polite voice and slowly extended her hand. Her eyes turned timidly to his.

Patricia frowned. She had hoped to hear a certain waver in her sister's voice, or some sign of kindled emotion.

"And I am more than pleased to meet you," Tony said with emphasis. He gladly accepted her hand and held it a moment longer than was necessary. Turning to Clayton only a moment before returning his gaze to Catherine, he stated, "You never told me Catherine was so beautiful and I had foolishly thought Patricia the most beautiful woman ever. It would be almost impossible to try to decide which was more attractive. You certainly must be proud of yourself for having two such lovely daughters."

"Indeed I am," Clayton said, puffing his chest out slightly and pulling his chin in.

Patricia always thought he looked a lot like a rooster when he did that but decided to keep that assessment to herself. Someone needed to thank Tony for such nice compliments and since no one else seemed to want to, she took it upon herself to do so. "Tony, you are too kind."

William frowned at the easy way Patricia had just used this man's given name, but said nothing.

"Kindness has nothing to do with it. I pride myself on being totally open and honest." Tony's eyes never left

Catherine even while he spoke to Patricia.

"Such unusual traits in a man," Catherine replied. A pinkish blush crept along her cheek when she noticed how he continued to stare. She found she had to look away in order to keep control of her responses to this man. She must not allow herself to feel such things.

"I don't know if those traits are so unusual," William said, sounding a little offended. "I like to think of myself as being very open and honest."

"Well, you go right on thinking that, William," she said without as much as a flinch to indicate it was meant as a barb. Not wanting to give him time to consider and respond, she quickly suggested they all sit down and make themselves comfortable until Minnie was ready to announce supper. She found it a little unsettling when Tony followed her to the sofa and sat down right beside her. He was so close to her that she had to move a few inches away from him in order to be able to turn her knees toward his and face him. Patricia and Clayton smiled in unison as they watched the two. William seemed to be the only one in the room unaware of how Catherine was reacting to Tony.

"Patricia told me you are planning to buy some of Father's land and build an office on it," Catherine said, eager to get an impersonal conversation started. She could feel all the attention was on her and she hoped to direct it elsewhere as quickly as possible.

"Yes, I think the spot would be perfect. It is in the business district and since I intend to practice commercial law, I think my office should be there," he explained, but wanting to return the focus to her, he asked, "Don't you agree?"

"I suppose it makes sense," she said and wondered if that had sounded as dim-witted to him as it had to her.

"Well, it makes perfect sense to me," Clayton put in. "He needs to be accessible to his clients. This young man knows what he's doing all right. He's my type of man. He knows what he wants and then does what he can to get it. And he doesn't waste any time in doing so."

Tony looked up at him and wondered how the man could possibly have evaluated him this quickly, but decided to use that statement as his cue to say what was on his mind. "And what I want now is to know if you would mind if I came calling on Catherine."

"You what?" Catherine gasped, finding this interest very sudden. They had only met each other fifteen minutes ago.

"I want to call on you, that is if it is all right with you and your father. He told me earlier how you were not married and did not have a steady beau at this time, but as pretty as you are that is bound to change in a hurry. I don't want to take any chances by dragging my feet on this. I want to call on you." Seeing the stricken look on Catherine's delicate face, he added, "I am sorry if I shocked you, but I've already told you that I have this tendency to be open and honest. Sometimes I also have a tendency to be a bit too forward. It is all right with you, isn't it?"

Catherine did not know what to say. How could she gracefully tell him that his calling on her would be out of the question? She did not want to offend him but she certainly could not have him calling on her. It would not be right. She looked to Patricia for help, but could tell where her sister's heart lay. Patricia was smiling like a sated cat. Obviously, she considered it to be a wonderful idea. If only Patricia could be told everything.

"I—I think this is a little too sudden," Catherine said when she finally spoke. "I just met you."

"Of course, I should have known you would feel that way. Tell you what, I'll spend the rest of this evening letting you get to know me then ask you again before I leave. How's that? Still too soon?"

The smile he gave her was dazzling. Patricia could not understand how any woman could turn him down. She hoped her sister would find her good sense by the end of the evening and agree to see him. It would be such a mistake to tell him no. Almost ready to throttle her own little sister, Patricia quickly answered in Catherine's place, worried her sister was about to say something foolish that would make Tony give up even before he had gotten started. "I think that by the end of the evening Catherine should be able to judge you well enough to know if you are suitable to come calling."

137

"Yes, I think she should know by the end of the evening what a nice person you are," William put in, obviously glad Tony's interest had fallen on Catherine and not Patricia.

Catherine closed the mouth she had barely gotten parted. Staring first at William then at her oldest sister with open exasperation, she finally agreed to let Tony know by the end of the evening whether she would permit him to come calling or not. At least she would have several hours to think of a polite way to turn him down. Then she could use her time trying to think of a way of letting Patricia know how complicated such meddling could make her life without actually telling her everything.

Chapter Nine

Originally Patricia had intended to leave as soon as everyone was through eating, but she found she was too curious to know what her sister would decide about Tony. When they all retired back to the front salon after having had a final cup of spiced coffee, she went right along with them. She could put up with William a little longer in order to learn if Catherine would finally have a suitor or not. What she really wanted was for the men to retire to the study to talk about their business like they had claimed they were going to so that she could have a few moments alone with her sister. She would love a chance to point out more of Tony's many attributes. But to her disappointment, her father never mentioned their business again and neither did William or Tony. It was as if they had forgotten all about the property on Franklin Street that had been so important before. Finally, once the night began to grow very late, she decided to remind them of the original intent for this evening as subtly as possible and waited for the next lull in their conversation.

"Tell me, Tony, why did you choose Johnstown for your law practice? I would think a young man like you would lean more toward the larger cities like Pittsburgh or Philadelphia," she began casually.

"Several reasons," he replied and glanced at her a moment before his eyes traveled back to where Catherine sat beside him. "This may sound childish, but I wanted to find a prosperous city that had a lot of potential for commercial expansion, but at the same time I also wanted to be as close as possible to my family. My parents and my two brothers still live in Altoona and I do want to be near them. I probably would have opened a practice right in Altoona but there were too many lawyers there already. So I looked over the prospects in the immediate area and picked Johnstown and am I ever glad I did."

He gave Catherine such a meaningful smile when he made that last remark and left her no doubt of his meaning. It felt as if he was setting some sort of a trap for her. She tried to think of a way to get around that remark without giving him a reason for taking any comment personally. "Yes, I think Johnstown is a very progressive city. You should do very well here."

"I hope so," he said in earnest.

A sudden shattering crash from the kitchen followed by a low Swedish mutter gave Catherine the means for escape she wanted. "What was that?"

"Sounds as if Minnie broke something." Clayton frowned. "I hope it was not one of Hilary's lovely plates."

"I'll go see," Catherine quickly volunteered, but before she could get up, Patricia had risen from a chair near the door and was already on her way out of the room.

"No, Catherine, you just stay put. I'll go see what happened," she said over her shoulder.

"I'll go with you," Catherine put in, still wanting to use it as an excuse to get away from Tony. She needed to put distance between them, not because she found his company so loathsome, but because she did not. She was starting to like Tony and knew that liking him would only make matters worse.

"No need," William said immediately and started to rise from his chair. "I'll go with her. Minnie may need a man's help."

"Then maybe I should go with you both," Clayton put in. This was a way of getting these two young people alone. Upon catching a glimpse of William's terse expression, he realized he had the same as declared William was not man enough

140

and gave him an apologetic shrug when he hurried to catch up with him.

It took all the control Patricia had not to laugh as she hurried toward the kitchen to make sure Minnie had not hurt herself in any way. There was always a chance it had been a real accident, but she doubted it.

"Wonderful, I finally get to be alone with you," Tony said as soon as the other three had gone. Without realizing it, he leaned intimately toward her. All he wanted though was to get a better whiff of her floral perfume, a closer look into her deep blue eyes.

At first Catherine had felt a sense of panic and thought of fleeing the room for some pretended emergency but then realized it would be easier to turn him down while everyone else was not around. At least he would not have to feel as disgraced by her refusal. "Yes, it does seem we are suddenly alone and this is the perfect opportunity for me to try to explain why I don't think it would be a very good idea for you to be calling on me."

"Oh? Why is that?"

The hurt was so evident in his greenish-blue eyes that Catherine wanted to reach out and comfort him. She had never wanted to hurt him and tried to think of some way of letting him down easy. "For one thing, I'm not like most girls. I hate to socialize. I hate crowds. I prefer quiet evenings to myself and I don't like to talk very much. You would find yourself bored to tears with me. One evening in my company and you would be looking for the nearest door."

"Why not let me find that out for myself? Give me that one evening. We don't have to go anywhere that will be too crowded. I'm not that fond of crowded places myself."

"But I assure you, I am not fun to be around. I am a very dull person."

"In that case, you won't have to worry about me asking a second time, will you? Just give me that one evening with you to find out for myself."

Catherine could see that she was not going to be able to persuade him any differently. He refused to simply take her word for it. She would either have to lie and tell him she

141

found him repulsive and hurt his feelings, which she really did not want to do, or go out with him once and prove herself to be the dullest and most boring companion he could ever possibly be saddled with. She decided she would do less harm in disillusioning him than by insulting him and finally agreed to go out with him once, but warned him again how disappointed he was going to be.

"But you will go out with me?" he asked, excited. His eyes sparkled with renewed hope and his smile returned full depth.

"Provided we have an escort," she said and smiled back despite her trepidation.

"I'll find us an escort. You just pick the date and the place. Wherever you want to go."

"I will have to think about that. I'll let you know when I have decided."

Another clattering crash came from the kitchen and Tony turned to stare curiously in the direction of the sound. "What was that?"

"Sounded like a pan of some sort," Catherine said with little concern. Pans did not easily break. If Minnie felt the need to drop something, she was glad it was something not breakable. It meant she was no longer as angry as she had been when she had dropped whatever that first thing had been.

"Your father's housekeeper may be a terrific cook, but she certainly can be clumsy," he observed, his eyebrows drawn with concern.

Catherine laughed. "Yes, at times she can be extremely clumsy."

"I hope she doesn't hurt herself or someone else through her clumsiness," he mused worriedly, then returned his attention to Catherine. The tense lines softened when his gaze once again met hers. "Back to what we were talking about a moment ago. I am very eager to call on you. How about next Saturday?" he suggested with enthusiasm. "I know a small restaurant that is usually not very crowded. They serve great Italian-style food. A second cousin of mine owns it and he's always after me to bring my friends by. It's not a very lavish place, but you'll love it. I know you will."

"I thought you were going to let me pick the time and the place," she complained. She really had hoped to put it off long enough for him to meet some other lovely young ladies in Johnstown. It would be easier to convince him how dismal she was if he had someone interesting to compare her to.

"Just trying to be helpful," he explained. Reaching forward and taking one of her hands in his, he said with a sheepish shrug, "I'm afraid patience is not one of my better virtues."

The intimacy of his touch affected her much as a hot branding iron might and she quickly jerked her hand away.

"Tony, don't do that!" she cried out. Without looking down at her hand, she began to gently massage it as if it had truly been injured. He had barely held her hand a second, yet she had felt something special inside her jolt awake, sending waves of alarm through her. He should not have affected her that way. She must not allow him to touch her like that again. It was not right.

"I'm sorry. I really am. I knew better than to do that. I realize we just met and I should never have been so bold," he said with true sincerity. "Please forgive me for that."

Unable to watch him suffer for something most girls would have wanted to happen, she quickly said, "Just see that it doesn't happen again." Then she smiled at him to let him know he was forgiven.

"Will you at least decide on what night we can go out before I leave?" he asked. He did want her to commit herself so that it would not be very easy for her to back out of it later.

"All right, I guess Saturday night will be as good as any," she finally conceded. She might as well get it over with. "But who are you going to have accompany us?"

"I was thinking of William and Patricia."

At that moment, William reentered the room. "What were you thinking of me and Patricia? About what a handsome couple we make?"

The two turned, surprised to have heard his voice. Neither had been aware of his return. "I was hoping you and Patricia would provide escort for Catherine and me next Saturday."

Catherine's initial response was to protest, but decided adding William to the evening could only help make it that much more dull. For once, William would be doing her a favor simply by being his usual obnoxious self.

"Then she has agreed to go out with you?" The eagerness in Clayton's voice was heard even before he had entered the room behind William. "She really has agreed?"

"Yes, she has." Tony beamed. "Provided I can find someone willing to go with us, which is only proper."

"No problem there. Patricia and I will be happy to join you," William inserted quickly. He was eager for another evening with her since she couldn't seem to find enough time for him these days. How could she ever come to realize how much better he was than that Gifford fellow if she did not have him around to compare the man with?

"Join who?" Patricia asked. She had just returned and caught the tail end of what William was saying. She tried to keep the irritation from her voice, but was not at all pleased with the way William proceeded to make plans for them without bothering to check with her first.

"Catherine and Tony need an escort. She's agreed to go out with him Saturday. I was telling him we would be happy to be their escorts."

"But I already have plans for Saturday," Patricia put in without as much as a flinch. That was such a lie, but she did not want to spend her Saturday night with William. Not when Cole had insinuated they might be going to the park again this Saturday evening if everything worked out. He had not notified her the plans were definite just yet, but as far as she was concerned, they were as good as set. Then realizing she could be ruining an opportunity for Catherine and Tony, she added, "I guess I could see if my plans can be rearranged." Sadly, her visions of sitting beside Cole in the park listening to music and laughing over silly jokes and wayward glances faded slowly away. They were very close to winter weather now; this could very well be the last concert in the park until spring. But for Catherine she would make the sacrifice. She would explain it to Cole.

"I should think you would be more than willing to change

144

your plans for your sister. Whatever they are," Clayton admonished, certain these plans of hers included that horrible Cole Gifford. "If your Mr. Gifford is half the wonder you think him to be, he will fully understand your wanting to call off your plans."

"Are your plans with Cole?" Catherine wanted to know. When Patricia did not immediately answer, she knew that they were. "No, I will not have you disappointing him because of me. I don't see why you and Cole could not be our escorts, that is if Cole would be agreeable to it. I know I find no objection to it. In truth, I've been wanting a chance to meet him. Ever since I heard how he bid so high against William for your basket when he hadn't even met you yet, I've been anxious to meet him."

William stiffened when he realized now just who this Gifford was and glared first at Patricia then down at Catherine but said nothing. He couldn't have if he had wanted to, for Clayton was already arguing with his youngest daughter in a barely controlled voice. "How dare you be so rude, Catherine Marie. William was kind enough to volunteer to be your escort Saturday and there you sit suggesting someone else right in front of his face. You really should be ashamed of yourself, young lady."

"Well, Father, if he would be so kind as to turn around I would gladly make the suggestion again behind his back. Would that suit you better?"

Seeing Clayton was about to explode with anger, Tony quickly rose from his seat and stood between them. "I don't suppose it has to be this Saturday. We could make our plans for the following Saturday. I certainly don't want to be the cause of any dissension in this family."

"You are not in any way the cause," Catherine assured him and he turned to look down at her. "There was dissension long before we met you and I see no reason for us to change our plans to go out this Saturday night unless it becomes absolutely necessary." Then looking over at Patricia, who stared daggers through their father for such an outburst in front of Tony, Catherine asked in a sweet conversational voice, "Patricia, do you think you and Cole could act as our

145

escorts Saturday? I would be very much obliged."

"I'll have to ask Cole to be certain, but I don't see any reason why we couldn't," Patricia replied, equally as calm. Even if Cole could not come, she would rather escort them alone than have William at her side all evening. She liked him less and less with each day's passing until now she could barely tolerate the man. She could not understand how she had put up with him as long as she had.

"Good, then it is settled." Catherine smiled pleasantly and gazed up at Tony, not daring to glance at their father. "What time do you plan to pick us up, Tony? Is seven o'clock all right?"

Patricia felt her insides coil as tight as the spring in a new watch while she waited for her father's anger to burst out of him again. The vein in his neck stood out stark blue against his pallid skin, yet he said nothing. Patricia could scarcely believe Catherine had gone against him like that. It would have been in character for her to have done what Catherine had just done, but for dear sweet little Catherine, it was such a shock. Maybe that was why her father did not shout out his anger again. He too was too stunned to think of what to say. Everyone was. It was Catherine's gentle voice that sounded next.

"Would seven o'clock be all right with you and Cole, Patricia?"

"Yes, I'm sure seven o'clock will be fine. Where should I tell him we are going?"

"Tony said he has a cousin that owns a nice Italian restaurant in Johnstown and he wants to take me there. Is that all right with you?"

The tension in the room grew taut as the two casually made their plans. Tony stood between William and Clayton with his gaze nervously shifting from one to the other. Neither looked his way to see the sympathetic apology his eyes offered. He had not expected a simple invitation to dinner to cause so much commotion.

"I love Italian food. It's so rich and spicy. I love things that are spicy," Patricia continued and sat down beside Catherine, where Tony had been seated. It was as if they had grown oblivious to the others in the room. "And maybe we could stop by the park afterward and listen to the music for a while."

"Sounds lovely. I haven't done that in years. I wonder what I should wear."

Perfect cue to save their necks. "I don't know. Let's go on up to your room and decide right now."

As they both rose Patricia offered one of her nicest smiles and said, "You gentlemen won't mind if we leave you now. We have plans to make."

No one replied. Clayton and William were too angry and Tony felt like he had better not.

"Why don't you three go ahead and discuss your business now. I promise you won't have us women to bother you," she suggested over her shoulder while she and Catherine headed for the stairs. "I may just stay the night in my old room, if that's all right. I'll see you in the morning, Father."

Knowing Clayton would not want to display his temper any worse than he already had in front of Tony, Patricia was almost certain they would go ahead and discuss their business as if nothing had happened and by the time they had finished and Tony had left, she and Catherine could both feign being asleep.

Although Patricia was not asleep, in fact far from it, she did not respond when someone knocked at her door a few hours later. She waited another full hour before daring to open the door and slip out into the darkened hallway still fully clothed. Having rumpled the bed, she would simply tell her father she had wakened early and gone home to change into a fresh dress before work. It was more to her liking to tell a little white lie than to have to digest her father's anger so early in the morning. When she slipped past her sister's room, she could just imagine the headache Catherine would fake in the morning. Minnie would have her bedridden all day with cool compresses and a brothy vegetable soup.

When Patricia arrived at her office the following morning, she was not surprised to find her father already sitting in her desk chair waiting for her. He had been there long enough to have removed his coat. It lay carefully folded across the

147

desk. Having had a few hours of sleep and a good breakfast, Patricia felt more up to facing his anger now than she would have otherwise. Cautiously, she stepped inside the room and laid her handbag down on the corner of her desk next to his coat.

"Good morning, Father," she said sweetly as she swept her own coat off and hung it on a large brass hook near the door. Rather than face him right away, she took a few more moments than were actually necessary to straighten her burgundy-colored skirt and the thin waist jacket she had chosen to wear.

"I want to know why you allowed Catherine to treat William like that last night," Clayton said right out. "And why you went along with it the way you did."

"What was I to do? You know as well as I do how Catherine feels about William. She detests him. It would have ruined her evening out with Tony to have William tagging along. And it has taken her so long to finally agree to go out with anyone that I did not want to chance it being ruined for her." My but that sounded reasonable. Sometimes she impressed herself with what came out of her own mouth.

Clayton mulled over his daughter's words a moment. "Will you at least explain it to William. He thinks you have turned against him. It was bad enough what Catherine did, but when you became a part of it . . . well, he was very upset when he left the house last night."

"I don't doubt it. Yes, I will apologize to William and explain it as best as I can. I'm sure he must be aware that Catherine doesn't exactly treasure his company. And I have never known him to try to do anything that might change her poor opinion of him. He really is partially to blame for the way she treated him, but I won't go into that with him. I'll just explain the obvious and try to soothe his wounded pride."

"Good, then at least he won't think it was your idea," Clayton said and shook his head while he recounted what had happened. "I just don't know what got into Catherine last night. I can't believe the way she spoke to me."

148

"Did you like it any better when she refused to speak to you at all?"

"Yes, I believe I did. She made such a display. I haven't had a chance to speak to her yet, but you can be assured I intend to have a long and hard discussion with her this evening when I get home. I am really going to give her a big piece of my mind for acting the way she did."

"Father, don't."

"But she has to be reprimanded for her behavior. I can't have her behaving like that toward my guests, my friends. She needs to be punished. She deserves it."

"Father, she is twenty years old. She is too old for you to punish. And if you stir up her anger any more than you already have, she might decide going out with Tony is not worth it at all. And we both want her to start seeing young men again, don't we?"

Clayton sat staring at Patricia a long moment before he finally grunted his displeasure. "I guess you're right. I am tired of her sitting up there in that damn room of hers every weekend when she should be out getting herself a husband."

"I don't know how important a husband is just yet, but she should be out there having fun, enjoying her youth. And I intend to see that she and Tony have a wonderful time Saturday night."

Clayton's eyes grew cold as he continued to stare up at Patricia. "You and Cole Gifford. Damn! When will you see that rogue for what he is?"

"Father, would you like some coffee?" she asked. She was not about to discuss Cole with him yet, not until he was much more receptive. "I'll see if Iris has any brewing yet."

"Patricia, I'll tell you again. I don't like you seeing that man. He is a troublemaker. Him and that damn petition of his. You are making a big mistake. I only wish I could make you see that. Why do you have to be so stubborn? That's probably where Catherine learned it, from you." His voice rose as he leaned his elbows heavily on the top of her desk and looked her squarely in the eye, waiting for her response.

Having just stepped through the door, Patricia turned and said in a mild voice, "I'll bring your coffee to you in your office. Would you care for any sweet bread with it?" She knew full well where Catherine got her stubbornness from—the very same place she had.

"No," he muttered and sank his chin into his hands. As he watched her walk out of his sight, he issued a low warning that he knew she could not possibly hear, but he had to say it just the same, "You will be sorry, young lady. Truly sorry. You never should have started up with that man. That was one of the worst mistakes you ever made." Shaking his head with resignation, he slowly stood and went to his own office with his coat carefully tucked over his arm. There was no use in his brooding about it now. He would just have to wait and see what the outcome of all this would be. Sadly, he wished she would come to her senses before anyone got hurt.

Cole had seen no problem in Patricia's request that they tag along with Catherine and Tony Alani. He had agreed to it without any protest whatsoever. In all honesty, he was looking forward to the evening. This was an opportunity to meet someone from Patricia's family besides her father and that other sister of hers. He just hoped he made a far better impression on Catherine than he had on Clayton or Jeanne. It would be nice to have the support of someone in Patricia's family. He already had enough of them disliking him.

They were all to meet at the Mackey house at seven but Cole arrived for Patricia just a little after six-thirty. Patricia had mentioned wanting to get there a little early to help Catherine get dressed and Cole had gladly agreed to oblige. He thought it odd that a twenty-year-old girl could not dress herself, but was not one to argue when it meant being with Patricia that much sooner. He had been looking forward to the moment he would see her again ever since he had left her last Saturday.

Patricia was ready to go when he arrived, wearing a dark brown dress made of silk and velvet. It was a little extravagant for the sort of evening planned, but she did so want to impress Cole. She wanted him to think her the prettiest woman and that might not be too easy with omeone as pretty as Catherine around.

After grabbing a velvet cloak that matched the dark trim f her dress, they were on their way to her father's within ninutes. Despite her eagerness to help Catherine, Patricia as feeling a little uneasy about their early arrival. Should er father be home, he would be far from cordial toward Cole. She was certain of that. He might even go as far as to efuse to let him enter. She hoped he would not be that rash, ut when it came to her father's moods, she could never redict what might happen.

Because she did have Cole with her, Patricia chose to enter he house through the front door and waited patiently to be et in after having knocked. To her relief, Minnie was the one vho answered the door. At least, Cole would not be refused ntrance.

"Come in, missy, your little sister is upstairs putting the nishing touches to her hair. She should be down in a spell," Minnie said while eyeing Cole with unrestrained interest. Iolding out her hand for his overcoat and her cloak, she told hem, "You can either wait in the front room with your entleman friend or you can go on up and let me have the onor of showing him where he can wait."

"His name is Cole Gifford," Patricia said in a way of ntroduction. She was so tempted to also say "and he is no entleman," but managed to keep the retort to herself. And I'll show him on into the salon myself. Tell Catherine 'll be up in a minute."

"Go on up," Cole said, giving her a nudge. Looking at the notherly smile on the woman's wide friendly face, he added, I figure I'll be safe enough with Minnie here. It is all right if I all you Minnie, isn't it? As many wonderful things as Patricia has told me about you, I feel I already know you."

Minnie sputtered her appreciation of Cole's kind words nd assured him she would be proud to have him call her Minnie. She actually blushed. None of Patricia's gentlemen allers had ever bothered to compliment her before. Patricia vanted to stay and watch but decided Minnie would just ave to try to hold her own against Cole's many charms and vent on up the stairs to see Catherine.

151

When Minnie had shown Cole into the front salon, she proceeded to ask him questions without any show of reluctance. "Missy sure does set high stock by you, Mr. Gifford. I hope your intentions toward her are perfectly honorable. It would break my heart if you were to hurt her in any way. She may not look it and she may not act it at times, but she is truly a very vulnerable woman. She could be hurt very easy."

"Rest assured. I don't intend to hurt her in any way, Minnie, I promise you." Seeing such deep concern on the woman's creased face prompted him to tell her more. "In fact, I'll share a secret if you promise not to tell a living soul."

A living soul? Well, that meant she couldn't be telling her sister Eva, but she could still share it with Mrs. Hilary on her next visit to the cemetery should she decide to. Turning and stepping closer, she eagerly asked, "What is your secret? I promise I won't tell—not a living soul."

"I'm not completely sure of all my feelings just yet, that's why it is a secret for now, but I think I am falling deeply in love with your missy. I've thought a lot about her lately and that is the conclusion I've started to come to. So you see I would not want to hurt her in any way. I care for her too much to ever want to see her hurt."

"You do?" Minnie's eyes were wide with excitement as she studied his face. Such a handsome man. So much more the type of man she would like to see her missy with than that uppity Mr. William. "Bless your heart, I think you really do. Are you going to ask her to marry you?"

"I don't know. One step at a time." He wanted to laugh at her directness but held back. She reminded him of his grandmother, only younger. She even looked a little like her with that head of snow-white hair tied back into a tight bun and those big curious blue eyes. "I have just now discovered how much I care for her and I'm not at all certain she cares for me in the same way."

"She wouldn't let you know if she did," Minnie said bluntly, deciding such information would be safe with this man. Besides, he needed to know just what he was facing. "She's one of those women that sees marriage as a millstone

152

around the neck. She was hurt awful bad when her first husband died. She was beside herself with grief. I didn't think she was going to ever get over it. I think she finally quit crying over it, but I'm not sure she ever got full over it. She was so young when it happened."

"I know how she feels. I suffered the loss of a wife," he admitted solemnly. "And a son."

"Then maybe you will understand and be patient with her. I think she will come to see marriage again for what it is supposed to be. Oh, and while I'm at it I want you to please try and understand that bold nature of hers. Having been raised much of her life without a mother has caused her some problems and sometimes she just does not realize she gets too bold and far too outspoken."

"Understand it? That is one of the things I like best about her," he said, laughing. "I never know what to expect from her, but I love it. She is so full of surprises. She's one of a kind."

"That she is," Minnie admitted with a conspiratorial nod. "But if you actually like that in her, I'll quit my trying so hard to change her."

"No, don't try to change her at all."

"Couldn't anyway," she muttered, then grinned. "What is your favorite dessert? I have a feeling you are going to be eating around here during the family gatherings soon enough and I sure would like to have your favorite on hand."

"Strawberry pie when it is in season, but I like apple pie almost as much," he told her, realizing he had made a friend. Knowing Minnie was just the same as family, he felt he already had one on his side. Now if he could win Catherine over, he would have two for him and two against. It would better his chances should he find he truly did want to make Patricia a permanent part of his life and it looked more and more like he just might want to do that very thing.

Chapter Ten

Cole sat in a high-backed, richly upholstered chair facing the doorway and waited patiently for Patricia's return. He kept his hands busy by searching out tiny pieces of lint on his black trousers and carefully inspecting the grain of the small table beside him. Every now and then he could hear her laughter directly overhead and wished he could be up there with them and witness what went on between sisters in the privacy of the bedroom. Never having met Catherine, he wondered what she would look like. Would she have the same captivating green eyes and thick dark brown hair as Patricia? He smiled to himself when he realized that if Catherine was even half as lovely as her oldest sister, she was going to be extremely beautiful. But if she looked anything like Jeanne, or acted like her, there was no wonder she was twenty years old and not married. One sister like Jeanne was enough. He hoped Catherine took after Patricia: beautiful, exciting, and full of life.

Absently, he let his thoughts drift back in time to how captivating Patricia had looked in that black gown of hers and how much he had wanted her, still wanted her. As he remembered what-all had happened that first evening, he felt his need for her growing. Shamelessly, he recalled how her rounded breasts had strained against the material and beckoned him when he had pinned her to the bed. How he would love for that opportunity again, only under different circumstances. He had a feeling that Patricia would make a passionate lover. A passionate wife.

That last thought took him a little by surprise. He had thought he would never want to marry again, but now the idea of marrying Patricia was growing ever stronger in his heart. He wondered what it would be like to be able to come home every evening to her warm embrace and generous smile, to be able to make love to her whenever the urge struck them. He knew it would be ecstasy. He smiled to himself. Then he remembered what Minnie had said about Patricia. She was against marriage. What would it take to change her mind? Maybe the years had mellowed her pain enough that she would be willing to consider it again. After all, here he was considering it and he too had thought he would never want to marry again.

The sound of the front door slamming shut brought him quickly out of his reverie and he focused on the hallway to see if anyone was about to enter. He hoped it would not be Clayton. Patricia had warned him of her father's continuing dislike of him and he did not want to start the evening off with an ugly scene. He would do what he could to avoid any such confrontation. Much to his relief, it was Minnie's smiling face that appeared in the doorway.

"Mr. Cole, I don't believe you've met Mr. Tony here," she said as she stepped closer and held her thick green skirts to the side so the tall young man could enter without tripping on her hem. She let a deep smile plump out her wide face as she explained, "Tony is Katy's—er, Catherine's gentleman caller. You two best be getting to know each other. I got a feeling you two are going to be seeing quite a lot of each other from now on."

"Hello, I'm Tony Alani," the handsome young man greeted in a friendly voice and extended his hand as he stepped on inside the room. "Pleased to meet you. I've heard a lot about you."

"And not all of it pleasant, I'll bet." Cole laughed, knowing that if he had gotten his information from Clayton it was far from it.

"No, not all of it," Tony admitted. "But I like to make my own personal judgments about people."

156

"Cole Gifford here, ready to stand trial and be judged," he said with a genuine smile and accepted Tony's handshake. "Let me know when you reach a verdict."

"Hmmm, my initial inclination is to say 'not guilty,'" he remarked and they both laughed.

Minnie joined them in their laughter. "I guess it is safe enough to leave you two alone. Katy is just about ready, but I think I should go up there and make sure everything is going all right. Wait until you see her. She's wearing a divine dress of ivory and pink. She looks like an angel."

Tony could hardly wait. His eagerness showed in the sparkle of his eyes as he watched Minnie's plump figure rush from the room.

From where the two young men stood just inside the doorway they could watch Minnie's dark green skirts swish up the stairs and decided to stay where they were so they could be able to watch when Patricia and Catherine came down. Awkwardly, they stood staring at one another in silence, tapping their fingertips together lightly for several minutes before Cole finally thought of something to say.

"I'd ask you a question about yourself, but I'm afraid Patricia's already filled me in on everything I'd want to know. I just can't think of anything to ask. Sorry to be such a dull conversationalist."

"Well, after what happened around here the last time your name was mentioned, I'm almost afraid to ask you questions," Tony admitted. "I guess you know Clayton is not exactly fond of you."

"Yes, that is my general impression." Cole grinned and just as he was about to explain the day in Clayton's office, the front door slammed shut again and heavy footsteps were heard coming their way.

Tony leaned out into the hallway, then quickly ducked back in and spoke in a hushed voice. "Speak of the devil . . . here he comes." He then turned to greet the man when he entered. He might be a little wary of him, but the man was Catherine's father and it would pay well to be on his good side.

Glad for the warning, Cole braced himself for what was to

157

come. He would do his best to try to change the man's opinion of him, but was not about to grovel in order to win him over. If nothing else, though, he would try to avoid an argument with him, especially tonight. Patricia so wanted tonight to be special for her sister.

"Tony, it is good to see you," Clayton said with a warm smile as he entered the room with his hand outstretched. "I was hoping I would get a chance to speak with you before you left. I wanted to tell you that the title to that property can be officially in your name as early as Monday afternoon. All you have to do is show up at the bank around three."

"That's good to hear," Tony said, and accepted the handshake. "I have already started looking for a builder. I am anxious to get my office building under way."

"Yes, it would be nice to have it ready to move into by next spring." Clayton nodded, still smiling, until his gaze fell on Cole. Suddenly the huge smile wilted and he gave Cole a terse nod of recognition. "Mr. Gifford, isn't it?"

"Yes," he replied as cordially as he could when faced with such open rudeness and offered Clayton both a friendly smile and his hand, neither of which the man wanted to acknowledge. Feeling awkward with his hand outstretched, he reached his other hand up and began to slowly rub them together as if trying to get a little feeling and warmth back in them. They did feel suddenly cold, right down to the bone.

"How's your petition coming along?" Clayton asked while he placed his hands behind himself in an effort to show the young man he wanted no part of a handshake from him ever.

Cole wished he could report progress on the petition, just to be able to rile the man as much as he had just been riled, but answered honestly. "I haven't spent too much time on it lately. I'm afraid I've neglected it."

"Good. If you ask me it is a waste of time," he told him, his meaning direct.

Cole wanted to point out that no one had asked Clayton for an opinion whatsoever, but instead he politely replied, "We see things differently."

Tony could sense that whatever this petition was, it was one of the main sources of conflict between the two and decided a change of subject would be best for them all. "Tell me, Clayton, is Catherine usually punctual in getting ready or should I expect her to make me wait. Some women have a notion that waiting makes a man appreciate them more."

Clayton let his attention be drawn from Cole for the moment. It had been so long since he could remember Catherine ever getting ready for anything besides work and church that he was not sure. But realizing she was never late for either of those, he responded, "She is usually very punctual. I can't say that I ever remember her having purposely made any man wait."

"Good," Tony said, smiling. "I like a woman that is punctual. It shows consideration."

At that moment the large cabinet clock sounded from the hallway with seven loud chimes. Expectantly, all three of them turned toward the stairs, as if the clock had announced the approach of the women, but no one came. They waited in silence for a few minutes, but still no one came. Finally Minnie appeared at the top of the stairs and smiled apologetically. "We seem to have a problem up here. Katy has torn her hem and has to change dresses. Missy is already pressing out another but it will be a few minutes."

Once they had watched her disappear again, they turned to stare at each other. Again, everyone seemed to want to pass the time idly tapping their fingertips together.

Cole decided to be the one to break the silence. "A torn hem can't be helped. I guess we will just have to wait."

"No, a torn hem can't be foreseen at all," Clayton put in, and it was as close to agreeing with Cole as he ever hoped to have come. "Tony, my boy, how about a drink while we wait?"

Realizing he did not intend to offer Cole any similiar refreshment, Tony declined. Instead he walked over to the sofa and made himself as comfortable as being in the room with a time bomb could allow. Cole followed and eased himself into the same chair he had been seated in earlier while Clayton remained standing and staring everywhere but in Cole's direction. As Tony had stated earlier, he was well used to making his own judgment about people, and

159

when he compared Cole to Clayton at this moment, he noted that Cole might happen to be the younger of the two, but that he was also the more mature. Cole pretty well kept his irritation to himself and Tony thought that showed a lot of character. Tony pulled in the corner of his lower lip and chewed on it absently, as was his habit whenever he felt nervous. Quietly, he wondered just what this petition of Cole's was all about and why Clayton thought it was a waste of time.

After several futile efforts at a civil conversation among the three of them, footsteps and the soft fluttering of skirts could be heard on the stairs. Cole and Tony quickly stood and the three men turned to greet the women, very relieved their moment of torture was over.

The women could sense the tension in the room and did not linger over inconsequential conversation. As soon as Catherine had been introduced to Cole and the proper compliments had been bestowed on Catherine's dress—which was a lovely combination of lampas and surah silks in different shades of light blue that brought out the sparkling color of her eyes—Patricia mentioned how late it was getting to be and they left immediately.

At first, the conversation in the carriage on the way to the restaurant was slow and very stilted, but by the time they had arrived, their moods had started to lift and they had begun to laugh and enjoy the evening. The restaurant Tony had chosen was on the outskirts of Johnstown near Kernville and not far from Stony Creek. It was a small place like he had promised Catherine it would be, and although almost every table was taken, they were spaced far enough apart that the room did not seem crowded.

"How lovely," Patricia remarked as they entered. And it was. Bright red linen cloth covered the tables and windows and each table had its own candle flickering in a wine bottle in addition to the gaslights that burned softly overhead. Although the waiters were dressed in regular street clothes, they each had a red cloth tied around their waists to act as an apron, which gave them a somewhat uniformed appearance. The room was filled with the sounds of easygoing con-

160

versations and the rich aromas of fresh bread and garlic. "Mmmm, I like this place."

Catherine wanted to agree that the restaurant was very charming, but had vowed to be as silent as possible for the evening. She had to convince Tony she was the worst company imaginable and she had to convince him of that before the night was over. It was bad enough Patricia had not allowed her to wear the gray and black dress she had intended to wear. That's why she had torn the ivory dress in the first place. She did not want Tony to find any reason to invite her out again. It would complicate her life too much.

"Marco," Tony called out when he had finally spotted the man he had been looking for bent over a table of giggling young ladies.

A tall dark man who looked to be about forty years old glanced up at the mention of his name, quickly excused himself, and hurried in their direction with a broad smile to greet them.

"Marco, your best table, please."

"And which of these beautiful young ladies is foolish enough to be with you, Antonio?"

"Antonio?" Catherine asked, her vow of silence broken by her own curiosity.

"Yes, my given name is Antonio. I changed it to Anthony when I became a lawyer."

"True, he is ashamed of his name."

"It's not that, but there are four other Antonios in the Alani family, three of which live in Altoona. It was getting a little confusing."

"Well, you'll always be little Antonio to me," Marco insisted and bent over to give Tony a warm hug. "You look as healthy as a bear cub. How's my favorite first cousin? Is she still doing well?"

"Last letter I got from Mama, she was good," he assured him while he helped Catherine off with her cloak. "She plans to come visit as soon as I am fully settled."

"Then she must come and eat here," Marco insisted as he took the women's cloaks from the men. "I will show her how well her cousin Marco is doing."

161

"She will surely be impressed," Tony agreed. "Now, will you give us your best table and bring out your finest bottle of wine?"

No sooner had he spoken than Marco had both Patricia and Catherine by the arms and was leading them toward a table in the far corner. He gallantly pulled out opposite chairs for the two and seated them one at a time, then left the men to seat themselves while he went to hang up the cloaks and get the wine and menus.

The food was as delicious as Tony had promised and Marco kept it coming even after they had sworn they were full. Everyone was having such a good time that Catherine was finding it hard not to join in the conversation, but generally succeeded in keeping quiet most of the time. She realized Patricia kept looking at her with a worried expression, but tried to ignore it just like she tried to ignore everyone else at the table.

"Catherine, aren't you feeling well?" Patricia finally asked, and rose to feel the side of her sister's neck with her wrist. She was concerned.

"I'm fine," Catherine assured her, keeping her gaze away from her sister's. Patricia had an uncanny way of knowing when she was lying if she ever got a look into her eyes.

"You are usually not this quiet," Patricia commented. "We've barely heard a peep out of you. This is not like you at all. I know you tend to be shy at times, but this is ridiculous."

Tony listened intently to what Patricia was saying and wondered if it was true. Was she behaving out of character? Maybe his company bored Catherine so that she did not want to join in, but he could scarcely believe that. There was too much laughter, good food, and entertaining stories for her not to be enjoying herself. He wondered what the problem was. "Maybe we have been talking so much that we haven't really given her a chance to speak." Then seeing how uncomfortable she seemed at having all this pointed out, he decided to change the subject entirely. "After all, I myself have been wanting all evening to ask Cole about that petition of his, but haven't had the chance. We've been so busy discussing other things. What exactly is this petition

162

Clayton mentioned earlier?"

Cole explained as briefly as possible about the sub-standard condition of the Lake Conemaugh dam and how much danger Johnstown could be in because of it and why he was having to resort to a petition. "I've already tried the local government and have even written the state government at length, but with no real results. I now intend to bring this to the attention of the national government. I am hoping to have my case ready by sometime in July, but with this stupid 'I'll-believe-it-when-it-happens' attitude I find I'm up against, I'm going to have a hard time getting a very impressive number of signatures by then."

Tony grew very serious while he listened. "You realize that a petition alone might not be enough to get you the action you really want. You are up against some very powerful men."

"It's a start," Cole said defensively, feeling Tony was about to take Clayton's side in the matter.

"True, it is a start, but what we need to do is have some real experts examine that dam and declare in writing that the dam is unsafe and specifically state what the faults are and what, in their professional estimation, the dangers are. If we can get several signed affidavits from unbiased professionals in the area, your case will be that much stronger when you present it in Washington."

"We?" Cole repeated curiously.

"Certainly, we. This is serious and Johnstown is now my home too. Don't I have a right to be as concerned as you?"

"Yes, you definitely do," Patricia put in, delighted Tony was on their side in this and especially delighted that Cole was still as enthusiastic as ever. This was the first time Cole had even mentioned the dam since the day they first met and she had started to worry he had decided to let the matter drop due to lack of public interest.

"We all do," Catherine put in, again forgetting her vow of silence. "Cole, I want to sign that petition. I want my name on it. And I want to help in any way I can. The thought of that dam breaking and sending all that water down on us terrifies me. I can't even swim."

163

"Most people around here can't," Tony put in. "Of course, I want to sign it too." He was adamant. "I had no idea that dam posed Johnstown any threat whatsoever. But if what you say is true, and I have every reason to believe you know what you are talking about, we need to get on this right away. I've seen that lake. It's huge. I will see if I can round up a couple of reputable engineers to survey the dam up there as soon as possible. And maybe even a government official of some sort. Someone with known experience in dams."

For hours, the four of them remained at the restaurant discussing tentative plans to right the problem with the dam. Catherine completely forgot all about her decision to remain quiet and got just as involved in the conversation as the others. The next time anyone noticed the hour, it was after ten o'clock and too late to go to the park and expect to listen to music. The concert would be over by now. Instead, they opted for a moonlit ride along Stony Creek—that is everyone except Catherine.

Because there would be four of them and Cole's personal carriage only sat three comfortably, he had decided to rent a cabriolet with a canopy top for the evening. He and Patricia sat up front, which gave Catherine and Tony full privacy in the rear seat, something Catherine was not too fond of but Tony was delighted with.

Because of the chilly autumn night air, each couple was forced to share a large lap quilt. Patricia did not mind at all, but Catherine felt awkward having to sit so close to Tony and share his body's warmth in order to keep some measure of comfort and not get chilled. She kept reminding herself it was more practical than allowing herself to become ill from the cold, but her thoughts came without much conviction. She was enjoying herself for the first time in years and she felt very ashamed of herself for allowing it. She was well aware that Tony had his left arm outstretched on the back of the seat behind her and all she had to do was lean back and enjoy more than his body's warmth. She quickly shunned herself for considering it.

"Shouldn't we be getting back?" she called to Cole when

she realized they were leaving the well-lighted streets of town behind them.

They were headed up a narrow lane that curved and wound along the side of Green Hill and were soon surrounded by miles of burly forests and peaceful babbling streams. The chugging sounds of the iron mill grew ever fainter. With the moonlight shimmering on the darkened treetops and in the rolling meadow and the gentle warmth of the lap blanket keeping the cold night air at bay, the ride was very pleasant, too pleasant. Catherine sat forward and remained on her guard, heedless of the fact that sitting upright the way she was, was exposing her shoulders and back needlessly to the cold.

"What's your hurry?" Cole and Patricia responded in unison then laughed because they had. They were thoroughly enjoying the ride and the fact that their legs were pressing firmly against each other.

"It is just that it's getting late. Father will be worried."

"And since when do you care if Father worries or not?" Patricia asked pointedly, but good-naturedly.

That was a ridiculously hard question to answer. If she lied about that one, everyone would know it. Finally she sat back and sighed. "You are right. But let's not stay out too late. There is church in the morning."

"And what church do you attend?" Tony wanted to know. He hoped she would answer Catholic.

"Methodist."

"The Todd Street Methodist Church?" he asked. He knew the minister there very well.

"No, I am a member of that big stone Methodist Church that sits on the corner of Franklin and Locust. You've probably seen it. It's right next to the park."

"Yes, I have, many times. I pass by it every time I have to go to the post office, which is almost every day. By the way, I think I saw you there the other day. I was too far away for you to notice me, but I saw you come out of the post office smiling gaily as you hurried along your way, pretty as a picture. That was you, wasn't it?"

Catherine stiffened. "Probably. That must have been the

day I went by in search of postcards."

"Postcards certainly must delight you. I never saw a brighter smile," Tony teased, unaware the chord his words would strike. "You looked so lovely, so joyous, you brought nothing but shame and misery to the other women on the street."

"I was just happy, that's all. It was a pretty day," she said defensively, her voice growing stilted.

"That it was," Tony responded, wondering why the sudden show of emotion. Catherine was certainly a moody person. He would just have to learn to adjust to these moods. "Actually, we have been pretty lucky with the weather this season. I dread the first really bad cold spell. I'm not exactly a winter person. I've always been rather partial to warmth."

At that moment, the rear wheel of the cabriolet hit a chug hole in the graveled road and jostled Catherine sideways, causing her to fall hard against Tony. She reached for the far side of the carriage in order to keep from falling any further about the time his arm came around her to steady her. Their gazes met. They were just inches apart, and she was well aware of the deep desire glimmering in Tony's eyes. It scared her, but for the moment she could not pull away. Her breasts were pressed against his chest, but still she did not immediately break the light embrace. It was as if he had cast a spell on her that refused to let her move. Her heart hammered out its message of alarm but the warning went unheeded.

When he leaned forward to gently press his lips against hers, she trembled slightly, but met the kiss, still mesmerized. Shame flooded her, but she did not prevent his other arm from coming around and completing the embrace. She allowed him to hold her close, firmly pressed against his chest until the kiss deepened. At that instant, she wanted him. Had they been alone, she might have been lost. It was so long since she had been held, been tenderly kissed. Hot tears welled in her eyes. She squeezed them closed so that they could not escape down her cheek and embarrass her. She did not want Tony to know of her anguish.

Shyly, she let her own hands come around and lightly

grasp his shoulders from behind. A passion that had lain dormant and hungry inside her drove her to part her lips and allowed him entry to the sensitive edges of her inner mouth. She could hear Patricia and Cole deep in conversation and knew that they would not be looking back. When Tony's hand came up to cup her breast beneath her cloak, she did nothing to stop him. In fact, she found herself arching her back in order to give him easier access.

Tony pulled the lap quilt up higher to shield them from view and while his lips continued to work their magic on hers, his fingers began to frantically undo the cloak ties and work the three tiny buttons between her breasts. Soon he was able to reach in and feel her softness through the thin material of her chemise. She did not make a move to stop him. He wished fervently that they were alone. His whole lower body ached with his need.

Catherine felt as if his touch had set her on fire. She quivered in response while his fingers continued to play at her breast, fanning the many flames that engulfed her. She realized she would give herself to him readily if they were alone at that moment. Despite her closed eyes, her tears found their way down her cheek. She desperately wanted to be made love to, to be held and coddled. She could pretend her circumstances were different until it was all over, but the realism of knowing they were not alone kept them from being able to carry their actions any further. She was safe, but not at all sure she truly wanted to be.

It was not until Tony pulled back to stare into her passion-filled blue eyes, his own eyes dark with desire, that she started to bring her senses back under control. When he opened his mouth to speak, she was so afraid of what he might have to say that she was able to pull away from him at last. She must not let him whisper words of love to her. Quickly she worked to re-dress herself, while his eyes questioned what had gone wrong. She was ashamed by her own wanton behavior. Her heart was supposed to belong to another and she had honestly wanted to make love to Tony. And deep down inside her, she knew that desire was still there.

"We really should be starting back now," she called out to Cole as soon as she had her clothes fastened again and the lap quilt tucked back around their waists like it was supposed to be. Her voice sounded strange even to herself. Tony said nothing, he just continued to stare at her with his brow drawn and his body rigid.

Much to her relief, Cole complied this time and at the next bend where there was room, he turned the carriage around and they headed back toward Johnstown. This time Catherine had no trouble remaining quiet. She was busy with her thoughts of deep shame and trying to figure out why she had been so willing to give in to her passions. Why had she lost control like that? She dared not look at Tony. His look of confusion and hurt was like a thunderbolt to her heart. She never had intended to cause him any pain. She had grown very fond of him. She never should have let him talk her into going out. Reaching up a delicate hand, she wiped away yet another tear.

Chapter Eleven

Tony had very little to say when he bid Cole and Patricia good night. His expression was solemn, the laughter was gone from his eyes. He and Cole had already made plans to meet and discuss the dam situation later on the following week and Cole had promised to stop by Tony's the first chance he got so there was nothing really to be said about that. Tony did not even speak to Catherine when he turned to walk her inside. Cole and Patricia waited in the carriage at the street side until Catherine and Tony had stepped safely through the front door. Both had noticed the sudden change in Tony's behavior, but neither had any idea what had caused it.

Once they were on their way again, Cole spoke off-handedly, "I like that Tony Alani. He's a very friendly fellow. And I like your little sister, too. She's a lot quieter than you, but she seems nice enough."

"And what about me?" Patricia probed, then leaned toward him so that she could clearly see his facial expression when he answered. She was not above digging for compliments. "Don't you still like me too?"

"Not really," he commented, his voice thoughtful, and he felt her bristle beside him. "I don't know why, but a few days ago, I realized I didn't like you anymore. I don't even know when it happened for certain, but my feelings for you have definitely changed." He was deliberately baiting her, but felt she wouldn't mind after she learned the outcome of this conversation. "I can't help it, but that's the way it is."

That was not the sort of response Patricia had expected. Her heart constricted, sending a twisting ache right through her, and she fought the sudden urge to cry. He didn't like her anymore. He was about to tell her they would not be seeing each other for a while or something polite like that. He would be the type to try to let her down easy. She had never felt such a hollow pain.

"Somewhere along the line, my liking you changed—into loving you. I'm afraid, my dear Patricia Morgan, that I have fallen deeply and hopelessly in love with you. I'm sorry."

She felt a strong sense of relief but at the same time an intense alarm. He was not supposed to actually fall in love with her. She wanted for them to be friends, close friends, nothing more. "That's ridiculous. We haven't even known each other two weeks. How can you possibly believe you have come to love me in such a short period of time?"

"To tell you the truth, I don't know how it came about at all," Cole said, realizing she had tensed and drawn away from him. He suddenly worried that he had read tonight's mood all wrong. "It just happened. I'm just as surprised as you seem to be."

"But in less than two weeks? That's impossible!" The thought of his loving her frightened her far more than it should. Something inside her quivered in response.

"I don't suppose it is so impossible. After all, it happened. I've had a lot of time these past two weeks to think about it and each time I see you, I'm more convinced. What I feel for you is special, very special. I know what I feel. Why do you doubt it so?"

"Because it isn't natural. What you are feeling can't be true love."

"True enough that I've started to consider what it would be like to be married to you," he told her as he looked away from her to the shadows of the street ahead. The sternness in his voice did not match the tenderness he had been feeling in his heart. "I've thought about it many times, a half dozen times just tonight."

Marriage. That was the last thing she wanted him to

170

consider. It felt as if everything had started to close in on her. She felt panicky. "That's absurd! You don't consider marriage to someone you barely know."

"I think I have come to know you very well in such a short time, and until this moment I have loved everything I have learned about you. But I'll confess, right now I'm getting more than a little angry. I don't like having my personal feelings questioned."

"See? How could you even think of marrying someone who can make you angry so easily? It's absurd."

They had pulled up in front of her house and were sitting facing each other with their fists coiled so tight that their knuckles had turned white. Cole's features had gone rigid and the muscles in his neck and jaw flexed as he fought his anger. He had told her how he felt and she had shunned him. "Maybe you are right. Maybe I was a fool for thinking I'd be happy married to you. I should have better sense when it comes to a woman like you."

That remark hurt. "A woman like me? Just what sort of a woman am I?"

Cole did not answer; instead he climbed out of the carriage and walked around behind it. He stood at the side, staring at her with his hand outstretched to accompany her down. His eyes bore into her like cold shards of steel.

"Don't bother," she responded icily, then added, "Especially with a woman like me!"

Not wanting to pursue this argument further, he stepped back and shoved both hands into his pockets. "Okay, I won't. Get out of my carriage on your own, but hurry. I want to go home."

"Oh!" Grabbing up her dark brown skirt, she leaped to the ground, unaware of the length of leg she had lent to his view. So much anger welled up inside her as she traipsed toward the porch that she thought she would burst. When she did not hear footsteps behind her, she turned sharply around and glared at where he had been standing. But he was no longer there. She glanced around and discovered he was already climbing back into the carriage. When he was well situated, he turned and saluted her with a tip of his finger to his forehead. His face was stone and before she could voice her opinion of what he was doing, he flicked the reins and was on his way.

Not wanting to stand there gaping after him, Patricia turned and flounced inside. Duchess appeared at the top of the stairs as soon as she had heard the door open, but quickly ran for cover when she noticed her mistress's foul mood.

"How dare he!" she hissed and slammed the door shut as hard as she could. Without bothering to lock it, she yanked up her skirt and ran up the stairs. "How dare he tell me he loves me! How dare he not escort me to my door. He let me off at the street like I was a common trollop. Damn him!" She gasped at her own expletive, but it had felt so good on her lips at the moment that she repeated it again and again.

Duchess decided that being under the bed was not nearly safe enough when her mistress was this angry and made a wild dash for the door just as Patricia stormed through it, almost causing her to fall backward in the darkness.

Violently she jerked her cloak off and began tugging at the many ties, buttons, and stays of her dress, until she finally had it off too. With a shrill cry of anger, she flung the dress into the corner, turned, and fell face forward across the bed in only her chemise and stockings. She could not remember ever having been so furious with anyone in all her life, not even her father. With loud wails of anguish, she began to pound her pillow with her fists and screamed her newly found curse word over and over until her voice started to grow hoarse. Finally she dropped her face into the deep pit her fists had made and wept bitterly.

After having fully vented her rage, she rolled over and faced the dark shadows on the ceiling. Calmer now, she began to sort through what had happened and wondered why she had gotten so angry. She had wanted to prove to him that he could not possibly love her and had obviously succeeded. He surely hated her now, so why had she gotten so angry? Why did she feel so much pain now that the anger had subsided? What was wrong with her? Slowly the answer dawned on her. Despite her every effort not to, she too had

172

fallen in love. With Cole. Incredible as it might seem, it was true. She honestly loved him.

"Damn!" She cursed again, getting very good at it by now. Here she finally realized she was in love with him and had just moments ago driven him away. If he never forgave her for her outburst, she would deserve it. She had reacted childishly. Why did she have to be so impulsive? Would she ever learn to curb her tongue? The man had bravely proclaimed his love to her and she had practically rammed his declaration back down his throat. She had the same as called him a fool and a liar. Would he ever forgive her? Would he even give her a chance to apologize? That's what she needed, a chance to tell him how sorry she was now that she had had the opportunity to cool down. Would he even give her that chance? Her heart twisted with the tormenting anguish she felt.

Her wild display of anger and now her deep feelings of remorse caught up with her and she realized she was overheated and sweating lightly. Her chemise clung to her damp body. Grudgingly, she rose from the bed and walked over to the window to open it. A blast of cold night air was just what she needed to soothe her frayed nerves. Quickly, she jerked the curtain aside and flung the window open wide. To her amazement, the cabriolet Cole had rented was sitting in front of her house. The light of the nearest streetlamp fell in such a way it left a dark shadow on the front seat. She could not see if Cole was still in the carriage or not. If he wasn't, he had to be nearby. She dared not let him leave again without first talking to him.

The excitement of knowing he had returned hurried her steps as she ran down the stairs. Here was the second chance she had hoped for. Though she did not deserve it, she was getting it and dared not risk losing it. She started calling out his name, her voice sobbing with relief even before she reached the door. When she flung the door open and saw him standing there in the dark shadows of her porch, she cried out, "I'm sorry, Cole. I'm so sorry. I love you too. I just didn't want to admit it, not even to myself, but I love you too. I do."

173

His arms opened and she went into them, undaunted by the fact that all she wore was her scanty underclothing. "I'm so sorry, Cole. Please forgive me. Please don't be angry with me anymore. It's just that the thought of being married to someone again and then losing him terrifies me, but the thought of losing you and never having known the joy of marriage to you, of loving you fully, terrifies me just as much."

"Then you will marry me?" he asked, just as surprised by the suddenness of all this as she was.

"Yes, yes, Cole, I will," she said and reached up to pull his lips to hers. She wanted to seal the promise with a kiss.

Realizing they were standing in the doorway where a passerby might notice them, Cole bent down and gathered her into his arms. Their lips never parted as he kicked the door shut behind them, giving them the privacy they needed. The sound of the door shutting seemed to intensify Patricia's emotions, for her lips pressed harder into his, giving him an idea of the measure of emotions that had overtaken her. Eagerly, her tongue sought his and she wrapped her arms securely around him, binding them close.

Cole stood in the darkness for a long moment returning her fevered kiss until he could feel his need for her start to grow. Rather than pressure her into something she might regret later, he pulled his lips free of hers and reluctantly set her back on the floor. Taking a tiny step back, he could not help but stare down at her near naked beauty while he strived to get his emotions back under control. A dim light filtered through the window and fell across her. There was even more of her exposed to his view than had been when she had worn that black gown. He wanted to strip away the tiny garment and know her complete beauty, but carefully restrained himself.

Patricia was well aware of where his hungry gaze had gone and stood proudly before him, her nipples taut against the thin fabric.

"I'd better get out of here," Cole growled, sounding almost wounded. "I'd better get out of here right now."

When he turned to do exactly that, Patricia reached out a

174

restraining hand. He glanced first at the delicate hand on his shoulder, then back into her smoldering green eyes.

"Stay," she said simply, then slowly began to pull his coat from his shoulders. She did not want to wait until she had made him her husband. That would take too long. She wanted him desperately. She wanted him now.

Their eyes locked as Cole took over the task of removing his coat. He carefully hung it on the clothes tree near the door then walked back over to stand in front of her. "Are you sure?"

A timid smile crossed her face when she nodded. "Yes, Cole, I'm sure."

"I do love you," he said as he bent down and scooped her back into his arms. Well remembering how to get to her bedroom, he headed for the stairs.

"And I'm afraid I love you too," she muttered playfully.

"Well, you won't be afraid of your love after tonight," he promised and paused on the landing long enough to kiss her once tenderly. Then, as his eagerness grew, he hurried on upstairs and into her room. The same moonlight that had entertained them on their long ride now streamed into the open window, pouring a soft island of silvery light across the bed. Reverently, Cole placed the woman he loved into that delicate light and stared longingly at her a moment before starting to get undressed.

When he returned to her, he was naked. She had gotten a glimpse of his strong masculinity just before he lay down beside her. He was such a virile, handsome man. It amazed her that she would have a man like Cole for her husband. She adored him, wanted him, and had considered undressing herself while he was undressing, but she had waited. She wanted to enjoy the slow sensual torment of having him do it for her.

Propped up on his elbow, Cole stared at her again for a long moment, cherishing every little detail before reaching for the delicate little sashes that held the garment at her shoulders. He gently pulled on each bow until the ties had given way, then he ran a fingertip beneath the garment's lacy edge and pulled the front of it down until he had exposed

175

first one creamy round breast, then the other. Pulling himself to his knees, he bent over her and slowly worked the garment on down over her slender hips and beyond, until he held the wisp of fabric in his hands. He pressed it to his face and breathed deeply the gentle scent of her before tossing it lightly to the floor.

"You are exquisite," he told her, his voice golden with desire. "Truly exquisite. I don't deserve such a wife."

Patricia responded to his tender words by raising her arms to him. She pulled him gently down. As she closed her arms around him, she knew it was where he belonged. It felt as if he had always belonged there, in her arms, in her bed. A smile curved at the corners of her mouth when she angled her head slightly to meet his fiery kiss. This man was to be her husband. He loved her as she loved him. She was to have his pleasure at her beck and call for the rest of her life. She could not remember ever having known such joy.

The warmth of his body spread quickly through her, bringing her a deep languid pleasure as their lips once again explored each other, first sampling then devouring. Soon the languid warmth turned into molten desire as Cole's mouth left hers and began to make a trail of tiny, hot kisses down her throat, across her collarbone, then down again to her breast. Patricia cried out as she savored the sensations that stirred deep within her the moment his mouth descended over the tip. She thought she would never be able to bear the swirling torrent of fiery need that grew wild inside her when he had begun to draw lightly on the breast until it was taut with desire. She clutched helplessly at his back, letting him know her urgency, but instead of moving to fill the need that consumed her, he repeated the same loving act on the other breast.

Writhing beneath him, Patricia grew desperate to find release from the splendid torture he was putting her through. She had never felt anything like it, ever. Not even during the many times she and Robert had made love. Cole was bringing her to sheer madness with her exploding need of him. She bent forward and began to kiss the top of his head and tried to bring his mouth back to hers in an effort to slow down the whirlwind that spun inside her.

Instead, Cole moved to drive her into further ecstasy. While his mouth continued to arouse one breast with tiny suckles and nips, his hand gently teased the other, shooting pure rapture through her, until Patricia was not sure she could bear it any longer. Finally she cried out, "Now, Cole, please, now."

"I love you" was all he said as he moved to fulfill the needs he had so expertly brought to life within her. His lips claimed hers once more and their tongues hungrily sought the sweet depths of each other's mouths while they worked together to meet their splendorous goal, soaring ever higher, higher, until they crested the top. Having shared the ultimate height of lovemaking, they came gently down again, bound together in each other's arms, their energies spent. Again, Cole whispered just above her ear, his warm breath gently falling across her temple, "I can hardly wait to make you my wife."

"And I can hardly wait to become your wife," she replied and lifted up to kiss him lightly.

"Why wait at all?" he responded eagerly, smiling as he bent low to nip at the sensitive edge of her earlobe.

What a marvelous sensation that created.

"Patricia, let's get married just as soon as possible. Is yesterday all right?"

"Don't be silly. We can't get married now," she said, laughing. "It will have to be later, much later. You know that."

"You are not backing out on me, are you?" His body stiffened beside her as his smile dulled.

"No, Cole, not at all," she said and raised up on one elbow in order to look into his eyes. "It is just that you have that petition to worry about now. It is extremely important that you get that finished first. Once that is out of the way and those people are hard at work repairing that dam, I'll be glad to marry you."

Cole stared at her a moment. It was obvious she meant every word of what she just said. "But I can marry you and still work on the petition."

"No, you can't. You wouldn't have the time. I want a nice wedding with both my sisters as bridesmaids. It can't be a big church wedding since I have been married before, but it can still be special, which it should be. Our marriage is going to be very special. But in order to be special, the wedding will take time to prepare. More time than you realize."

"But you can do all the planning. I'm no good at that sort of thing anyway."

"Maybe so, but I also want to help you with the petition. I can't do that and plan a wedding too. We are just going to have to wait until next summer to get married."

"But you will marry me next summer?"

"The day you get back from Washington. I promise."

"Why can't we go ahead and get married now, tomorrow, and just not tell anyone. Then you could go ahead and have your special wedding anyway and I wouldn't have to worry about you changing your mind and backing out on me. I'm not going to rest easy until I know you are mine."

"I won't be backing out on you. As far as I'm concerned, we are already eternally bound to one another. We became one just a few minutes ago, here, in this bed. I've made my commitment. You know it and God knows it. You don't have to worry about me backing out or changing my mind. I already belong to you."

"I love you," he said again, and drew her back into his arms for another leisurely kiss, but when his hand moved to cup her breast, the kiss took on new meaning and once again they soared to their passions' limits, and beyond.

Catherine paced wildly about her room. She was too immersed in her intense shame and extreme mortification to even think of trying to sleep. She had tried reading to force her mind off of what had happened that night, but had been unable to concentrate enough to comprehend the words. After having reread the same paragraph a dozen or more times, she had finally tossed the book aside and given up.

She never should have allowed Tony to kiss her, much less take such liberties with her. And worse, she never should have agreed to go out with him next Saturday. Where had her mind been? She knew she should not see him again, yet when he had asked, his eyes so solemn and full of hurt and confusion, she had said yes. Even worse still, she had not thought to demand an escort this time and was not sure he planned to provide one. They could very well end up being all alone next Saturday. She was terrified by what might happen. She had to find a way out of it. She just had to. What excuse could she use? She must never allow herself to be alone with him.

Sunday morning dawned bright and beautiful. An early morning mist hung over the hillside but quickly burned away as another Indian summer day began. It amazed everyone in Johnstown how nice the weather had remained this fall. By now, the days usually were cold and the nights were freezing, but so far, they had experienced mostly mild weather. Although many birds had already started their long trek southward despite the warmer days, several still sang cheerfully in the huge elm outside Patricia's window, heralding the wondrous new day. It was a lovely serenade for the two of them to wake up to.

"Good morning," Cole said, leaning up on one elbow and smiling down at Patricia.

"Oh, are you still here?" she asked, trying to sound unconcerned as she stretched beneath the sheet.

Finding her action terribly provocative, Cole reached for the cover's edge and jerked it off her. He stared at her beauty for the first time in daylight.

"See anything you like?" she asked when all he could seem to do was stare. She ran her fingertip over the soft swell of her breast invitingly. "Anything at all?"

"Vixen," he growled and made a move to devour the breast, but was thwarted when she rolled out of his way and quickly swung her legs over the edge of the bed in an attempt to escape and torment him.

"Oh, no you don't," he warned and reached for her arm just in time to prevent her from getting away. "You are mine, remember?"

"How dare you try to take advantage of me like this," she said, her nostrils suddenly flaring. With her lips pressed determinedly against her teeth, she spun around to face him on all fours. His look of surprise spurred her on. "You think that simply because I was lying in bed with you without any clothes on that you can do as you please with me. How wrong you are."

"I—I." Cole tried to speak, but couldn't. He was overwhelmed by this sudden change.

"You think that simply because I let you have your way with me last night that you can do the same thing again this morning, don't you?"

Cole remained speechless. He had no idea what had gotten into her.

She flung her leg over his hips and pinned him to the bed. "Not this time, fellow." She grinned proudly. "No, sir. It's my turn to pursue you. So there."

This time she was quite proud of her impulsiveness and felt it paid off remarkably well, for she not only brought them both to full arousal but also provided both of them complete satisfaction; it let him know what he could expect from a marriage to her. With lovemaking as wild and passionate as they shared, it deserved a little variety, and variety they would have. She would see to that. Her husband would never be in want of anything more than what he would have with her.

When they again lay in each other's arms, exhausted from their lovemaking, she suddenly thought of church. "Cole, get up and get dressed, I want to go to church."

"Now?" he asked, still groggy from his passion.

"Yes, now. There's still an hour before services. We can get ready in that time. I want to go to church so that I can thank God properly for bringing us together."

Cole stared at her a moment, then smiled. He liked her reason. "All right then, church it is." Quickly, he got out of bed and started to get dressed. He just hoped that if they ran into Clayton, the man would not be aware that he was wearing the very same clothes he had worn last night.

"The carriage!" Patricia gasped. She had gone to shut the window and noticed that the rented cabriolet was gone. "It's been stolen."

"No it hasn't," Cole assured her as he worked to get his tie straight. "I went down last night and pulled it around to the back. I put it in one of your outbuildings."

"Horse too?" she asked and wrinkled her nose at the thought. Both of her sheds had planked floors.

"No, the horse is tied to your clothesline," he muttered, having to start all over on his tie. He had enough trouble getting it tied right without all these distractions.

"But why?"

"I didn't want your neighbors talking. Some of them saw us drive away yesterday in that very same carriage. It just wouldn't have seemed right to them if that same carriage stayed out front overnight. What would they say?"

"I really don't care what they say," she said, but knew that was not all together true.

"Well, I don't want them talking about my future bride like that." He grinned. "Even if it is the truth."

He ducked just in time to avoid the pillow that suddenly sailed in his direction, but found he had to start all over again on his tie.

Chapter Twelve

"Catherine. Patricia. I'm so glad I found you before you left."

Patricia turned around to see what Jeanne wanted. She had been unsuccessfully trying to get Catherine to admit that she had enjoyed her evening out and was becoming more than a little disgruntled when she discovered her sister had almost nothing to say on the matter. The more questions Patricia asked, the more evasive Catherine became, and frustration was quickly getting the best of her. Had Catherine enjoyed herself or not?

Cole kept himself busy staying out of it, nodding to the curious church members who stared pointedly in his direction when they passed by on their way from church to home. Gazing at the brilliant cobalt sky overhead, he wondered when he and Patricia would ever be on their way. Church services had been over with for more than ten minutes and, after having skipped breakfast, he was starved. But he was also determined to be a good sport about having to wait and continued to smile pleasantly as two older women eased forward along the rock and mortar sidewalk that passed in front of the church until they had come to stand right beside him. They seemed to want to get a closer look at him. No doubt they wondered who he was and why he was with Patricia, but neither of them bothered to speak.

"I need to ask you something," Jeanne called as she rushed toward them and almost tripped on her heavy woolen skirt in her eagerness to catch them. "Harrison and I won't be at Father's for dinner later so I need to ask you now."

Cole too turned around when he recognized the high timbre of that voice. He put on a hardy smile and could hardly wait to see what Jeanne's reaction would be when she realized exactly who was at Patricia's side. He loved to intimidate the woman and watch her grow flustered. There was just a mean streak in him somewhere that seemed to be directed right at this little busybody.

Not having noticed Cole yet, Jeanne hurried on toward them and was only a few feet away before she bothered to look up at the tall man standing beside her oldest sister. When she saw his face, though, she let out a startled gasp and her eyes flew open wide with alarm. Her breath held in her throat until she had turned to see just where Harrison was, still worried he might find out what an awful thing they had done to this man. He would not like the way they had behaved, not at all. She finally exhaled when she noticed that her husband was busy talking to Othell Shattles on the far side of the churchyard. It would be awhile before he would be free of that man. Othell had more ailments than an active squirrel stored nuts.

Though Jeanne's already rosy complexion had turned even rosier from the exertion of having had to run in order to catch up with her sisters, she suddenly paled everywhere but her neck, which gave her a sickly color. "What are you doing here?"

"Good morning, sister dear," Cole said, running his fingers along the smooth black lapels of his semicutaway suit coat. His dimples dipped at the corners of his upturned mouth when her expression became even more unsettled. "I am waiting for Patricia to finish her talk with Catherine. You know how women love to talk. Most of them seem especially partial to gossip." That remark must have hit home, for Jeanne winced and drew in her shoulders. He pretended not to notice. "Did you enjoy the sermon?"

"You were at church?"

"Does that amaze you?"

"With Patricia?"

"Of course with Patricia." He smiled and wondered why her hand kept patting her breastbone spasmodically. "She was kind enough to invite me. But we got here a little late and had to sit near the back, otherwise I'm sure we would have joined you near the front."

"Oh, my," she uttered, then fell silent as she thought about that. Slowly, a wicked little glimmer entered her wide hazel-colored eyes and some of the color returned to her cheeks. "Did William see you?"

"William who?" he asked, screwing up his face as if earnestly trying to figure out who she was talking about. He wanted to laugh at the exasperation she displayed. "Oh, the William that bid so extravagantly for Patricia's picnic basket last month. I can't say whether he has seen me or not, but I can say that I definitely haven't seen him. Why? Are you looking for him?"

"No, of course not," she bristled and indicated her sisters. "It should be obvious I am looking for Patricia and Catherine."

With a smile as sweet as molasses, he shrugged and asked, "Do you want me to help you?"

"Help me what?" she asked, confused, but already certain that whatever it was, she most assuredly did not need his help.

"Do you want me to help you look for Patricia and Catherine."

"Of course not, I've found them," she said, waving her arm for emphasis. With all the brightly colored plumes in her stylish black English-style felt hat, her motions made her look a lot like a plump peacock trying to take flight. "I just wish I'd found them alone."

"You didn't do it alone? Then you *did* have help?"

"Cole, quit aggravating her," Patricia finally inserted and raised a brow in warning. "I want you two to get along, not try to outwit each other every time you get close. Come on. Both of you. Pull in your barbed tongues and try to be friends. I know you got off on the wrong foot, but I want you two to shake hands right now and say something civil to one another." Seeing Cole's eyes twinkling with mirth, she

185

emphasized, "I said *civil.*"

Jeanne and Cole looked at each other doubtfully, then slowly Cole stuck his hand out. "She's right. I'd much rather be friends." When he noticed her wary look, he added with a roguish grin, "Especially when it's with a beautiful woman like yourself."

"I suppose we just got off to a bad start," Jeanne admitted and stared at him a moment longer before she finally accepted his flattery and lifted her own hand. "Yes, I guess we should make an attempt to be friends, especially since it looks like you could be seeing quite a lot of Patricia in the future."

"As you probably recall, I've already seen quite a lot of her, but I wouldn't mind seeing a little more." He chuckled. He couldn't help it. That one just slipped out.

"Cole!" Patricia admonished, but found herself wanting to laugh too.

Jeanne was horrorstruck, her hazel eyes quickly scanning the area to see who might have heard his comment.

"Sorry," he said, then quickly grew solemn. He folded his hands humbly at his waist and bowed his head slightly. "I get carried away sometimes."

Catherine looked at the three of them with a puzzled expression. "You two already know each other?"

"We've met," Cole explained. "I guess you could say a mutual friend introduced us."

"Patricia?"

"No, a fellow named Ben Butler." The devilish gleam in his eyes totally contradicted his humble stance.

"Catherine," Jeanne interrupted, deciding to ignore that last remark of Cole's. "What I wanted to talk to you about is Harrison's birthday party."

"What birthday party?"

"Next Saturday. I want to give Harrison a nice little dinner party for his birthday."

"How old will he be?" Patricia wanted to know. She never could keep up with ages. It was hard enough for her to keep up with her own.

"Thirty-two. And I want the evening to be special. I want

186

all the family to be there, including you, Catherine. No excuses. And I want you to bring that young man Father has been talking so much about."

"Tony?" she responded hesitantly. In her mind, she could already see this as a way out of having to be alone with him next Saturday, but she worried that he might jump to the wrong conclusions when she explained to him she wanted him to take her to a family function. But then again, it would be much safer to be surrounded by lots of people, family at that, than be alone with him somewhere. "I guess it will be all right. He's planning to come over and see me Saturday anyway."

"Wonderful," Jeanne replied, beaming. "I am so looking forward to meeting the young man who has finally managed to get you out of that silly shell of yours. And of course I want you there, Patricia."

"We'd love to," she replied, then glanced up at Cole to be sure it was all right with him. She could tell by the warm, loving smile he gave her that anything she wanted was just fine with him.

Jeanne looked a little flustered when Cole stated that it was fine with him. Running her tongue nervously over her lips, she hesitated to tell them, "There's one problem you should know about."

"What's that?" Patricia wanted to know. If Jeanne planned to tell her Cole was not invited, she intended to refuse to go without him. She did not want to hurt Harrison's feelings, but her place was now with Cole.

"I sort of invited William," she said and flinched.

"What on earth for?" Catherine asked, beating Patricia to it.

"I didn't mean to, believe me," she explained. "I saw Father talking to Gorden James right after church. Since Father does not usually linger long after church, and since Harrison and I won't be able to join him for dinner today, I hurried over to tell him about the party before he could get away."

"Gorden James was at church?" Patricia asked. "I didn't know he even went to church, much less that Father was

187

friendly with the likes of him."

Jeanne thought about that a moment. The man was not exactly known for his good deeds or his saintly heart at that. "Well, he was at church today and he was talking with Father."

"What has all this got to do with William?" Catherine wanted to know. She didn't know who this Gorden James was, and at the moment did not care.

"Because I was in such a hurry to speak with Father, I interrupted them a moment in order to go ahead and tell him about the party. Just as he was agreeing to come, William came up and Father quickly included him. I had little choice really than to agree. Not with him standing right there."

"So—let William be Father's guest. Cole will be mine," Patricia said adamantly.

"Surely William won't come once he learns Cole will be there with you," Jeanne said with sudden hope.

"You won't be able to keep him away," Catherine muttered, then gave a timid smile. "Too bad Harrison wasn't born on the Fourth of July."

"Why do you say that?" Jeanne asked.

"Because of all the fireworks we are sure to see at his birthday dinner." Catherine's smile turned into a devil of a grin when she looked up at Cole. "And let me warn you, Father has a very short fuse."

"I'll try not to light it," he said and grinned back at her.

Later, when Cole and Patricia were headed for the Hulbert House for lunch instead of her father's as she usually would be at this time, she offered him a chance to get out of going to the party. He certainly couldn't be looking forward to it. "We don't really have to go, if you don't want to."

"I wouldn't miss it," he assured her.

"Neither Father nor William are going to be very cordial toward you," she warned. That was putting it mildly.

"I can handle it. Besides, it's time everyone started getting used to us being together. After all, we love each other and we are to be married soon."

Marriage. Why didn't it sound so terrible anymore? What a difference a couple of weeks could make. She smiled as she thought of herself as Mrs. Cole Gifford. She could hardly wait for summer. She wondered how long she should wait before she told her sisters.

"You'd better hurry, Harrison, or you are going to be late for your own birthday party," Jeanne warned as she put a touch of rose-scented toilet water on either side of her neck. She had spent all day getting herself ready and now that she was, she felt the effort was well worth it.

Proudly, she stepped back from her huge gilt vanity mirror and admired the dark green gown that glittered from the tiny gold brilliants running through the bodice. It had been one of the most elaborate gowns in Akard's dress shop and she had not felt the least bit guilty in spending such a large amount for it. After all, she was going to be the hostess for the evening, she really should look her very best. Besides, Harrison could afford it.

"You would think with all the advancements in modern medicine that someone could come up with a cure for baldness," Harrison muttered as he tried to arrange his thinning hair so that the narrow bared spots above each temple did not show. He wished he could just forget it and wear his derby, but Jeanne had already ruled that out.

"I don't know why it bothers you so much," she said and shook her head. Why did he think having a thick head of hair was so important? It would not matter to her if he lost every hair in his head. Hair did not make the man, heart did, and her husband had a wonderful heart. "Harrison, you are a very handsome man. Even if you do go bald, you are still going to be very handsome."

"Maybe," he said begrudgingly, frowning—not thoroughly convinced but hoping it was the truth. As long as Jeanne still found him attractive, it didn't matter as much. "At least I won't have to worry about turning gray. Scalp doesn't usually turn gray."

Jeanne laughed and came up behind him to place a light kiss on his cheek. "Don't be too much longer. I will need you down there tonight, not only as the man of honor, but also as

189

a mediator."

Harrison smiled, still peering into the mirror. "Yes, tonight should prove to be quite interesting if that Cole fellow does show up. You certainly were brave to invite him."

"I told you, Patricia invited him," she reminded him. "I had little choice in the matter. He was standing right there."

"Then if you didn't want him to come, you shouldn't have extended the invitation while he was there. It could have waited."

"It never occurred to me that she would invite him. I hadn't realized at the time that they were getting so serious. But now I hear he's been seeing quite a lot of her." She cringed when she remembered the remark Cole had made last Sunday to that very same comment. Yes, he had indeed seen quite a lot of Patricia. Jeanne blushed right to the very roots of her perfectly coiffed hair. How she hoped Harrison did not find out. That's what worried her the most about Cole's coming tonight.

"Yes, they do seem to have hit it off pretty well. I saw Patricia Thursday at the mercantile and she seemed to light right up when I asked her how her new fellow was doing. Poor William. I think he has met his match. No doubt he's going to find that out tonight. It won't set well with him," Harrison said with a note of concern. Reaching for his tie from the pole inside his wardrobe, he promised, "But I'll do my best to keep the two apart. I'll be on down in a minute."

"Be sure that you are," Jeanne said then hurried downstairs to make certain Ruby had everything in hand. Although she had surveyed the tables in the dining room and the parlor earlier, she decided to give them one last inspection before going into the kitchen to check on the progress there.

The dining tables in the parlor were all set and the banquet tables in the dining room were coming along just fine. Some of the food was already out. A fresh lettuce leaf salad with four choices of dressing oils sat at the head of the largest table and next to it was a colorful fruit salad drenched in sweet cream. Space for the turkey, ham, and the many vegetables had been left at the far end of that same table and the different desserts had already been set out on a smaller table nearby.

On yet another table sat an enormous cut glass bowl filled with a ruby red punch and surrounded by a ring of tiny glass cups. A three-tiered birthday cake that read "Happy Birthday Harrison" in bold letters around the base had a table of its own not far from the punch table. She smiled at the cake with its sculptured layers of white icing. Harrison had not seen his cake yet. She hoped he would be pleased with it. Because he seemed so irritated at having become thirty-two, there were just three candles for him to blow out. One had been carefully placed in each of the centers of the three sugared rosettes that adorned the top and matched the ones that encircled the bottom.

Everything was perfect. Jeanne could hardly wait for someone to arrive so she could hear the compliments. Being a good hostess was very important to her.

She did not have to wait too long, for just moments later Catherine and Tony arrived. Jeanne was delighted to find that Catherine's new gentleman caller was so handsome and utterly charming. She wondered why Patricia couldn't have found someone as likable as this Tony was. She frowned when she thought of Cole. Would he let what she and Patricia had done to him slip out? Harrison would never understand. In fact, she had a hard time herself understanding how they could have done such a thing. She cringed at the thought of it.

Harrison came downstairs before any more of the guests had arrived. Hearing the doorbells jingle just as he passed through the foyer near the front door, he paused to let the newest arrivals in.

"Michael! Come in," he said with a warm welcome then held out his hand to take his young colleague's wife's coat. "Hurry and get out of the cold."

"Cold is right." Michael shivered as he stepped inside behind his wife. "Hard to believe, isn't it? At this time yesterday I was outside repairing the hinge on the front gate in just my shirt-sleeves and vest. When the weather finally decided to change, it didn't dally."

"And I think this weather is only going to get worse," Ruth put in with a knowing nod. "Much worse."

"Oh? And why is that?" Harrison asked as he closed the door and turned back to face his guests.

"Every time we have a lengthy spell of good weather it is always followed by an even longer spell of bad. Having had such a lovely summer and fall, I'm afraid we are in for one nasty winter."

"I certainly hope not," Harrison remarked and held his hand out to accept her coat. He wondered where Michael's overcoat was. After all a doctor should know better than to traipse around in weather like this without one, but he made no comment. Instead he told them, "I believe everyone is in the parlor. Do go ahead and join them while I hang this up."

"But you are the birthday boy," Ruth protested, then handed her coat over anyway. "You shouldn't have to play host too."

"Ruth's right, old boy, it's just not fair," Michael put in as he pulled his favorite bent briar pipe out of his suit pocket and began to search his other pockets for his pouch. Being a frequent guest in the Rutledge home, he knew his pipe was acceptable, and since he was not allowed to smoke at the hospital, he took immediate advantage of the places where he could. "You really should complain."

"I agree, Doctor," Jeanne said as she came out to greet them. Reaching to take the coat from Harrison, she ordered him into the parlor with the rest to enjoy his party.

She stood and watched as Harrison escorted his friends toward the main room. The huge smile on his face let her know that he was really enjoying himself. He liked being the center of attention now and then. What man didn't?

Jeanne turned to put the coats in the closet below the stairway when the bells outside the door jingled again. She quickly opened the door and found Clayton and William waiting to come in. Her father had brought William after all. Jeanne's insides coiled into a knot when she saw the grim expression on both men's faces. It was obvious they were prepared for the worst.

"Hello, dear, is Patricia here yet?" Clayton asked, trying to sound casual, but failing miserably. William's eyes searched the large double doorway ahead for sight of the guests that had already arrived.

"No, Father, she is not here yet. But Catherine is. So are Dr. and Mrs. Michael Mack. You remember Michael, don't you?"

"Yes, he's that new surgeon Harrison brought in. Who else is coming?" he wanted to know as he tugged out of his heavy wool mackintosh and handed it to her.

"Since the Fagans can't make it tonight, there will be Clifton and Shirley Randall from next door, Perry and Lorretta Sutcliffe from down the street, and then there's Patricia and, ah, Mr. Gifford, and that's it."

Clayton scowled.

"Father, please, don't make a scene. I want this night to be special for Harrison."

"Would I make a scene?" he wanted to know and made an honest effort to smile. "I am just here to enjoy myself. You always throw such wonderful parties, my dear. Doesn't she, William?"

William responded by nodding his head. His mind was obviously elsewhere at the moment.

"Well, go on in and get yourself a cup of punch while I hang these coats up," she said, not fooled by her father for a minute. She had never seen him look so ready for an argument. "William, may I have your coat too?" Quietly, she waited for him to remove his dapper new box-tailed coat with its narrow upturned collar and watched as they went together into the parlor.

Soon everyone had arrived except Patricia and Cole. Jeanne flitted from group to group making certain everyone enjoyed himself, offering to refill any cups that became empty. At first she was not concerned over the fact that Patricia and Cole had not arrived, but the closer it got to time to eat, the more concerned she became. Had they backed out? She should feel relief at such a possibility, but she had prepared herself for this night all week. She felt ready to handle any problems that might arise and wished they would come on so everyone could eat while the food was hot.

The doorbell sounded just as Ruby started to bring in the steaming platters of food. Jeanne hurried to the door. She wanted to get right back and make certain Ruby set everything in its proper place. The woman was competent but not above making mistakes.

Jeanne sighed with relief. It was Patricia and Cole all right.

"You're late," she told them as soon as she had the door open and had practically pulled them inside. "We were just about to eat."

"Sorry, but we had to make a stop first and were detained far longer than we had anticipated," Patricia tried to explain, but found Jeanne was in too much of a hurry to stay and listen. Patricia was eager to tell her about the three new signatures they had gotten on the petition, even though she was not sure her sister would really care.

"I've got to get back. Put your coats in the closet and come on," Jeanne said over her shoulder. Then when she entered the main room again and saw the way everyone paused and looked up with uncommon interest, she realized what Patricia and Cole were in for and waited to escort them inside and personally began to introduce Cole to the ones he did not know. She may not have fully accepted Cole yet, but she was not about to allow one of her guests to be mistreated and he was one of her guests.

Although an almost tangible undercurrent of tension continued to build throughout the evening, the dinner itself went smoothly. Because there were so many guests, Jeanne had not bothered to try to seat them all at one table. Instead she had two dining tables set side by side, one set to seat eight and the other six. She arranged it so that Catherine and Tony as well as Clifton and Shirley Randall sat at the table with Patricia and Cole. She felt they would all be compatible.

She personally escorted her father to his seat beside Harrison and claimed that her motive was purely selfish since she liked to keep him near her. Although he had eyed the chair across from Cole, he allowed Jeanne to steer him on past. Reluctantly, William realized he would have to sit at the same table as Clayton or make the seating arrangements come out odd. He made certain that the seat he did choose would allow him to watch Patricia, and she him.

Well, after everyone had eaten and sampled the many desserts, the first incident occurred. Jeanne had asked that someone bring the cake over and place it in front of Harrison. William and Cole had both jumped up to volunteer and arrived in front of the cake at the same time. They stood there a moment eyeing each other like two fighting cocks about to do battle until finally Jeanne spoke. "Hurry you two, bring the cake over here so we can light the candles."

Somehow the cake reached its destination whole, but Patricia had held her breath the entire time the two of them had it in their hands. When they set it down in front of Harrison, she expected to find that the candles had gone limp from the heated stares the two men had exchanged the whole time they carried it. But once everyone had gathered around the birthday boy and the candles had been lit, Cole drew his attention away from William and joined right in when the group sang out the birthday song. But William's narrowed eyes never left Cole.

Patricia was well aware of William's continued interest in them both. If he wasn't gazing longingly at her, he was glaring at Cole. It made her extremely uncomfortable.

Jeanne sensed William's growing discontent and managed to monopolize what she could of his time after that. If something was going to happen, she wanted to make sure it happened after most of the guests had left. She could not hope that Patricia and Cole would leave early and she certainly would not ask them to. William and her father were the type to consider that a form of victory in this silent battle of wills. No, something was going to be said tonight. She knew that. She just hoped it would be later.

The hour finally grew late and the punch, which was found to have an added ingredient or two after supper, still flowed freely. Eventually, Michael Mack noticed the clock and decided it was time to leave. Soon there was just the family, Tony, William, and Cole remaining. Tony suggested he and Catherine go on and take their leave, well aware that something was about to blow, but she seemed to want to stay and be in on it. He had no way of knowing that she merely wanted to avoid being alone with him just as long as she could. She no more wanted to witness whatever was about to happen than he did.

"I sure do love my new watch," Harrison said when he realized the conversation had all but died in the room. Hoping to divert the pointed stares to himself, he made a great show of pulling it out of his vest pocket by its bejeweled black ribbon for yet another close inspection. He smiled at the craftsmanship. "And you say everyone chipped in and bought it for me? That's nice."

"You're more than worth it," Jeanne assured him.

That was just what Harrison had wanted to hear. Looking at her with a special glimmer in his eyes, he said, "You're a special woman for organizing such a wonderful birthday party, Mrs. Rutledge."

"I think that's our cue to leave," Patricia said, avoiding a grin, and quickly set her empty cup down. "I believe these two would prefer to be alone now. Cole? Would you be so kind as to get my coat for me?"

"Right away." His eyes caressed her a moment, giving her the courage to see these final moments through.

As soon as he left the room, Patricia turned to her father and said with an appreciative smile, "Thank you for not causing a scene. I know you don't like Cole and were upset that I invited him. It can't have been easy for you. I just want to say how glad I am of the way you handled it."

Clayton frowned. Obviously he had not planned to let the evening pass so uneventfully. "You are right. I don't like Cole and I can't see why you invited him instead of coming with William, but"—he paused a moment—"I didn't see that as any reason to upset Jeanne's party. After all, it's Harrison's birthday."

Patricia smiled again, knowing better than to believe all that. "I just wanted you to know how much I appreciate it."

196

Bending forward, she pressed a light kiss to his cheek and offered William a friendly smile. After saying an overall good night to everyone once more, she turned to join Cole in the foyer.

"Patricia?" William called out before she had gotten through the doorway.

"Yes?" She stopped to see what he wanted.

"May I have a moment with you?"

"Would you care to walk me out?" she offered and waited for him to catch up with her. She saw no reason why she should refuse to talk with him for a moment. Maybe if she tried to stay on his good side, he would keep his temper in check.

They were already within Cole's sight, but still out of earshot when William reached out and pulled her to a stop, turning her to face him. He held her by the shoulders and stared at her a long moment before finally speaking. "I want you to know that I'm not giving you up. I've just been giving you time to realize the mistake you have made, but I haven't given up on you by any means. I'll do whatever has to be done in order to keep you."

"William, you never truly had me. How can you keep what you never had?"

"That's not true, but I won't argue with you. I just want to warn you that I don't intend to let you go. I keep what is mine."

He was so solemn and so sincere that Patricia's heart went out to him. "I'm sorry, William, but I've never thought of us as more than very good friends. And I still consider us good friends but I don't love you. I never have."

The first flaring of anger reached his eyes. "I know you can't mean that. He's turned you against me."

"No, he hasn't."

"Yes, he has and he'll be damned sorry he ever tried—and you will be just as sorry you ever let him."

The muscles in William's lean cheeks worked furiously as he waited for her response. There was something so intensely evil in his glowering expression that it sent a shiver right through her to her very toes. She had never seen William quite so angry. But despite the tremor and the sudden danger she felt, she remained calm and spoke in a cool, level voice. "The only thing I'm sorry about is that you feel the way you do. Good-bye, William."

Without waiting for his response, she pulled herself free of his grasp and hurried to where Cole stood watching her, patiently holding her coat along with his temper.

Chapter Thirteen

Over a month had passed and still William did nothing to carry out the angry threats he had made right after Harrison's birthday party. Patricia had finally quit worrying about them, very glad William turned out to be a man of mere words and not action, which in this case she felt was to his credit. The most he had done to show his anger was to stop speaking to her and that worked out fine. She had enough to worry about without having to deal with William.

The petition was not going as well as they wished it would. No matter how hard they tried, they found it almost impossible to convince the many people they approached to support the petition. They had hoped for a better response.

There were now four working with Cole on the project to save the dam. With the plans for his building already well under way, Tony seemed to be able to find the most time of all to devote to the problem and as a result had become Cole's right-hand man. And it was Tony who had unwittingly solicited Andrew Edwards's help and, between the two of them, they had managed to get almost all of the one hundred and twelve signatures they had thus far.

Andrew Edwards was the new minister for the Todd Street Methodist Church near where Tony lived. Just days after Tony had moved into the neighborhood, he and Andrew had both been called on by some of the neighborhood children to help little Dottie Cross get her kitten down from a huge mockernut tree in her backyard. After they had managed to rescue the kitten and calm the little girl, Andrew had invited Tony back to the parsonage for a cup of hot coffee in order to celebrate their joint success.

It did not take them long to discover they had a lot in common and a friendship quickly began. They became such good friends that when Andrew learned about the problems with the dam and what Tony and Cole were trying to do about them, he immediately volunteered to help. Since then, Andrew had spent almost as much time as Tony trying to reach as many people and get as many signatures as possible.

Just recently Andrew had filed a written request with his church's leaders which asked for their support in the matter and was waiting for a response to that. With their permission, he could bring the problem before the church body and be able to approach hundreds of people at one time.

Patricia had not had the same luck as Tony and Andrew. She had trouble getting people to even listen to her. The ones she did find willing to at least discuss the matter usually ended up just wanting to argue about it. Most seemed to believe the dam was doing all right just the way it was and saw no reason to tamper with it. Even after she had eventually managed to persuade a few people into believing that a problem did exist, they almost always balked when it came to actually putting their names on the document. She could certainly see why Cole had gotten so frustrated in her father's office. On one occasion, she came very close to throttling a particularly closed-minded old codger with her own bare hands. The more she had tried to explain the problems to him, the less he understood the point she was trying to make until she wasn't even sure he was discussing the same thing she was at all.

Catherine experienced similar trouble. The only signature she had managed to get on her own was that of Jeb Sobey, the postmaster. No one else paid much attention to what she or Patricia had to say. After a while, they came to realize that it was because they were women. In order for them to get anyone to take them seriously, they had to have one of the men with them. It reached the point where Patricia would not go out soliciting names at all without Tony, Andrew, or Cole at her side. It proved to be a complete waste of time and effort to venture out alone. Catherine too found she did better when she teamed up with one of the men. She tried to avoid Tony as her partner whenever possible, but if he turned out to be the only one available, she did not refuse his help. The cause was too important to be hindered by such pettiness. She was terrified by the possibility of the dam breaking. Besides, Tony had quit pressing her to go out with him and had not tried to get intimate with her again in any way.

Tony now seemed content just to be a part of the same project with her and any time they spent together was almost always project-related. Last night, the two of them had joined Patricia and Cole to see if by teaming up they might finally be able to persuade Jeanne and Harrison to sign their petition.

Although the evening had had a purpose, Catherine had to admit it had also been fun. Tony was the first man able to draw laughter from her in years. She could not deny that she enjoyed his company more and more as time passed and was becoming more at ease whenever he was around. She was certain that was because she had finally quit thinking of him as a danger.

Last night had also been a success as far as getting Jeanne and Harrison to sign. Until then, Jeanne had refused to even listen to what she termed were "silly accusations," and Harrison too had remained uncommitted, although he had at least heard them out. But, desperately needing to get someone with the social influence of Harrison to support them, even if in name only, in order to help draw others to their side, Tony had devised a plan that would convince Harrison to sign. It had worked beautifully, so well in fact that even Jeanne had eventually signed, something they had truly not expected. Jeanne rarely did anything that went against her father's wishes and signing the petition had certainly done that.

Having taken Jeanne and Harrison to Marco's first and plying them with good food and wine had no doubt helped

201

lessen their resistance, but it was the first typewritten report Tony had finally managed to get that had cinched Harrison's involvement. Reading what the two experts had to say about the inadequacies of the dam had impressed him. It was proof positive that the problems existed. No longer was it the undocumented opinions of a few local men. As far as Harrison was concerned after having read the twenty-six-page report, the issue concerning the dam was an actual fact.

The drive they had taken along the Little Conemaugh River on the way back to his house had only helped to convince Harrison that something really should be done. After several days of steady rain, the water was again raging nearly out of its banks. It reminded him of how treacherous the river could be, especially when it passed the flood level and washed through the streets of lower Johnstown, which it did at least once every spring. He could not help but worry what it would be like to have that whole lake come crashing down on them. The thought was frightening.

By the time the evening had grown late, they not only had Harrison's signature on the petition, but he had asked what he could do to help. Even Jeanne wanted to help in some way. Plans were already in the making for a large social to be held at their house sometime that following spring, as early as the weather might permit, probably about mid-March. Jeanne was especially excited about it. She wanted to give Cole and Tony the opportunity to meet their friends and see if they could convince any of them to sign. They hoped that the relaxed atmosphere of a large party would aid them in gaining lots of support. Harrison was almost certain the doctors could be persuaded to sign. It was their nature to be concerned with anything that threatened the community.

But that would not be until at least March. Meanwhile they continued to approach the people on the street and with little success.

"I heard from the trustees of the church today," Andrew said in a melancholy voice as he pulled a chair out and slumped into it, still wearing his heavy overcoat. He had not

202

even bothered to brush the snow from his shoulders.

"And?" Tony asked and leaned forward, his face revealing his concern as he studied Andrew's unhappy expression.

"And they refuse to let me bring it up before the church body at all. In fact, they strongly urged I not continue to aid you in any way. They want me to stay well out of it. They hinted that my position with their church just might be in jeopardy if I was to continue to openly support the petition or bring up the problems with the dam. Seems they are all very opposed to what we are doing."

"They would take away your position as minister?" Catherine interrupted. "Why would they want to replace you over something like this? You're only trying to help."

"I don't know," he replied peevishly, raking a hand through his sandy-colored hair. "It could be a bluff. You can never tell when it comes to the dictates of the trustees."

"That's all right," Tony said in a strained voice. His hands formed tight fists on the table's surface as he spoke. "Don't concern yourself. We'll do all right. Even though you won't be able to get out and talk with the people anymore, we will know that in your heart you are behind us."

"No, I intend to continue right on with this," Andrew said firmly. His slightly protruding chin had never made him look more determined than he looked at that moment. "I have to do what I feel in my heart is right."

"But it's not worth your livelihood," Catherine put in.

"Isn't it?" Andrew smiled at her with reassurance. There was no fear, no regret in his dark blue eyes, only a strong dedication to his cause. "Isn't insuring the safety of my neighbors and friends worth a job that is governed by such a group of narrow-minded businessmen? I would gladly trade that job, or any job, for a chance to save the lives of those I care about."

Tears filled Catherine's eyes at such open sentiment. She was not so sure her own motives would prove to be as pure. Until now, she had thought mostly of her own personal losses should the lake come tearing down on Johnstown. She had thought very little of the suffering it could cause others. Mainly she had worried for herself. Now she felt ashamed.

"You are sure of this decision?" Tony asked, his own eyes moist with admiration. "Here it is, barely a week into December and we already have nearly three hundred signatures and come next spring when we get the support of Harrison's many friends in the medical community, and I feel certain we will, getting another several hundred names should not be too hard. I honestly think we are going to have this thing licked in plenty of time for Cole's trip in July."

"Yes, Tony, I am very sure of my decision. Until we have at least a thousand signatures on that petition, I won't rest. Even then, I will strive to get more. Until the very day Cole leaves for Washington, I will be out there trying to convince people to sign. Like you yourself have said again and again—the more signatures we can get on that thing the better the impression it will make. And now that we have that report to show everyone, I think we might even manage to get two thousand signatures. It's a goal worth considering."

"Don't get too optimistic too soon. True that report will pull some weight, but we are still going to have a hard time getting people to even read it."

"Why don't we approach the newspapers with it?" Catherine suggested. Her eyes lit up as the thought occurred to her. "We could show them the report and they could condense the information and print it for everyone to read."

"I already have. The only one that will touch the story is Swank down at the *Tribune,* but he refuses to do so until he has conducted his own investigation."

"How long will that take?"

"I really can't say. He claims he is going to get someone on it just as soon as possible." Tony shrugged. "I guess it depends on how thorough an investigation he makes, but it also depends on the weather. They can't very well inspect the thing if it is covered with snow. Besides, as cold as it is, those leaks are surely frozen, which will prevent anyone from finding them anyway. It'll be awhile, but at least Swank has said he will do what he can. That's better than anyone else would promise."

"Why won't the other newspapers agree to write a story on

it?" Catherine wanted to know. "This is news that affects their readers too."

"Seems the men that run the other paper are afraid of losing some of their best advertisers. Your father is one of them. And they are right. It could cost them a lot of advertising income. I know your father would pull his advertising the moment he read anything that might be derogatory to the dam or the hunting club and there are lots of others who do business with those people that would do the same."

"Then why is Swank so willing to do a story on it?"

"Swank's a good man. He prints what he feels his readers need to know. He's not easily intimidated," Tony explained and laughed. "He's a true journalist."

"I wonder if I could get the church to take their printing business to the *Tribune*. Swank seems like just the man to be printing out our Sunday notices," Andrew said and nodded with thoughtful appreciation. "I certainly do admire people like that."

"You would." Catherine said, laughing. "You are just like him."

"Yes, we are all such do-gooders. We really should pat ourselves on the back for our wonderful deeds." Andrew chuckled, obviously not taking anything he was saying seriously. Then he changed the subject entirely and asked, "Do we have to wait for Patricia and Cole to get here or can we go ahead and order?"

"I'd say go ahead and order but Cole is bringing his sister with him tonight. I guess since we have never met her, we should at least try to make a good first impression. Let her learn what horrid creatures we really are later," Tony said with a wiggle of his dark eyebrows.

"His sister is joining us?" Andrew asked, interested. "I've heard him talk about her. I gather she is quite a character. A real rabble-rouser. Is she interested in helping us with the petition or is it purely a social visit?"

"The way I understood it, she wants to help."

"I don't know what good it will do," Catherine muttered. "No one believes anything a woman has to say anyway."

"Now don't be bitter," Tony told her, then upon looking up and seeing the three enter the restaurant, he added with a slow grin, "You may have had trouble getting people to believe what you have to say enough to listen, but I have a feeling they are going to be more inclined to believe anything this woman has to say."

Andrew and Catherine turned to see what Tony was grinning about just as Marco escorted the three to the table. Andrew and Tony quickly rose to greet them, but Catherine sat staring up at them dumbfounded.

"I don't know which is wider," Patricia said, amused, "Catherine's eyes or her mouth."

"I think it's her mouth," Cole remarked and sounded serious in his assessment as he bent down and stared. "If you look close you can see that little thing that hangs down in the back there."

Catherine's mouth quickly shut and she blushed for having reacted like that. "I'm sorry. I didn't mean to gape."

"But you were not expecting a nun," Faye surmised, turning to jab an elbow at her brother. "I'm sure your failure to mention it to your friends was purely accidental."

Cole shrugged. "I thought they knew."

Patricia laughed. She had been just as guilty of forgetting to mention it as Cole was. "Faye, let me introduce you to my sister, Catherine."

She next introduced Tony and Andrew, then suggested they all sit down and order before Cole wasted away to bones.

"Good, I'm hungry too," Andrew said and immediately signaled for a waiter. He held a chair out for Faye before finally removing his overcoat and taking the chair next to hers.

By the end of the meal, Andrew and Faye seemed far removed from the rest of them as they discussed the similarities as well as the differences in their theologies. Andrew was especially curious to learn all about the sacrifices she'd had to make in becoming a nun. He found her to be truly admirable and was pleased to learn that she supported what they were doing about the dam whole-heartedly.

206

"And is it going to get you in trouble to help us?" Tony wanted to know as they all rose to leave after having eaten their fill.

"No, I have Father Tahncy's blessing," she assured him. "In fact, I have already recruited his signature. All I have to do is take the petition by St. John's sometime soon and he and Father Ald will gladly sign."

"Good, we'll do that tomorrow," Andrew said quickly. "That is if it's all right with you." He looked forward to being the one to work with Faye. He found her company stimulating.

"Tomorrow will be fine," she assured him. "I have all afternoon free to spend on it. I am eager to get started."

"Great, then tomorrow it is."

James Seale had set his large flat-topped oak desk only a few feet away from a narrow window facing the lake. Although the beveled pane was frosted over and night had long since set in, he sat and stared idly at the reflection of the fire roaring in the rock and mortar fireplace behind him. The faint smell of burning hickory permeated the room as he let his mind wander at will.

He had only two more days to complete his work before he headed back to Pittsburgh for a month. He looked forward to seeing his family again but he looked just as forward to meeting with Robert Pitcairn. Mr. Pitcairn was not only a prestigious member of the South Fork Hunting and Fishing Club, and the man who had hired him as the club's engineer, he was head of the Pittsburgh division of the Pennsylvania Railroad, and since the railroad traveled along the valley floor below the lake, he should be very interested in any potential problems with the dam. James doubted he would find Mr. Pitcairn to be as apathetic or as antagonistic toward discussing it as the captain and the few members of the club who he had met. In fact, he was counting on Mr. Pitcairn's interest.

For the past few weeks James had spent many of his off hours painstakingly drawing up the changes he personally recommended for the dam. He was proud of the work he had done. He just hoped Mr. Pitcairn would take time to see him and look over his sketches. Once Mr. Pitcairn saw the sketches and had been told of the dangers the dam presented in its present state, James felt sure the man would do what he could to help him. If they followed his well-thought-out suggestions the club could start draining the lake near the end of summer and have everything repaired and in working order in time to start refilling it by the first of the following summer. It should only take about ten months. It would be expensive, but at least it would not inconvenience the club members very much. They could be boating and fishing again by mid-summer.

"How is it going?" Captain Reid asked when he came to stand beside James Seale's cluttered desk.

James came to with a start and quickly began to straighten the many large drawings and note papers spread out across the wide surface before him. He had not heard the captain enter. He had been too deep in thought.

"The plans for the plumbing are almost finished. In fact, I was just about to call it a night," James told him as he gathered his pencils and laid them to the side in a neat pile. Leaning back in his chair, he raised his arms, slowly stretched his tired muscles and succumbed to an honest yawn. "I think that we will be ready to start digging a trench for the piping just as soon as the ground thaws. I may go ahead and start marking it off when I get back from my holiday."

"Looking forward to seeing your parents, are you?" the captain asked and lifted one of the more important-looking pages for a better look. It was the plans for the Moorehead cottage.

"Yes sir, I am," James admitted. "Although I love it here, I do miss my folks. I especially miss my mother's cooking. No offense intended, but Cody's cooking leaves a lot to be desired, and as you know, I certainly can't cook." He was referring to his attempt to make a simple chowder the day Cody had taken ill. They never were able to make that pot serviceable again and eventually had had to throw it out.

"What's this?" the captain asked as he glanced down at a

208

page that he had uncovered.

James felt his insides knot. The captain had discovered one of his drawings for the dam. He was not going to be pleased.

"That's just something I was doing in my spare time," James said, trying to sound unconcerned as he reached for the page, but the captain jerked it from his grasp. "It has nothing to do with the plumbing, sir."

"It looks like it has something to do with the dam." The captain scowled down at the paper and then looked accusingly at the young man. "What exactly is this thing? What's it for?"

"It's nothing really. I was just playing with a few ideas."

"What's this about discharge pipes here?" he asked and pointed a stubby finger at the places where James had indicated a trio of discharge pipes near the base of the dam.

"To tell you the truth, sir, I think the dam needs discharge pipes of some sort. There needs to be a way to let excess water out other than that spillway. I hear there used to be discharge pipes but that they were carelessly filled in years ago."

"Where'd you hear that?" he asked, reaching for another page and discovering more work that concerned the dam.

"From the inspectors," James said firmly.

"What inspectors?" The captain's wide face hardened to stone. "When?"

"Early last month, I happened to be near the dam when the inspectors came so I had a talk with them. When I mentioned how little control we had over the water level, they told me about the filled-in discharge pipes. They agreed with me that we need some better way to control the water level, especially in the springtime when it rains so much. They also said they intended to suggest that those fish screens across the spillway be removed because they tend to collect debris and clog up until the water can barely get through. They also agreed with me that what you think are natural springs are actually water leaks seeping right through the dam's surface."

"Why didn't you tell me about all this?" the captain

shouted. His eyes narrowed and caused downward creases along his wide cheeks. "Who were these men?"

"I didn't get their names, and I didn't mention them because you are so sensitive when it comes to discussing any problems concerning that dam. Besides, I thought you knew they were out there. You told me how they come and inspect it twice a year. Don't they tell you when they are coming?"

"Yes, they do and those men were not sent here by the club."

"Well, who else would have sent them here?"

"I don't know, but I'm sure as hell going to find out." Angrily he rumpled the plans James had worked so hard and long on into a single fat wad and slung them into the fire. He turned and glared at James a moment then stalked out of the room, slamming the door behind him. James stared sadly at all his hard work being consumed by flames and curling into a small black mass. He would have to start all over. It would be weeks. He would not be seeing Robert Pitcairn over the holidays after all.

Chapter Fourteen

"There's no better way to bring in a new year than to be surrounded by my closest and dearest friends," Cole said while his thumbs carefully squeezed the cork out of the tall, dark green bottle that had been chilling in a bucket of ice for the past few hours. Water dripped from the base onto the highly polished wooden floor in dozens of raised droplets, but Cole did not particularly care. His floor had suffered worse treatment and he knew he would have all the following day to clean up after the party.

"Isn't that the truth," Harrison agreed as he helped by handing out the glasses to everyone. "There's nothing like family and friends."

Midnight was only a few minutes away and everybody was getting ready to toast the coming year. They all had gathered around the tall Kingsland clock that rested on Cole's thick, intricately carved mantel and waited patiently for the last few minutes of 1888 to tick away.

One by one Cole circled around and filled their glasses, starting with the ladies. Once Patricia, Catherine, Jeanne, and Faye had been served, he began to fill the men's glasses. He started with Andrew and Tony, then poured the sparkling white champagne into the glasses Harrison held for himself and Cole. With barely a minute to go, he set the bottle down on the sideboard and took his glass from Harrison.

Everyone held a glass out in readiness, exchanging brief

glances and bantering lightly as to who would get to kiss whom. Although Cole had teased Jeanne several times during the course of the evening that he was going to steal his kiss from her, he placed his hand on Patricia's shoulder when the moment grew near.

Harrison walked over to stand only inches away from Jeanne and smiled down at her lovingly. She responded with a smile of her own.

As she had expected, Catherine found herself facing Tony, but for some reason, maybe it was the festivity of the moment, she did not particularly care if he did steal a New Year's kiss. After all, there was nothing wicked in a simple little New Year's kiss. Friends were expected to exchange kisses at New Year's. It was tradition for a man to take a kiss from the woman nearest to him when the clock struck midnight. She shouldn't be one to tamper with tradition.

The room fell silent as the last seconds passed. All that could be heard was the faint sound of the clock ticking and the light crackling of the small fire in the fireplace below. Everyone's eyes moved to the tiny ornate hands as they edged ever closer to the elaborate number twelve painted at the top of the bulging round face. At the sound of the first gong, everyone cheered in unison and clinked the delicate edges of their glasses together.

"To 1889," Cole shouted out in that deep golden voice of his. "May it be a year of happiness and surprises."

"Here, here," Andrew chimed in. "And may it be a year of changes . . . and the year that dam finally gets repaired so we will no longer have to worry about that."

"Here, here," everyone called out as they lifted their glasses to their lips and drained them dry.

The clock slowly continued to chime.

"Happy New Year," Cole called out while he placed his glass on the mantel. In one smooth motion, he pulled Patricia close and quickly lowered his lips to hers to sample her familiar sweetness in what he knew would be the first kiss of many for the year. It was a long, tantalizing kiss that might have led to other things had so many others not been around.

Harrison did likewise with Jeanne. "Happy New Year, darling." Jeanne snuggled close.

With a timid smile, Catherine closed her eyes and leaned forward for Tony's kiss, but it did not come to her cheek as she had anticipated. Instead she found herself drawn into his embrace and kissed soundly on the mouth. More than the quickly downed champagne warmed her as she felt herself being drawn into the magic of his kiss. She was barely aware that the clock was still chiming away. All she could hear was the pounding of her heart and the soft moan of pleasure that welled in her own throat. His kiss was far more welcome than she had wanted it to be.

Andrew chuckled at how long the New Year's kisses were lasting. He glanced down at Faye and could see she was equally amused. Tilting his head toward her, he looked at her questioningly, "May I?"

"Indeed, you may." She laughed and accepted the brief kiss he placed on the corner of her mouth. She smiled at his gentle show of friendship.

When the clock finally stopped chiming, no one seemed eager to pull away. One by one, the couples came apart. Cole's eyes were dark with passion when he finally withdrew. "Now, shall we tell them what you've been dying all evening to tell them?" he asked, glancing first at Patricia then around at the curious stares of their family and friends. "This is the moment you've waited for, isn't it?"

"It most certainly is," Patricia said and boldly linked her arm with his, pressing her cheek against his shoulder. "Friends, sisters, and what have you," she said with a huge grin as if preparing to make a long and formal speech. "I have an announcement to make."

"Why do I have a feeling this has nothing to do with the petition?" Tony asked, chuckling, already having guessed what this announcement was going to be. He had been expecting them to announce an engagement for weeks now. He wondered what had taken them so long to realize how much in love they were.

"Hush, you are ruining the ambience of the moment," she said and laughed. Her green eyes sparkled with more than

213

the reflection of the glittering chandelier overhead.

"Yes, shame on you," Cole said and shook his finger playfully at the dutifully sullen Tony. "Go on, dear."

"If you two will let me," she said with exasperation. She had already waited three months to make this announcement. Now that the decision had been made to finally let everyone know about their plans, she did not want to wait a moment longer. "I want you all to know that standing before you now is the future bride of your friend, Cole Gifford. Come next August, if the problems with the dam are finally all solved and if there are no major disasters, I, Patricia Morgan, will proudly become Mrs. Cole Gifford."

"Is that all?" Andrew asked and frowned in pretense. "The way you were carrying on, I thought it was going to be something important."

"Yes, me too," Faye said, trying to sound disappointed.

"Oh, you!" Patricia yelped and stamped her foot. "Isn't anyone going to say congratulations or wish us well?"

"I will. Congratulations, my dear," Harrison said gallantly. "And let me be the first to offer my deepest sympathies to your future husband. The poor man obviously has no idea what he is getting himself into. Look at him. He's smiling. Ah, the bliss of the ignorant. It's bad enough that he has decided to get married at all, but to a stubborn, bull-headed woman like you ... I do offer my innermost sympathies. I know from many years of personal experience exactly what the poor man is in for." Pulling in his head, he turned to see if Jeanne had picked up on his meaning. She had. And before he could duck out of her reach, she had popped him soundly on the top of his head with her opened hand. He looked at Cole beseechingly. "See? See what you are in for?"

Cole did not respond more than to laugh at his friend's antics and offer a crooked little smile. He reached his arm around Patricia's shoulders and gave her a brief squeeze then kissed her lightly on the cheek.

"Say, doesn't this call for another toast?" Tony inquired and glanced at the bottle to see if there was enough left for another go-around.

214

"I should say it does." Harrison was quick to agree and reached for the bottle still resting on the sideboard. "Retrieve your glasses, we are going to toast these two properly."

"To August," Andrew said as he raised his glass. The others quickly followed, again clinking the edges together. "May the month find these two happily wed and facing a bright and wonderful future."

"Here, here," everyone called out in unison and they tapped their glasses together again. Cole looked down at Patricia and smiled adoringly.

"Speaking of facing, Andrew, old man," Cole said after he had once again set his empty glass on the mantel. "Patricia and I have discussed this matter thoroughly and although we like Reverend Chapman and all, we would really rather be facing your ugly mug when the time comes. Will you officiate at our wedding?"

"And have you blaming me for the rest of your lives?" he asked with a raised brow, sounding offended. "Of course I will."

Then everyone started talking at once, asking questions and wanting to know the exact date. Patricia answered as many of the questions as she could and let Cole answer the rest. Jeanne immediately announced that she wanted to give them an engagement party, but Patricia insisted that the big gala she was already planning in order to give them a chance to sway her friends and Harrison's co-workers to sign the petition was more than enough for her to do. Even when Jeanne insisted she plan to announce the engagement at that same party, Patricia declined. She did not want to take away from their cause. Tonight's announcement was the only announcement they planned to make, formal or otherwise.

"Besides, if I know you, everyone in Johnstown will know of our engagement by the end of the week," she said with a playful shrug. "Why bother with a party at all?"

Jeanne narrowed her eyes and opened her mouth for a rebuttal, but could not immediately think of anything to retort. Finally she simply smiled and said, "Give me credit for better than that. Five days should be sufficient and if I can get a hold of Lola Bellmont early on, it'll only take four."

"By all means, tell Lola." Patricia laughed, remembering she was the one who had insisted Cole was really Ben Butler. "I credit her for helping us get to really know each other a lot sooner than we might have otherwise."

Only Jeanne, Cole, and Patricia laughed at the comment, but no one bothered to question them. Instead, they were each naming off the people they wanted to tell. With this entire group at work on it, all of Pennsylvania and half the eastern seaboard would know within a matter of a couple of days.

It was well after two o'clock before everyone prepared to leave Cole's house. Catherine and Tony waited patiently for Cole to tell Patricia good night before leaving. In order for Cole to be home and greet his guests as they arrived, Tony had brought both sisters and since Catherine was staying the night at Patricia's, he had volunteered to take them both back home as well.

Because Faye planned to stay the night in his spare bedroom, Cole had agreed it would be best to let Tony take Patricia home and had to make do with a brief kiss in a darkened hallway when what he wanted to do was whisk her upstairs to his bed and make passionate love to her. It had been since Christmas Eve and he was not sure how much longer he could last. He wanted her desperately, but he had to be sensible.

During the short ride to Patricia's, Catherine was bubbling with excitement about the wedding plans. Having learned that she again would be a bridesmaid at her sister's wedding, she was eager to know all the details and this time she wanted to help.

"Have you decided what color you are going to use?" she asked. "I think you should go with a soft green to highlight those beautiful eyes even if it is the same color you used before."

"It's not going to be that elaborate," Patricia assured her, smiling at Catherine's enthusiasm. Catherine was only

216

fifteen when Patricia and Robert were married in a very large and extremely ornate wedding, a gift from their father, but little Katy had been terribly overwhelmed by the grandeur of it all. "I won't need to select a color. We are going to keep this wedding simple, just our dearest friends and closest family. After all, we've both been married before."

"Cole's been married before?" Catherine asked, surprised.

"Yes, years ago, back when he lived in Pittsburgh. Her name was Vella and she died in childbirth. The baby died too," Patricia explained as she let her gaze wander to the tall, narrow houses that closely lined the street. Through the decorative iron fences, she could see where an occasional lighted window cast a soft glow over the freshly fallen snow. It seemed so very peaceful, so serene, so detached from the sadness she suddenly felt.

"I didn't know that," Catherine said in a low whisper. Looking at Tony, she asked, "Did you?"

"I knew he'd been married before, but I didn't know she'd died trying to give birth," he said, equally saddened. "I didn't know anything about the child." The muscles in Tony's face tightened as he watched the deep ruts in the snow-covered road ahead. He hated to think of the sorrow his friend must have gone through. How painful it must be to face such a loss.

Wanting to change the sudden gloom that had overtaken them at the mention of Cole's previous marriage, Patricia smiled and changed the subject back to what it had originally been. "So, my dear little sister, if you want to see a huge, elaborate wedding, you are just going to have to have one of your own. After all, Father is just aching to give you the finest wedding Johnstown has ever seen. And if I know him, nothing will be spared. All you have to do is find someone foolish enough to marry you."

Tony's gaze fell on Catherine, aware of how tense she had become over her sister's offhanded remark. He had expected a lighthearted retort, but she said nothing. He frowned when he noticed how Catherine's clasped hands were flexing restlessly in her lap. She had become very uncomfortable at

217

her sister's mention of her own wedding. *Why?* he wondered. Personally, he had liked the idea. What could *she* have against getting married?

Patricia had fully intended to tell her father herself, but when she and Catherine arrived at the house early that following afternoon, she realized she was too late. Minnie greeted her with a warm hug that enveloped her whole body and wanted to know how big to make the wedding cake.

"How'd you find out?" she asked as she readjusted her hat. "No one else knew but Cole and me until early this morning."

"Little birdies like to talk." She laughed happily, a grin spread wide across her face. "Tall, handsome little birdies with curly dark hair and big round eyes just like to chirp away."

"Tony was here?" Catherine asked. There was no mistaking that description and she was curious to know why. Surely he hadn't stopped by just to be the one to tell the news. Tony was not much on gossiping or telling tales.

"Yes, he was here right before lunch. He came by to bring the gloves you left in his carriage last night. He had hoped you would be home by then. I had to tell him you weren't but that you might be back at any time. He then told me how you two may have stayed up extra late talking about Missy's plans and that there was no telling when you would get back, so he handed me the gloves and started to leave. And you know me, I had to know what these plans were you and Missy would be discussing to all hours."

"Does Father know?" Patricia asked.

"Oooo." Minnie's pale blue eyes widened as she pressed a hand to her upper breastbone as if trying to steady the heavy pulse that throbbed at the base of her throat. "Indeed he does."

"Not too pleased is he," Patricia surmised.

"I can imagine," Catherine muttered. "I'll bet he's having regular fits over this."

"Where is he now?" Patricia asked as her eyes scanned the

218

house. She expected to find him barreling toward her at any moment.

"He left right after Mr. Tony did. He just grabbed up his hat, scarf, and overcoat and marched out of here without even taking the time to put the coat and scarf on. He didn't say where he was going or when he would be back. Are you going to wait for him?"

"I might as well," Patricia sighed. "We need to have this out. He's got to know that I am serious about marrying Cole and he might as well start trying to accept it."

"Love Cole, do you?" Minnie chuckled with glee. "That's a right nice fellow you found yourself. I like him. And your father will come around eventually. It may take months for him to adjust, but eventually he will, especially with all of us working on him. Why don't you two girls go on into the front salon and I'll bring you a tray of tea and cakes to enjoy while you are waiting. Or would you rather have lunch? Have you two eaten at all?"

"Yes, we had a late breakfast," Patricia admitted. "Tea and cakes will be fine, and bring enough for yourself. You may as well plan to join us, I can see that you are just dying to ask me a lot of questions."

She was right. Minnie was a continuous fountain of questions for the next two hours and, big wedding or not, Patricia was going to have the fanciest cake Minnie could make, with sugar bells and tiny ribbons all over it. And Minnie also demanded to be in charge of making the bridal bouquet. It too would be something special, something to be remembered for years to come.

It was after five o'clock before Clayton finally returned home. After he had carefully hung his overcoat and scarf on a hook near the front door, he went in search of Minnie. When he discovered Patricia and Catherine seated in the kitchen watching and talking while Minnie prepared supper, he did not waste any time venting his anger. He had already gone by Patricia's house on his way home from William's and had been very irritated to find her not at home.

"I hope what I have heard is not true," he began as soon as he had fully entered the room. Shoving part of his coattail

219

back out of the way, he planted the backs of his hands firmly on his hips with his elbows out. He was clearly ready to give Patricia an ample piece of his mind.

"If it's that I've agreed to marry Cole Gifford, it is very true," Patricia said firmly. "I plan to marry him in August if everything goes well. I happen to love him very much and would really like to have your blessing. And I also would like for you to be there."

"How can you want to marry a man like him? And what makes you think you love him at all? You only met the man a few months ago. How can you possibly think you know him well enough to agree to marry him?" he asked as his blue eyes snapped in anger.

She considered telling her father how she had already decided Cole was the man she wanted to marry after only two weeks, but decided such knowledge would only serve to enrage him more. "How long did you know mother before you asked her to marry you?"

"That was different," he sputtered. His hands came off his hips and crossed defiantly across his dark blue pin-checked vest. "I was not, in all practicality, engaged to someone else when I met your mother. I was fresh out of college and had no commitments and she was special." A faint smile softened his stern features for a moment. "She was very special."

"Yes, Father, she was. And Cole is very special too. If only you would give him a chance and at least try to get to know him, I know you would find him just as special."

"How can you compare that rogue to your own sainted mother?" he asked. His features grew hard again; his eyes narrowed until they were two slits of cold steel.

"I'm not comparing him to anyone. It's just that he is very special and you would realize that if you'd ever take the time to get to know him. You have continuously refused to have him here for any of our family get-togethers. Why not at least invite him over for dinner on Sunday and give him a chance?" Her eyes grew moist as she spoke and she had to blink to keep tears from forming. "To tell you the truth, Father, I've missed coming to our Sunday dinners. I've missed them a lot."

"I never told you that you were not welcome," he reminded her.

"But you told me not to come if I intended to bring Cole with me and that is the same as telling me not to come at all."

"That's not exactly so. Besides, I must consider William in this matter. He still comes to our family dinners faithfully. He would be terribly uncomfortable to come and find Cole here as well."

"You don't have to let him find anything. Warn him ahead of time that I intend to come and plan to bring my fiancé with me. Then he can decide for himself if he wants to join us or not."

"You never have given William any true consideration, have you? That man is devoted to you, always has been, and all you can do is flaunt that Gifford fellow in front of him. If you are not careful, I'm afraid you are going to lose William forever. As of now, he has been very tolerant of your little dalliance with this Gifford, but now that he knows how far you have carried your silly act of rebellion, he is going to be far less tolerant. You had better watch yourself. You are about to push William too far," he warned, waving a finger staunchly in her face.

"Forget it then, Father. Cole and I will continue to stay away from family dinners here at your house and we will continue to have our own private family get-togethers without you. As for William, I don't need his tolerance. I don't really care what he thinks of me anymore. I don't love him and never have."

"That's not true," Clayton shouted, his pale eyes narrowed as he drew in a sharp breath. He honestly did not want to believe that. He would much rather believe she was just having another one of her stubborn spells and would eventually tire of the whole matter and come to her senses.

"Yes, it is. We were never more than good friends. If he ever truly believed there was anything more than friendship building between us, he conjured it up out of the blue. I never led him to believe that I was serious about him. In fact, I can't tell you the number of times I tried to explain to the man exactly how I felt or rather how I didn't feel. After all, how many proposals did I refuse?" She had raised her voice until she was almost shouting, but didn't care. She was hurt, deeply hurt, that her father seemed to consider William's feelings even over her own.

"Father, I just came over to tell you that you are invited to the wedding, but if you don't care to come, I'll understand. Believe me, I'll fully understand." Having said that, she leaped from the tall stool she had been sitting on and ran from the kitchen, almost tripping on her long woolen skirts in her haste.

"Patricia, you come back here," he shouted and hurried after her. "I'm not through with you."

"Oh, yes you are," she cried out over her shoulder, never once looking back, even as she jerked her cloak from the hook where Minnie had hung it. "You will find you are through with me forever."

Hot tears streamed down her cheeks. She did not want him to see them. She never should have let herself hope that she might be able to reason with him, to win him over to their side and make him understand how much in love she was. He was too stubborn for that. Much too stubborn. She never should have come.

"It doesn't matter. It just doesn't matter," she sobbed as she made her way along the less traveled streets, all the time knowing that it did matter. It mattered a lot. Her tears continued to run steady streams down the sides of her face, burning hot trails that quickly chilled along her neck. Once the tears reached her crisp white collar the icy moisture disappeared into the thick fabric. She tried to ignore her tears as she made her way along the snow-covered walkway that Tuesday afternoon. She pulled her cloak tighter in an attempt to cover the damp material freezing at her throat. It had begun to chafe her neck, only adding to her misery.

Undaunted by the freshly fallen snow or the approach of darkness, Patricia plodded along, hoping not to meet anyone she knew. Whenever she approached someone who might recognize her, she turned her face away and hurried past.

It was only a matter of minutes before she had Cole's

222

house in view. The large two-and-a-half-storied structure draped in its fluffy white cloak was a welcome sight. When she got nearer to the tall iron fence capped in white that surrounded his yard, she felt her pulse quicken. She prayed he would be home. She so needed him to be home.

The streetlight in front of his house sputtered to life just as she approached. Glad that none of his neighbors were outside where they could watch her enter, she hurriedly grasped the lever on the heavy, narrow gate and slipped inside his yard. Her bootprints led a path directly to his door. She never hesitated. Although it was not at all proper for her to call at his door alone, she didn't care. She needed him.

Fumbling with the heavy knocker, she worked it with only one hand. She raised the other hand to try to partially cover her tear-stained face. She wondered how swollen her eyes were by now and how red her nose looked even though she knew it would not really matter to Cole.

"Patricia?"

She heard his voice even before he had the door fully open. Slowly she looked up to see the concern on his face.

"Patricia, come in."

He never asked her what was wrong. It was not essential for him to know. He knew enough. She had been crying and she looked very cold and so very miserable. As soon as the door was closed, he reached out and pulled her into his warm embrace. He said nothing. He simply held her close. When it was time for words, he knew she would speak. Until then he would simply hold her.

Fresh tears filled Patricia's eyes as she let herself be comforted. How dearly she loved this man. She waited until she was certain her voice would hold before finally speaking. "Cole, you are my only source of strength."

"I can hardly believe you need a source of strength. Not a woman as strong and courageous as you are," he said and leaned back just enough to be able to look into her eyes. He smiled and gently caressed her cheeks—still pink from the cold—with the warm tips of his fingers. "But I'm glad that you think of me in that way. I hope you will always come to me when you need someone."

223

Returning his smile, she blinked back the last of her tears and sniffed. "For as long as I live. I shall always come to you."

"Ah, yes, there's that smile. I knew it was there somewhere," he taunted her, making her smile more. "You were just hiding it from me."

Never had she known such warm consideration from a man. "I love you so much, Cole."

"That makes it kind of nice, since I love you too," he told her and bent down to kiss her lightly. He was rewarded by the sound of her soft laughter.

"Have you had supper?" he asked, already untying the sashes on her cloak. "I just happen to have that ham that was left over from last night's celebration already warming in the oven and I was just about to reheat the potatoes and beans. Would you care to join me?"

"Yes, I'd like that."

"Good. I thought you looked a little hungry."

"You aren't even going to ask me what I was crying about, are you?" she asked, curious as she turned so he could lift the cloak from her shoulders.

"You'll tell me if you feel I should know."

She thought about that a moment. He was far more understanding and caring than anyone she had ever known. "It has to do with my father."

"I felt like it might," he said, and offered her a sympathetic hug around her shoulders. "I take it he didn't care for the idea of us getting married."

"Not at all." She smiled at that understatement.

"Give him time. I'll bet he will eventually come around."

"That's more or less what Minnie said."

"Smart woman, that Minnie. She should know if anyone does."

"I don't know. Sometimes she is prone to wishful thinking. Too bad wishes rarely come true."

"I don't know about that. I've been wishing all day that I could see you tonight, and here you are. Just like in a fairy tale. I got my wish."

"I thought in fairy tales, you always got three wishes."

"That means I still have two left," he mused, tilting his head as he thought about that. "I'll have to be sure and use them very carefully if I want to get that kiss I've been aching for."

"A kiss is it? Why, Cole, I think you are about to have another wish come true." Reaching up, she slipped two large pins from the high crown of the small but widely brimmed hat she wore and pulled it off of her head, revealing a thick array of curls piled high on her head. Tossing the hat aside, she slowly eased her arms around his neck and pulled him toward her.

"And that still leaves me with one more wish," he warned her as his lips slowly descended to hers.

Chapter Fifteen

Gently, Cole pulled Patricia against him and enveloped her in a warm, tender embrace. His lips played lightly over her mouth, across her cheek, and up to close one tear-dampened eye with a delicate kiss, then across to the other. Then he simply held her close. When he finally spoke again his warm breath fell gingerly across her forehead. "Just how hungry are you?"

"For food? Not very," she said softly and opened her eyes again to look up at him. A timid smile spread across her face as she slipped her woolen jacket off and tossed it on a nearby table, not caring in the least that she had knocked her hat onto the floor in the process.

Cole responded with a smile of his own. Deep, narrow dimples formed in his lean cheeks and his blue eyes sparkled with the love he felt for her. For a long moment, he stood gazing affectionately into her dark green eyes before his smile finally faded and his lips once again returned to hers in another series of gentle but passionate kisses. His strong arms continued to surround her and hold her close while his hands tenderly massaged the still tense muscles along her upper back and shoulders.

Patricia held on to him as if he was her lifeline, as if she was afraid he might disappear. It was very hard for her to believe a man this loving, this caring, actually existed. It was easy for her to see that his every action, his every tiniest movement, was for her. He knew she was just getting over something that had hurt her deeply and because of that he took special care to soothe her pain, slow and easy. She appreciated it far more than she could ever express in mere words. Simply telling him how she loved him was too inadequate for what her heart wanted to convey. Words that would actually describe what she felt for him at that very moment just didn't exist for her. All she could do was hope that he understood the true depth of her love.

Slowly, Cole's hands continued to work and relax the tense muscles along her shoulders. Deliciously warm and extremely tantalizing sensations rippled through her, delighting every inch of her. The misery and heartache that had totally consumed her earlier was gradually melting away. Pure joy and a deep need for this man hurriedly took its place. How truly lucky she was to have a man like Cole love her. He was far more affectionate than she had ever known a man could be. Even Robert, who had always been attentive in his lovemaking, had never been this tender, this gentle. It had never even occurred to her that a man as strong and powerful as Cole was could be quite so gentle, so giving, so loving in his touch. How she yearned to show him the true depth of what she felt for him.

With a love that had taken on a new dimension, she pressed her fingertips into his back, urging him on. Her mouth tried to devour each and every kiss that he offered. She had a deep need to be closer to him than she had ever been, but did not know how that could possibly be. They had already shared so much of themselves. Did she have something more to give of herself?

Cole realized that the passions in Patricia had ignited and flamed deep within her but he continued to move very slowly. His lips lingered at her sweet mouth as his hands eased downward along her rib cage. He was well aware that her breathing became more labored with each movement he made. It delighted him that he was able to bring her such pleasure and arouse such an intense need of him. There was a beautiful sense of accomplishment in giving her pleasure. He held back his own responses while he worked to bring her to one new height of arousal after another. Tonight would be especially for her.

Letting his hands massage their way ever closer to the breasts that pressed firmly against him, he continued to work his magic with more plundering kisses. His tongue entered her mouth in slow degrees, going deeper and teasing different areas with each gentle thrust. She responded in kind by allowing her tongue to follow his every time it retreated into his own mouth. Having her tiny tongue tease the sensitive inner areas of his mouth made him groan out his pleasure and made keeping his desires under control almost impossible.

Leisurely, he slipped a hand between them and cupped one of her breasts through the thin fabric of her blouse. Lightly his fingertips played with the tip until he felt it grow rigid with desire for more. But he waited to begin to undo the many buttons that would finally allow him to touch her soft skin. Instead, he continued to let his hand prowl about the outside of her clothing, seeking, searching, but never quite finding.

Patricia became lost in a deep, swirling torrent of emotions. Liquid fire coursed through her veins and her ever-growing arousal quickly possessed her entire being. Every part of her yearned for more. Why didn't he try to undress her? Never had he taken this long. Unable to bear the flames that burned deep to the very core of her, she reached for her own buttons.

"No, let me," he whispered softly into the depths of her mouth, sending another delicious wave of pure ecstasy through her.

She trembled with expectation as he stepped back and slowly began to undo the buttons, allowing himself a view of the low-cut lacy white camisole that barely hid her thrusting breasts from his sight. He pulled the delicate Sicilian blouse free of her skirt and gently slipped it from her shoulders. Carefully, he placed the blouse over the woolen jacket that still lay on the small table near the front door. Then he turned his attention to the wide waistband of her heavy woolen skirt. The buttons he found there were far more contrary and the drawstring almost impossible to untie, but soon the skirt and underskirt were nothing more than a puddle of golden brown and white on his light gray carpet.

As he stood and stared longingly at her, she bent down and gathered up her skirts and hung them on a shiny brass coat hook near the door. Then, feeling awkward to be dressed in just her camisole and bloomers and still have on her boots, she sat down in a nearby chair to hurriedly pull them off.

"Let me," he said again and quickly knelt at her feet. As he pulled the boots, still damp from her long trek through the snow, from her feet, then rolled her delicate cashmere stockings down her creamy white legs, he impulsively leaned forward and kissed her well-shaped ankles.

Patricia gasped out a delighted surprise. His warm, moist lips felt good against her cool skin.

After he placed her boots and stockings beside the chair, Cole rose and held out a hand to her. As soon as she too had risen, he bent down and lifted her into his arms. He said nothing as he carried her up the carpeted stairs toward his bedroom. His eyes were dark with his desire and his lips dipped down to take brief little kisses which she accepted hungrily.

Having seen his bedroom before, Patricia did not pull her gaze from his in order to view her surroundings. She had already seen the maple high-chest with its dome-shaped top and slippered feet as well as the dressing table that proudly held his shaving mirror and his tall shaving cup. She knew where the side chairs were and where his large maple wardrobe sat. And she also knew that in the far corner, where they were headed, sat a sturdy poster bed with mattresses as soft as down but that accepted their weight graciously.

After he carefully placed her in the very center of his bed, Cole leaned over her in order to light three candles in a candlestand that stood on the small table at his bedside. Until then, the only light had come from a dimly burning gaslight in the hallway. Once he had the candles lit, he turned to look at her and smiled.

"I want to be able to see you," he told her simply.

Before he returned to her waiting arms, he rose from the bed and began to undo his own buttons. In the flickering glow of the candlelight, she watched him undress, mesmerized by each movement he made while he quickly removed his every article of clothing. Soon he was naked and she could once again see just how splendid he was. Such true masculinity. He was perfection. When he returned to her, she held her arms out to receive him.

His lips came down on hers gently as his hands slid beneath the thin fabric of her camisole. His fingertips teased and taunted as they came ever closer to the sensitive peaks of her breasts in light circular motions. She arched her back to accommodate his touch, wishing his hands would hurry and reach their destination. Eagerly, her own hands began to roam over his body, exploring the firm muscles along his back and down his arms. When he rose just enough to be able to pull her camisole off her, she reached out to feel the crisp texture of the hairs on his chest that glowed golden in the candlelight. His body's warmth seemed to intensify the already sensitive tips of her fingers as she felt first the flat plane of his stomach then moved on to caress the hardened muscle along his hips.

A deep sound welled up in Cole's throat that very closely resembled an animal's growl as he quickly removed her bloomers. He lingered only a moment to stare at her glorious beauty before bringing his body's weight down on her with an agile ease. Sighing aloud her pleasure, she let him know that she delighted in the feel of his naked body against hers.

Her hands continued to roam freely over the firm solid muscles of his back and strained to be able to feel the taut, lean muscles of his hips and upper thighs. His lightly haired skin felt good to her touch. She marveled at the fact that this magnificent man was soon to be her husband. How dearly she loved him.

While his lips sampled again and again the sweetness of her mouth, he too allowed himself the pleasure of exploring every feminine curve of her body. Slowly, he let his lips leave hers to trail tiny kisses downward until he finally reached one of her breasts. Deftly, his tongue teased the tip with

231

short, tantalizing strokes until she arched herself upward, eagerly seeking more. Slowly, he moved to take in the neglected breast.

Such sweet ecstasy. She was not certain how long she could bear this tender torment, nor was she able to coax him to stop his delicate torture and bring her the relief she sought. She pulled gently at his shoulders, but his mouth continued to bring her breast unbearable pleasure. She shuddered from the delectable sensations building in her, degree by degree, until she was sure she would explode. A delicious ache centered itself somewhere low inside her and had reached that same unbearable intensity. Her body craved release from the sensual anguish that burned within her.

"Love me, Cole. Love me now," she moaned, only vaguely aware that she had said the words aloud.

Drawing on first one breast, then the other, one more time, he moved to fulfill her. With lithe movements, he brought their wildest longings, their deepest desires, to an ultimate height. When release came for Patricia only moments before it came for Cole, it was so wondrous and shattering that she cried out with pleasure.

Their passions spent, they lay still in each other's arms and slowly sank into the warm depths of supreme satisfaction. Smiling contentedly, Patricia still marveled at the fact that this man, this exquisite man, would soon be her husband. Such happiness was to be hers forever. She was blessed, truly blessed.

"At times like these, it seems just too good to be true," she murmured, not really aware she spoke her thoughts aloud.

"What's that?" he asked and raised up on one elbow beside her in order to be able to gaze into her beautiful eyes as she spoke. He loved to look at her.

"Sometimes I worry that I will wake up and discover that you were just a dream, a wonderful dream." She reached a hand up to caress his cheek as if reassuring herself. "It just seems too good to be true." Seeing the questioning look in his eyes, she finished the thought. "That come this summer, you will be my husband."

"We don't have to wait until this summer. We already have over two hundred signatures and with Tony and Andrew working so hard to help me, my time is not as essential as it once was. They hardly need me anyway."

"You know that's not true," she put in and frowned. She did not like for him to sell himself short.

"Okay, maybe I'm still needed. It's just that I'm not as pressed to spend every spare moment I can manage to get on it now that I'm not the only man on the job. We could go ahead and get married and I could still find enough time to do my part with the petition. I too have worries like yours. I worry that something will happen between now and August that might prevent us from ever getting married."

"What could happen?"

"I don't know. It's just a gut feeling. Something is going to happen that will put a strain on our relationship or even change the way you feel about me. Maybe it will be due to your father or maybe it will be something I just can't foresee right now, but the feeling is there, in the very pit of my stomach."

"You are such a worrywart. I thought I was the world's worst, but you outdo me by far. What could happen that would make me love you any less? What could happen short of death that could stop me from marrying the man I love?"

"Don't say that!" he shouted gruffly, his arm tightening around her. "Don't even think such a horrible thing."

"Don't say what? Death?"

"Yes, don't say such a thing. Don't speak it aloud. I don't know what I would do if you should die and leave me too."

Patricia's heart went out to him. She should have known better than to say something like that to him. "I'm sorry. I didn't think. I, of all people, should know how painful the thought of another loved one dying can be. It is one reason I never wanted to fall in love again. I never wanted to chance going through such devastating heartache ever again. I'm sorry. How about if I promise to live to be at least ninety years old instead?"

"I can almost see you at the age of ninety," he chuckled as he conjured up an image.

"Sitting in a rocking chair crocheting doilies for our grandchildren?"

"No, wearing that black gown of yours and driving this old man crazy as you hobble around on the opposite side of the bed, just out of my reach."

They both laughed at the thought, then Cole bent down and kissed her affectionately. He stared at her a long moment before he asked, "But wouldn't you really like to move the wedding date up? Say to April?"

"In a way, yes, but then, in another way, no."

"That's what I like about you. Decisive answers," he teased.

"It really would be better to wait until the matter with the dam has been settled one way or the other. Besides, I've already told everyone August. They will wonder if I suddenly move the wedding day up. They will think I did it because I was afraid I might lose you or worse—that I was with child."

"Let them think what they want," he shrugged, then as he thought about what she had said, he asked, "Doesn't it worry you that you could become pregnant? Isn't that as good a reason as any to go ahead and get married?"

"Or I could always simply refuse you and keep you at arm's length until we do finally get married," she said offhandedly. When she saw how quickly he frowned, she smiled. "No, I doubt I could at that. I need you too much."

"So wouldn't it be wiser to go ahead and get married?"

"I'm not really worried about getting pregnant so easily. In fact, I worry more with not being able to at all. I know you will want children and lots of them. What if I can't give them to you?"

"Why would you worry about that?"

"I was married before, remember? And I wanted children then, but I remained childless."

"But you weren't married that long. Two months is hardly long enough to base such a notion on."

"And there's my sister, Jeanne. She and Harrison have wanted children ever since they got married, and as of yet, she has been unable to conceive a child. And consider my

234

own mother, she was married four years before she was finally able to conceive."

"So you believe it is an inherited problem?"

"Would you be terribly disappointed if I was unable to bear you a child? Would you come to despise me for it?"

"I would be disappointed, yes. But I could never despise you. And I think you are worrying far too prematurely. Maybe you are the master worrywart after all. I just hope being a worrywart is not an inheritable trait. With the two of us for parents, our poor children won't have a chance. They would be totally gray before their time."

Patricia laughed at his silliness. "What I hope is that insanity is not inheritable."

"What are you insinuating?" he demanded with a scowl. "Maybe you think I'm insane to have fallen for a woman like you." He paused, widening his eyes in a frightful manner. "Maybe you're right. Maybe I am insane. After all, I was mad about you." Having said that, he bent down and began to kiss her frantically about the face and neck, causing her to squeal out a delighted protest. But soon his kisses slowed their pace and her protest was lost as their passions once again overtook them both.

"Thanks for bringing me home," Patricia said as she quickly looked around the dim streets in front of her house for signs of a neighbor. When she decided the street was deserted, she leaned over and stole a tender kiss from Cole's smiling lips.

"I couldn't very well let you walk home in this weather," he said, then reached out a gloved hand to pull her back for yet another kiss. "True, it was quite a sacrifice on my part to forge my way to the carriage house in such a raging blizzard in order to hitch up the buggy, but you are well worth it."

Patricia looked around them at Cole's blizzard. Huge fat snowflakes drifted delicately to the ground. There were no howling winds, only the faint clanking sounds of the mill and the light sputtering of the electric lights as the feathery snowflakes struck them. "I just hope we can make it to my door safely and not be lost to the elements."

"I'll do my best," he assured her.

After refusing to be carried, Patricia walked beside Cole while they made their way through the foot and a half of snow toward the front porch. It was late. Probably after midnight by now.

"Someone's been here and left," Cole told her, then indicated several trails of large footprints that the snow had just begun to fill in. "Looks like two people came by. Both men."

"I know Father said he was by here earlier," she remembered, looking at the four sets of indentations curiously. "I can't imagine who might have been with him."

"The other person might not have been with him. Someone else may have been by here separately." Eyeing her with mock suspicion, he demanded to know, "Is there another man, Patricia?"

"There are lots of other men, Cole. The world is full of them. But none as wonderful and handsome as you," she reassured him. "And there is no one I would rather marry. I'd be a fool to even look at another man and chance losing you."

"You are an intelligent woman, Patricia Morgan," he said, raising himself up to his tallest height as he made his way up the steps. Because of the overhang of the porch the steps were clear of snow, but he held his hand out to secure Patricia's balance anyway.

"And you are a vain man, Cole Gifford," she taunted, then as she stepped onto the wooden porch her foot skidded on something solid, making her clutch on to his arm to avoid falling. Lifting her boot, she discovered a burnt match. When she knelt down to pick it up, she discovered three more. "Someone was here all right. Evidently, someone who smokes."

Cole looked at the four matches in her glove and frowned. "Yes, and either he had a hard time getting his smoke lit, or he was here for quite some time."

"I wonder who it could have been," she said as she tried to figure out just who would have come by on a holiday. Many of her friends were quickly ruled out because most of them did not smoke. Then she thought of William and his occasional cigar, but discarded him because he was no longer speaking to her. Who could it have been? "I hate mysteries."

"Me too. So whenever you do find out who it was, be sure to let me know. Especially if it was a gentleman caller. I will want to have a nice little chat with him."

Patricia could imagine what sort of chat Cole had in mind and laughed as she opened the door. "For a man who believes in fairy tales and wishes, you certainly do worry about your happy-ever-after."

He laughed along with her and bent down for a long and lingering good-night kiss.

"By the way," she said after he had pulled away and was headed for the steps. She waited until he turned back around and looked at her before finishing. "Did you ever get that third wish of yours?"

"Indeed I did." He chuckled lightly and grinned. "Indeed I did."

Although Patricia never gave her New Year's Day visitors little more than a passing thought, she was soon to find out just who it was that had come by. As she had remembered, her father had been one, and the other, it turned out, was William after all. As soon as he had learned of her engagement to Cole, he had decided to break his lengthy silence and pay her a call.

That next evening, when Patricia got home from work, she discovered William sitting on her doorstep smoking one of his imported cigars and knew immediately who her other visitor had been. He rose after he looked up and noticed her coming but did not walk out into the melting snow to meet her. She could tell by his rigid stance that he was angry. And there was no doubt in her mind that it had to do with her engagement to Cole. Her stomach twisted into a tight knot of anticipation as she continued toward her house. She was in no mood for any of his silly rantings.

237

"Hello, William. I'm surprised to see you here," she said politely and extended her hand as she came close.

"Are you?" he asked, accepting her hand and giving it a firm squeeze. When he did not let go of her right away, she forcefully pulled her hand free.

"Yes, after all, I haven't seen very much of you lately. How have you been?" She decided to try not to stir his anger in any way.

"I've been miserable without you," he said bluntly. "I've tried to be indulgent with you, giving you the time I thought you needed in order to get all your silly rebellions out of your system and come to your senses, but after hearing what I heard yesterday, I'm afraid my patience is at its end. I'm tired of all this waiting for you to stop your silly pretenses and realize your mistake. I want you back. I want you back now."

"I thought I had already made it clear that you never really had me. You may have taken it for granted that one day you might, but that one day never came and never will. Yes, if what you heard is that I'm engaged to Cole Gifford, you heard right. Try to make yourself understand that I love him. He asked me to marry him and I accepted. We will be married in August."

"But I asked you to marry me first," he pointed out with growing indignation.

She let out an exasperated breath and stared at him a long moment. How could she ever get it through that thick head of his? "Yes, you asked me to marry you first. In fact, many times, but I always turned you down because I didn't love you. True, I liked you and still do to some degree and I certainly enjoyed your company there for a while, but I don't and never have been in love with you. I'm sorry, but feelings like I have for Cole were never there for you."

"Why do you lie to me like that? What purpose do such lies serve you?"

"What lies? I'm telling you the truth just like I always have."

"I happen to know differently. I well remember how breathless, weak, and wanting I left you the last time I kissed you. You can't deny it."

"Oh, yes, I can."

"Go ahead then, deny it, but I know the truth. I felt your pulse pounding at my touch and I saw the dazed expression my kiss had left you with. If I had wanted to pursue the moment, I could have easily had you in your very own bed. I know it and whether or not you are willing to admit it, you know it too." Having said that he reached out and yanked her to him. His left hand grasped her hair, holding her immobile while his lips and tongue quickly plundered her mouth. She could taste heavy traces of whiskey on his breath.

"You're drunk," she hissed as she tore her lips free, wincing with the pain his grip on her hair had caused. She tried to push him away from her, but his grasp tightened on her hair and the pain was so severe she froze, with her head tilted at an awkward angle.

"I may have had a drink or two, but I'm not so drunk that I can't perform, I assure you," he slurred as he hurriedly crushed his lips to hers once again. This time his tongue dove deeply into her mouth, almost gagging her, and his right hand roamed up and began to untie the sashes of her cloak. She panicked and did the only thing she could do without bringing herself worse pain. She bit down hard and held his tongue prisoner between her teeth.

She waited until his grip on her hair lessened before finally relieving the pressure on his foul tongue. When she was certain he would free her altogether, she released him. "William, you have had far too much to drink. I don't think you realize what you are doing. You had better get out of here before I start to scream for the neighbors. And you had better hope that I don't tell my father what you tried to do to me."

William stared down at her in anger, rolling his tongue around in his mouth. Delicately, he reached up and placed a finger to the surface of the injured tongue and came away with a drop of blood on his fingertip. He frowned. "All I wanted to do was remind you how you feel about me."

"Well, you certainly did that," she spat.

"No, I didn't. You didn't give me the chance."

"William, you've had all the chances you are ever going to have. Please leave."

"I'll leave. But I will return and I will make you see just how much you do care for me. I may have to wait until an opportunity arises when you don't have the neighbors around to threaten me with. But then once I show you what love really is, you won't even consider calling someone to intrude. You have so much to learn and I have so much to teach you. And teach you I will." Having said that, he quickly turned and left.

Patricia's heart pounded against her ribs as she fumbled with the door latch. She felt suddenly weak. Could he have really been serious? Did he truly intend to catch her alone somewhere and force himself on her? Or was that simply the whiskey talking? He had made idle threats before, never bothering to actually see them through. Taking a deep breath to steady herself, she decided to be extra careful for a while, just in case.

She started by making sure every door and window in her house was securely locked and never went anywhere where there might not be a lot of people around. But as the days went by and she saw nothing of William, she became less cautious and decided the threats had indeed been the whiskey talking and not William himself. Soon she came to believe he would no more act on that last threat than he had on the first and did not bother to tell Cole or her father of his visit. Yet, she did continue to lock her door whenever she was home—just in case.

Eventually, she considered the matter closed. Until William did something to cause her to believe differently, she would continue to give him the benefit of the doubt. William staked too much on his reputation and she would not want to take that away from him unnecessarily. She felt like she had already taken enough of his pride. She would leave him with what she could.

A week later, a letter arrived for her in the mail. It was from William. In the letter, he apologized eloquently for his actions and admitted that he had had far too much to drink and that having heard how she had promised to marry Cole had driven him to the point of madness. He asked for her to forgive him and tried to assure her he never meant her any harm. He ended the letter by once again declaring his love and promising that one day he would prove his love and devotion to her. As she folded the letter and placed it back into the envelope, she felt a renewed sense of fear but had nothing to really base it on but her womanly intuition. William was going to cause trouble again. She would have to be very cautious.

Chapter Sixteen

March first began a bright and cloudless day. After such a miserable winter, the sunshine and higher temperatures were more than welcome. Patricia eagerly dug into the back of her armoire to find her lighter clothing. It was such a beautiful Friday, she wanted to go for a short walk before work.

She donned a yellow and gold lightweight cotton and wool dress with the latest wrap-around-styled overskirt drawn back and gathered into large protruding pleats in the rear which produced a small bustle behind her. The fitted jacket she wore was made from matching material and accentuated her trim figure nicely. A high-crowned hat with a wide sloping brim in the front colorfully adorned in colorful yellow and brown feathers and gold satin ribbon completed her outfit. A quick check in a mirror assured her that she looked just as pretty as she felt.

Afraid the sun might become unbearably warm before the morning grew very old, she also grabbed her yellow parasol and tucked it under her arm before heading for the stairs. Duchess walked with her to the top of the stairway gazing up at her with big, sad eyes and mewing pathetically. Patricia felt so sorry for her cat, having to be cooped up inside on such a beautiful day that she went back upstairs to open a window for her. Patricia had been keeping her doors and windows securely locked for the last several months, ever since William had made his threat against her, but since he had stopped bothering her and she had not caught him even as much as trying to follow her for over a month now, she decided it would be safe enough to leave one of the upstairs windows open enough to allow Duchess a way in and out.

"Now don't you go out there and get into any trouble," Patricia warned the fluffy white cat as it quietly explored the opening. "And I don't want to have to go looking for you after dark either."

Duchess gazed up at her mistress and meowed as if agreeing to those terms before slipping through the narrow opening and heading along the short stretch of roof toward the nearest tree limb. With an agile leap, she was on her way.

After Patricia left the house, she decided to take her walk through the business district and then down by the river. She still had almost an hour before time to be at work and wanted to enjoy every minute of it out doors enjoying this lovely springlike day. She wished Cole was not already at work. She would love to share her walk with him. Just thinking about it brought a smile to her lips. She could scarcely believe that their wedding was only five months away. It seemed like they had just met, yet at the same time it felt as if they had known each other forever. It never ceased to amaze her that she had been lucky enough to have found a man like him.

As she passed along the boarded sidewalks, Patricia greeted the many shopkeepers who were outside busily sweeping off their sections of the walkway, getting their day under way. Patricia felt happy to be alive. How she loved Johnstown and the people who lived there. She loved the hustle and bustle of the business district and the serenity that could be found in the neighborhoods just blocks away. It was more than the beautiful weather that brought a broad smile to her face and a song to her heart.

"Good morning, Patricia," she heard behind her when she stopped at a corner to allow a huge flatbed wagon carrying a tall load of lumber to pass by. She turned to greet the familiar voice.

"Well good morning, Tony," she replied. "What are you doing out and about so early this morning?"

"I'm on my way down to Franklin Street to see how the

244

builders are coming along on my building. With all the bad weather we've had lately, the going has been very slow. But if we could have more days like today, they just might be able to complete it in another couple of months. I am anxious to have it finished. I'm ready to open my practice. I can't keep working out of my house the way I have been."

"Mind if I walk along with you?"

"Not at all. I love to have beautiful women for company," he said and motioned for her to walk on the building side of him. Once they were under way again, he asked about Catherine. "Is she any better?"

"Yes, as a matter of fact, she is. I went over to see her last night. She still has a nagging cough, but the fever was completely gone and her appetite was definitely back. She plans to go on back to work later this week," Patricia told him while nodding a friendly greeting to Othell Shattles as they passed. "Why don't you stop by for a visit this evening. I'm sure she'd be glad to see you."

"I don't know if she would be or not. Sometimes she does seem glad to see me and we seem to have a great time together, but then again sometimes she acts as if I carry some sort of dreaded disease. It's so strange." He frowned. "One night we can go out and have an absolutely wonderful time and the very next night she will refuse to even see me. I never know what to expect. She's a hard woman to understand."

"Cole would tell you it runs in the family." Patricia laughed, hoping to reassure Tony somehow. "But Catherine is particularly moody. I'm her sister and I love her dearly, but I'll be the first to admit how moody she is. She always has been. Even with me. Sometimes she is very talkative and open, but then some days she seems downright secretive and keeps to herself."

"You mean it's not just me?" he asked. His eyes widened with hope.

"By no means is it just you. Surely you didn't think you somehow were causing those odd mood swings of hers, did you?"

"I didn't know what to think," Tony said with a heavy raise of his shoulders. He paused a long moment before he asked, "Did she tell you I asked her to marry me?"

"You did?" Patricia asked, then smiled. "No she didn't tell me. When was this?"

"A couple of weeks ago. Just before she took ill. We had gone to see a play at the Opera House and she seemed to have had a wonderful time. On the ride home in the moonlight with her looking so beautiful, I couldn't seem to help myself. You know how impatient I can be. I proposed. I simply blurted out that I wanted her to marry me. I'll admit I could have led up to it with a bit more subtlety and with more romanticism."

"What did she say?" Patricia asked. Her smile faded. She could tell by his expression that Catherine's response had not been what he hoped for.

"She told me she was the wrong one for me, that I could do far better than her. It was as if she thought she wasn't good enough for me. That's when I told her how much I love her."

"And what did she say to that?"

"She told me we shouldn't see each other anymore, that it was unfair to me. Then she told me I was wasting my time on her and should spend it with someone else, someone who could love me the way I should be loved. Someone I could have a future with. She wants to be my friend and nothing more." Tony's pain was evident in his tight expression.

"I see," Patricia said slowly, even though she did not see. She did not see at all. Tony was the perfect man for Catherine. How could her little sister not see that? "And are you now spending your time with other women like she suggested?"

"I don't want any other woman. I want Catherine. I love her," he said and waved his arms helplessly. He stopped walking and looked Patricia in the eyes. "I think I've loved her from the very first moment I saw her. There can be no other woman for me. But how can I make her see that?"

"I don't know. Catherine is strange." Patricia paused a long moment before she decided to tell Tony about Franklin. Maybe in knowing a little about the past, he would be better able to cope with the present. "She was in love once before. Back when she was very, very young and extremely impressionable. She loved the man deeply and when it was over, she was terribly heartbroken. She hasn't dared love anyone else since. In fact you are the first man she had even gone out with more than once since then."

"Did he shun her love? Is that why she doesn't want for us to become serious? Is she afraid I will do the same? I won't. I assure you," he said, his eyes almost pleading with her to believe him.

"No, he didn't shun her. As far as I know he loved her just as much as she loved him."

"Then what happened?" he asked, then he lifted his hand to cover his mouth and inhaled with a rushed gasp. "He didn't die, did he?"

"No. Father drove him away. You see, Father did not approve of Franklin. He did not feel Franklin was appropriate for my sister. Not only was he much older than Catherine, he was a common worker at the iron works who had spent his youth in a rather boisterous manner—in trouble more times than not. But all that was in his past. He had started trying to change for Catherine's sake, but Father just couldn't see that. He wanted better for Catherine and demanded she not see him anymore, but Catherine was too much in love. When Father found out she was still seeing him, he took matters into his own hands."

"What did he do?"

"I'm not really sure. I do know that Franklin was arrested for something he couldn't have done and spent several days in jail because of it. In a brief trial, he was convicted of the crime. The next thing we knew, he was gone. Catherine was devastated. I think she has been afraid to fall in love again ever since then. I had similar fears of loving and losing again after I lost Robert. Heart wounds are very slow to heal."

Tony started walking again. He did not speak for several minutes. "And she has never heard from this Franklin again?"

"Not that I know of. He left a note for her which told her to try to get over him, to forget him, that their being together was never meant to be and then he simply disappeared. Right out of jail."

247

Tony walked in silence again. It was all beginning to make sense now. No wonder she seemed so inhibited whenever he showed even the slightest aggression toward her. She was afraid of being hurt again but that was now understandable. It was hard to openly subject oneself to a situation where he or she could easily get hurt, especially after having experienced such pain before. He realized that if he truly wanted her, and he knew he did, he would have to take things very slowly, give her more time to adjust to him. With a feeling of renewed hope, he knew he would never give up on her now. He loved her too much. He would just have to be patient. Even if her father decided he also was not the man for Catherine, he would not give up. True love could always find a way.

A smile spread slowly across Tony's face. "Thank you for telling me all this. It certainly helps me to understand better. What she needs is time. Eventually she will come to trust me and know my love is true and that I won't ever leave her." His smile turned into a broad boyish grin. "In time she will come to see just how wonderful and dedicated I am to her and will eagerly agree to marry me. I'll just have to bide my time."

Patricia was glad that she had brought a flicker of hope back into Tony's eyes. Like Tony, she also believed that eventually Catherine would come to realize, just like she herself finally did, that being in love was well worth the risk. No pain, however great, could ever undo the true happiness she and Cole now shared.

When Patricia heard the loud knock at her door, she hoped to find Cole on the other side. Flinging the door wide open, her bright smile quickly fell to an annoyed pout. "Oh, it's you."

"Fine way to greet your sister," Jeanne said with an indignant shake of her head. "Aren't you even going to ask me in?"

"Since when do I have to ask?"

"Since you started locking your doors."

"Well, come on in. You know you are always welcome,"

248

Patricia conceded and stepped back to let Jeanne pass. Aware of the unusually tense expression on her sister's face, she asked immediately, "What's on your mind?"

"Father," she replied as soon as she had stepped inside. Draping her light shawl over a hook on the coat stand near the door, she turned and Patricia could see Jeanne's concern deepen. Whatever it was, Jeanne felt it was serious.

"Father found out the real reason behind the party next weekend. He knows it is so that Cole and Tony can persuade some of our friends to sign the petition and he is furious with me."

"We didn't expect to keep it from him forever," Patricia pointed out.

"There's more. When he claimed that the petition was not worth the effort, that it was doomed to fail anyway, I told him how wrong he was—that there really was a good chance Cole would be able to pull this thing off. I told him that even without our help that the petition already had several hundred signatures on it. He grew livid. He seemed to be under the impression that no one was signing it."

"In a way he's right, when you consider how many people we have approached," Patricia pointed out with a twisted frown. "I guess because I never mention it to him at work, he doesn't realize just how dedicated we still are to this."

"At any rate, he knows now and is furious. I think he intends to come by here and issue ultimatums. I know he has already told me to call off the party."

"Oh? And what did you say to that?" Patricia's insides tightened as she waited for the response. They had all been looking forward to the opportunity the party offered, but Jeanne had a way of doing whatever she could to please their father.

"I told him it was too late, that the invitations had already gone out," she said with a worried look. "It's true. The invitations went out last week."

"And what did Father say to that?" Patricia wanted to know.

"Let's just say that he has invited himself to the party and I don't think it is because he is eager to socialize."

"No, he wants to keep an eye on things now that he knows just how serious we still are about this. But that's all right. He's our father. He should be invited. We will just have to figure out a way to handle this." She made it sound so easy.

Later that evening, when Patricia relayed the problem of her father to Cole, his comment was that it might be easier to handle a swarm of angry bumblebees and he laughed.

"You don't seem too concerned." Patricia eyed him warily.

"What can he do? I don't think even your father would risk causing a scene at such a huge party just to be able to get his way in this matter. About all he can do is try to convince people not to sign and he is already doing that. We will just have to be more convincing is all."

"That won't be easy. Father can be terribly convincing when he wants to be," Patricia explained, hoping to show him that the fear building inside her was justified.

"You worry too much," he said, and pushed the matter aside. He had more important things on his mind at the moment. Her perfume was far too intoxicating and she was far too beautiful in her pale green dress with its peaked sleeves and wide, flowing skirt to ignore for long. Reaching out and draping his arms lightly over her shoulders, he pressed his forehead against hers. "Fine thing. Here we are in your house all alone and all you can talk about is your father."

A smile finally began to play at her lips. "And what would you have me talk about?"

"I'd rather you didn't talk at all, but if you really must speak, I would prefer that it be about me."

"What would you have me say?" she asked as she closed her eyes to better enjoy the warm sensations his touch always caused in her.

"Say whatever wonderful thing crosses your mind," he coaxed, then leaned forward to place a light but lingering kiss on her lips. "You could tell me how much you love me. That's always nice to hear."

"Don't you grow tired of hearing the same old thing time and time again?" she asked softly, her voice thick with emotion as she tilted her head back and awaited more of his tantalizing kisses.

Cole did not make her wait long. Pulling her gently to him, he brought his lips down to claim hers in a series of powerful and demanding kisses. Patricia leaned toward him and moaned aloud with the overwhelming pleasure his kisses always brought her. Willingly, her mind sank into the swirling sensations he always aroused in her. The familiar sweet taste and spicy scent of him only served to intoxicate her further. She was barely aware that he had removed the pins from her hair until she felt his fingers running gently through the long silken tresses. Slowly, her hand eased up and wrapped around his neck, drawing him closer to her. It was amazing the power he had in his kiss. Although her heart raced vigorously and her pulse was vivid in her throat, her body turned weak and yielding to his touch.

In one easy motion, Cole swept her into his arms and headed for the stairs. Their lips rarely parted. While he carried her the distance to the bedroom, she began to unbutton the dress she had put on barely an hour ago.

Upon seeing their approach, Duchess quickly abandoned her mistress's bed, aware she had little choice. With an indignant raise of her furry head, she slipped quietly through the open window and perched herself on the ledge outside. Neither Cole nor Patricia noticed.

When Cole gently laid Patricia on the pale yellow coverlet, all he was aware of was her. He could see that the jaboted bodice of her dress was already undone. A smile came to his lips as he helped her out of her garments. His eyes boldly moved to caress her beauty once she lay naked before him. He never grew tired of looking at her. Eagerly, he reached for his own buttons.

"No, let me," she said softly, then rose to a kneeling position while she slowly began to undo the tiny buttons of his shirt and deftly worked to unfasten his britches. Soon he too was naked and just as eager to share their love.

As the two of them fell back into the softness of the huge feather mattress, Cole's lips again claimed hers in another fiery, passion-filled kiss. They marveled in the wonder and delight of holding each other, caressing each other, loving each other to the fullest. Each moment was savored, each new height of arousal explored and treasured until the ultimate height was finally reached and shared breathlessly between them.

It was after midnight when Cole pulled into his own drive again. He felt as lighthearted as a young boy. With a crooked little smile beaming across his face all he could think of was how beautiful and loving his Patricia was and how in just a few months, she would become his wife and he would not have to leave her in the middle of the night like he did now. He could hardly wait. Just the thought of it warmed him so that he was totally unaware of the slight chill in the air as he rode back home.

In just over ten minutes, he had the horse bedded in its stall and was headed from the carriage house to his back door, his thoughts still on Patricia. He stopped a moment to stare up at the almost full moon. In a few days the moon would be completely full. It occurred to him how nice it would be to make love to Patricia under the silvery glow of a full moon. He certainly hoped the weather would cooperate by continuing to be mild. A tremor of excitement wafted through him.

Cole was so deeply engrossed in his arousing thoughts that he almost did not notice that a letter that had been tucked into the tiny crevice between the door and the doorframe. Plucking it from the spot, he eyed the bold print on the envelope and wondered who it could have come from. Quickly unlocking the door, he waited until he had his coat off and the top buttons of his shirt undone before he opened the envelope and read the brief message inside. He felt every muscle in him grow taut as he read:

Gifford,
    It is time to put an end to that petition of yours. If you don't, someone is going to get hurt—badly hurt. Consider this a friendly warning.

252

The letter was not signed. Cole read the message twice, unable to believe someone would actually threaten him like that. Anger boiled up inside him as he tried to figure out just who the letter could be from. His first thought was Clayton. Clayton had clearly let his opposition be known. But that's what bothered Cole. Clayton had openly stated his position. Cole did not believe the man was the type to resort to leaving anonymous letters at his doorstep. Clayton would have delivered his message in person. Who else would be likely to do such a thing? Someone from the club? Someone who benefited from the large amounts of money the club always spent in the area? The question plagued him far into the night.

Early the next morning, Cole hurried over to Patricia's and pounded on her front door until she finally awoke and answered his knock. As soon as he stepped inside, he showed her the note. She was horrified, but agreed that the bold yet precise print was not her father's. Even taking careful pains, her father's scrawlish print could never be made to look so neat, so nearly perfect. She had no idea either as to who could have written the note.

"Well, I'm going to have everyone meet tonight at Marco's. I think we need to discuss this."

"You're not thinking of calling off the petition because of that childish note, are you?"

"No, but I think we should all be aware that there is someone out there so opposed to what we are doing that he is making anonymous threats to try and stop us."

"How do you know it's a man?"

Cole thought about that a moment. "I don't. I guess I feel it is a man because of how masculine the print looks. It could be a woman. At any rate, it is someone to be concerned about."

"True. I'll stop by and tell Catherine about the note and about the meeting. She'll want to be there tonight." Patricia knew that her sister secretly wanted a reason to see Tony again, even if she herself didn't know it. Why did love have to be so blind?

253

"I'll get in touch with Tony and Faye. Tony can tell Andrew. We'll all meet there around seven. I'll be by for you just before that."

"Be careful," Patricia said as he reached for the door to leave. "You're the one who received the note. You're the one that's in the most danger."

"If there is any danger. We could be worrying needlessly. This could be from some old crackpot," he told her, hoping to put her mind at ease.

"Just the same, be careful."

"Yes, Mother, I will. I promise," he told her teasingly, then crossed his heart in a solemn oath before he left, leaving her wanting to pout but smiling at the infuriating way he was treating the matter.

Just minutes before seven, Cole arrived safely back at her door with the news that Tony had also gotten an anonymous note. His was a little less threatening. It had stated that he would never be able to get a law practice started in this town if he continued to work against the good of the community the way he was. It warned him to pull his support before it was too late, but did not threaten that he might get hurt if he failed to comply.

While the six of them got together over supper, they tried to remember everyone who had shown the most resistance, but there had been so many that it was impossible to come up with any true prospects.

"How many of you feel there is any real danger?" Cole wanted to know. "If anyone decides he or she wants out, I will fully understand. After all, none of you undertook this project thinking there might be danger involved. I want your opinions."

"Well, I for one am more determined than ever," Andrew said as he pounded his fist on the table and almost upset everyone's water glasses.

"I agree," Faye inserted, her eyes flashing with quiet anger. "I can hardly wait to get out there and show them just how hard I can work."

"Me, too," Patricia said emphatically. Meeting Cole's admiring gaze she smiled and added, "I'm not about to be frightened by such silly letters."

"I feel the same way," Catherine put in. Although until now she had kept completely quiet, she wanted them to know she still fully supported the project. "We will show this person that we are not to be bullied."

Tony smiled and shrugged as he picked up the letters and stared at them. "Looks like it's unanimous. Seems none of us is very easily frightened. Cole, your crew is not about to abandon ship over spineless letters like these."

It was agreed. They would continue exactly as they had been but with certain precautions. For now, they would work solely in pairs and try to keep a careful eye out for trouble.

Chapter Seventeen

Just days before the outdoor party Jeanne planned for Cole, Tony, Andrew, and their petition, Harrison was called to a special meeting of the hospital's board of directors. Being head of the surgical department, he was automatically a member of the board and was expected to attend. He had no idea what the meeting was about, although he had been told it was urgent, but then they always claimed every special meeting they ever called was "most urgent."

It always annoyed him that he had to take time from his work in order to be there for these meetings. Usually they amounted to little more than the usual bickering between the doctors and the administration. They never could seem to see eye to eye. Harrison had little use for such meetings and it really did not bother his conscience that he was a few minutes late for this one.

"Come in, Harrison," Dr. Laurence Pyle said when he looked up from the notes on the table before him and noticed Harrison standing in the doorway looking around. "Although the seating is informal today, I would prefer it if you would take a chair here by me since what we have to discuss today mainly concerns the surgical department."

Harrison looked around at the solemn faces of the doctors already in the room and knew that whatever it was they had to discuss, it meant trouble. He wondered if he had done something wrong. Was one of his patients causing a ruckus? As he took the seat to Laurence's left, he noticed Michael

Mack was among the doctors in the room. What was he doing there? He was not even a member of the board. Neither was Harold Vicke or Christopher English. They were all part of his surgical staff but none of them was a member of the board. What was going on?

"It looks like everyone is here now," Laurence said with a heavy sigh as he adjusted his thick-framed glasses and looked apprehensively at a tri-folded piece of paper before him. "Might as well get right to the problem at hand. None of us has time to waste."

Harrison exchanged curious glances with Michael and knew by the shrug of his friend's wide shoulders that he was just as much in the dark about the purpose of the meeting.

"Harrison, since this does affect the surgical department the most, I have asked that your entire staff of doctors be present and as you see all but Duane Flores is already here. Dr. Flores said he would be late because of a patient with a few complications he has to take care of, but we can fill him in on everything once he gets here."

Harrison felt that for someone who wanted to get right to the problem at hand, Laurence was stalling a little more than was necessary. Now that he had been made aware something was wrong, he wanted to know exactly what it was so it could be dealt with and they could all get back to work. "Exactly what is this problem?"

"I know you all remember the large donation the surgical department is supposed to be getting in order to build those two new fully equipped operating rooms," Laurence said. He still did not get right to the point. "We discussed it at the last general meeting. Some of you weren't there, but I know news of it has spread all over. It's the best thing that has happened for us in a while."

"If you're talking about that anonymous pledge you told us about last week, sure we remember," Harrison interrupted before Laurence went to the trouble to detail all that information again. "But why do you say 'supposed to be getting?' I thought it was definite. I thought that money was going to be transferred to an account in our name sometime at the end of the month."

258

"So did I," Laurence said solemnly. He paused to pull off his glasses and lay them aside. Wearily he massaged the tender indentations his glasses had left along the upper sides of his nose while he explained the situation as it was now. "I learned today through the man's attorney that there is a stipulation. Nothing was said about a stipulation when he first told us about the money. It has something to do with a petition that is going around town concerning the dam up at Lake Conemaugh."

"Lake Conemaugh?" Harrison repeated under his breath. A cold, prickling anticipation crept over the sensitive skin along his neck.

"Yes, whoever is donating this money now claims that the pledge will be withdrawn if any of you doctors or if any member of the hospital administration sign this petition. I'm not really sure what the petition is all about, this is the first I've heard of it, but if even one doctor signs it, the hospital will be refused the entire three thousand dollars. Now I know I don't have the authority to demand that none of you sign the thing, but I do want you all to consider the hospital in this matter if any of you are approached to sign. That donation is very important. Not only can we add the two new operating rooms, we will be able to staff another surgeon and with all the accidents out at the mill lately, we certainly could use another surgeon. You all know that. What I want you all to do is to talk to the other doctors and convince them not to sign. Once we explain the situation to everyone, I know they will all cooperate."

There was a muttering of agreement among the doctors before Harrison finally spoke up. "I've already signed it."

The room grew deathly quiet except for Michael Mack. "I've signed it too."

Laurence covered his face with his folded hands for a moment then pulled them slowly downward, distorting his features when he did. Once his hands were finally clear of his face, he sighed heavily and spoke in an extremely controlled voice. "Is there any way you two can have your names removed from the petition?"

"I'm not sure that I want to," Harrison said stubbornly.

"Don't want to?" Laurence raised his voice in disbelief, clearly angered by that reply. He practiced no more restraint and nearly shouted when he asked, "Don't you care about the money? Don't you want the new operating rooms? Can't you see how badly we need them?"

"Yes, of course I know how badly we need those operating rooms and, yes, I do care. I care a lot. But I also care about the safety of Johnstown and with the dam being the way it is at the moment, this whole valley could be in danger."

"I don't know anything about any of that. The petition may very well represent a very worthy cause—but does your particular name have to be on the thing in order for whoever is sending it around to succeed with whatever it is they are trying to do?"

"Probably not," Harrison conceded. He realized his was just one name and even with Michael's, it only amounted to two names. And the last he had heard Cole and Tony had over three hundred names. "But I like having my name on it. Especially now. I don't take kindly to being told what I can and cannot sign."

"Harrison, please, for the hospital's sake, reconsider. See if you can get your name off that petition," Laurence pleaded and put his glasses back on in order to look Harrison in the eye. "Surely you can make them understand how important it is to get your name off that petition."

"I'm not so sure I understand myself," Harrison said quietly, then gazed around the room, taking a visual consensus of his colleagues. By the irritation he could see on so many of the faces, he realized they had mostly sided with Laurence. And with good reason. The whole hospital needed money for improvements. This donation would not only bring the surgical department up to date, the money appropriated thus far from the general funds for his department could be infiltrated into other areas. Eventually every one of these men would benefit. Finally, Harrison stared down at the dull wooden floor of the dimly lit conference room and said, "Let me think about it."

"And what about you, Michael?" Laurence asked and turned the focus on Harrison's newest staff member. "Do you think you can have your name removed from this petition?"

Michael dared not look at Harrison. Staring down at his own tightly interlaced fingers, he replied in a low voice, "I can try."

That evening, Harrison took a long ride through the streets of Johnstown, oblivious to the cold wind curling down the valley from the northeast. He circled by the river twice and let his thoughts visualize exactly what might happen if the dam broke and all of Lake Conemaugh came rushing through the unsuspecting town. He wondered how many of his friends would be hurt, or killed. How many businesses and homes would be ruined? He tried to judge whether the hospital would be in any danger from the onslaught of water. Not being an expert in such matters, there was no way for him to tell. He did not have any way of knowing if the water would reach that far or not. But he had read the report Tony had and knew that the danger was tremendous. He just wished he could know for certain how tremendous.

Finally, as it grew dark, Harrison drove over to Cole's house and pulled into his drive. He waited a long time before getting out of his carriage and tethering Rebel to an iron bar of the tall fence surrounding Cole's yard. He knew he needed to talk with Cole about this but did not know where to begin or how to explain. He hesitated to tell Cole about it at all. Yet he needed and wanted his friend's opinion and knew Cole needed to know in order to combat such actions in the future.

When Harrison finally approached the door and knocked, Cole was upstairs busily trying to tie his ever-stubborn tie. He had plans to take Patricia to the Hulbert House for dinner. It took him a moment to answer the door.

"Harrison. Come in," Cole greeted him warmly once he had swung the door open and found his friend standing out in the cold. "My, hasn't the weather taken a nasty turn?" When Harrison did not reply and entered the house without saying as much as a word, Cole realized something was terribly wrong. "Make yourself comfortable in the next

261

room and tell me what the problem is."

Harrison accepted his offer and took a seat facing the fireplace in the front room. He turned his eyes toward the small glowing fire, the only light in the room, and waited until Cole was seated too before he explained the whole situation to him even down to the part about Michael. "And I just don't know what to do. I honestly don't want to take my name off that petition, but then I don't want the hospital to lose this donation. Three thousand dollars is an awful lot of money."

"I agree. And I know how you were looking forward to having those two new operating rooms. It's all you could talk about last weekend. I also remember how outdated you said your equipment is. Mind if I offer a suggestion?"

"That's why I'm here. I need your advice. I simply don't know what to do about this," he said and pulled his gaze away from the fireplace to look at Cole. His attention seemed drawn to the strange shadows flickering across his friend's face.

"Let me mark your name off the petition," he told him.

"But that petition is important," Harrison protested, exasperated that Cole had made it sound so simple.

"The hospital is important too. Either way, you are attempting to save lives. Look at it this way, if the dam does break and all that water comes crashing through Johnstown, there are bound to be casualties—lots of them. You would be able to do so much more for the wounded if the hospital was better equipped. As I see it, you will still be backing us, only in a different way," Cole said in earnest.

Rising from his chair Cole walked over to stand in front of Harrison. The glow of the fire behind him outlined his powerful frame in the darkened room. "Harrison, we are all fighting for the safety and future of Johnstown, aren't we? We are trying our best to prevent a potential disaster from ever happening with that petition and those reports, but if we fail to do so, that's when you will be needed the most. And the hospital. Don't jeopardize the money needed to make that hospital the best it can be."

"I know you are saying all this for my benefit, and you do

262

make sense," Harrison began and gave Cole a grateful smile. "And I do appreciate it. But I feel like I'm letting you down."

"You aren't letting me down. The only way you would be letting me down is if you pulled your name because you wanted to, because you had changed your mind about what we are trying to do. You still do believe in what we are doing, don't you?"

"You know I do."

"Then go back to the hospital tomorrow with a clear conscience and tell them that your name is no longer on the petition. Tell Michael his name is no longer on it either. What about your wives? Should we take their names off too?" he asked, trying to keep the disappointment from his voice.

"I don't see why. The attorney who represents this anonymous donor said only that the doctors were not to sign. He didn't say anything about the doctors' families. I'll have certain satisfaction in knowing that at least Jeanne's name is still on there."

"You don't have any idea who this anonymous donor is, do you?" Cole asked, wondering who would be against what they were doing enough to do something like that. He also wondered if the same person was connected in any way to those anonymous letters. Slowly, he realized that the man who had threatened them might be far more powerful than they had presumed. That thought worried him.

"No, I don't even think Laurence knows who the man is. The only communications we've had with the man that I know of have come through his lawyer, a Mr. Lansdale."

"Do you think the party this weekend will threaten the donation in any way?"

"Not that I'm aware of," Harrison replied, rubbing his chin thoughtfully. "Besides, hardly anyone even knows the real reason behind the party. They just think Jeanne is trying to get the jump on everyone else and have the first party of the season. We figured that the less the guests know, the fewer reasons they will find to stay away."

"Good, then the party goes on as scheduled?"

"Exactly as scheduled," Harrison told him with a

determined nod. "You just remember to bring that petition and those letters and reports with you."

"How many guests did Jeanne end up inviting?"

"Over a hundred and fifty, but judging by the usual turnout to these sort of things, only about seventy will actually show up. Especially if the weather continues to be as cold and dreary as it has been these past two days. Most people will choose to stay inside."

As it turned out, Harrison greatly underestimated the number of guests who would decide to come that following Saturday afternoon. Luckily Jeanne didn't. She had ordered Ruby to prepare enough food to feed a hundred and twenty people and by three o'clock there were already almost a hundred men and women milling about the backyard. When Cole and Patricia arrived shortly after three, they were surprised and delighted at the turnout.

"What did you promise them to get them all here?" Patricia asked Jeanne as she entered through the narrow iron gate at the side of the brick wall that surrounded the entire backyard. The gate had been left open for the guests to come and go freely throughout the afternoon.

"Just chicken and potato and bean salad." Jeanne shrugged. "I guess everyone is simply tired of being cooped up inside. Even with the sky threatening rain the way it is and the slight chill still in the air, I estimate I'll end up having about an eighty percent turn out." She paused as she thought about that. "Oh, I know the reason. Maybe it's my magnetic personality that drew them here," she said and batted her hazel-colored eyes coquettishly. When she noticed Patricia's eyebrows shoot up and her smile press into a flat line, Jeanne laughed and conceded, "But then again, maybe not."

"Chilly enough for you?" Harrison asked as he came up to say hello to Patricia and Cole with his hand extended in greeting.

"Yes, I believe it is," Cole said as he reached out and accepted Harrison's firm handshake.

"Well, if you think it is chilly here, you should be over there standing beside Clayton." Harrison gestured toward the house.

264

"Is he already here?" Patricia asked and quickly scanned the crowd for a glimpse of her father.

"Yes, he's up on the veranda talking to a few of his friends and keeping a keen eye on that gate. You can bet he already knows you are here."

Patricia searched the many people on the veranda but was unable to spot her father among the crowd. But then it occurred to her that he did not want to be spotted just yet. When she did happen to see him, she planned to hug his neck and greet him as she normally would, despite the cold shoulder he had given her over the past few weeks. She would act as if nothing had passed between them. That ought to throw him off his guard for a while.

"I had hoped the weather would be better," Jeanne commented, and frowned with irritation. "I had hoped the sun would come out and push this chill aside."

Looking up at the gray cloud-filled sky churning threateningly overhead, Cole remarked, "It's chilly all right, but then it is not so cold that anyone really needs a cumbersome overcoat." He took a deep breath of the invigorating air before adding, "Actually, I think the weather is just about right."

"You mean if it doesn't rain," Jeanne interjected, still frowning.

"No, I mean if it does. A little rain might be just the thing we need. Rain seems to encourage people to think in my direction. Whenever the sun is shining, it is harder to get people to consider the dam giving way to a flood," Cole explained and narrowed his eyes as he scrutinized the clouds overhead. "When the river rises again this spring the way it always does and overflows its banks, flooding the flats and some of the business district, I expect to really rack up the signatures."

"I never thought of it that way," Jeanne said with a crafty smile as she too looked heavenward. "I guess a little rain wouldn't hurt after all. We can always move everyone onto the veranda and inside."

"It's too bad about the doctors not being able to sign today. We could certainly use their prestige," Patricia mentioned and found herself looking up too. She never had been able to judge a rain cloud successfully, but studied the clouds overhead as if she knew what to look for. Although there was not much breeze on the ground, the dark, heavy clouds rolled dramatically across the sky.

"I know," Jeanne said with a frown. "It really is too bad about the stipulation to that donation, because I'll bet we have twenty doctors here this afternoon. But there are lots of other people here too." Nudging Harrison, she asked, "Why don't you start introducing Cole around to some of them while I find Father and keep him occupied elsewhere?"

"Will do," he said conspiratorially and motioned for Cole and Patricia to walk with him. "We will start with Pemberton Smith. He's a civil engineer with the Pennsylvania Railroad. Since a flood is sure to do a lot of damage to that railroad, I figure he might be interested in what you have to say. And the man with him puffing on the big cigar is James Quinn, president of the Electric Light Company. I think he will be interested too. He also is half owner of Foster and Quinn Dry Goods and Notions. Not only could the electric company suffer considerable damage if that dam was to break, that store is over there by the Hulbert House and not very far away from the river. He's also a member of the school board and an active Catholic, you know, an all-around concerned citizen."

"Sounds like likely prospects all right," Cole said, and smiled an earnest greeting as they approached the men.

Ten minutes later, Harrison and Cole were leading James and Pemberton over to one of the large tables that had been set up for eating so that they would have a flat surface to sign on. While they were signing, Andrew Foster, James's brother-in-law and business partner, walked up and wanted to know what was going on. This time it was Pemberton who gave the pitch, with James inserting how he had personally seen that lake. He explained just how large it really was. Five minutes later, Andrew Foster had signed too.

Although several of those approached refused to discuss the matter at all, many more than Cole had dared hope cooperated. Meanwhile, Jeanne did her best to keep Clayton involved in conversations with other people. She was aware that his attention was constantly drawn to Cole and Harrison and she knew that when this day was over, Harrison's place in Clayton's heart would never be quite as dear, but that could not be helped. What they were doing was for his benefit too. It would save Clayton's business as well as most of downtown Johnstown. She felt no regrets. She only hoped that the party would prove to be a tremendous success for the petition despite the doctor's inability to sign.

"There's James McMillen, president of the First National Bank," Harrison said as he steered Cole and Patricia clear of a man deeply engrossed in a conversation with two other immaculately dressed middle-aged men. "I don't think you'll get much sympathy from him or those men he's talking with. They are trustees at his bank and some of those club members who own the dam have big fat accounts in their bank in order to have easy access to some of their money while they are vacationing at the lake."

Cole made a mental note not to approach a group while any of those men were present. They looked like types who would express their opinions and he didn't need that. Quickly glancing toward the veranda, he was glad to see that Jeanne was still successfully keeping Clayton busy, even though it meant neglecting her guests.

"We must do something very special for Jeanne when this is over," he commented to Patricia. "I know what emphasis she places on being a good hostess and there she is ignoring the rest of her guests and the new arrivals in order to keep Clayton occupied and away from us."

Patricia glanced admiringly at her sister. "Maybe I should go stand by the gate and at least greet her guests for her. People will probably continue to arrive until at least four." Without waiting for Cole or Harrison to comment, she turned and headed for the gate to do just that. She made good use of the opportunity and primed the late arrivals with innocent little comments like, "I hope it doesn't rain. With the luck Johnstown's been having lately, it won't stop raining for days and we'll have an early flood this year. It

267

makes me so nervous. I just hate it when it floods." Even if it didn't rain, Patricia intended to at least put the idea of rain clearly in their heads. Most of the arrivals left her with a cautious eye on the clouds overhead.

Patricia felt like she was accomplishing something, however subtly, but she missed being with Cole, even for this short a time. When there were no guests to greet, she watched his lively animated features as he tried to persuade people to sign. Occasionally, he would look up and notice her staring at him and would give her a playful wink or a leering smile that let her know that he missed her company too and that he could hardly wait until he had her alone. Shivers of delight wafted through her at the mere thought of being alone with him.

At 3:45, Patricia noticed Tony's carriage had pulled up and watched as Andrew climbed out of the passenger side and held his hand out for Catherine. The two of them waited until Tony parked the carriage about a block away and had walked back to join them before heading toward the gate.

"Where's Faye?" Patricia asked when the three of them approached.

"She couldn't come," Andrew explained with a look of disappointment. "She has her hands full these days with a very precocious six-year-old named Alan."

"How'd that come about?"

"Thursday night, the authorities showed up at St. John's with the boy and asked if they would take him in and give him a place to stay for a while. Seems his stepfather got drunk, beat him severely, then locked him out of the house and made him sleep under the porch steps all night. A neighbor spotted him and reported it. It wasn't the first time something like this has happened to that boy either."

"Why didn't his mother do something?" Patricia asked, horrified by such a ghastly tale. She didn't even know the boy and wanted to hug him to her breast to comfort him and protect him.

"His mother died over a year ago. All the boy has is that cruel drunken stepfather of his. And until the courts can get the stepfather legally declared incompetent to raise the boy, they can't put him up for adoption. They can't even put him into an orphans' home until he is legally made an orphan. So the church agreed to take temporary custody of the boy and Faye has taken him under her wing," Andrew said proudly, then with a slight chuckle, he added, "I've met the boy. Cute child, but is he ever a handful."

"How's that?" Patricia wanted to know.

"Friday, I volunteered to keep the boy a couple of hours while Faye tended to some urgent matter or another in town. I only left the boy alone in my study for fifteen minutes while I talked with a visitor in the hallway just outside the door. When the visitor had finally left and I stepped back inside, I discovered that the boy had rearranged one whole wall of my books according to color instead of subject and had started on a second wall. He was busily putting the brown books together in one section and blue books together in another and the black ones . . . and so on and so on. He's quite an active little fellow. It took me most of last night and part of this morning to get all those books back the way they were supposed to be."

Catherine and Patricia laughed and agreed that Faye was going to have her hands very full for a while. Patricia wondered if she dared volunteer to help with the child. She hadn't much experience when it came to children, so in the end she decided to forget it.

"How long have you and Cole been here?" Tony asked, breaking into her thoughts. Already he had spotted Cole and Harrison busy courting a small group of young men near the punch bowl.

"About thirty or forty minutes," she said, not really sure.

"How are they doing?" Andrew wanted to know.

"I know they have gotten at least six signatures so far and probably more. I've been greeting people here at the gate for the past ten or fifteen minutes and haven't been able to keep a constant eye on them."

"Why are you greeting everyone? Where's Jeanne?" Catherine wanted to know, perplexed that Jeanne would allow such a thing.

"Trying her best to keep Father occupied and out of Cole

and Harrison's way. I'd do it myself, but he isn't talking to me these days. When I walked over to greet him, all I got was a terse nod and a very meaningful glare. Jeanne is the only one he still seems to tolerate, but judging by the agitated expression that's been growing on his face, I'd say he won't tolerate her interference much longer."

"I might give it a try and let her rest a while," Tony said. "For some reason, he is still speaking to me."

"Because you have money and clout," Catherine muttered. She knew full well why Clayton willingly made allowances for Tony when everyone else involved with the petition was on his black list, even his own daughters.

"Maybe I should think of some business to discuss with him," Tony said thoughtfully.

"Good idea," Patricia agreed. "Tell him you are interested in purchasing that rooming house he owns next to the land you just bought so that you can expand. Tell him you've had such an interest in your office building that you believe a second building just might be called for. Talk high dollars. That should take his mind off of what we are doing for a while."

Turning to Andrew, Tony said, "Take care of Catherine while I'm gone. Don't let any handsome men flirt with her and don't you go flirting with her either."

Andrew saluted his agreement and neither man noticed how uncomfortable Tony's request had made Catherine, but Patricia did. She wondered why her sister couldn't just accept Tony's attentions and enjoy them.

"Why don't you two go over there and lend Cole some support," Patricia said to Andrew and Catherine once Tony had left. "I'll be over as soon as Jeanne has relieved me here." She noticed how Catherine's eyes followed Tony even while Andrew escorted her over to where Cole and Harrison were talking.

While she waited for more late arrivals, Patricia let her gaze travel across the yard to the diverse group of people that Jeanne had invited. When her gaze temporarily lighted on a large group of doctors huddled together along with Pemberton Smith and James Quinn near the foot of the wide

270

stairs below the veranda, she felt a pang of anger toward whoever had ruined their chances of getting the doctors to sign. They all had so hoped to gain the support of the medical community during this party. She just wished she knew who was behind that donation. She too felt like whoever it was, he or she was also behind those two poison-pen letters. How she would love to give whoever it was an ample piece of her mind if not a good part of her boot.

Eventually, Jeanne worked her way through the crowd and came to stand beside Patricia. "Thanks for taking over as unofficial hostess. I appreciate it."

"It's the least I could do. After all, you were busy diverting Father's attention." Looking toward the veranda, where Clayton had been held captive for the past hour, she was unable to locate him. "Where is he now?"

"He and Tony stepped inside for a while. I think they wanted to talk a little business," Jeanne said as she beamed a crafty smile. "If you would like to go over there and join the others, I'll keep an eye on the gate now."

By the time supper was served at five-thirty, Cole counted thirty-one new signatures and they felt that was just the beginning. During the meal itself, he and Harrison carefully selected who they should sit by. They chose Philip Cooke, another employee of Pennsylvania Railroad, and George Heiser, the owner of a mercantile on Washington Street that was only about a block from the river and already suffered a lot from the floods. Both would have a reason to listen and Harrison had just turned the conversation in the direction they wanted when Clayton appeared out of nowhere and placed his plate right beside the mercantile owner.

"Hello, George, who's minding the store?" Clayton asked with a broad smile.

"Victor is," George replied proudly. He loved a chance to brag about how capable his teenaged son was. "He is a better salesman than I could ever hope to be."

"And how has business been?" Clayton asked as he pulled out the wooden folding chair in front of his plate and sat down. He flashed a determined smile to Cole, Patricia, and Harrison, who sat directly across from them, then turned to offer Andrew and Catherine a similar smile. Andrew and Catherine had seated themselves on the far side of Philip Cooke and were ready to insert their opinions if they felt they were needed.

"Fine, Clayton. In fact, Mathilde claims we made such a fine profit last month that we might be getting us a new counter with one of those glass fronts to show off some of our finer things. It's something she's been wanting for quite some time," George said as he shoved a forkful of bean salad into his mouth. "We'll even have some money left over to put into Victor's college fund."

"I guess with the fishing and hunting club getting stocked up soon for the upcoming season that you will have another good month next month as well."

"Should do it," George agreed, unaware of the crestfallen expressions on the faces across the table from him. None of them had been aware that the club bought any of their supplies at George's store and now that he had been reminded of the profit those purchases could bring, they had little hope of persuading him to sign and if they tried to convince Philip Cooke with George and Clayton sitting there, they seriously doubted they would have much success with him either. Except for an occasional remark made by George, Philip, or Clayton, the remainder of the meal passed in silence.

After that, they could pretty well count on Clayton's interference. Even Jeanne found she could not draw him away nor could Tony. He was wise to them and with Clayton there to argue against them, they were unable to convince even one more person to sign. Eventually they gave in to their frustration and decided to wait before approaching anyone else with their proposal. With Clayton around, they were doing more harm than good.

Cole had securely placed the petition inside one of his inner coat pockets with little hope of bringing it out again when Michael Mack approached the group of them standing near one of the bonfires and asked if he could speak to Harrison and Cole alone. This time Clayton was unable to follow. Nor were any of the others. They all stared curiously at each other, wondering where Michael was taking them. They watched with keen interest when Michael led Cole and Harrison into the house. Cole turned to give Patricia a shrug that let her know that he had no idea what it was about either before he turned back and followed the two of them out of everyone's sight.

Catherine was the first to realize that several of the doctors had followed them inside at inconspicuous intervals. Looking around, she noticed that soon none of the doctors she worked with and had seen ambling about the yard earlier were to be found. She wondered just what was going on.

Chapter Eighteen

"We've all talked about it and that's the way every one of us feels," Michael said adamantly as he waved his pipe a few inches from his mouth in perfect time with the syllables he spoke. There was a loud round of agreement from the twenty-some-odd doctors crowding around them in the small, book-lined study near the front of the house. It was Harrison's private room and they had chosen it because it had a lock and the many books seemed to muffle any sounds going to the outside. "We've decided not to be bullied. We've discussed the petition and what it stands for and have decided we want to sign it. All of us."

"But what about the donation?" Cole asked. "You can't just throw three thousand dollars away like that. The hospital needs it."

Before Cole could go on to explain how much a good hospital with adequate equipment would be needed should the petition fail, Michael put up his empty hand to silence him. "We've discussed that too. Should that donation really be pulled, we've decided that we would all come up with at least a hundred dollars each out of our own money to donate in its place. Even if we have to eat sausage and beans for a year, we have all agreed. And we feel certain we can get most of the other doctors that are not here today to agree to help cover the loss of the donation too. It didn't sit too well with any of us that some nameless person out there was trying to tell us what we could and couldn't do. Next thing you know we will be making more concessions, and more, until we will have lost all our self-respect. No, we've talked to several people tonight. We've heard several different views. And we have decided we want our names on that list."

Cole looked from face to face and could see the determination on each and every man in that room. Glancing over at the huge grin on Harrison's face, he laughed and reached into his pocket for the petition. "Who gets to sign first?"

"Let Harrison," someone called out. "He's already signed once and had to have his name removed. Let him be the first."

"Then Michael should be next," someone else pointed out.

Soon they all crowded around Harrison's desk for a chance to put their names on the petition. Cole couldn't believe it. By the time everyone had moved away from the desk and grouped into individual conversations, he picked up the petition and counted twenty-two new signatures. All in all, the party had netted them fifty-three signatures.

"So, how many signatures does that make?" Christopher English wanted to know when he came to stand behind Cole and peered over his shoulder.

"Close to four hundred. We may even have as many as five hundred signatures before I go to Washington this summer. That may not seem like many coming from a valley of ten thousand, but it is far more than we had hoped for."

"Expect to have a few more doctors looking you up. Once they find out what we've done, I'm sure they will want to have their names on it too," Michael told him. "Nurses too."

"Don't forget about our wives and friends. I for one am going to try to convince everyone I see to sign that petition. I don't particularly care for the idea of having to tend to hundreds of injured at one time. It would take forever to care for them all. And with my luck, it would happen on my bowling night," Harold Vicke said with a scowl.

Everyone laughed, knowing how seriously Harold took his bowling.

"Who's going to tell Laurence about this?" Harrison asked once the laughter had died down.

276

"Why you are, of course," Michael said as if that had been understood.

"Me?"

"Yes, you. And about twenty of the rest of us. We've decided to call our own special meeting Monday afternoon."

Harrison felt the sudden tension drain from his body. He had not relished the idea of facing Laurence alone with this, but he would have.

"And you are also going to come up with a hundred dollars if that donation falls through because of this, aren't you?" Michael asked, as if needing the fact verified.

"I'll donate two hundred," he promised and laughed. It felt wonderful to discover just how good-hearted and noble his colleagues really were.

"So, how many names did Cole manage to add to his list last Saturday?" Clayton asked when he entered Patricia's office early the following Monday morning.

It had been so long since Patricia's father had voluntarily spoken to her, much less made a special trip into her office, that it startled her for a moment. Without meaning to, she sent her pencil flying across the room where it bounced off the apricot wallpaper and landed on the polished wooden floor with a loud clatter.

"Good morning, Father. I didn't hear you come in," she replied in as cheerful a voice as she could produce at that particular moment. Her heart still jumped from having been caught off guard that way.

"How many?" he asked again, not easily swayed with petty conversation.

"Fifty-four by the time we left," she said, remembering how Ruby, Harrison's housekeeper, had demanded to sign after she had overheard some of the conversations at the party.

"Fifty-four!" he repeated in disbelief. His face twisted into a rough scowl. "I figured he'd only gotten about a dozen or so. I had no idea he had managed to get that many. Are you sure?"

277

"Yes, I'm sure. You remember when Michael Mack called Cole and Harrison away? That was so every doctor there could sign as a group," she said and carefully watched his face for a reaction. Even though she was pretty sure it was not her father's handwriting on those notes, she realized he could be the one behind the shady donation. He certainly had the money and the motive.

"And he came away with fifty-four more signatures?" he asked, obviously more concerned with the number than the fact that the doctors had signed.

Patricia felt relieved to know that. Although he was openly against what they were doing, she did not want to believe he was the type to secretly try to sabotage their project. She could tolerate his opposition as long as it was out in the open. After all, he was entitled to his opinion no matter how wrong it might be.

"Yes, Father, fifty-four signatures."

"That makes over three hundred, doesn't it?" he probed.

"That makes nearly four hundred," she said proudly.

"Damn," he muttered and quickly left the room without saying another word.

The scowl on his face told Patricia exactly what he thought of their progress. She felt an odd satisfaction in watching his agitation grow. They were succeeding despite the odds. Even her father would have to admit that.

Later, when she relayed to Cole what had happened in her office, he too was glad to hear that Patricia felt certain Clayton was not the unknown opposition. Clayton would be his father-in-law one day. Eventually they would need to be friends. He'd hate to think of him as deceitful. Despite the obvious stubborn streak and despite Clayton's terribly bullheaded ways, Cole believed the man at least had a sense of honor and Cole had never honestly courted the thought that the anonymous saboteur was his future father-in-law. He just couldn't believe that the man who had spawned someone as strong and courageous as Patricia could be cowardly in any way. No, it wasn't Clayton, but then who was it? He decided to make a trip down to this Mr. Lansdale's office on his very next day off and see if he could find out from the lawyer himself who was out to sabotage their efforts.

Thursday, Cole did just that. He made an appointment to see Voncille Lansdale at his office on Main Street but was unable to learn anything other than Mr. Lansdale was a true believer in protecting his client's rights as well as his identity. About all Cole managed to find out was that it was definitely a man and that this man truly intended to withdraw his pledge. The hospital had indeed lost the donation.

When Cole left, he had so much pent-up anger and frustration he felt like he was going to explode. He desperately wanted to know who had offered the hospital that sizable donation with the sole purpose of keeping the doctors from signing the petition but had no way of finding out. He liked to know just who his enemies were so he could confront them or at least watch out for them. How did someone deal with a nameless enemy?

Needing someone to talk to and knowing Patricia would not be home for hours yet and that Tony was busy getting his office building finished and ready to move into, Cole stopped by the Todd Street Methodist Church to see if Andrew was around. When he pulled up into the paved area near the street, he noticed Andrew crawling around in the shrubbery just outside his office on his hands and knees.

"What on earth are you doing?" he wanted to know, his blue eyes wide with curiosity when he approached.

"Looking for footprints," Andrew said offhandedly, as if anyone should know that.

"Footprints? In the bush bed? What kind? What for?"

"I happen to have risen in the ranks since last we talked. I am now on equal status with you and Tony," he said while he carefully tried to back out of the tightly knit holly bushes without getting badly scratched. When he stood to face Cole, his sandy blond hair stood out in a dozen different directions with several broken twigs poking out and there was a large rip in his vest.

"Would you care to explain that remark? How have you risen in the ranks?"

"About an hour ago, I found a note in my office, on my

279

desk. It was from our friendly anonymous letter writer. And because I had locked my door when I left the room and it was locked when I returned, I can only assume the person who delivered the message entered through one of the windows. He had to. That's the only other way in."

"You locked your doors but not your windows?" Cole asked with a raised brow as if questioning the logic in that.

"I know. I know. It doesn't make very much sense, but then I never thought anyone would be willing to climb through four feet of prickly holly bushes to get to one of those windows either."

"What did the note say?"

Thrusting his hand into his trouser pocket, Andrew came out with a folded piece of paper and handed it to Cole. "See for yourself."

Cole quickly unfolded it and noticed the handwriting was very similar if not exactly the same as the other two notes. After reading the threats inside, he folded it back and held it out to Andrew.

"No, keep it. I already have it memorized. Whoever this fellow is, he sure thinks he has the power to have my church taken away from me," Andrew said with a frown. "And who knows, he just might. The trustees are already upset with me for continuing to help out when they had just the same as ordered me to stop months ago."

"And did you find any footprints?"

"No, but I found a half empty box of Smith Brothers cough drops. I can't say for certain that the box came from my intruder, but I do know it hasn't been there long. The box doesn't look as if it's been rained on and, as you might remember, it rained yesterday morning. I guess this means the fellow who has been harassing us has a cough. But then this time of year lots of people have bad coughs."

"True. That intruder could have been anybody. Be extra careful for a while. This fellow could be harmless but then again, he could be very dangerous."

"Don't worry. I'll be careful. I'm even going to start locking my windows."

*   *   *

280

"Father, since Iris didn't come into work today, could you take the deposit by the bank?" Patricia asked nicely when she entered his office just before lunchtime. Although he had not been extremely friendly toward her, their short conversation last Monday had at least put them back on speaking terms.

"No, I'm busy," he told her, and looked up from the work on his desk only a moment. "And I have an appointment at one. You'll have to take it over yourself."

Patricia was afraid of that. If it wasn't such a large deposit she would be tempted to wait until the next day when Iris might be back, but it was very large and she could not chance leaving that much money in her office. Even though a trip to the bank meant chancing a run-in with William, a deposit needed to be made. Reluctantly, she tucked the huge leather pouch under her arm and headed for the front door.

Had her destination not been the bank, Patricia would have enjoyed the short walk more. Although a heavy mist had clung to the ground early that morning when she had gone to work, the warm sun had burned the moisture away and a bright sunny day had prevailed. Birds sang cheerfully overhead and spring flowers had suddenly made their appearance in flowerboxes, yards, and along the riverside. It occurred to her that this was the sort of day that should be shared by lovers. She thought of Cole and smiled but the smile quickly faded when she found herself in front of the First National Bank. She hardly noticed the noon whistle from the iron works as she took those final few steps. With little enthusiasm, she pushed the heavy wood and glass doors open and slowly stepped inside.

When she first glanced toward the window to William's office and noticed his chair was empty, she finally realized the time. It was quite possible he was already out to lunch. She might not have to face him after all. But no such luck, for while she stood in line to have her money counted, she heard his familiar voice directly behind her.

"Hello, Patricia."

Turning to greet him, she was startled to see how pale he looked. Deep gray semicircles curved downward below his eyes and his eyelids looked heavy from lack of sleep. His usually intense hazel eyes looked dull and lifeless and, even as thin as he already was, she was sure he had lost weight. He looked terrible. "Hello, William. How have you been?"

"As if you care," he said with a sharp thrust of his jaw. His nose flared slightly as he waited for her reply.

Patricia felt he was behaving childishly and wanted no further part of this conversation. "I see you are still too angry to want to talk with me. I understand. It's nice to have seen you." Then she quickly turned back around to face the teller. She wished the man behind the window would hurry. She was next in line and she wanted to get out of there.

"Yes, I'm angry," he grated through clenched teeth as he grabbed her by the arm and turned her so she had to face him again. His large ornate ring was turned around on his finger and the emerald stone bore painfully into her skin. "But I want to talk to you. In private. Come into my office."

"But I have a deposit to make."

"I'll count it and fill out a slip for you in my office," he said in a determined voice. Then realizing by the pained expression on her face that he was hurting her, he quickly released his grip on her arm.

With a look of true regret for having lost his temper so easily, he reached up and lightly ran a fingertip over the soft contours of her cheek. The touch sent a strange feeling of sadness through her.

"I'm sorry, Patricia. But I do want to talk to you. Would you please come with me? Just for a moment?"

Rather than make a scene and possibly because she felt a little sorry for him, she agreed to go with him to his office for a moment. She did not consider herself in any real danger since William's desk was in full view of the main part of the bank. He would be unable to pull any stunts like the one he had pulled the last time he had wanted to talk. Besides, she could use this opportunity to tell him to quit following her, for if he was still hoping to catch her out alone in order to prove his love, he was going to be out of luck. She was not about to give him such an opportunity.

"Here, hand me your pouch," he said once they had entered his office and he had closed the door. While she made herself comfortable in one of the large upholstered chairs across from his desk, he sat down and counted the money in a businesslike manner. After he finished, he filled out a deposit slip and signed it. When he looked up from his desk, he smiled and remarked, "You look as beautiful as ever."

"Thank you, William," she replied sincerely. "A woman always likes to get compliments."

He stared silently at her a moment more as if wanting to memorize every little detail about her, then he let his gaze drop back down to what he was doing. Carefully, he tucked the deposit slip inside a pocket in the pouch and folded it. He took his time tying it securely closed. "I've missed you more than you can ever know," he said when he looked back up, his voice so tight with emotion that it made him cough. "Please come back to me. I still want you to be my wife. I need a woman like you at my side."

Patricia could hardly believe this was William. She had never known him to sound so sincere, so humble, so utterly heartbroken. Usually he demanded to have what he wanted and made threats when things didn't go his way. Her heart went out to him as she stood and reached for the pouch. She decided not to mention that she knew he was following her. That would ony make him feel worse. "I'm sorry, William. I am very much in love with Cole and I'll never leave him for anyone else."

"Never?" he asked and she thought she saw a glimpse of the old William before the expression gave way to the total sadness that seemed to engulf him. "Never is a long time."

Patricia did not know what to say. She could see that he was hurting but felt there was nothing she could say or do to really help him. Taking the pouch from him, she offered him a sympathetic smile and said, "It was nice to see you again."

When she turned to leave his office, she heard his chair scuff back across the thick carpet so she paused and waited for him to open the door for her. When she stepped out into the lobby, she heard him speak again, but his voice was so low this time she only caught part of what he had to say, ". . . and I won't give up. I still want you and someday very soon you will be mine again."

Rather than try to reply to his comment, she continued to walk toward the door, pretending she never heard any of it. But when she stepped outside, his words and his strange attitude plagued her. She had never seen him like that and had never heard him sound so hurt, so defeated. She felt a twinge of guilt for having had a part, however involuntary it was, in the anguish William seemed to be feeling. She wished he would find someone else before he suffered a complete emotional breakdown.

That evening when she and Cole joined Andrew and Faye for a short walk through the streets of Johnstown, Patricia did not mention William or how depressed he had seemed. She still felt too guilty for having been a part of his problem. And especially for not having shown him any compassion whatsoever until today. Selfishly, she had never given his feelings a second thought. Rather than tell her friends any of what she was feeling guilty about, she showed her interest in the fact that Faye was finally able to get out again now that the abused child she had been in charge of had finally been placed in an orphanage and she was curious about the note Andrew had received.

"I had hoped those two notes were just a one-time thing," she told them, compressing her lips into a pout. "I wish we could catch whoever it is."

"Or whatever it is," Andrew commented. "The man has to have the agility of a cat to have gotten through those holly bushes and up into one of those tiny windows."

"And he must not weigh very much," Cole added. "I noticed not one bush had been broken except at the bottom where Andrew had been crawling around, not even where the man would have had to use a limb for a boot up."

"So all we really know is that he is probably very small, writes extremely neat, and likes Smith Brothers cough drops," Patricia recounted, trying to match that with anyone she knew. It certainly was not much to go on.

"And we know he doesn't like what we are doing about that dam," Cole added thoughtfully.

"And that he has plenty of money to use against us," Andrew put in as he rubbed his chin. He was so deep in thought trying to remember if there were any other clues they should have noticed that he almost walked into a lightpole. "Three thousand dollars isn't chicken scratch," he said and looked a little sheepish as he stepped back and circled around the pole.

"That is if the donor and the note writer are one and the same," Faye cautioned them. "They could be isolated incidents."

"True," Patricia admitted. "But I have a feeling they both are one and the same."

"So does anyone know a small, rich man that writes very well and coughs a lot?" Andrew asked with such sincerity that everyone laughed.

"Maybe it is one of the members of the club. Why don't we write them and ask for a listing of any members who weigh practically nothing and cough a lot?" Patricia suggested.

"I don't think they will cooperate with you on that one, Trish," Cole said, laughing. "What we need is another clue. We will all have to keep our eyes and ears open. Eventually, I think we are going to figure out just who this guy is. It's just a matter of time."

"I just hope it's before he hurts someone," Faye said seriously. "I worry about it. This man might not be in full command of his faculties. I worry that he might actually try to hurt one of you men."

"I almost wish he would," Cole said, his eyes narrowed. "Then maybe we could find out who he is. Once we know that, then maybe we can deal with him."

"True, we can't catch him until he does something," Andrew agreed, then decided it was time to change the subject before it got too serious. "Did Tony tell you that he expects to be able to move into that new office building of his sometime next week? He's already started moving some of his things over there."

"No, I knew it would be soon, but I didn't think it would be that soon," Cole replied. "But I should have guessed. He's been spending a lot of time down there these last two weeks. Getting ready for the move, I guess. What say we all go down there next week once he's all moved in and surprise him with

285

a good luck party—a celebration of sorts."

"That'll be fun. I'll see if I can talk Minnie into making a special cake," Patricia said excitedly. She would love to do something special for Tony. "If I didn't like Tony so much, I'd bake the cake myself." Everyone laughed at such a ridiculous comment.

"And I'll bring plates, forks, and napkins," Faye quickly volunteered. "And something to cut the cake with."

"And I'll bring the champagne and the glasses," Cole offered quickly. "So what does that leave Andrew to bring?"

"My appetite," he said with a bold grin and chuckled with delight when everyone groaned in playful misery over his remark.

A week later, Patricia learned that Tony planned to have his office furniture, records, and books moved into his building the following Friday. They made plans to surprise him late that afternoon after everyone got off work. To be sure he was there when they arrived bearing their food and drink, Patricia convinced Catherine to pay him a visit earlier that afternoon and find a way to keep him there late. Normally, Catherine would have balked at the thought of being alone with him at his office, but because it was for such a good cause, she agreed.

"If I have to tie him to his desk, I'll keep him there," she promised, but knew she would not have to resort to anything so drastic. Tony would stay just to be with her. He made no secret of the fact that he liked her and enjoyed her company. She wished he didn't, but he did. For once, she would work that to her advantage.

Friday afternoon late, Catherine dressed in one of her most frilly daytime dresses, a creation of pink gingham and pearl lace, picked up a matching pink parasol, her pink and white handbag, and headed for Tony's office building. When she arrived on Franklin Street, she found the front door was locked, but that the back door stood wide open. Remembering he had mentioned how his office would be on the ground floor near the front, she made her way down a small tiled hallway toward the front of the building.

When she neared the front, she peeked into every door

until she finally found the right one. Tony was busy pulling books out of large cartons and placing them neatly on the shelves when she stepped just inside the door. Startled at the sound of her voice when she finally spoke, he fumbled the books he had just picked up. They hit the floor in front of his feet with a loud clatter.

"Need any help?" she asked and smiled at his reaction.

"Catherine! What are you doing here?" he wanted to know, kicking the books out of his way so that he could hurry to greet her. His eyes sparkled with delight.

"I wanted to see what your office looked like. You told me I would be welcome anytime."

"And you are. You are," he said with a cheerful smile. "Please, come in."

"I'm in." She stated the obvious while she looked around at the crates that still needed to be unpacked. "But if you are busy, I can come back another time."

"No, no. I was just putting some of my law books on the shelves. I can do that anytime. Please," he said, pushing several empty cartons from a nearby chair, "sit down. Make yourself comfortable."

"First I want to see the rest of the building," she said, in hopes the tour would take up a lot of time. Everyone was due to arrive at five-thirty. That was over an hour away. Placing her handbag and parasol on the chair, she looked around and told him, "I want to see it all."

"Sure, come on," he said excitedly and took her hand to lead her. "Let's start with the third floor."

Catherine's heart jumped when he took her by the hand and gently pulled her toward the door. A warm, vibrant sensation spread quickly through her. She frowned. She thought she had managed to get these wild feelings that linked themselves to Tony back under control. Then why had his touch ignited such pleasurable sensations in her? Why was her unruly heart pounding furiously against her breast when it should forever belong to another? She decided it was the fact that they were quite alone in this huge building and might be for as long as an hour. She tried not to think about it as he led her up the stairs with her hand still firmly clasped in his.

"There are four offices up here on the top floor," he began as he stepped over to the door nearest the stairs and flung it open so that she could see inside. "These rooms are not quite finished but should be in another week or two. As you can see, the walls still need paper and the gaslight fixtures have not been installed yet nor has any of the shelving nor the furniture brought in." Pulling her further down the hall, he reached for another door and opened it. "And look at the storage areas. Each office has its own separate storage room with shelves from floor to ceiling and bins that lock individually."

Catherine watched the pride and excitement Tony displayed over his building and couldn't help but share in his enthusiasm. "You certainly didn't scrimp on space. You should have this office building filled in no time at all."

"I hope so. Come on, let me show you the offices on the second floor. They are completely finished and ready for businesses to move into," he said and pulled her back the way they had come. He had never once let go of her hand, enjoying the physical contact and the feelings just touching her could arouse in him.

"And the offices are even larger on the second floor," he went on to explain as they made their way back down the stairs. "Instead of dividing the floor into four offices like I did up there, I have it divided into three. The ones on the ground are the smallest. There are six offices down there."

When they reached the second floor, he led her to the nearest door which was already open. Inside was an empty room with highly polished mahogany shelves, durable oak furniture, including a desk, file cabinets, a sofa and two chairs, and pale green wallpaper that went beautifully with the dark green tile on the floor.

"This is lovely," Catherine said as she stepped inside for a better look. "I'm impressed."

"Are you?" he asked. When her gaze left her surroundings to look at him, his broad smile slowly faded and she could see his expression grow very serious. His eyes seemed to bore into hers when he spoke. "I did so want you to like it. I value

288

your opinion." When Catherine said nothing, just remained standing before him staring at him, he continued softly. "I also value your friendship."

Catherine felt herself blushing and looked away. "And I value yours," she admitted shyly. When she braved another glance at him, she found he had moved closer. He now held both her hands. The flutterings inside her gained momentum as she watched him take still another step toward her.

"Catherine, it's more than that. I know how you hate for me to say it, but I love you. I love you so much." Without giving her time to protest his actions, he pulled her to him and held her close against him as his lips came down and claimed a tender kiss.

Catherine's first impulse was to resist, pull away. This was exactly the thing she needed to guard against. Quickly, she pressed her hands against his chest in an attempt to free herself from his gentle embrace, but as the kiss deepened and she felt herself responding, she found that her traitorous hands had quit pushing all together. Instead they eased their way up his masculine chest and felt of his broad shoulders as they moved to encircle his neck. Something inside her warned her to stop this before it went any further, but her body refused to listen and she found herself pulling him closer in order to better sample the excitement of his kiss.

It was as if her body and mind had somehow become separate. And she gave up trying to figure out why. Hungrily, she devoured his kisses. When his hands moved to take her tiny hat from her head and loosen her hair which was held back by two small combs, she knew that she wanted him just as much as he wanted her. Shame still flooded her, but so did her need for this man. Despite her every effort not to, she had fallen in love with him. It was wrong and she knew it, but she loved him dearly and wanted him more than she could ever remember wanting a man. She could no longer deny what she felt, but she knew she should not give into it either.

"Catherine," he said in a husky voice. "I need you."

"Oh, Tony, please don't," she responded in a trembling voice, tears already beginning to form. There was such confusion and turmoil inside her, she could not begin to sort out what-all she felt, but she knew that she wanted him desperately yet must not lose sight of the fact that their love should never be. Where was the strength she needed to pull away? She knew she would never be able to deal with the guilt and the shame tomorrow would bring. She had to keep her wits about her.

"Tony, I—" she started to say, but found her words quieted by yet another passion-filled kiss. A warm tide of pleasure surged through her as his ardent kiss began to drug her senses further. Her lids grew heavy and she felt herself being pulled into a turbulent sea of emotions so powerful, she was no longer sure she could fight back.

Slowly, tenderly, his hands roamed along the gentle contour of her spine then around to caress one of her breasts through the soft material of her dress, bringing the sensitive peaks to life. Wildfire raged through her. She felt herself clinging to him as her strong resolve weakened more. It had been so long since she had been held in a man's arms. She wanted to feast on the sensations that had overtaken her if only for a moment. But she knew she must not give in. When his hands moved to undo the many fasteners at the back of her dress, she realized that if she didn't act then, she would be forever lost to the flames that engulfed her. She allowed herself to savor one last moment before she let her better judgment win out and pulled quickly away.

Tony looked so bewildered and confused that she knew she should say something to explain, but she never got the chance. At that moment, they heard a loud crashing sound directly below. That noise was immediately followed by another loud clattering crash, again just below them.

"Someone's down there," he said breathlessly, not having fully recovered from the moment of passion. Still another sound came from downstairs and a look of pure disappointment washed over him. Quietly, he walked over to the door and pushed it shut. With a pained expression of regret, he pressed himself against the door and said, "I guess you had better hurry and comb your hair and get your hat back on before whoever is down there decides to come upstairs looking for me."

Sadly, he diverted his gaze to the window while she hurriedly ran the small decorative combs through her hair and anchored it back into place. Moments later, she had her hat back in place and looked exactly as if nothing had happened. A deep ache welled inside him as he slowly reached for the door handle.

Chapter Nineteen

Wordlessly, Tony moved to the door and opened it just enough to slip through. He stepped quickly out into the hallway and looked both ways to see if anyone had come upstairs that might be witness to the two of them coming out from behind the same closed door. Another loud noise below put his mind to rest and let him know that whoever had come by was still downstairs in his office. He reached back and pushed the door open wide to let her know it was safe to come out.

"It's clear," he verified when she did not at first respond, his voice hushed, his manner apologetic. He had not planned for any of that to happen.

Catherine's gaze did not meet his when she stepped through the door and joined him in the hallway. Instead she kept her eyes trained on the shiny tiled floor in front of her. Her muddled thoughts tried to sort through the deep whirlwind of emotions that consumed her.

In a self-conscious gesture, she felt through the soft fabric of her dress and played nervously with the necklace that hung there. Everything inside her was in a vast turmoil. Her emotions had come very close to betraying her. She had almost done the unforgivable. Had there been more time . . . she didn't want to think about it. And as for the time, she could hardly believe that an entire hour had passed in so brief a span. But it must have. Or else everyone had decided to come a little early for some reason.

She fought the tears of confusion and shame that stung her eyes as they made their way down the stairs side by side. She tried not to show any of the utter chaos she suffered inside. It felt as if she were floundering helplessly in a swirling sea and there was no one to help her, no one she could really turn to. How could she have come so close to giving in to the temptation she felt whenever Tony was near? Would she be able to stop herself if the opportunity ever presented itself again? She must not let it. Now that she knew she loved him as much as she did, she must avoid being alone with him at all cost.

"And so you now have had a first class grand tour of my new office building," Tony said overly loud, obviously giving whoever was in his office a reason for their sudden appearance after so long an absence.

"Thank you," she replied sincerely. "It was lovely." Her eyes traveled up to meet his and they exchanged searching glances for a brief moment, but her gaze dropped before she went on to finish what she had to say. "It was truly lovely."

Something pulled at Tony's heart and he spoke in a voice not quite as loud as the last. "I'm glad you thought so. I was worried that you might have been displeased and I never want to ever displease you." She looked back up and their eyes held for another moment, then he escorted her down the narrow corridor toward his office, unaware of what he would find inside.

Just before they reached the doorway, they stopped to give each other one last questing glance but their attention was quickly captured by the sound of glass breaking from inside the office and then the grinding sound of someone stepping on the tiny shards of the broken glass.

"What's going on in there?" Tony demanded as he hurried past her toward the opened door. "You are going to ruin my new tile if you're not careful." When he stepped inside, he fell immediately silent then ran to the window and stuck his head outside to see if he could spot whoever had been there.

Catherine entered right behind Tony expecting to find everyone standing apologetically over a broken bottle of champagne, but what met her eyes was an empty room of mass destruction. Someone had ransacked Tony's office and done a thorough job of it.

Books and papers were strewn everywhere. The drawers of his desk had been removed and the contents scattered across the floor. The empty drawers had then been tossed haphazardly against the far wall. A small wooden chair lay broken beside the smashed-out window, which obviously gave whoever had done this a quick means of escape. Even Catherine's handbag had been pulled inside out and tossed on the floor, the contents thrown aside. Her parasol lay in a rumpled heap on a nearby chair as if it too had been searched. Someone had been looking for something and did not care if Tony knew.

Tony was speechless when he turned back around and his expression unreadable as he quietly bent over and began to gather up some of the papers and stack them neatly in his hands. His eyes scanned the room, looking for something that might give him a clue as to who had done such a thing. His brow furrowed when he was unable to find anything. His face finally grew rigid and displayed the anger he felt.

"Shouldn't we go for the police?" she wanted to know, and stepped closer to him while her eyes studied their surroundings. She reached out to touch his shoulder, suddenly wanting physical contact with him. She needed the security his male strength offered. She was frightened. She knew that whatever madman had done this could return at any moment.

"Yes, I guess we should," Tony said, then straightened and looked around him again. His lips pursed into a tight flat line as he surveyed the damage. "Who would do such a thing and why? Did someone think I would have money in here already?"

A small sound just outside the door caught both their attentions. Their eyes met briefly, then Tony's cut to the door. Catherine felt her heart leap to her throat and wanted to scream aloud the terror that suddenly gripped her, but Tony lifted his finger to his lips to warn her to be quiet.

Bending over and picking up a large brass bookend out of the rubble on the floor, he raised it high into the air and cautiously made his way toward the door. When he passed the only chair left standing, he reached down and picked up the parasol still lying there by the cloth end and carried it like a club in his other hand. Without causing a sound, he stepped over the debris, carefully choosing the places he laid his feet, until he finally had reached the door. Every muscle in him tensed and prepared to do battle against whoever was out there. He hoped the element of surprise would work to his advantage. Above all else, he had to protect Catherine.

As he pressed his back against the door and took a deep steadying breath, he could sense that someone was on just the other side of the wall listening. Tightening his grip on the bookend and the parasol, he lunged out into the hallway ready to fight.

"What the . . ." Cole cried out when Tony suddenly flung himself through the door with a bookend and a pink parasol raised high in the air ready to come down on him. Patricia was so startled, she screamed.

"Cole, Patricia." He breathed out with relief when he realized who they were. As the tension drained out of him, he fell against the wall for support. His knees felt suddenly weak. The bookend clattered to the floor as the parasol fell limp and hung loosely from his hand. "I didn't know it was you."

"I should hope not," Cole stated as he tried to get his heart rate back under control. Tony had frightened a full year's growth out of him. "Is this the sort of reception you give your friends when all they have come to do is celebrate your having moved into your new office?"

Catherine came to stand in the doorway, looking just as relieved as Tony did. "I'm so glad you are here."

"That's much better than the greeting Tony tried to give us," Cole commented and looked curiously back at Tony. Then noticing the parasol still hanging loosely in his hand, Cole stared pointedly at it and grinned. "Lovely color. Quite becoming. Goes well with your complexion. Especially the shade it was just a moment ago. Petal pink, don't they call it?"

Patricia laughed when Tony quickly dropped the parasol

to the floor. "Yes, quite becoming. You and Catherine do have a lot in common. You both like the color pink and you both look good with it."

"But I think blue would go better with your outfit," Cole put in when he discovered Tony was still too unsteady to reply. Still unaware of the seriousness of the situation, he went on in a light manner, "If you're so afraid of intruders, why do you leave the back door unlocked?"

Still grinning, Cole bent over and picked up the bookend and parasol for Tony. When he straightened up, he heard Andrew and Faye coming down the hall and turned to greet them. Knowing he looked just as ridiculous with the parasol as Tony had, he quickly handed it to Catherine. That was when he got his first glimpse of the destruction in Tony's office. His amused grin fell into an expression of deep concern. "What on earth happened here?"

"I had a visitor," Tony commented simply and followed everyone into the room. "While I was showing Catherine the upstairs, someone slipped in and did all this."

"And you didn't even hear them?" Cole asked, perplexed.

"I heard noises, loud noises, but I figured it was one of you down here pulling some sort of joke so I didn't hurry back."

"Some joke," Andrew muttered as he set down the cake he carried on the desk and walked over to stick his head through the window in order to see if there was any sort of clue out there that would let them know just who did this. There was nothing but broken glass.

"When we did come back down and he heard us talking in the hallway, he immediately busted out the window with that chair and hightailed it out of here."

"Did you get a glimpse of him?" Cole asked as he took the large basket Faye held and cleared a place for it on the desk next to the cake.

"No, I didn't. I was still down the hall a ways when I heard the glass break. By the time I got to the window, he was gone. Did any of you happen to see anyone suspicious-looking when you came up? Perhaps a man running?"

"No, we came up around on the other side," Cole muttered. He wished they had accidentally run into the guy.

He would love to have gotten his hands on him. "How about you two?" He turned to ask Andrew and Faye. "You were still in the carriage gathering up everything; did you see anyone suspicious?"

"I really wasn't paying attention," Andrew admitted and frowned.

"The only man I really noticed was a young man dressed in a brown pin-squared suit walking down the street. He had a brisk pace, but I'd hardly think he was running from something like this," Faye said with an apologetic shrug.

"What did he look like?" Cole and Tony asked at the same time.

"He hardly looked the type to do anything like this," she pointed out. "But like I said, he appeared to be young. But then I didn't really get a look at his face. He was walking away from me. I guess it was the way he walked that gave me the impression he was young. He had on a derby, but of what I could see of his hair, it was brown and cut short. Very upright looking."

"How tall was he?" Cole wanted to know. So far the description fit half the men in Johnstown, even himself since he had taken the time to go by the barber's last week and have his hair trimmed back.

"Not very tall. I doubt if he was as tall as Andrew." She placed her hand on her chin and thought a moment before she added, "No, he was definitely not as tall as Andrew."

"I'm six foot," Andrew offered.

"Then he was possibly about five-nine or five-ten," she deduced. "But, seriously, he was probably just a business-man taking the back lane home. I didn't see anyone that looked in any way suspicious."

"I wonder what this person was looking for," Cole questioned aloud as his gaze swept the room again. "You didn't have any money here, did you?"

"Not a cent," Tony replied.

"Anything missing?"

"I'm not sure," Tony said as he looked around at the mess.

"You don't think this was a warning of some sort, do you?" Andrew wanted to know. "Those notes did say there

298

would be trouble if we persisted and we have persisted. Maybe this was just the man's way of reminding us."

"That's always a possibility," Cole answered thoughtfully, then threw his hands up. "I really don't know what to think."

"Have you told the police yet?" Andrew asked.

"Catherine and I were just about to go do that when we heard Cole out in the hall."

"Why don't you go do that right now," Patricia suggested. "The sooner they see the place and make their reports, the sooner we can get all this cleaned up."

"I'll look around and find something to board up that window," Cole volunteered. "Andrew, why don't you go with Tony instead of Catherine. The man could still be out there. He would be less likely to do anything if there were two men to contend with."

"We'll be right back," Andrew told them as he nudged Tony through the door.

"And do me a favor," Cole shouted out so that they could hear him down the hall. "Lock that door on your way out."

It was after ten o'clock before the office was clean and everything back in order. Feeling that they had definitely earned it, Cole broke out the now warm champagne while Patricia cut the cake into huge slices and they had their celebration after all.

When they finally finished, they left the office building as a group. No one truly believed the man was still out there since the police had promised to keep a close watch on the building, but they decided it was best to be cautious. They stayed together as they let the women off one by one until it was just Cole, Tony, and Andrew left. With the women gone, they would be able to discuss what had happened more thoroughly without having to worry that they might frighten them. They decided to go over to Cole's house and talk.

When they turned the corner just two blocks from his house, they noticed a dull amber glow flickering in the darkness just ahead and large pillars of smoke billowing high into the blackened sky. Fire wagons blocked the street and a loud din of noise could be heard. As they got closer, they came to realize it was Cole's house that was on fire. All three of them jumped out of their carriages and started running even before they had come to a complete halt.

"What happened?" Cole demanded as he ran up to where several men were holding one of the three hoses on his house.

"Stay back, sir. We're a little too busy right now to talk," one of the men said as he kept his eyes trained on where the water was targeted.

"But this is my house, I want to know what happened," he shouted.

"All I know is we got a call telling us there was smoke coming out of this house but by the time we got here there was a lot more than smoke. It sure caught on quick. Could have been arson. We won't know that until we can get in there and see. Now if you'll just step back, we'll finish getting that fire out."

Tony pulled Cole back out of the way and stood beside him watching as the men worked to put the last of the flames out.

"It looks like most of the damage is being done over there on the right side," Andrew commented when he came to join them.

Except for the smoke curling out of a broken window on the bottom floor of the left side, that part of the house did not seem to be involved. Cole watched in horror as they slowly managed to put the flames out. Even after there were very few flames left, there was still enough light coming from the lanterns scattered around the yard for him to see the blackness of the rooms inside and the huge charred streaks above the windows where smoke had stained the walls. Not waiting any longer, he ran up to the front porch and crawled through one of the windows the firemen had broken out when they needed a way to get water inside. Tony and Andrew were right behind him, careful not to touch the areas where spattering embers still glowed red.

Paul Taylor from next door followed them in with one of the lanterns so that they could better survey the damage. Two firemen followed just moments later with another lantern.

"Don't touch anything until we have had a chance to

investigate," one of the firemen cautioned as he lifted his lantern high and peered questioningly at the mess. The only fire damage to this room was a large black hole that had burned through the far wall but smoke had covered the room and the ceiling in a thick layer of soot and water puddled the floor. Peering into the hole, they could see straight into the dining room, which was a total loss.

The two firemen stepped through the large hole and carefully picked their way through the smoldering remains of the room. Tony and Cole walked around to the doorway and peered in.

"Something's wrong here," the older one said as he looked through another burned-out wall then up at the burned-out ceiling. "It looks as if both these rooms went up at almost the same time. You got any enemies, Mr. Gifford?"

"I can think of only one," he muttered through clenched teeth.

"And who is that?"

"I don't know who he is yet. But I'm going to do everything I can to find out."

"Well, we'll do what we can to help you," the fireman said, nodding. "Yep, this certainly smells of arson. Look at this table. The top is completely burned but the insides of the legs are not. That looks definitely like someone poured kerosene or something over the top and lit it."

"Cole, come here," they heard Andrew call out from another room.

"Where? Where are you?" he shouted back.

"In your study. Come look at this."

The firemen followed Tony and Cole down the hall and into a room further back. The room had been searched but not as thoroughly as Tony's office had been. This time, though, there was a strong odor of kerosene in the room.

"You're lucky this room didn't go," the oldest fireman said in earnest. He watched curiously as Cole ran over to his desk and yanked on the top drawer so hard that it came out and fell to the floor.

"Damn!" he cried out once he had searched through the papers that had fallen from the drawer. "The petition.

It's gone."

"What?" Tony and Andrew cried out together. They knelt down and began searching through the papers themselves.

"It's no use. It's gone. That drawer was locked but it just now pulled out with no problem. It's been jimmied. That's why the rest of this room was not ransacked. Whoever did this found what he wanted in my desk. He was after the petition."

"That's why he searched my office," Tony said with quick realization. "He thought I might have it down there."

With a feeling of total defeat, Cole leaned heavily against the desk, his head bowed. "We are going to have to start all over."

Andrew reached over and placed a supportive arm around his friend. "But this time we won't have to work to try to convince them. We will just have to explain about the theft and ask them to sign again. It shouldn't be as hard."

Cole raised his hands to rub his tired face. When he did, he caught the scent of kerosene on them and felt a rage surge through him more powerful than he had ever known before. "But we only have three months until July. We had almost five hundred signatures. Do you honestly believe we can get them all back by then? After all, the appointments have already been made."

"All we can do now is try," Tony said, hoping to sound enthusiastic.

The firemen did not ask about the petition. They both already knew about it. One of them had signed it just the week before when a nun had approached him after mass. Shaking their heads, the oldest one went on to say, "I guess he set the fire to cover up his theft. You really need to thank whoever the boy was that called in this fire. It was his prompt action that saved most of your house. You really are very lucky."

"Who was it? I would like to give him a reward," Cole said earnestly.

"Don't know myself. I didn't talk to him. But Joshua Tillery would know. He took the call. The only reason I know it was a boy was that I remember how afraid Joshua

302

was that it was going to be another one of those prank calls we've been getting lately. Those are nothing but a waste of time and money," he muttered.

Later, Cole learned that the boy who had made the call was his next-door neighbor's oldest son, Joe. He had come home late from playing at a friend's house down the street when he thought he smelled smoke. It didn't take him long to discover the smoke was seeping out of Cole's house. Remembering that Mr. Cohen across the street had just had a telephone installed, he rushed over and made the call. The fire department had gotten there in a matter of minutes. If it hadn't been for the neighbor's new telephone, Joe would have had to run two and a half blocks to the nearest fire bell. Cole decided it was time he got himself a telephone. He might consider getting Joe's family one too as a means of a reward.

The next morning, several fire examiners and a law officer worked together to sift through the charred remains of the damaged area and also the other rooms that had been tampered with, looking for clues. To Cole's frustration, they found nothing more than an empty kerosene jug in the neighbor's yard, which must have been dropped in the arsonist's haste to get away and could have belonged to anybody. By the time they finished investigating, they were able to determine that the fire started at the back door and spread quickly to the two rooms that received the most damage and the rooms right above with the help of the kerosene. Two other downstairs rooms had been doused, but luckily had not yet caught fire when the fire wagons arrived. Otherwise the house would have received far worse damage.

That afternoon, Tony came by with the foreman of the crew that still was working on his building. After a long look around, the man agreed to put aside the work on Tony's building in order to repair Cole's house. With his full crew on it, he felt that they would have it back as good as new in less than a month. The only problem he could see would be matching the outside brick, several having cracked from the heat. Cole's house was an odd color of brown and he might have a hard time finding brick that same color. Meanwhile, Cole worked to secure the house enough so he could still live in it even while the work was going on. He also decided to purchase a small handgun that he could slip easily into his pocket or his boot.

"Can you believe this weather?" Captain Reid grumbled as he struck a match on the rough surface of the rock fireplace in the main parlor of the clubhouse. Placing the match to the tobacco packed loosely in his new pipe, he drew hard until the bowl glowed bright red. "Here it is April already and instead of bright sunshine and any evidence of spring, we suffer the heaviest snowfall of the year. If it doesn't hurry up and melt, you are never going to be able to get that plumbing in by the time everyone starts arriving this summer. You are already running behind schedule from all that rain and snow we had last month."

"You don't want that snow to melt too quickly," James pointed out as he sat down cross-legged on the thick braided rug in front of the fireplace with a hot mug of spiced tea. When he saw the captain's curious expression, he explained. "There's a lot of snow out there in those mountains. If it melts too fast the lake is going to fill up faster than the spillway can drain it off. The lake is already up. And since we don't have any other way to drain the lake and keep the water level stable, that lake will probably overflow and you will be left with a lot of pier and boathouse damage to repair."

"And I suppose you are going to bring up those drainage pipes of yours again," the captain replied sharply. "Even if the lake fills to the brim, the pier damage won't be so bad. Those piers have been under water before and held up just fine."

"Have they? How often?" James wanted to know. Was flooding a common occurrence?

Realizing what James was thinking, the captain refused to be a part of it. "It's none of your concern. The piers are my problem. You just worry about getting that plumbing finished before the guests start to arrive. And a few of them will start coming as early as Memorial Day so you had better get it moving just as soon as the snow does melt and the ground is dry enough to dig. I'd hate for you to lose your job because you weren't able to complete the work on time."

James did not believe a word of it. He had a feeling the captain would not hate to see him lose his job at all. Ever since the man had discovered the plans he had drawn to rework the dam last December, the captain had barely been tolerant of him. If he knew that he had already redrawn the plans with hopes of approaching the president of the club when he visited this next summer, the captain would probably have his head. Sipping cautiously on the hot spicy brew, James hoped the man never discovered his hiding place. It was bad enough that Cody had.

Chapter Twenty

"I don't understand. You were more than willing to sign just a month ago," Cole said, trying not to let his frustration lead to anger. "You and your wife both were."

"That was then. This is now," Micah Mitchener said and looked down at the invoices he had been going through when Cole and Tony had dropped by. His eyes were unable to meet Cole's. "I just don't feel as strongly about signing that thing as I did then."

"Why? The problem still exists. That dam didn't repair itself and those club members certainly haven't done anything toward making the thing any safer," Cole went on to say. "Why is it that you don't feel the same about signing this petition now?"

"I have my reasons," Micah said solemnly, still not looking up to face Cole who loomed over his desk like an angry shadow. "I can't is all."

"You can't? Or won't?" Tony asked, determined to get to the true bottom of this. He had tried to let Cole handle this one since he had blown his own temper with the last one, but found he was unable to stand quietly back and stay out of it. This was getting to be more than he could take.

"I can't," Micah restated softly. He pressed his lips together a moment and glanced around as if trying to decide whether or not to tell them any more than he already had.

"Why can't you?" Cole asked, also bringing his voice down. He sensed that this man was finally going to shed some light on why so many of the people who had signed before were refusing to sign now.

"I got a letter a few days ago warning me not to," Micah finally admitted, glancing only briefly up at Cole. "You see, I had to borrow money against this place last fall and the letter said that my business here might be foreclosed on if my name shows up on that petition again. It claimed that the bank could call in my loan and demand immediate repayment at any time. I don't have that kind of money. That's why I had to borrow money in the first place."

"The bank wrote you a letter like that? Why that's practically blackmail! Which bank was it?"

"It didn't come from the bank necessarily. The letter had no return address and it wasn't signed. It came in the mail as a friendly warning."

"Was it written in bold but impeccably neat hand print?" Cole asked, already putting a connection together.

"No, it was typewritten," Micah told him. "And I don't have any way of knowing if whoever sent it has the power to make the bank call in my loan or not, but I can't take that chance. You understand, don't you?"

"Yes," Cole said, breathing a reluctant sigh of agreement. "And I can't blame you. Sometimes threats are hard to ignore." His voice was calm, but his jaw flexed spasmodically as he tried to control the rage that continued to build inside him. It was a rage directed toward an unknown enemy and because the man was still unknown to him there was no real outlet for this rage. It burned deep within him and it took all the self-control he had not to let it blacken his very soul.

"So that's it," Tony remarked, relieved to know that the problem was not that everyone had simply lost interest or no longer believed. "Someone's going around behind our backs delving into everyone's problems or looking for their weaknesses and taking advantage of them. And I'll just bet it is our own Mr. Anonymous Firestarter. And since he now has the full list of names in his possession, he can work to head off a lot of these people before we can even get to them."

Cole's hands contracted into tight fists as he thought about that. Whoever was working against him was certainly going to a lot of trouble in order to do so. He was beginning to wonder if it wasn't a personal vendetta of some sort. Or else it was someone who had something major to lose if the petition was to succeed. But who? Those men at the club could certainly afford the cost of repairing the dam. It hardly seemed it could be so major a loss to them. Who then?

"Thanks for being straight with us, Micah. We appreciate your honesty," Cole said as he folded up the two petitions, handed one to Tony, and placed the other he was to keep inside his inner coat pocket. Just to eliminate their being left empty-handed again should someone try to steal the petition again, they intended to have a back-up copy this time.

One copy was being kept in one of the empty offices in Tony's building and the other was alternately being kept with Patricia or Faye at the women's insistence. They believed most men would not expect them to leave the petition in the safekeeping of a woman and felt their homes would be the last place the culprit would look for it. Yet they did not feel it would be safe with Catherine. Not with Clayton in the same house and still so clearly against what they were doing, even though Patricia did feel he was starting to mellow. They had to be very cautious. That's why they also had a few fake petitions hidden around for their anonymous friend to find should he go looking again. This time they were not going to be such easy prey.

When Cole stopped by Patricia's that evening to leave her one of the copies of the petition, she wanted to know how the day had gone. He followed her upstairs to watch her as she placed the petition at the bottom of a dresser drawer beneath several layers of her delicate undergarments.

"The day went terribly," he said in response to her question. "We talked to at least twenty people who'd signed the first petition and only seven were willing to sign again," he said dejectedly.

"Seven?" Patricia asked. Taking the petition back out, she unfolded it and looked down at the list of names. In the three weeks they had worked to get the new petitions to where the first one had been, they had only managed to get a little over a hundred of the original signatures back. "I just don't understand it. Why are they changing their minds?"

"It's not that so many of them are changing their minds, not exactly. Their minds are being changed for them. I suspect most of them have been blackmailed in some way or another and are now afraid to sign."

"Why would you think that? Just because the doctors were offered all that money if they wouldn't sign? Do you think everyone is getting offered money not to sign? That's ridiculous. Blackmail indeed," Patricia said with a disbelieving twist of her face, not fully understanding. "Where'd you get such a silly idea?"

"From Micah Mitchener at the feed store," he said, then told her about the letter Micah had received and how effectively the threat had worked. "We can only assume there were other such letters and other such threats."

Patricia could see that Cole's anger continued to eat away at him and it worried her. She wished there was something she could say that would ease it, but then she too was angry. It was so frustrating to know someone was out there sabotaging their efforts and not even know who he was. She had finally reached the point where she suspected almost everyone. If someone gave her even a sideways glance, she'd find herself wondering if he was the culprit.

Later that night after Cole had left her bed and she lay staring up at the darkened ceiling, her mind continued to worry with the problem. It was the fact that the man had known Micah Mitchener owed money to the bank that seemed to bother her the most. She could remember seeing Micah at the First National Bank before. Was that the bank he owed money to?

Slowly, she came to suspect William. He had clearly shown opposition to what they were doing when he had first learned about their plan to force the club members to repair the dam, but she had heard very little from him concerning the matter since. But then she heard very little from him at all these days. She knew he still followed her at times, always from a distance. Yet he never tried to make contact with her.

It was as if he tried to be content with admiring her from afar. Now she wondered about that. Maybe he had simply been keeping up with the comings and goings of their petition instead. It was a possibility and one she would look into that very next day.

The following morning, Patricia chose to take the brewery's deposit to the bank herself despite the heavy patches of snow that still lined the sidewalks and the cold gusts of wind that had a tendency to catch a lady's skirt and send chills right through to her bones. She wanted to have a little talk with William. She had to see if any of her suspicions were true and she did not want to wait any longer.

Spotting William seated behind his desk, deep in thought with his head bent over his desktop, she marched right into his office, only nodding briefly at the secretary who looked curiously at her when she passed. Without a word of greeting, Patricia closed the door behind her and waited for him to realize she was there. He looked up with a start when he heard his own door close without having requested it.

His eyes lit up with instant delight when he recognized her and he quickly rose from his chair to greet her. "Patricia, what are you doing here?" He glanced over at the closed door then back at her and a look of hope crossed his face.

"I want to talk to you," she said simply.

"Great," he responded happily and gestured to the up-holstered chairs facing his desk. "Please sit down." He had yet to notice the anger in her eyes.

"I'd rather stand," she told him sharply.

It was her tone that let him know she was not there to socialize or make up with him. His expression fell and suddenly he looked pale and gaunt, his facial features sunken in around his high cheekbones. He clearly was not eating right. He looked ill.

"You can sit, though, if you want," she said. "It is your office."

"No, I'll stand," he told her, then came around his desk to be closer to her. There was still a trace of eager hope glimmering deep in his eyes.

Patricia looked down at the many papers scattered across

his desk. Picking up one of the handwritten messages, she held it up and studied it carefully. Although the letters were not boldly written, they were undeniably neat. She was unable to determine though if it was the same hand that had written those notes, but that didn't matter. He could have tried to disguise his handwriting. Tossing the paper back down, she brought her gaze up to stare pointedly at him with such impact that he stepped back and leaned against the desk for support.

"I want to know why it is you're doing what you are doing," she said, hoping to trap him by acting like she was already certain of his guilt.

"I'm vice president. I have to go over the loans," he said and looked curiously down at the paper she had just read. It was an in-house memo he was about to send over to Sam Neely. It said nothing that should concern her.

"You know very well I'm not referring to what's on your desk," she said impatiently and crossed her arms, an action that brought his attention to her breasts. The red and brown woolen dress she had chosen to wear that morning had a fashionably low-scooped neckline that allowed the upper swell of her breasts to be seen and the pressure she had just put below them made them even more noticeable. Realizing where his gaze had wandered, she uncrossed her arms and placed her hands on her hips instead. "William, you know exactly what I'm talking about."

"Which is?" he prompted her, his eyes widening with concern.

There was just enough guilt hidden in his forced look of innocence to give Patricia the confidence to state her accusations. "I know you are the one who wrote those notes. I also know that you have been going around blackmailing people into not signing our petition, using bank foreclosures as a threat among other things. And you are doing such a thorough job of reaching everyone that I suspect you have the original petition in your possession and are just going down the list of names seeing who you can manipulate." She studied his face for reaction, but he showed nothing. He continued his wide-eyed expression of innocence but now

312

peppered it with a show of mild outrage.

"What on earth are you talking about?" he asked and threw his shoulders back as if he had just been falsely accused and was deeply insulted.

It was the flaring of his nose that gave him away that time. Patricia knew him well enough to realize that when he had been caught at something deceitful or was lying, his nose flared out at the back. Now she was certain of his guilt and so furious with him that it took all her control not to attack him with all her might and slap him until he was left silly.

"Damn you, William," she hissed. This time his eyes widened with true surprise.

He had never heard such language from her. He had never seen her so angry.

"Damn you for all you've done. I want that original petition back and I want it back today or I'm going straight to the authorities with this."

"And tell them what?" he asked with a sly lip-curling smile. Slowly he dropped his innocent facade as his arrogance took over. "All you have are a few far-fetched suspicions that no law officer is going to listen to. They will want proof. There is no way you have any solid proof of what you are trying to claim."

"Oh, yes I do," she lied, boldly staring him in the eye, hoping he would not be able to tell she was lying.

"No, Patricia, you don't. I've been too careful. No one has seen me do anything out of hand and I've left nothing behind that can link me to either the letters or the fire."

"So you admit you set the fire?" she asked, stiffening.

"I admit nothing, sweetheart. And you can forget about getting the petition back. Such a thing would be too dangerous to have around. It no longer exists. And all the threats you can think of won't help you get it back. I couldn't return it if I wanted to."

"Then at least quit blackmailing everyone into not signing the new petition. You can do that," she demanded, her hands clenched at her side. She no longer had an urge to slap him silly. She wanted to slug him one, right across the jaw. But knowing they were in full sight of everyone in the bank,

313

she refrained.

William's features softened for a moment. "What if I did agree to that? What if I agreed to retract the many," he paused for just the right word, *"suggestions* I've made to so many people whose names were found on the petition. What would be my reward? Would you be willing to come back to me?"

"What?" Her forehead furrowed until her delicate brows nearly met and her mouth gaped open with disbelief. He couldn't have said what she thought he just said. Even William wouldn't have such gall.

Gently, he reached out and caressed her face with the soft curve of his hand while he explained. "If you would just promise to come back to me and quit parading around town with that pompous Cole Gifford, I would not only start to encourage everyone to sign that blasted petition of his, I would sign the thing myself. That means my risking several *good* accounts. Our very biggest depositor happens to be a club member. But I'd do it, and would, in fact, start sending letters out right away encouraging everyone I know to support Cole's cause. Cole would be insured a success. All you would have to do is break your ridiculous agreement with that man and return to me. I don't even ask that you make your promise to marry me right away. We can wait a few months before we announce that we plan to be married."

"How very big of you," she said sarcastically, scarcely believing even he could make such a preposterous proposal.

"It would give you enough time to see that I made good on my part of the bargain. Just think of it. You have the power to stop all the harassment, all the blackmailing, all the problems Cole and his friends have suffered since the onset of their project. You hold the key to their success. If you truly believe in what they are doing, you should seriously consider what I'm offering."

Patricia reached for a nearby chair and sank into its soft depths. She stared up at him dumbfounded. She didn't know what to think. He had indeed given her a way to help save the petition and be an intricate part of getting that dam repaired. She felt as if the safety of the entire town lay in her hands now. What if she only pretended to break up with Cole? What if she also pretended she would marry William? He himself had promised her a few months before announcing the engagement. That was all the time they needed. In a few months, Cole would be presenting the case in Washington.

Realizing she had honestly considered what he had suggested, he knelt at her feet and looked up at her with huge doe eyes. "Please, Patricia. All you have to do is come back to me, promise to marry me, and I'll guarantee Cole's petition will be a success. Not only will he be able to get all those original signatures back, I have the power to get him hundreds more."

"By blackmailing people?"

"By finding their weaknesses and working on them." He nodded. His eyes pleaded with her to understand and say yes. "And those that can't be blackmailed, as you so crudely like to put it, can be bought. I have the means to buy lots of signatures." He continued to stare hopefully into her bold green eyes. "Just think about it. You alone have the power to make or break that petition. I am giving you that power. And once we are married, you can have your pick of the houses in Johnstown. You will be able to have anything you want. There's nothing I can't give you."

She stared back down at him with a strong sense of pure horror slowly seeping into her, gripping her by her very bones. "William, there is something terribly wrong with you," she finally said. "You can't honestly want me to come back to you and marry you if I don't love you."

"But you do love me," he told her emphatically. "You just don't realize it. You've fought your love for me for so long that you don't even know it exists and has for quite some time."

She could tell that he honestly believed what he was saying. "I know what love is, William. I loved Robert. And I love Cole. But I've never loved you. In fact, I don't even respect you anymore. And I can't compromise my feelings, not even for the safety of Johnstown."

"But the petition—" He started to remind her as he stood up. Anger once again filled his dark eyes.

"We will succeed in spite of you. At least now we know who our enemy is and I for one am no longer afraid," she said defiantly and rose to her feet. Turning on her heel, she headed for the door, then stopped and spun back around. "Is Father in this with you?"

William debated on whether or not to answer that. Something in him wanted her to be suspicious of her father, but in the end he answered honestly, "No, other than to innocently supply me with needed information, he has had no part in any of it. It is all my own ingenious doing. He's just as curious as you are about who stole the petition and set Cole's house on fire."

"Thank heavens," she sighed out with relief and felt some of the tension inside her release. "I'd hate to think that my own father could stoop so low." Having said that, she turned back around and reached for the door.

"You are making a big mistake, Patricia. Cole will never be able to get enough signatures as long as I'm working against him. Without my help, his petition is doomed. And you and you alone will be responsible for its failure. Can you honestly live with that hanging over your pretty little head?"

"Quite nicely, thank you," she said bitterly.

"What if one of your friends ends up getting hurt? What if it's your precious Cole?"

"Cole can take care of himself," she spat, then yanked the door open and marched out of his office. Her legs felt weak, but she never showed how deeply he had affected her. She managed to walk briskly toward the main door and never once faltered in her steps.

"When you change your mind, I'll be waiting," he called out after her in a voice loud enough that she would be certain to hear him and laughed sardonically at the mere thought of it. When a few of the people in the bank looked curiously at Patricia then at him, he winked to them as if it had merely been a lovers' spat. He spent the rest of the day with a huge smile on his face. He knew she would come back to him. He knew her weakness too well. It was just a matter of time.

*　　*　　*

316

Patricia went straight to the police and told them exactly what William was up to but, just as William had warned her, she got absolutely no action. They wanted tangible proof. Without it, they claimed their hands were tied. It would just be her word against his. And knowing William and Patricia's circumstances, they could not be sure she wasn't seeking reprisal for some lovers' tiff they were having.

Until she could get her hands on tangible evidence, she could not expect any help from the police. They claimed to be shorthanded as it was. Because of some monetary cutbacks forced on them by the city council, they did not have the man power to check out every claim that came across the station's desk. By the time she left the police station, she was seething with frustration. There was no way she could return to work. She would not be able to concentrate on anything. Instead, she went to find Tony. She knew she could not get inside Cambria Iron without a special permit or she would have gone straight to Cole.

After she told Tony all that had happened, they spent the afternoon visiting some of the people they suspected were being blackmailed but were unable to get them to admit to anything. Even Micah Mitchener, who had previously admitted he had received a letter, refused to tell anyone else about it. He could not risk it. His business was all he had.

By the time Cole came home from work, they knew what they were up against—a brick wall. No one wanted to chance sticking a neck out, especially for a cause they claimed they never truly believed in in the first place. William had already made an example of one young man. Just days after Walter Wade had signed the new petition, his tobacco store was foreclosed on. It didn't take long for news of that to spread through the local grapevine and put fear in the hearts of everyone involved.

Cole's intense frustration gave way to an explosion of fury when they told him about William. He listened to what they had to say, but the more he heard, the more angry he became. Finally, he reached his limit and charged out of his house without so much as a word to Tony or Patricia about where he was headed. But knowing he would try to find

William, they hurried out of the house just moments behind him. They had no choice but to leave the doors unlocked. Cole had taken the key with him.

Since the bank was closer, Patricia suggested they try there first. Sure enough, as they rounded the corner on Main Street, they saw Cole's horse tethered to one of the iron rods outside. Cole stood in front of the building pounding on the door so hard Patricia worried that the glass might break. If it did, William wouldn't hesitate having Cole arrested for breaking and entering. Before he was through, Cole could be wanted for bank robbery.

"Cole, wait," Tony called out even before he was able to bring his carriage to a stop.

Cole turned around to stare at them. "What are you two doing here?"

"We thought you might want our support," Tony told him as he quickly swung down from his carriage. "You shouldn't speak to him alone. No telling what he might claim about you. With us there, you will have witnesses."

"Please, Cole, if you must talk with him, let us be with you," Patricia pleaded as she made her way around the rear of the carriage. "Tony's right. William's the type to conjure up some wild story about you. And if you don't have witnesses to deny such charges, he just might have everyone believing him."

"Let them," Cole said as he cupped his hands and peered into the window. "It will be my word against his. Just like it is now his word against Patricia's."

"Still, we want to be with you," Tony explained as he looked in the window too. All he could see was his own worried reflection.

"There's a light on in there off to the right," Cole said with a frown. "I'll bet he's in there hiding. He knows it's me and isn't about to come out until he sees me leave. I should have figured on that."

"So leave," Tony suggested. "We can catch him when he goes home. There's only two ways for him to enter his house. With both of us there waiting on him, we can cover both entrances."

318

Reluctantly, Cole agreed to let Tony go with him, but he refused to allow Patricia to. He ordered her home.

"I won't go home. I have just as much at stake here as either of you do," she said firmly.

"Did the man try to burn your house down? Did he smash up your office? Did he send you threatening notes?"

"Well, no, but—" she started to reply.

"The worst he has done to you is ask you to marry him. I'll admit, that had to be a little distasteful, but nothing like what he's done to us. No, we have a score to settle with this fellow. I don't want you there and that's final. Go home. Or at least go back to my house and wait for us there."

Patricia could sense that his mind was made up. It was pointless to argue any further. Cole did not want her there. Reluctantly, she agreed to take Tony's carriage and go back to Cole's house and wait for them.

Cole and Tony proceeded to William's house riding double on Cole's horse. Afraid William might recognize the tall black steed, they left the animal in an empty lot almost two blocks away and walked the last of the way to William's. It was just getting dark when they slipped into the side gate and entered his yard.

"I'll take the side door," Cole said as soon as he had looked the house over and decided William would most likely use the door closest to his carriage house. "You find someplace to hide up front where you can watch the main door but not be noticed."

"And if you see him, you will call for me, won't you?" Tony asked, uncertain of what Cole had in mind. He had never seen such anger from Cole before. Nor such cold intent.

"You'll know," Cole promised and turned to find a place to hide where he would have clear view of the door. What Tony didn't know was that he really did not want a witness around, at least not right away.

"Be sure that I do," Tony said in a loud whisper to Cole's retreating back before he turned around and headed for the front yard as told.

It was over an hour before they finally heard a carriage

pull up into the drive beside William's house. Cole could see the vehicle pass but was unable to tell if it was William or not through the brick and ironwork fence. He waited patiently at the far end of the narrow veranda that ran along the side of the house. A large bush growing near the corner hid his presence from the stone path that led from the carriage house to the steps. William would not know Cole was there until he had already stepped up on the porch and that would be too late.

Leaning back into the shadows, Cole listened as William's footsteps hurried along the path toward him. His heart pounded furiously in his chest as the moment he had been waiting for neared. He had not even considered that William would be carrying a gun.

Cole watched the dark form step quietly on to the porch and hurry to the door. It was too dark in the shadow of the porch to make out the man's features, but by the size and build of him, he knew it was William. He waited until he heard the key clank in the lock before he let his presence be known.

"I've been waiting for you," he said in a smooth, low voice. He didn't see the pistol until it was too late to make a move to try and take it. When William turned to face him, he was half in and half out of the shadow with the barrel already pointed right at Cole's heart. A silver ray of moonlight gleamed off the tip, making it appear larger than it was. Cole froze.

"I suspected you might," William replied after his initial gasp of surprise. "As you can see, I came prepared for you."

Cole silently cursed himself for having rushed out of the house without thinking of his own gun. Suddenly, he was very glad he was not alone. Without allowing his anxiety to show, he replied calmly, "How very astute of you."

"True." William laughed, truly enjoying the position he was in. He felt a sudden surge of power and stepped closer to Cole. There was still twelve feet of darkness between them. "Now, is there something you wanted to say to me?"

"The first thing that comes to mind at the moment is that you point that thing in some other direction," Cole said. He was relieved at how casual he had sounded with that remark.

He did not want William to know the alarm he felt at finding himself at the wrong end of a madman's gun.

"But why would I do that when I fully intend to put a hole through your bloody heart?" William asked cheerfully. Then he motioned with the gun, "Won't you oblige me by stepping inside so that it will look like you broke in on me in a rage of jealousy? Then all I'll have to do is tell the authorities how you tried to attack me in my own home. Self defense, I'll tell them. And since my secretary, Markeleta, was there when you tried to bust into the bank, and a half dozen people saw Patricia pay a reconciliatory visit to me this afternoon, no one is going to doubt me. They'll think you heard about Patricia's visit and went into a jealous fit and came charging into my home to kill me. Only I got you first. No one will be the wiser."

"I will," Tony's voice sounded from the darkness behind William. He had circled the house and come around to the back.

"Who's there?" William cried out as he spun to look. Unable to see anything but bushes, trees, and shadows, he cried out again. "Who's out there?"

"Did you think Cole would be foolish enough to come alone?" Tony asked, still not revealing just where he was.

Cole sensed that he was in the bushes just around the corner, safe from William's aim, but close enough to cause William some true concern.

"Pays to have good friends," Cole said. The breath he had been holding silently slipped away from him. "Now if you would kindly put down that gun, I will say what I came here to say."

"But if I put down the gun, you are liable to hurt me," William pointed out, fear clearly evident in his voice.

"And with just cause, don't you think?" Cole asked, waiting for him to put down the pistol. His fingers flexed. He was itching to get his hands on William.

"Hey, Cole, why don't you just set his house on fire instead?" Tony called out. "I'll keep my pistol trained on him while you step inside and light the curtains." Oh how he wished he did have a pistol as he said that.

321

"No, I think we'll start out just like he did. With a clear warning. Only I'll deliver mine in person. I'm not the cowardly type or I'd wait and slip him a note," Cole said pointedly. "The warning is this. Stop blackmailing people out of signing our petition or you could be the one that ends up getting hurt because I fully intend to fight back and I can fight just as dirty as you can."

"Blackmail? Me? What are you talking about? Where'd you ever get a foolish idea like that?"

"I don't play games, William," Cole grated out. "You know damn well where I got that idea. Patricia doesn't keep any secrets from me. She never has."

"Patricia? Patricia said I was blackmailing people? Why would she say something like that? Where did she get such an idea? What's going on here?"

"Okay, play your games. But don't expect me to fall for any of that. Just heed my warning."

"Why would Patricia say something like that about me?" he continued. "Just today she was in my office trying to convince me to be friends with her again. She even asked me to take her to dinner. That's it. She's mad at me for turning her down. This is her way of getting even with me."

"She came to you wanting you to take her out?" Cole asked, definitely needing that fact verified.

"Yes, this afternoon. She tried to apologize for all that she had done to me, but I was still too angry to listen. I told her she had fooled away her last chance with me. I knew she was hurt and angry when she left, but I had no idea she was upset enough to stoop to telling such lies about me just to get even."

"In other words, she came to you wanting you to take her back?" Cole asked, again wanting clear verification.

"Yes, but I refused. You don't have to worry about me ever taking her back. She hurt me one too many times. I wouldn't take her back if she came begging," he said a bit too proudly.

Suddenly Cole burst out laughing. With no further word to William, he lifted his leg over the banister and slipped down to the ground, landing with a crunch on a small plant of some sort. He continued the deep laughter as he slowly walked away from the house and headed for the gate, fully aware that William had never laid down the pistol.

Cole was laughing far too hard to hear William's next words of warning but Tony heard them clearly from where he was standing. The menacing tone of William's voice sent chills right to the very core of him. At that moment, he would swear the man was insane.

"You will be sorry you ever laughed at me, Cole Gifford," he hissed and raised the pistol level with his eye, pointed directly at Cole's broad back. "Damn sorry."

Chapter Twenty-one

Tony stepped forward but was too far away to do anything to prevent it. He watched in absolute horror, transfixed, as William raised the gun and bore down on Cole. He wanted to cry out and warn Cole but was too afraid he might startle William into pulling the trigger and with the gun leveled right at Cole's back, that could prove to be fatal. Instead, he held his breath deep in his chest and waited, a sick feeling squeezing the very life out of him. He had never felt so powerless. His mind screamed out at a deafening level, but his mouth barely formed the words. "Please, dear God, no."

The front corner of the house blocked the direct rays of the light from the curb across the street, casting a dark shadow on much of the yard, but the dull glow that radiated from the streetlight created a gray backdrop against which William's silhouette stood vivid and clear. Tony could plainly see that William had brought his other hand up to reinforce the pistol, his finger still on the trigger, while the barrel continued to bear down on Cole's back. Cole was nearly to the gate now. William stood tense, his legs braced, ready to fire while Cole's deep throaty laughter continued to ring out into the night.

Slowly and soundlessly, Tony sank to the ground to see if he could find a rock or a stick, anything he could throw to make a false target. He needed to distract William without

325

causing him to pull the trigger on Cole. When he neared the ground, his right knee popped in the joint and he looked up, terrified, certain William and half the neighborhood had heard the sound. When he did, he noticed William slowly lower the gun and turn to look in his direction. Would he have time to duck back behind the wall before William could aim and fire? He was only a few feet away.

"Are you still out there?" William called out and leaned forward as if trying to detect a form or a slight movement in the darkness.

Tony remained silent. He was still half hidden by the bushes. Placing his hands on the cold damp earth, he very slowly and carefully began to crawl backward toward the corner where he would be safely out of William's sight and gun range. With his eyes set on William, he inched his way back, gently testing the way with the tip of his boot. His movements did not make a sound. The only noise Tony could even hear at that moment was the heavy pounding of his own heart as the blood rushed through his ears. Another six inches and he would be able to stand up and make a run for the eight-foot brick and wrought-iron fence that surrounded the backyard.

"I asked if you are still out there," William repeated, then fell keenly silent as he listened for a sound that might give away the intruder's presence. "Well, if you are, take a message to that arrogant son of a bitch from me. Tell him that I have just begun to fight and that if he knows what's good for him, or what's good for Patricia, he won't bother to fight back. He'll quit while the quitting is good. You tell him that for me!" William was shouting now. His voice trembled with rage. "Tell him, you hear me?"

Tony didn't reply, but knew that he would definitely relay the message in whole, that is if he got out of there whole himself. Finally he edged his way completely out of the sight of William and the porch. He slipped immediately from the protection the bushes offered, stood, and ran as fast as his feet would go toward the back fence. He amazed himself with his own agility when he reached the tall fence and hurled himself over as if it had been a mere hedgerow. Once he was on the other side, he made a direct line for the lot where they had left the horse. He was not sure which traveled at a higher rate of speed, his feet or his heart. Both were being pushed to the limit.

"You idiot," Tony rasped out once he and Cole were both back on the horse and on their way toward Cole's house at a steady trot. Tony held onto the back of the saddle with wavering strength, "Were you trying to get yourself shot back there? Did you forget all about that damn gun in William's hand?"

"No, I knew he still had the gun," Cole told him over his shoulder. "But I also knew he wouldn't dare shoot me in the back. It would be too hard to explain away. William's far too crafty for that. Shooting me inside his house with no one to dispute his word about what happened was one thing, but outside where people would soon come to see what had happened and with you there to tell them everything, he would have a difficult time keeping himself out of prison. And, my dear friend, prison does not fit well into William's plans for himself."

Tony thought about that. As badly as William had wanted to pull that trigger, he hadn't. "I wish I had known that back then. He scared me half to death with that gun aimed squarely at your back the way it was. I was sure you were as good as dead and there wasn't a thing I could do about it."

"You mean you didn't throw yourself out into the open and demand that he shoot you instead?"

"And get us both shot?"

"Humph, some friend you are," Cole laughed and snapped the reins against his horse's neck, prodding him into a swift gallop.

By the time they reached Cole's house, Tony's heartbeat had settled down and he felt some of the strength returning to his legs. He was proud of himself when he slid off the horse and managed to stand on his feet instead of crumbling to his knees. He had never come so close to witnessing a murder.

He was amazed he had fared so well. Just before they reached the back door, Tony grabbed Cole by the arm. "Oh, by the way, William gave me a message to give to you."

"You stayed around long enough to take messages?" Cole asked and turned to look curiously down at Tony.

"Not exactly," Tony muttered, then went on to tell him about William's half-crazed warning.

"If he thinks he's going to scare me off with more of his threats, he's making a big mistake," Cole said, his face rigid. "I'm not about to knuckle under to him or his threats. We'll just see who gives up the fight first."

"There's something wrong with that guy," Tony commented with a concerned frown.

"That's why we are going to be very careful. There's no telling what he is going to do to try to get even. He's treacherous, but at least now we know who we are dealing against," Cole said as he tried to keep a positive outlook. "But do me a favor, don't tell Patricia about his threat. I don't want to worry her any more than she already is."

Tony nodded his agreement. "What are we going to do next?"

"I'm going to send you home so that I can be alone with Patricia," Cole chuckled and produced a crooked little smile. Then in a more serious tone, he continued. "And I'm going to see if I can't find something on William, something he wouldn't want the world to know about. If I can, I'm going to play the game his way. I'll blackmail him into not causing us any more trouble. If that doesn't work, I just very well may have to beat him to a bloody pulp." Cole reached for the door latch. "That is if I can ever catch him alone without that gun of his."

"So? How did it go?" Patricia asked just as soon as they had stepped inside the door and she was certain it was them. Because she had been alone in an unlocked house, she had armed herself with a heavy fire poker, but put it down when

328

she noticed Cole looking curiously at it. "I let my imagination get the better of me," she admitted with a sheepish shrug.

Tony let Cole answer the question about how it went, not sure how much he intended to let her know and how much he preferred to keep from her. Cole neglected to tell her about the gun or William's intention to force him into the house so that he could shoot him with provocation. He skipped all that entirely and went straight to the part where he warned William to stop his blackmailing. When he told her how William had immediately tried to convince him that he was innocent and how he claimed she had come to the bank in hopes of a reconciliation but had been turned down, Patricia became livid. She ranted and raved and stamped around with such anger that Tony stepped behind Cole and peered over his shoulder, pretending to seek protection.

"Cole, I don't think she saw the purpose of her visit in quite the same way William did," Tony pointed out, grinning when it brought another shriek of anger from her. Cole realized Tony was goading her and that he was being used as a shield. Quickly, he stepped out of the way, but Tony followed him immediately, not about to be left out in the open.

"That horrid man is so exasperating," Patricia screamed, her fist clutched tightly.

"Who? William or Tony?" Cole wanted to know and laughed when Tony narrowed his eyes.

"William, of course. How could he say such things? Did he honestly think you would believe such lies?" she asked, waving her arms for emphasis. "You didn't believe him, did you?"

"Not a word. The man loves to play on people's weaknesses. I think he hoped I was the jealous type and that by planting a seed of doubt in my mind, I wouldn't know who to believe."

"What did you tell him? Did you tell him what an obvious liar he is? You did, didn't you?"

"No."

"No? Why not? You just said you didn't believe a word he had to say," she asked, her face drawn with indignant anger.

"Because I was too busy laughing."

A grin played at her still tightly drawn lips. "You actually laughed? Right to his face?" When he nodded and smiled, she chuckled and threw her arms around him. "I'll bet that made him furious. I'll bet he turned beet red."

"I suppose. I didn't hang around to see. That's when I left."

Tony coughed as he viewed the loving looks the two suddenly exchanged. "Speaking of leaving, I guess I'd better be doing just that. I'll see you in the morning, Cole."

"Bright and early," Cole promised.

"If you make it too early, don't expect me to be very bright," Tony warned with a laugh, then quickly left. He was smart enough to know when three became a crowd. And that room had started to feel very crowded. He sighed with a slight feeling of jealousy as he walked across the yard toward the gate. Although he didn't begrudge them their happiness, he did wish he and Catherine could have a similar caring-type relationship. If only he could find some way to get Franklin Hitt out of her heart for good. Until he did that, there would be little room for him. The thought of that plagued him all the way home and far into the night.

"I thought he would never leave," Cole said with a devilish raise of his eyebrows once the door had shut and they had heard Tony's booted footsteps crossing the front porch. He still held Patricia loosely in his arms, his smile only inches from hers.

"But I thought you liked Tony. I thought he was one of your closest friends," Patricia said as if she could not understand why Cole had wanted him to leave.

"He is one of my closest friends, but not my very closest," he said with a special glimmer lighting his crystal blue eyes. "You are my very closest friend, and sometimes I just like to

330

be alone with you—and get closer still."

"Why is that?" she asked, spurring him on while she looked up through heavily lowered lashes. Her heart already thudded wildly at just the thought of what was about to happen. She loved the intimate moments they shared.

"That's really hard to explain in mere words. Why don't you let me show you," he said softly and drew her near.

"Then show me," she replied in a smoky voice before tilting her head back to receive his kiss. His arms tightened around her and Patricia responded with a delighted moan of ecstasy as his lips took hers in what was a very demanding and passionate kiss. When his tongue dipped into her mouth, teasing the inner edges of her lips, she returned the favor in kind, savoring his tantalizing taste. She loved everything about him, his strength, his gentleness, his honest caring.

United through their ardent kisses, his spicy male fragrance mixed with her sweet floral scent to create a heady, intoxicating aroma of sensuality. She was lost to the many sensations, lost to his love. He became a part of her very soul.

Eagerly, her lips sought other areas, exploring the taste of his cheeks, then his neck, while he ravished kisses on her silken hair. Slowly, his fingers moved to where two silver combs anchored her thick tresses of dark hair at the back of her head, away from her face. Carefully, he eased the combs out of her thick mass of hair and gently ran his fingertips through it until it fell freely forward in a riotous mass and gently caressed her face.

"You are truly the most beautiful woman I've ever known," he stated in a husky voice.

"And you are truly the most imaginative man I have ever met." Although she had come to accept his lavish praises, she found it hard to believe in her own desirous beauty. "Either that, or there's truth to the saying that love is blind." She smiled briefly before lifting her lips to his once again. Her hands roamed freely over the coarse texture of his coat until she could stand it no longer. She had to touch his skin.

331

Gripping the coat by the lapels, she pushed the thick material back and off his shoulders. He cooperated by tugging the coat off his arms then tossing it aside. Next she reached for his shirt and pulled on the shirttail until it came free of his trousers. She heard him moan with pleasure when her hands were finally able to plunge beneath the soft fabric and feel their way along the firm muscles of his back, then around and over the crisp texture of the hairs on his chest. His body warmth seemed to intensify the already sensitive tips of her fingers as she felt the flat plane of his stomach and even stopped a moment to play with his navel.

Another rasping sound of pleasure moaned deep in Cole's throat as his hands frantically began to work with the many fasteners and stays on the dress she wore. He silently cursed whoever had designed this dress. While his hands fumbled with their task, his lips continued to send tingling electric shivers down her spine, especially when he moved to kiss the sensitive area just below her ear and along her neck. Such sweet torment.

Patricia felt the material of her bodice slacken as Cole finally began to make progress with the many stubborn fasteners. Soon, she could feel his fingers against the skin along her back as he finished his task. Once he was through, he eased his hands beneath the material and slipped the dress from her shoulders, making it fall down around her waist. She responded by gently unbuttoning his shirt, then stepped back to allow him to tug her dress on past her hips to the floor.

She waited until they both were completely naked before she reached out for him again, welcoming her future husband back into her arms. Pressing against him, she felt the marvel of his firm, fit body against her soft, supple curves. The texture of his hair tickled the delicate peaks of her breasts when she moved against him. The sensual movements aroused him to a point of madness. Quickly, he bent down and scooped her into his arms. Leaving their clothing behind, he bounded up the stairs and carried her to his bed.

Gingerly, he placed her into the soft depths of the tan and brown comforter that covered his bed then quickly joined her. His lips came down to make gentle contact with her awaiting mouth while he eased his body weight down on her with agile ease. She pulled him closer. Her hands roamed freely over the muscles of his back and strained to feel the tautness of his hips and upper thighs. His sparsely haired skin felt good to her touch. A smile lighted across her lips as she marveled over the fact that in four months this man would finally be her husband. They would be together forever. Her heart overflowed inside her, spilling joy everywhere.

Cole had felt the smile in her kiss and raised his head to look lovingly down at her. Oh, how he adored her, desired her. His hands moved to caress her shoulders, then ran a smooth course down her sides, causing her skin to tingle with life. Slowly, he moved down so that his lips could gently caress the straining peak of one soft breast. His tongue teased the tip with short, tantalizing strokes that caused her to arch her back. Eagerly, his lips traveled to take in the other breast.

Such sweet ecstasy. A wondrous torrent of delicious emotions raged through her. She was not certain how long she could bear it. Nor was she quite sure how to coax him to stop the sweet torture and bring her the relief she sought. She pulled gently at his shoulders, but his mouth continued to bring her breast unbearable pleasure. She writhed from the delectable sensations building in her. The delicious ache that centered itself somewhere in her abdomen had reached an unbearable intensity. Her body craved relief. Just when she thought she could bear it no longer, Cole moved to fulfill her, slowly bringing their love to the ultimate height of passion. When release came for them, it was so wondrous and shattering that she cried out with pleasure.

Sinking into a sensuous euphoria as they held each other close, Cole spoke with a contented half-smile. "Patricia, you make me so happy that sometimes I wonder if I even deserve it."

"Well, what are close friends for?" She laughed softly and snuggled closer. "I enjoy making you happy."

"Promise me it will always be like this for us."

"Always, Cole. I promise."

The following morning when Cole left his house to meet with Tony over breakfast at the Hulbert House, he carried his revolver with him, tucked neatly out of sight in a small leather holster hidden inside his boot. He had warned Tony the night before they needed to be extremely careful and had meant it. He for one was not going to take any more chances where William was concerned but he was certainly not going to back down either. He was more eager than ever to recruit new signatures. With the petition in hand, his first stop after breakfast was to be the First National Bank. Although he did not think they would have much success there, he did want William to know that his threat had not frightened him in the least. If anything, it had motivated him further. Enough that he was willing to take a few risks.

Later, when they walked out of the bank with the signatures of two of the bank's patrons, which they had gotten right under William's very nose, Cole burst out laughing. "Did you see the expression on William's face when he looked up and saw the two of us talking to some of the people in his very own bank? I thought he was going to bust a gut."

Relieved they were finally out of there, Tony laughed too. "He did look as if he might be in pain. I do think he got your message."

"Loud and clear, I'd say. I'm not about to be bullied by the likes of him," Cole said and laughed again. Looking down at the two petitions, he asked, "Where to next?"

For the rest of the day, Cole and Tony approached anyone who would listen and before they realized it they had managed to get twenty more signatures. Things were finally looking up again. William may have blackmailed a good many of the people who had signed the original petition, but he had not managed to blackmail everyone in town. There were still many people they had never had an opportunity to approach before. People William would not be able to head off. That was the direction they decided to take with this. If they could rerecruit some of the old signatures, that would be fine, but what they needed was to find new people to interest.

Although it was Thursday and they usually met as a group at Marco's on Thursday nights, Cole and Tony made excuses to Patricia, Faye, and Catherine. They wanted a chance to talk to Andrew alone and let him know what had happened and just where they stood. They could not do that with the women present. They had already decided they did not want any of the women worried any more than they were. They would handle William alone.

It was when they stopped by to pick Andrew up that they learned of his pending dismissal. They found Andrew sitting in his office staring unseeingly at the wall. The church's council, which was made up solely of the trustees, had met the night before and had decided the time had come to do something about Andrew's involvement with the dam controversy. Sam Neely had stopped by earlier that afternoon to tell him of the outcome. Either Andrew stopped immediately or they would search for someone more cooperative to lead the congregation. "And since I don't intend to pay attention to their ultimatum, I'm afraid I'm soon to be out of work. You two don't happen to know of a church in need of a minister, do you?" Andrew asked calmly.

Andrew seemed to be taking the whole matter rather lightly. Cole and Tony were the ones who became furious with the way Andrew was being railroaded and showed it through their raised voices. "Doesn't the congregation have any say?" Tony wanted to know, drawing his hands into fists.

"Oh, if I pressed it I could ask that the matter be brought up before the entire congregation. I could ask that it be put to a vote, but I'm not sure it would help me much."

335

"Why not? You have right on your side," Tony told him. Anger forced his features to become tight and his voice strained.

"Sometimes right is not enough. I've only been with Todd Street Methodist less than a year. That's hardly long enough to have developed invincible bonds with the people. Besides, I already know that many of them feel the same way as the trustees do. They feel it is not my place to be out recruiting names for a cause that might take some of the bread out of their mouths. Many of them are businessmen, but it is more than that. Occasionally during the summer, some of the club members come down to Johnstown for Sunday services and when they do, they leave very generous offerings. That alone will work heavily against me."

"But you have to try, man," Cole said, pounding a fist on Andrew's cluttered desk. "Is Sam Neely the one who seems to be behind this? I'll bet he is. He's some sort of friend of William's. They work at the same place. I wonder if William had anything to do with this."

"It's not just Sam. The entire council voted and it was unanimous."

"What can we do to help?"

"Nothing. It's no use. Whatever the trustees decide usually goes for the rest of the membership. I'm as good as out." He shrugged. "It really doesn't matter. There are other churches."

"But won't being dismissed like this work against you in getting another church?"

"Maybe with some of the larger churches, but there are always the smaller churches that need competent leadership. I won't be without a church forever."

"Still, it's the principle of the thing," Cole muttered.

"Exactly. It is my principles that are at stake here," Andrew agreed. "And I'm not about to bend any of them for anyone." Then as was his habit whenever the topic was one that caused discomfort, Andrew changed the subject. "So, what was it you two wanted to talk about?"

On their way to the restaurant, Cole and Tony filled him in

on what-all had happened since last they had met. Andrew was more angry at the threat William had made against Cole than he had been about what the trustees had planned for him. He reacted in much the same way Cole had and he was more determined than ever to see their project through to the very end. He started to contemplate going to Washington with Cole come July. The more he thought about it, the more he liked the idea.

Despite Andrew's position at the Todd Street Church hanging in the balance, things went fairly smoothly for them over the next few weeks. The topic of Andrew's dismissal was not mentioned for a while and the signatures finally started to mount up. They again had hope. It looked like they might have quite an impressive number of names by July after all and the most William had done to try to stop them was to continue to send them threatening, unsigned notes. But because he never actually did anything to them, Cole felt that their little visit to his house had impressed him far more than he had let on. Even so, Cole hardly felt it was time to relax. Although they paid very little attention anymore to the threatening notes William continued to send them, they kept their guard up.

It was not until early May that Andrew finally got the official word concerning his job. He had until the end of the month. After that, he would no longer be the minister for Todd Street. It was suggested by the two trustees who visited him that he start looking for another position in another town right away but Andrew intended to wait until after the trip to Washington before looking for another church. Until then, he would dedicate all the time he could manage to the cause, and once he was free of the church, he would dedicate every single minute he had.

When Patricia saw William next, during a chance meeting at Heiser's Mercantile, she quickly pulled him aside and demanded to know if he had had anything to do with Andrew's dismissal. William, true to himself, looked deeply offended and reminded her that he did not even belong to the Todd Street church.

337

"No, but Sam Neely does. He's one of the trustees that decided to toss Andrew out of the church just because he is helping us. And we both know just how close a friend Sam is to you."

"True, he's a friend of mine." William shrugged as if the fact was insignificant. "And as my friend I imagine I would be able to sway his thinking, but so far I haven't bothered. Now if you would like for me to speak to him in behalf of your friend, all you have to do is fulfill the bargain I tried to strike with you a few weeks ago. Come back to me and not only will you save the petition, which I understand is doing rather poorly—you might even be able to save your friend's position at the church as well. I will admit—I do have quite a bit of influence over Sam and should I use that influence in your friend's behalf, there is a good chance it would do some good. All you have to do is throw away that silly pride of yours and come back to me."

Because they were standing in an aisle very near the main counter where several people stood waiting to make their purchases, Patricia tried to hold her temper. Gritting her teeth, she replied, "I'd rather eat maggots."

"I thought by now you would realize that your petition does not have a chance without my help."

"For your information, we are doing very well with our petition. We have nearly three hundred signatures again and we still have two months to go," she responded with a haughty toss of her head.

"What? You mean the people are signing anyway?" he asked. "I don't believe you."

"I don't have the petition with me right now or I'd show you," she retorted. "I counted the names last night and we had two hundred and eighty-seven. And with Tony and Andrew out today recruiting still more, I'll bet that by the time I get the petition back tonight, there will be over three hundred. So you see, your threats and your blackmailings only slowed us down. They by no means stopped us. We are not about to be stopped by the wicked likes of you."

William's eyes narrowed as he thought about what-all she had just told him. "You honestly think that by the time you

338

get that petition back tonight there will be over three hundred signatures on it?"

"Delightful news, isn't it?" she retorted, unaware that she had unwittingly supplied him with more information than she should. A broad smile beamed across her face as she nodded politely to him and turned to leave. "Have a lovely day, William."

Chapter Twenty-two

When Faye found out what had happened to Andrew, she was outraged beyond anything she had ever felt before. She wanted to do something, anything, to prevent such an atrocity of justice from happening but managed to bridle her anger once Andrew finally convinced her it was really for the best.

He did not like the idea of working for a church that issued such unfair ultimatums to its ministers. He was not a puppet to act solely on the whims of the trustees and felt certain that even if he was allowed to stay he would not be happy. Eventually, he would find a much more compatible church and be far happier in the long run.

"I wish I could be so clearly optimistic about everything," Faye told him when she finally started to calm down. "I must tell you that I do admire your values." What she failed to say was how she also admired him as a man. She was not supposed to have the sort of stirrings in her heart that Andrew caused but she felt he was such a noble man. It would be impossible not to care for a man like him.

"Coming from someone like you, Faye, that is the utmost in compliments." He smiled with earnest and reached out to caress her shoulder in a friendly gesture.

Faye closed her eyes momentarily and enjoyed the warmth they had come to share. She had never had such a good friend in the form of a man before. Except for her own brother Cole and a few priests she had worked with, she had never really cultivated a friendship with a man before. Not since her girlhood. And now she had both Andrew and Tony for friends, especially Andrew. No friend could prove truer.

"When do you have to have your things out of here?" she wanted to know, looking around at the book-lined walls of his office. It was not going to be an easy move. "I want to help when the time comes. I'm very good at organizing a move. After all, I've moved twice myself and helped Cole when he moved into that big house of his."

"I have until the end of the month. I probably won't start packing my books away for a couple of weeks yet. I'll put it off at least that long. Then I'll get my clothing and my personal belongings together shortly after that and be out of here."

"Where will you go?" Her heart ached to know the answer to that. How she hoped he would be able to stay nearby.

"I'm going to live with Tony until after we have this problem with the dam licked. Then it will depend on where I can locate a new position. I hope to remain in Johnstown, though. I've become too attached to the place and the people in it." He gazed down at her a moment, knowing full well that she was one of the people he had come to enjoy the most. He had never known anyone like her. "And I'd like to be around on the day the work finally begins at the dam. Or better yet—the day we all learn the work has been completed to our satisfaction."

"Yes, you must be in on the celebration Cole will want to have. You know Cole, he loves to celebrate," she chuckled. If Cole could think of a reason plausible enough, he was always ready to supply the champagne. "Once, when I first moved here, he even celebrated the rehanging of a door with such gusto that the following morning my dear brother found himself not much better off than the door. He was hung too—hung over, that is." She laughed with merriment when she remembered how miserable he had looked when he awoke the next morning to greet her with a bleary-eyed smile. "He has a lot to learn about moderation."

"True, Cole never has impressed me as being a very moderate person in anything he does," Andrew admitted and joined in her laughter. "Well, we'd better get a move on or we are going to be late," he said as he lifted her cloak from the hook near the door and placed it back around her shoulders. For the hundredth time, he caught himself wondering what color her hair was beneath that heavy woolen black and white headdress of hers.

Because it had started to rain again, Faye opened her umbrella and they made a wild run together for his carriage but did not reach it before they were both soaked to the knees. Faye for one had grown tired of all the rainy weather. She was eager for a few days of sunshine. She wanted to go on the picnic Cole had proposed last week but worried that if it didn't stop raining soon, the next picnic they went on might be as far away as Memorial Day, and that was weeks away.

When they arrived at Marco's, everyone else was already there and a decanter of wine had been brought to the table. Tony and Catherine had just arrived. There were still droplets of water glistening in Tony's dark curls and tiny dark water spots were splattered across the hem of Catherine's pink skirt.

"You wouldn't believe the success I had today," Tony was telling Cole when Andrew and Faye joined them. He pulled the two petitions out of his pocket and handed one to Cole and the other to Andrew while he explained. "I was able to convince almost everyone I talked to this afternoon into signing. Several argued with me about one point or another, but eventually almost everyone sighed."

"I think it has to do with the weather and the fact that the river is up so high already," Cole told him. "People seem to be more willing to listen when they are already worried with the prospect of normal flooding. It seems the closer the river gets to the flood stage the better the response we get to our petition. A couple more days like today and the river is going to spill over its banks, and that can only be good for us."

"That and the story the *Tribune* did on its findings at the dam. It may not have come right out and said the dam was a threat, but it did cast a doubt on the situation," Tony put in. "I've had several people mention having read the thing. With

343

that story having run and the weather the way it is, we are going to be far more successful than we had hoped."

Later, on the way to Patricia's house, Cole decided to take a short detour and drove by the river to investigate its present condition. The murky, fawn-colored water churned turbulently as it roared through the center of town, nearly jumping its banks in several places. There was nothing little about Little Conemaugh at the moment. It was only a few feet from flood level. Even if it stopped raining that very night, the drainage from the mountains would keep the river very active for several days, making the prospects good for continuing to recruit new signatures. As he turned the carriage toward Patricia's house, he fervently wished he had the following day or so off so that he could help Tony. It was a shame not to make the fullest use possible of such an opportunity.

"It certainly is cool tonight," Patricia commented, breaking the silence that had fallen between them during the short ride from the river to her house. As she shook the droplets of rain from her skirts that she had gathered during the run from the outbuilding where they had parked Cole's carriage to the shelter of the porch, she added, "Tonight would be a good night for a hot cup of mint tea." She handed her door key to Cole and watched as he quickly unlocked the front door before any of the neighbors could spot them going inside together. "I'll make some just as soon as I've put the petition away."

"Sounds good," Cole said as he shook his thoughts about the petition and responded agreeably. "I'll get a good fire going and we can enjoy our tea in front of the fireplace."

"How cozy," she murmured with a knowing smile.

Once inside, Patricia stepped into the main salon to turn up the gaslight she had left dimly burning. Cole stayed behind on the porch to shake some of the water from their coats before hanging them inside near the door.

"Oh my word," he heard her gasp just as he lifted her coat to the hook. "Cole. Come here. Quick!"

The urgency in her voice was all that was needed to set his feet in motion. Quickly, he slammed the door shut and ran to see what was the matter.

"What is it?" he asked before he stepped inside the room and discovered the answer for himself. His eyes widened. "What happened?"

Patricia stared with utter disbelief at the destruction before her. Her lower lip started to tremble and she reached out to grasp Cole's arm for support.

"William," she said simply, then looked again at the dishevel. As she slowly surveyed all that had been done, her eyes dulled and her expression appeared grim.

Not a chair or a sofa had been left standing. Drawers were pulled out of the tables and tossed haphazardly around the room, their contents scattered everywhere while the tables themselves had been pushed over on to their sides. Even her drapes had been pulled down, rods and all, and strewn across an overturned side chair. The huge beveled mirror that had hung over the fireplace in a large ornately carved wooden frame had been tossed to the floor upside down and pieces of silver-backed glass were everywhere. Nothing stood in its original spot. The walls had been plucked bare. Patricia was too stunned by it all to be angry yet. She stood transfixed, expressionless, clutching Cole's arm.

"Yes, evidently William is at it again," Cole ground out, his anger already consuming him to the point that his voice shook. "I wonder if he hit all our houses while we were out."

Patricia blinked as she thought about that. Her eyes filled with a horrifying realization when she spoke again. "No, he thought he would find what he was looking for right here. I the same as told him I would have the petition tonight."

"What?" Cole shouted with disbelief. "Why in the hell would you do something like that? When?"

"This afternoon. I ran into him at Heiser's and demanded to know if he had anything to do with Andrew losing his job. You already know how strongly I believe he had something to do with that." She paused as she tried to remember exactly what had been said that afternoon.

"And?"

"And he told me that he hadn't had a thing to do with Andrew's job trouble but that he would do what he could to help him keep that job if I'd decide to come back to him. He also said something about how I still could save the petition if I'd just come back to him. He was under the impression we were not doing too well with it. I was angry so I told him how wrong he was about that. Then I told him how I had counted nearly three hundred signatures last night." She paused again when she realized exactly what she had said next. Her green eyes grew wide.

"And?"

"And I then told him that by the time I had the petition back tonight, there would probably be over three hundred signatures on it. He even repeated that back to me in the form of a question, I guess to be sure he had understood me right. Me and my big mouth," she wailed and glanced around at the ruin again, then her eyes turned fearfully toward the door leading into the dining room. Hurrying to the door, she peered inside and discovered William had done just as thorough a job there. He had scrambled everything in the room into one large mess and sprinkled it liberally with broken dishes and shattered glasses.

Feeling sudden panic at finding her belongings ruined, she ran hurriedly on through the dining room to the kitchen and discovered that room was a disaster too. Every drawer and cabinet had been opened. Kitchen utensils were everywhere, some smashed beyond use. Even her canisters had been turned over, the contents dumped in huge piles across the counter.

About the time Cole entered behind her, she took off for the stairs. Huge tears filled her eyes as she made her way upstairs and to the doorway of her bedroom. Her bedside lamp had been lit and still burned brightly, enabling her to see the wreckage that was in her room. Her clothes had been pulled out of her armoire and drawers were flung everywhere. Some had been torn and shredded into rags while others fared better and had merely been tossed to the floor. The drawers to her tall dresser and her vanity table lay against the far wall, some badly broken as if they had been thrown there in anger. Her bed had been stripped of its clothing and the top mattress lay crooked with huge gaping rips down its length. Mounds of feathers bulged out of them. And right in the middle of the mattress was plunged a huge broad-bladed knife with its pearl handle gleaming menacingly in the lamplight.

"I guess he left the knife as a warning of some sort," she muttered through tightly pressed teeth while she stepped forward to pull the knife out of her mattress.

"Either that or we almost caught him in the act and he didn't take time to retrieve the knife," Cole surmised when he stepped over to the window and discovered that although it was closed, it was unlocked. "I thought you were locking your windows these days."

"All but that one," she admitted, then explained about her cat, Duchess. "I didn't think it would hurt to leave that one window open just enough for her to be able to get in and out, especially since it faces the street the way it does."

"Street or no street, it looks like this is how he got in. I didn't notice any doors that had been jimmied downstairs or any broken windows. This has to be how he entered."

"I know it is. That window was open about five inches when I left," she admitted. "Someone closed it." Suddenly her eyes grew wide. "You don't think he's still in here somewhere, do you?"

"Stay here," Cole ordered quietly, then picked up a piece of wood that had originally been a part of her vanity chair and slipped through the door, into the darkened hallway, and out of her sight. Several long minutes later, he returned assured that William was no longer in the house and wouldn't be getting back in quite so easily. "Not only did I check every window and door to be sure they were all latched shut, I jammed the windows with whatever I could find. Don't touch them until I can get over here tomorrow with extra latches for the windows. I want you to have at least two latches on every one of them and I want you to use them," he instructed her as he stepped over and utilized the chair leg he had been carrying as a club to blockade the window William had used to get in.

"Since he didn't get what he wanted, he will probably be back," he went on to say. "And now that he knows the

347

petition does still offer a threat, he will do whatever it takes to get his hands on it or else stop us in some other way." Cole's voice shook as he spoke. "No telling what lengths he will go to."

"Cole, you are trembling," Patricia noted when she looked down at his hands and saw how they shook. She had seen him angry before, but never before had she seen him actually tremble. It frightened her.

"I know. I was thinking what might have happened if you had been home," he told her and ran a shaky hand through his hair. "There's no telling what he might have done to you." Tears forced their way into his eyes and his mouth tightened. "I never really stopped to think about the danger I could be putting you in."

"But he didn't find me home and he hasn't harmed me," she said and reached out to dash one of his tears away with her fingertips. "I'm safe."

"No you aren't," he said adamantly. "You are not at all safe. In fact, you are in very serious danger and it's my fault."

"What do you mean it's your fault? How can what William does be your fault?" she tried to reason with him.

"William warned me. He told me that if I knew what was good for you, I wouldn't continue to pursue the matter with the dam. He the same as told me he would try to harm you in some way if I persisted, but I didn't listen. I just didn't think he would do anything to any of you women. I didn't realize how far he would go to get his way on this. There's no telling what he plans to do next. The man's a maniac. He may be planning to physically hurt you in some way," Cole said, his eyes transfixed on the far wall as if he saw visions there. "I can't let you continue to keep the petition here. In fact, I can't let you continue to be a part of this in any way. You, Faye, and Catherine are not to help anymore. Tony, Andrew, and I will take it alone from here. I'm not going to risk your safety anymore."

"But you can't push us out like this," Patricia told him, angry he had even thought about it. "I, for one, don't care what sort of threats William makes or what he does to my things. He can even try to burn my house down like he did yours, but I'm not quitting."

"Oh, yes you are," Cole said, deceptively calm. "William might not stop with damage to our property. He very well could go as far as to try to harm one of us. The man has no conscience to deal with. There's no telling what extremes he might go to. William wants a fight and he is sure going to get one and it just might get very dirty before it's over. I don't want you involved."

"I can hold my own against William. I have before and I can again."

"You won't have to. You are already out of it."

"I am not," she shouted, furious. "I'm not about to quit at this late date. And you can't make me."

"Oh, yes you are," he said with a firm nod. "And I most certainly can."

"I've come too far," she tried to explain, only to be interrupted. That infuriated her. He was not even going to listen to what she had to say.

"It doesn't matter. You are no longer involved with this."

"Then I'm no longer involved with you either," she spat, in such a rage she could hardly see straight. Cole had never denied her anything before much less refused to listen to her reasoning. Didn't he realize how important this was to her? "What if I refuse to marry you? What if I tell you that if you don't let me help with the dam, then I will simply refuse to marry you?" Surely that would make him see just how important this was to her.

"Is that an ultimatum?" he asked, feeling the pain of her words deep within him. He stared down into the stormy depths of her emerald eyes for a long moment before he spoke again. "Then so be it." He couldn't continue to let her life be in danger and if that is what it took to keep her safe, then that is how it would have to be. He would come back to her and try to straighten this all out after they had completed their work. He would see what he could salvage then.

"Just like that?" she shrieked, unable to believe he had said that. "Just like that and it's over between us?"

"Just like that," he said with such restraint that he sounded unconcerned, but inside he felt as if his heart had collapsed and stopped beating. A deep pain seized him. He knew that the wedge he was driving between them at that moment might be enough to separate them forever. "So long, Patricia."

He could feel hot tears building in the backs of his eyes and turned to leave before she could spot them. She stared after him in disbelief as he departed, unable to say anything. All she could do was watch his shadowy form slowly disappear from sight as he made his way through the hallway and down the stairs. Just before she heard him close the front door, he shouted loudly so that she could hear him upstairs, "Lock your door."

Then he was gone.

Patricia stood dazed. It was hard to realize the magnitude of what had just happened in so short a time. Blinking curiously at the bedroom doorway Cole had just passed through, she tried to sort it all out. It had happened too quickly for her to have a full grasp of it just yet. When she did slowly come to realize that whatever and however it had happened, the end result was that their engagement had been dissolved and her future happiness destroyed, her feet took flight and she flew down the stairs and to the front door. Yanking it open, she peered out into the rainy darkness.

Cole was already in his carriage and pulling away from her yard. He never once looked back. That angered her. Slamming the door shut again, she locked it like he had told her to, then turned around and pressed her back to the cold hard surface. When she caught a glimpse of the massive destruction that still lay around her and knew that it didn't hold a candle to the horrible devastation she felt inside, huge tears formed in her eyes and poured wet trails down her cheeks. With more pain than she had ever known before, she sank to the floor and cried aloud with large, rasping sobs.

Patricia did not go into work for the next three days. She reported the crime done to her house for the little good it would do, then spent the rest of the time alternately cleaning up the mess inside and mourning her loss. She kept hoping

Cole would reconsider and come to her ready to make up, but he never appeared. On the third day, Catherine stopped by to help Patricia with the clean-up and told her how Cole and Tony had come by the evening before and explained why she was not to help with the petition anymore. She had been horrified to learn what had happened to Patricia's house and even more horrified to learn that Cole and Patricia had argued and called off their wedding as a result.

Patricia finally had a release for the hurt and anger she had been holding in. For hours, she spouted exactly how she felt about what he had done and Catherine listened quietly. Finally, when it looked like Patricia was about to wind down, Catherine asked her right out, "Why haven't you told Cole everything you just told me?"

"And give him the satisfaction of knowing how much he hurt me?" She raised her voice, incensed that Catherine had suggested such a thing. Coming to stand beside the chair her youngest sister sat in, she explained in terms simple enough even Catherine would understand. "Like I told you, he was not upset in the least that I was willing to break up with him in order to preserve what I believed in. He simply said 'so be it' and left. That isn't love."

"I think you are wrong about that," Catherine said simply as she sorted through the silverware in her lap and placed the proper pieces in the narrow compartments of the velvet-lined box. "I think he was very upset."

"You weren't here. You didn't see how coolly he walked out of here and drove away."

"No, but I saw him just two days later and he looked dreadful, like he hadn't slept both nights."

"He did?" she asked, truly surprised to hear it. At the same time she felt hopeful.

"Yes, he was with Tony when he came to tell me I was no longer to have anything to do with the petition. He had dark circles below his eyes and his eyelids looked heavy, like they were swollen. The sparkle was gone from his eyes. At first, I feared that it was the petition that was causing him to lose sleep. I worried that it was in far more serious trouble than they wanted us to know, but then I learned that you two had

351

broken up, and I realized why he looked so miserable. It hurt him deeply. I've never seen a man look so down. I could tell by looking at his eyes that he had actually been crying. He looked like Father did right after Mother died."

Patricia's heart felt as if it was being wrenched right from her chest. Cole was hurting too. She hated the thought of him suffering in any way, especially since she was the cause, and wanted to put an end to it as soon as possible. As angry as she was, she still loved him. "Did you come in the buggy?"

"Yes, I did." She said, smiling. "Need a lift somewhere?"

"I want to be waiting on his doorstep when he comes home," she explained, even though she knew Catherine had already guessed. "Just give me a moment to change."

Fifteen minutes later, Patricia was dressed in a yellow and gold cotton dress with pale yellow lace across the scooped neckline and down the front in five even rows. The short puffed sleeves were also edged in the same yellow lace and two rows of it circled the billowing skirt, near the hem. Taking just enough time to locate a crocheted shawl in case night should fall before Cole came home, the two of them were soon on their way to Cole's house.

"Do you want me to stay and keep you company?" Catherine asked. "No telling what time he will come home."

"No, you go on home. I'm going to wait on his doorstep until he comes home if it takes all night."

But it didn't take all night, for about thirty minutes later, she saw him riding up on his horse. When he trotted the animal past, he happened to look over through the wide gaps between the iron bars of the fence and noticed her. With a wild leap of his heart, he pulled his horse to a stop and stared at her only a moment before jumping down and hurrying toward the gate. Patricia met him halfway and despite what the neighbors might think, they embraced a long moment, then he kissed her, long and hard.

"You've changed your mind?" he wanted to know as soon as their lips had parted. He kept one arm around her as he escorted her to the front porch.

"About not marrying you, yes," she started to explain. "But as for the petition, I have not. Someone I love and

352

respect very much once told me never to start anything I don't intend to finish. I believe that to be very sound advice. And ever since then I always finish anything I start."

Cole paused with the door key in his hand. He knew she was talking about the night she had lured him into her bedroom thinking he was a married rake. He had used those exact words. "But I wasn't talking about something like this. I don't want you hurt. I want you safe and out of harm's way."

"I'm willing to compromise," she finally said, suddenly aware of the darkened rings below his eyes and the unusually pallid color of his skin. Catherine had been right. He looked terrible. "I won't expect to keep either of the petitions at my house anymore, I won't even ask to hold it in my hands, if you will just let me continue to help recruiting signatures. I've come this far, I do want to be with you till the end of it."

"Will you promise to start locking all your doors and every window in your house until this is all over and done?"

"Yes, I already have started doing that despite Duchess's many loud complaints."

"And would you consider getting a pistol for your own protection?"

"No!" she answered emphatically, having always been terrified of them, but then admitted, "But I have started to keep a hammer under my pillow and have that knife where I can get to it should I ever really need it."

"Tell me something. Is the hammer to knock some sense into me or William?" he teased as he slipped the key into the lock and turned it.

"Whichever I feel needs it." She said, laughing.

"What if I say no?" He watched her closely as he held the door open for her.

"Then there is still one avenue open for me. I can always help you anyway by going to William and pretending to make the bargain he has suggested twice now. Not only will that get you more signatures, it will assure that William no longer fights you on it."

"You wouldn't dare!" His eyes narrowed.

"It would assure everybody's safety," she explained.

353

"You wouldn't dare!" he repeated in a low even grate. An angry muscle twitched in his cheek as he waited for her response.

Tossing her head back, she looked him in the eye with a bold "try-me" expression on her face then asked, "Do I still get to help with the petition?"

Knowing that whatever he answered, she could be getting herself into danger, he decided to let her have her way. He had already started to give in to her even before she had thought of that final threat against him. "Okay, you can still help us solicit signatures, but that's all," he stated with a firm nod. "I mean it."

"Anything you say," she responded sweetly and tiptoed to kiss him dutifully on the cheek. "Anything you say."

Chapter Twenty-three

A shadowy figure loomed just inside the dark alleyway across the street, watching and waiting. By now William knew he was there. It infuriated him that he was constantly followed, continuously being watched, and although he had no real proof since he did not know for sure who the man was who kept following him, William was almost certain Cole was behind it. A sardonic smile swept his aristocratic face as he peered through the slatted window blind, knowing he would soon bring an abrupt stop to so many of his problems and have the perfect alibi for himself. What could be better than to have the very detective or whoever it was Cole had hired to follow him be the one to verify that he was nowhere near when it happened. Cole didn't know it, but he had provided him with the perfect witness to declare his innocence. If he played this right, there was no way he could be implicated in anything. He would again be free to pursue life the way he wanted it and without Cole to interfere.

For weeks William had been suspicious that someone was following him, but last night he finally confirmed the fact. Everywhere he had gone, his newly acquired shadow had followed; sometimes hiding in alleys, sometimes slipping into shops across the street, and sometimes nowhere in sight, but always nearby. And because of the low-brimmed hat and the high-collared coat that the man wore despite the warmer temperatures of mid-May, William was not able to tell just who it was that followed him. He knew it was not Cole himself. The man wasn't tall enough. And he knew it wasn't either of Cole's friends, Anthony Alani or Andrew Edwards. The height wasn't right for those men either. But he knew Cole and his friends were behind him, paying him whatever it took to keep a close eye on everything he did, making it impossible for him to get his hands on that petition—or anything else.

When does that man sleep? he wondered with disgust. The man had followed him all the way home very late last night. William was sure of it. And although he had left the house at the break of dawn this morning, the man suddenly appeared behind him again, even before he had traveled as far as a block from his house. Whoever he was, he was good at his job. William had to give him that.

Stepping away from the window, William paced the thick carpeted floor in his office while he impatiently waited for Frank Gordon to show up. He glanced at the Jeffery clock on his huge rosewood desk with anticipation. It was nearly five-thirty now. If Sam got the message to him on time, Frank should arrive at any moment.

Finally he heard the rattling knock on the front door. He had decided not to try to sneak Frank in through the back way. Whoever that guy was out there, he was too good for that. It would look better if Frank was let in through the main door as if there was nothing whatsoever to hide.

"You wanted to see me?" Frank asked when William opened the door to greet him with a friendly slap on his shoulder.

Frank shifted uncomfortably in the three-piece suit he had been instructed to wear. Although the material and the cut were expensive, the fit was atrocious. He was too rounded in places where the suit was tucked and far too flat in other places to give him the dapper businessman look William had hoped for.

"Yes, come in, Mr. Johnson, I have those papers all ready for you to sign. There's not going to be any problem whatsoever in getting you that loan you wanted. Do come in," William said in an overly loud voice so that whoever was around who might be interested in what was being said would have no problem in hearing him. Then under his breath he added, "Don't turn around. I don't want to give the fellow that is watching us the opportunity to see your face."

Frank appeared confused, but being a cautious man by nature, did exactly as he was told. He stepped quietly inside and did not turn around even after the door had been securely locked behind him. Keeping his voice as low as William's had been a moment ago, Frank asked, "What's going on?"

"Step into my office and I'll explain," William told him and indicated the door to the only lighted office in the building. Everyone else had gone home.

"Mind if I ask why you called me Mr. Johnson? Is that why you wanted me to come dressed like this?"

"Yes. I'm being watched and I didn't want him to know who you were. I have a job for you that must be kept in the strictest of confidence."

"What kind of job and what does it pay?" Frank asked, always ready to get to the point. While he waited for the answer, he eased down into one of the upholstered chairs facing William's desk and made himself as comfortable as the narrow high-backed chair would allow his wide frame.

William continued to stand. "I want you to get rid of someone for me."

"Permanently or temporarily?" Personally, Frank didn't care which except for the fact that he could rightfully ask for better pay if it was to be permanent.

"Permanently," replied William without so much as a pause. His mouth tightened and his nostrils flared at the back as his jealousy and hate speared through him like a cold-bladed knife. "I've put up with the bastard as long as I intend to. He's a troublemaker that has gotten in my way one too many times and now that I found out he is having me followed so that I can't do a damn thing without him knowing all about it, I have reached my limit. I warned him not to mess with me. I warned him," William said aloud, more for his own benefit than Frank's. His usually fine, almost feminine features turned ugly—demonic in nature. "He should have backed off when he had the chance. And he

357

damn well never should have tried to take Patricia away from me and fill her full of no-telling-what-sort-of-lies about me. Everything was going along just fine until he butted in."

William looked toward Frank with his eyes expanded menacingly when he grated out the rest. "He turned her against me with all his lies and deceit. He is also trying to ruin everything else I've worked so hard to build up over the past few years. He wants to destroy everything. He's trying to alienate those rich men at the club. He wants to turn them against me and all of Johnstown. His stupid interference just could cost me some of my best contacts. I know I'll lose Captain Reid's account and probably several others. But he doesn't care if he's hurting anyone by what he does. He only cares about himself. And he doesn't really love Patricia either. Not like I do. He just wanted to see if he could take her away from me. It's some sort of game with him. Just like he tried to outbid me at the picnic last year; only I managed to win out on that one. That really must have burned him up because now he is out to get me. I don't know why, but he has some sort of vendetta against me. He has ever since the picnic. Or maybe even before that."

Frank watched William's jerking movements as he paced the floor in front of him and flailed his arms wildly in an effort to emphasize whatever it was he was trying to say. But the more William talked the less sense he seemed to make, although Frank really didn't care. It wouldn't make any difference to him if the man was daffy as a loon as long as he paid good money. "So who is it I'm supposed to do in and how much are you willing to pay me for it?"

"The man's name is Cole Gifford, he works for Cambria Iron, and I'll pay you three thousand dollars," William stated firmly. His jaw muscles flexed with extreme satisfaction when he noticed Frank's eyes light up at the amount mentioned. He could always count on Frank's greed.

"Man, you really must have it in for this guy," Frank said, laughing. His eyes glittered with approval. "For that amount you can have the man killed any way you want."

"I don't really care how you do it as long as you do it

without getting me involved. Be creative. Just don't get caught."

"For three thousand I'm willing to be creative as hell. And I don't intend to get caught. I'm not exactly an amateur, you know. I'll make it look like an accident just like I always do. When you want it done? Right away?"

"No, I don't want to take chances on that detective—or whatever that fellow is out there—becoming suspicious of anything. If Cole was to show up dead tomorrow, the very day after I had a mysterious after-hours caller at the bank, he might somehow put two and two together. No, better wait at least a week. Better yet, two. Use those two weeks to get to know his habits. Then the first time you catch him out alone somewhere where there can't possibly be any witnesses, you do it. Just be sure it gets done before the end of June. I hear he's headed for Washington sometime in July. And don't report back here to me when you are finished. I'll keep my ears open and as soon as I've learned about the bastard's untimely death, I'll send you a message through a courier of some sort. He'll tell you exactly where you can pick up your money."

"I get some of it now, don't I? Sort of in good faith?" Frank asked eagerly, running his tongue over the rough surface of his lower lip.

"Sure." William smiled. He had anticipated that. Frank was well known for his love of money. It was probably the one thing the two of them had in common. Walking over to his desk, he bent down and unlocked the bottom drawer and pulled out a large leather pouch with the bank's emblem on it. He flipped the top flap back and drew out a bulging unmarked envelope and tossed it on the desk near where Frank sat. "You'll find that there is one thousand dollars in that envelope. Take it with you. Count it if you like." Carefully reclosing the pouch, he patted its thickness and added, "You will get the other two thousand once I've learned the job has been completed."

Frank eyed the pouch curiously. The thought occurred to him that he could do William in right now and not only collect the other two thou right away, but would probably find more to boot. After all, this was a bank. But knowing William was always good for a quick job now and then and remembering that there was someone out there watching the place, he decided against it. He was not one to take chances.

Watching with keen interest as William locked the pouch safely back in the desk drawer, Frank made a mental note of the fact that William kept the key tucked away in his vest pocket. Such information could come in handy one day. Grunting from the forced movement, Frank slowly pushed himself up and out of the soft chair and made an attempt to straighten his suit. It was useless. No matter where he tugged at it, it really did not help. He just was not the type to wear fancy business suits.

Offering William one of his massive hands, Frank smiled heartily and said, "It's always a pleasure to do business with you, William. And you won't regret it. You just keep your ears open like you said. I don't want to wait too long in getting the rest of my money."

"Don't worry. You'll get it just as soon as I've learned that I won't have to worry about Cole Gifford anymore. I've never failed to pay you yet, have I?"

"Nor have I ever failed to earn it," Frank said agreeably and followed William to the front door. Keeping his derby pulled low and his head diverted toward the building, Frank hurried along his way, already thinking of ways to spend his money.

Although it felt more like March than the end of May, the rain had finally stopped early the morning before and it looked like Memorial Day was going to be a lovely day after all. The long shadow of Green Hill slowly slipped back and away as the sun climbed high into the sky, making everyone hopeful that the afternoon temperatures might climb a little higher than they had in the past few days. Even Cole had grown tired of the rainy weather and cool temperatures. Now that they had nearly five hundred signatures, he was not as eager to see the river over flow, especially not on

360

Memorial Day. Besides, many more rainy days and the lake itself might be in real danger of overflowing. They certainly did not need that happening. No telling what effect the strain of that would have on the dam.

He shuddered to even think about it as he drove his carriage through the crowded streets toward Patricia's house. Having kept a close watch on the dam during the long rainy spell that had followed that freak fourteen-inch snowstorm in April, he was well aware of how high the water level had risen at the lake. It worried him, but he hoped this would be the last year that he or anyone else would have to worry about it. It was almost June. They had the rainiest months behind them. He was certainly glad of that and tried once again to push such thoughts to the back of his mind.

Being a holiday, Johnstown was buzzing with activity. People had been gathering all along Main Street since well before noon in order to get one of the best spots to see the parade. Stores all over town had started to close for the afternoon's festivities. Even the saloons and restaurants would close down at two for the parade and not open again until after six. School was out and the workers from the mills had the afternoon off. A group called the Ancient Order of Hibernians was also in town for a state convention and filled the many hotels and rooming houses to capacity. Everyone had come to town to enjoy the holiday.

Just as he promised, Cole picked Patricia up promptly at eleven so that they could find a good spot to enjoy a picnic in the park and claim it before anyone else could. Faye, Andrew, Catherine, Tony, Jeanne, Harrison and Minnie, and even Minnie's semiinvalid sister Eva were all supposed to meet them there at noon, near the stretch of draping chain fence that was closest to the post office.

When they arrived at the spot, there was a much larger crowd gathered there than they had expected. They found they had to leave the carriage blocks away and would have done nearly as well just to have walked from Patricia's in the first place. Cole felt very much like a pack mule having to carry all the things Patricia had insisted they bring and wished they had had the foresight to arrive earlier so that they could have parked the rig a little closer.

All the best places beneath the spreading red oaks were already taken, but as cool as the temperature still was, it was just as well. The sunshine would help stave off the chill. Cole spread the three quilts Patricia had insisted on, one on top of the other, in an effort to keep the water-soaked ground from seeping through to their clothes. While Patricia walked across the park to stand at the designated meeting place, he went ahead and started to unload some of the things that were inside the huge basket Patricia had packed. She had brought enough to share with everyone. If they all brought this much, there would be far too much to eat. He just hoped Minnie remembered to bring the apple pie she had promised him.

"Don't you dare start eating before everyone gets here," Cole heard his sister's voice admonish just as he tore a tiny piece of chicken from a hefty-sized leg and popped it into his mouth. Startled at being caught when he had just glanced around moments before and not spotted any familiar faces, he looked up to find Faye, Andrew, Tony, and Catherine all standing at the edge of the quilts grinning down at him. Chewing guiltily in an effort to clear his mouth of the evidence, he motioned for them to join him.

"I only took a tiny taste," he defended himself once he had his mouth clear. "I just wanted to make sure it tasted all right."

"Yes, and if we hadn't come up when we did, you would have tasted that chicken leg right down to the bone," Faye retorted while she waited for Andrew and Tony to finish laying out their quilts to the side where they barely overlapped Cole's.

Soon they were all sitting comfortably on the quilts and exploring what tasty treats each had brought. Before long, they all had their plates filled to overflowing with the tempting delights, which included everything from ham to smoked turkey to fried chicken. The men were piling on seconds when a large shadow fell across the corner of one of the quilts. Looking up, they were all surprised to see Clayton standing quietly over them.

"Father! What are you doing here?" Patricia gasped. She lifted her hand to press against her breastbone where her heart had leaped when she had first recognized him. His appearance had been so unexpected, it had truly frightened her.

Cole immediately rose from his place and indicated the spot where he had just been seated. "Please, sir, sit down and join us. There is more than enough."

Clayton looked at the spot a long moment as if he was truly considering the invitation, but eventually took his eyes away and answered, "No, but thank you. I don't want to intrude."

"Intrude?" Cole responded quickly once he had glimpsed Patricia's hopeful eyes. "On family and friends? How can you call that intruding? Especially since you were just invited?"

Clayton looked at Cole a long moment, then down at the spot where the young man's hand still indicated he should sit. "But where would you sit?"

"We can make room for you both," Minnie stated quickly and began to scoot over toward her sister. Patricia quickly did the same, as did Catherine and Tony. Almost immediately there was room for both men to sit comfortably.

"Are you sure you don't mind?" Clayton asked, still hesitant.

Patricia and Catherine exchanged disbelieving glances. This was not like their father. Even Jeanne's mouth had gaped open at how polite and undemanding Clayton was trying to be.

"No, Father, of course we don't mind. If I had realized you would accept, I would have gladly invited you," Patricia told him. "We would have even offered you a ride. It just never occurred to me . . ." She paused for lack of a tactful way to continue, feeling like she was backing herself into a corner as she tried to explain. Finally, she decided to be blunt and come out with it. "Frankly, Father, I thought you and I were still not speaking."

"Who, me?" Clayton asked with such mock innocence that everyone burst out laughing, Clayton included. Then after he had settled in, he admitted, "I guess I have been a little stubborn about a few things lately."

"A little stubborn?" Patricia came back quickly. "Other than at work when you need something done, you've barely spoken to me for five months."

"Haven't thought of anything to say." He shrugged and offered an apologetic smile. Then, pulling his shoulders back, he took on his usual cool demeanor and wanted to know why he hadn't been served yet, letting them know that that was as close to an apology as they could expect.

"Coming right up," replied Minnie as she quickly piled a huge assortment of foods onto a plate. Since no one had brought a spare, she had taken the plate that had been used to cover the bean salad. It was not fancy, but it certainly held an ample amount of food. "Eat up, but just you save room for some of my apple pie."

Cole's ears picked up on that. "Apple pie? Where? I didn't see any apple pie."

"Hidden away so that you would eat other, more proper things first," Minnie scolded with a wag of her finger. "I know all about that hollow sweet tooth of yours. Desserts are for last."

"Don't feel too bad," Clayton muttered, giving Minnie a meaningful look that was supposed to chastise her but served to bring a huge smile to her lips. "She does the same thing to me and I'm supposed to be her boss."

Patricia couldn't believe it. Her father had actually spoken to Cole, and in a friendly tone no less. Would wonders never cease? Again the three sisters exchanged looks of delighted surprise. What had come over their father?

Realizing that everyone was staring at him with the most amazed expressions on their faces, Clayton began to feel uncomfortable. He decided to see if he could turn the attention elsewhere. "So, what was everyone talking about when I walked up? I certainly didn't mean to interrupt."

"We were talking about Andrew's move," Patricia explained. "For the past few days, Cole and Tony have been helping Andrew move out of the church and into Tony's house."

Clayton looked up and started to ask something, but decided against it. Instead, he picked up a small deviled egg and placed it into his mouth whole.

"Yes, Cole and Tony have been so busy helping me get packed and moved that I'm afraid they haven't had even a moment to themselves for almost a week," Andrew said quite frankly. "In fact, we kept Cole so busy that he's slept the last three nights at Tony's house."

"Too exhausted to go home," Cole put in good-naturedly.

"And what about me?" Faye piped up, looking insulted. "I've helped too, you know."

"Yes, let's give credit where credit is due. Faye was the brains of the outfit. I never would have thought of putting my towels and linens in with my books in order to keep certain crates from being far too heavy to lift," Andrew said with a loving smile.

"I appreciated that too," Cole said with a light chuckle. "After all, it seems I ended up doing most of the heavy toting."

"And you did it very well, I might add," Tony inserted. "Far better than Andrew or I could have done. You were so good at it that if I ever have any moving to do again, I'll be sure and call on you."

"It's so nice to be appreciated," Cole muttered with a raise of his brow and everyone laughed, even Clayton.

"I hate to interrupt such stimulating conversation," Harrison put in as he snapped the case of his watch shut and slipped it back into his vest pocket. "But we need to start packing up all of this if we intend to watch the parade at two-thirty. It's after two now."

"Is it? No wonder I feel like an overstuffed pillow. We've been eating for almost two hours," Cole said and patted his midsection soundly.

"No, you've been eating for almost two hours," Faye corrected her brother. "Most of us quit over an hour ago."

Cole scowled at her. "Thanks for pointing that out to me, Sister dear."

"Don't mention it," Faye teased. "And if you can still move after having eaten all that, Harrison's right. We need to get these things packed up and loaded back into our carriages so that we can get on over to Main."

"Okay, the women can do the packing and the men will then carry everything to the carriages," Andrew said quickly, ready to get this thing organized.

While Patricia, Faye, Catherine, Jeanne, and Minnie worked to get everything back into the baskets and the quilts properly refolded, Cole and Andrew helped Eva up and led her over to one of the park benches that had just been vacated. Then while the men, including Clayton, gathered up everything, the women stood around talking to Eva and waited for the men to return. The sisters pretended not to be keenly interested, but could not keep from watching with undeniable interest while Clayton helped Cole carry part of his load. The two men walked side by side off toward Cole's carriage in congenial silence.

It was not until they reached the carriage, put down their loads, and Cole had turned to leave that Clayton captured him by the elbow and finally spoke. "Cole, I want to speak to you a moment about William."

Cole felt a twinge in his gut. So all of this show of friendship had been a ruse to get him alone. "And what do you have to say about William that I might care to hear? He's not exactly a favorite subject of mine."

"I know, and with good reason," Clayton admitted, at first unable to look up into Cole's steely gaze, but as he made up his mind to say it, he stared up at the proud young man and boldly met his gaze. "But I have to tell you something."

While Clayton paused for just the right words, Cole wondered if he was about to give one last plea for his young friend. Cole didn't want to alienate his future father-in-law, but he also did not want to hear how William would be a better choice for Patricia. Especially not now that he knew William's true colors.

"Cole, William stopped by the house last night for a visit. I realized right away that he had been drinking, but at first he seemed his usual self, only a little slurred in his speech and a bit shaky on his feet. But after a while, he started to say things that were a little odd, even for William. He was keenly interested in your welfare and didn't like hearing that as far as I knew you were the same as ever. It was as if he was hoping, maybe even expecting, to hear that you had met with an accident of some sort. He never actually said as much. It was just a feeling I got. The man is losing his grip on reality. Some of the things he said last night frightened me. I never saw so much raw hate in a man before. He was obsessed by it. I'm really afraid of what he might do."

"Are you warning me to be careful of him?" Cole asked, surprised at the thought.

"Yes, I am. I know I have acted like a horse's ass in the past where you are concerned, but with reason. I honestly thought I had Patricia's best interest at heart," Clayton said defensively. "I didn't think you would be a good man for her."

"And you've changed your mind?" Cole felt a little leery of all this.

"Somewhat," Clayton said and threw back his shoulders. "I still think you are far too arrogant for your own good and extremely overzealous when it comes to that damn petition of yours, but I've come to realize that you truly do love my daughter." Clayton paused then grinned slightly when he added, "So you can't be all bad. At least you have good taste."

Cole stared down at Clayton with a glint of admiration. The man was trying to bridge the first gap that lay between them. There was hope for the two of them to eventually become friends after all. Nothing would please him more. "Thanks, sir. I'm probably going to surprise you by this, but I agree. I am far too arrogant and I am very overzealous when it comes to that dam. But the dam is very important to me as is your daughter. They are both things I truly believe in. I hope that when we get married in August, you will change your mind and be there to hand her over to me. It would mean a great deal to Patricia and to me."

"To tell you the truth," Clayton confessed. A light glimmer touched his eyes as moisture collected around the edges. "I had already decided to be there even before William came by last night and showed me how much I had misjudged his character. Patricia is my oldest daughter and the only one that seems to have any of my blood flowing through her veins. She's as bullheaded as they come and refuses to bend to anyone's rules but her own. I'm proud as I can be of her but I don't envy you having to tame her into being a wife."

"I don't intend to tame her. I like her just the way she is," Cole stated proudly.

Clayton gave him an appreciative nod and smiled. Then the two of them started back toward the park to rejoin the others, only this time they talked as friends would along the way.

Although the sky started to cloud back up before the parade even began, the rain held off until the parade was over and Clayton had left with Minnie and Eva to help get Eva back in her room. The afternoon outdoors had done wonders for the woman, but had tired her considerably. The rest of the group decided to convene at Marco's and although the place was already crowded to capacity, Marco somehow managed to find them a table within a few minutes.

That's when Cole announced that Clayton planned to be at their wedding to give the bride away. The tears Patricia shed touched his heart and he stated with a broad smile, "I think this calls for a celebration."

"You would," Faye said jokingly, then gave Andrew a knowing look. "Didn't I tell you. He loves a celebration."

"But this time I think he has a legitimate reason," Andrew said in defense of his friend. "I know what this must mean to Patricia." They all did and agreed that a celebration was in order.

They stayed at Marco's far longer than they had expected. It was not until they finally decided to take the women on home so that they could approach a few of the men still in town celebrating the holidays in the various saloons, that they realized it had grown dark outside and rain was still coming down steadily. Suddenly, the conversation took a serious turn.

Looking skyward as they stood out under the wide awning

in front of Marco's, Cole shook his head. "Except for the break we got yesterday, this makes eleven consecutive days with rain. I'm worried."

"Me too," Harrison replied. "That river is bound to overflow this time and as fast as it has been running these past few days, it will mean serious injuries. Never fails that the curiosity seekers don't get a little too close and get themselves hurt."

"I was thinking more about the dam," Cole explained. "I sneaked up there just the other day and took a look around. That lake is already way up and with the ground being as soaked as it already is, the watershed off the mountains above the lake is going to be tremendous. I honestly don't think that small spillway of theirs can handle the volume of water that's going to be coming in. Especially if it continues to rain like this all night."

"And it doesn't appear to be breaking up," Harrison commented, his brow furrowed with concern as he stared up at the blackened sky.

"What can you do?" Tony wanted to know. "They won't let you near enough to that dam to do a thing to help should there be a problem.

"To answer your question, I don't know what I can do, but I'm going up there just the same," Cole explained to Tony. "Are you going with me or do I go alone? I know Andrew has to report to the trustees for that final meeting tomorrow afternoon."

"I'm afraid you'll have to go alone. I have to catch a train to New York in the morning. I—I've got personal business to attend to." He intended to explain his reasons for the sudden trip to Cole later. He just didn't want Catherine to know that he had located the whereabouts of Franklin Hitt and his reason for going was to find the man and persuade him to come back with him to settle matters with Catherine once and for all.

Later, after they had safely delivered the women to their doors and had visited several saloons in order to get another twelve signatures, the three of them climbed into Cole's carriage to go home. That's when Tony finally told Cole and

Andrew about having located Franklin's address and what his intentions were.

"But aren't you taking a big risk? What if you get there and find out that this Franklin fellow still loves Catherine? What if you end up just reuniting the two lovers—leaving yourself out in the cold?" Cole asked, wondering if Tony had thought this thing through.

"It's a risk I'll have to take. I can't have Catherine's heart for my own as long as she pines away for someone from her past," Tony explained. "As long as her memory of Franklin Hitt stands in my way, I haven't a chance. I either have to eliminate him from her heart somehow or reunite them and graciously step out of the picture. But I can't go on the way things are. Almost having her, but not quite." Tony paused a moment to get a grip on the emotions that flooded him.

"That's very noble of you," Andrew said quietly.

"Not so noble," Tony replied with a sad shake of his head. "Besides, Ralph, the investigator I hired, believes that Franklin is now married. Ralph never was able to catch the woman at home in order to talk to her, but did hear rumors about how Franklin had built himself a big new house for his wife and how devoted he was to her. Having heard that, Ralph checked it out. He did see the house. It was a white-framed house with pink trim. Only a man who loves his wife would be willing to live in a home that's trimmed in pink."

Cole thought about that. It certainly made sense. "And if he is married, you intend to make him come back here and tell her?"

"He may not be willing to come back. There are still those trumped-up charges against him. I'll settle for a long letter explaining to her that it is over between them and how he has found another. She needs to know. I want him to let her down easy, but she must know the truth so that she can start to get over him and maybe find a place in her heart for me. You don't know what it's like to love someone the way I love Catherine and know that her heart belongs to someone else, someone from the past."

"How do you know the charges were trumped up?" Cole

asked as he pulled the carriage up into the drive beside Tony's house. He tried to get as close to the front door as possible so that they wouldn't have to get too wet.

"I investigated the records myself. Seems he was arrested for setting a fire that got out of hand and ended up burning half a block and killing a small child. Franklin had an alibi— a woman who swore he was at her house repairing a broken pump for her at the time. Her name was Jane Thomas and there was no real reason to suspect her of lying. But there was also a witness who swore he saw Franklin at the scene of the crime—a one disreputable Frank Gordon. The trial was poorly handled and Franklin Hitt was found guilty. Somehow, although it's never been quite clear, Franklin escaped that very day from jail and was never seen again. It all sounds pretty shady."

"Indeed it does," Cole agreed solemnly. He remembered how Patricia had once mentioned that she believed her father had had something to do with the whole thing. It seemed hard to believe that the same man who had warned him that very afternoon of William and showed such true concern of the danger Cole might be in could have set anyone up like that. Shaking the thought, he turned to Tony and wished him luck on his trip.

"You too. Don't you go getting yourself into trouble while snooping around that lake tomorrow," Tony warned him.

"Yes, you be careful. They might have you thrown in jail if they catch you trespassing," Andrew said over his shoulder just before he made a dash for the front door.

"Or worse," Tony cautioned him, then turned and stared at Cole a long moment as if needing to memorize every feature of his face. There was a loud peal of thunder that caused them both to jump and gave them an eerie feeling. For some reason Tony felt suddenly compelled to touch his friend. Reaching out and embracing Cole's shoulder with a firm grip of his hand, Tony said in an emotionally strained voice, "You are a true friend. Take care of yourself."

Then he pulled his coat collar up against the rain and hopped down from the carriage. Without looking back, he hurried toward the house where Andrew had left the door open for him, leaving Cole staring curiously after him. There was another loud clap of thunder just as Tony closed the door behind him. Cole felt extremely apprehensive as he pulled the carriage back out onto the street. He wondered why he was so jittery. Thunderstorms didn't usually affect him that way.

Chapter Twenty-four

Before heading for home, Cole made a slight detour down Mockingbird and passed in front of Patricia's house. He wanted to see if she might still be awake. For some reason, maybe it was the storm, he did not want to be alone tonight. He needed Patricia's company, her special comfort. Oh, how he wished they were already married. August seemed so far away.

Spotting a faint light in her bedroom window, he realized she was still awake. Hurriedly, he drove on down the street and parked his buggy in front of a church a couple of blocks away then walked back. His hopes were to spend the entire night with Patricia as he hastened back along the stone walk to Patricia's. By the time he finally reached her house and knocked, he was soaking wet, in spite of his oil slicker and wide-brimmed hat.

"Cole!" she exclaimed with delight when she pulled back the lace curtain and peered through the beveled pane of the narrow window beside the door and saw his rain-drenched form standing on her porch. Throwing the door open, she ordered him inside and out of his wet things. Closing the door behind him, she yanked his wet hat from his head when he passed and hooked it on the door latch to dry.

Due to the heavy, early morning chill for the past few days, Patricia had left a small fire burning at the back of the fireplace in the kitchen, which also served to heat the bathing room. Staunchly, she ordered him in there to undress immediately and followed him to make sure he obeyed. In her mind's eye, she saw herself as being very wifely at the moment.

"You'll catch your death if you're not careful," she admonished as she slid his coat off his wide shoulders and worked hastily to undo his tie and the buttons of his vest and shirt. He offered her no resistance as she quickly began to undress him. He knew he would be more comfortable without the clinging wet clothing.

While she carefully laid the damp coat, shirt, vest, and tie across a chair in front of the fireplace to dry, he went ahead and slipped out of his soaked shoes, socks, and pants then handed them to her to place near the fire too. Feeling a slight chill on his damp skin, he reached for the poker and jabbed at the low burning embers, then added a split log from the pile nearby. Soon he had the fire flaming brightly and Patricia felt compelled to move his clothing back some. It wouldn't do for his clothes to catch fire.

Once Cole was sufficiently warmed again and his clothes carefully placed, Patricia paused to gaze at the masculine physique that was now so familiar to her and noticed how enticing he looked with the golden glow of the firelight reflecting off his muscled form. Reaching out and touching the band of his underwear, she gave in to a wicked little smile and wondered if she was forever lost to the demons.

"These are wet too, Cole. They have to come off."

"Yes, ma'am," he said and stood dutifully still while she slipped the final garment from his body. Once he was naked before her, she was well aware that he had become just as fully aroused as she was. When he bent over to take the hem of her flannel gown in his hands, she willingly lifted her arms so that he could pull it up over her head. Once he had her only garment in his possession, he let it drop quietly to the floor, forgotten.

Without hesitation, Cole swept his future wife into a powerful embrace, his mouth meeting hers hungrily. Never had he felt such a need to possess her and he made love to her right there on the braided rug in front of the fireplace. Patricia sensed his need and met it with an equal passion.

374

Hungrily, they sought to meet each other's desires and soared quickly to the lofty heights, their hearts pounding in a wild furor.

Once the wild frenzy of their sudden passions had been fulfilled, they went upstairs to make leisurely love in the soft depths of her bed until sleep finally overtook them. They spent the remainder of the night clasped in each other's arms, sleeping peacefully, contented with each other's love.

The rain fell all night and despite their original plans to spend that entire Friday together, since they both had managed to get the day free, Cole followed through on the trip up to the lake to check on the dam. He promised her he would get back as quickly as possible so that they could still spend the afternoon together, but until he had examined the lake for himself, he would not have the peace of mind to enjoy the day. He had to know what condition the lake was in. If there was a problem, he wanted Johnstown to be warned. He left even before she could prepare him breakfast, stopping by his house just long enough to change into heavy work clothes, unhitch his carriage, and saddle his horse.

Although the rain finally stopped just after daybreak, Cole was extremely worried about what he was going to find once he reached the lake. He wondered if his struggle to force the club members to make that dam safe before anything terrible could happen would end up having been in vain. He felt uneasy, apprehensive, as he rode along the main road out of town.

Unaware he was being followed at a distance, Cole attributed his unusually skittish mood to the weather and his worries about what he would find once he got to the dam. He had no reason to suspect more.

Half an hour after the last of the guests at Lake Conemaugh left for the South Fork depot to catch the evening train to Pittsburgh, James Seale stepped out onto the porch to enjoy the peace and quiet. It had been quite a holiday and although he had enjoyed the people being there for the day's festivities, he was glad for a moment alone

375

at last.

There had been a cool dampness in the air all day and heavy overcast skies most of the afternoon, but by some stroke of luck, Memorial Day had passed without so much as a drop of rain coming down to destroy the day's festivities at the lake. With all the rain they'd had lately, it was certainly a welcome relief, especially as far as James was concerned. The escalating height of the lake worried him. He wished the president of the club had been one of the holiday guests that afternoon. The present height of the lake would have made quite an impression on him. And James felt he might have found a chance to show the man his drawings of the dam and the improvements it needed.

Staring up at the cloud-filled sky, James's thoughts returned to the weather. He hoped that the threat of rain would pass them by this time. The wind was up and it looked as if it might have rained to the west much of the afternoon, but so far no rain had fallen on the lake. There was still the possibility that the clouds would blow right on over and the rain would miss them entirely. When James went on to bed just after ten he was hopeful—there still had been no rain and the wind had let up some.

The rain began again right after he went to sleep, just a few minutes past eleven.

When James awoke from a sound sleep around six the following morning, he heard the heavy rain hammering against the lofty windows of his room and became instantly alarmed. He quickly left the warmth that clung to his bed and padded across the polished wooden floor to look out at the weather. It was raining so hard he could barely see the shape of the nearest tree. But by the time he had gotten dressed and stepped outside onto the front veranda, the rain had suddenly stopped and a thick, almost white fog hung heavily to the ground. He could not see the lake for the fog, but heard a sickening roar of water off toward the head of the lake to the southeast. Hurrying to the water's edge, he discovered it had risen at least another two feet from yesterday and now had to be only about four feet below what he figured was the crest of the dam. He could not tell exactly

376

how fast the water was rising, but was not encouraged by the crashing sounds that came from the head of the lake.

"Damn," he muttered even though it was completely out of character for him, then turned to go get a rowboat from the main boathouse. He needed to see what was happening at the southeast end of the lake where several rivers and streams emptied down from the northwest side of the Allegheny mountain range.

Finding one of the Italians who was hired to help install the plumbing already awake and rambling about, he sought the young man's help and the two of them took off for the head of the lake in a matter of minutes.

As they rowed across the foggy lake, they passed all manner of floating debris. That worried James. Small trees and bushes had been completely uprooted and planking from the sawmill upstream had been washed right off the banks and into the water. It didn't look good at all.

The situation was far worse once they reached the southern shore and discovered that the two largest rivers there were swollen and sweeping down through the woods at such a rate that they were stripping branches and leaves from the trees as high as six feet from the ground. After docking on the driest land they could find, they walked into the woods toward the four other rivers and streams that fed into the lake and discovered that for almost half a mile, the woods literally boiled with foaming water. It came crashing and curling in at every angle.

James felt a cold fear coil inside him as he realized what was happening. Hurrying back to the boat, he was terrified to discover that in the short period of time they had been gone, the water had risen enough to put their boat afloat. Rushing out into the frigid, churning water, they rescued the boat and headed back for the docks in front of the clubhouse to see if Captain Reid had arrived yet.

When he reached the clubhouse and discovered that the captain had not even been in for breakfast, James wasted no further time. He rushed to the stables for his horse and, within minutes, was galloping through the heavy mist toward the dam a mile and a half away. As far as he could tell, the lake was rising about an inch every ten to fifteen minutes and if this was so, the water would reach the top of the dam in a matter of hours unless something could be done to release more water than the spillway was now handling.

There was already a dozen or so people there when James reached the dam. A clump of bystanders, mostly from neighboring farms and the small borough of South Fork a couple of miles away, stood well out of the way as several of the Italian workers worked frantically with picks and shovels in a futile effort to throw up a small ridge of earth across the top of the dam in order to heighten it some. Rafe Buie, the captain's personal hired man, was doing the same with a horse and plow, but with very little success. James felt that the task was ludicrous. The loose dirt would wash away almost instantly. They were doing more harm than good. The grooves they made would only weaken the top of the structure and they certainly did not need that.

At the southwest end of the dam, James soon noticed several more of the workers busy trying to cut a new spillway through the tough shale of the hillside several feet beyond the other side. They had managed to cut through about half the width of the dam, but the trench was barely knee-deep and the breadth was no more than a couple of feet wide. That would hardly help.

Next James noticed Captain Reid sitting on a horse in his black gum coat and oiled boots issuing orders at the top of his lungs. James headed straight for him.

In Johnstown, the situation had just started to get serious. There had been a small landslide that caved in a stable at Kress's Brewery sometime before sunup. By seven o'clock the two rivers that flowed into Johnstown were rising so rapidly that Cambria Iron sent its men home to look after their houses and families. There were cellars to be cleared and furniture to be carried upstairs in case the river should actually flow out of its banks again, which it looked like it had a good chance of doing. Having dealt with this before on an almost annual basis, everyone pretty well knew just what

378

to do. It was bothersome, but nothing more.

By ten o'clock the water started to pour into the lower business district. Main Street, which was several blocks away, soon filled with water. People in houses higher up, who usually did not worry about flooding from the rivers, started to clear their cellars. It looked as if this was going to be one of the worst ever.

Tony and Andrew took just such precautions at Tony's house before they left for the depot. They cleared the entire lower floor of everything but the largest divan and a piano which the two of them not only couldn't lift but would have had a hard time getting up the stairs because of its width. They finished the work just in time for Tony to make the train to New York.

Promptly at ten o'clock, Andrew pulled right up to the steps of the depot platform and waited until Tony had boarded the train before leaving. Since he was already out, Andrew decided to drive down by the flood area and see just how bad it really was before going back to Tony's. It was far worse than he expected. Being new to Johnstown, Andrew had only seen the river leave its banks once, last spring. He was surprised by what he found when he tried to reach Main Street. A small lake had formed. The muddy water swirled everywhere. Buildings on Main Street were already a foot underwater while people waded around helping move things from the lower floors to the upper ones.

Spotting a man he recognized from the Todd Street church tromping through the water with his britches legs rolled up past the knee, Andrew asked if there was anything he could do to help.

"No, Reverend Edwards, not unless you have a boat," the man replied with a laugh and a shrug then gazed out at the murky water. "I was hoping to get across to the other side before it got too bad. But it looks like I'm out of luck this time."

Andrew could scarcely believe the man was taking this so lightly. When he glanced around at the people he saw milling about, he realized they were all taking this in a very easy manner. He heard comments like: "Another two feet and it will be the worst flood in history. It'll even beat the flood of 1887. I sure wish I had my fishing gear. Too bad it's so cold, it would be rather sporting to swim across Main Street, don't you think?"

When he turned the carriage around and headed back to Tony's house, Andrew wondered how they could seem so unconcerned. For the next few hours, he sat on the front porch with an eye toward the flood area many blocks away, glad Tony's house was on higher ground.

The train Tony had boarded for Philadelphia was scheduled to leave Johnstown precisely at 10:20. When it did not move by 10:40, Tony went in search of the conductor to see if he could find out why there was such a delay. He was anxious to get to New York and find this Westchester County where Franklin was supposed to be living now. He hoped to be on his way back to Johnstown with either Franklin or at least a letter from him by early Monday morning.

"We've been delayed because of a washout on the eastbound track on up the valley a ways," the conductor explained tiredly. "Part of the mountainside gave way because of all the rain lately. But don't worry, they are working on the problem. We should be on our way directly."

Knowing the man was being evasive because he didn't know any more than that, Tony decided not to question him further and went back to his seat and waited. It was just after eleven before the train finally lurched forward and started to move. Looking out the window beside him, he realized they had eased out onto the westbound tracks headed east, right behind a small mail train. Looking back, he noticed another train followed. With a sharp exhale of breath, he fervently hoped they knew what they were doing and prayed someone had cleared the way before attempting such a venture. But after about only ten minutes of travel, they slowly came to a stop and Tony glanced out the window again to see why.

They had barely gotten as far as East Conemaugh, which was two miles beyond Johnstown, and stopped. Tony could see the huge roundhouses of the railroad yards just ahead. Curious as to the unscheduled stop, he went in immediate search of the conductor and soon learned that the trains had again been delayed because of another washout, only this time both tracks were gone and until the proper repairs could be done, no one was getting through. He was also told that another train, a daily express called the Chicago Limited, was on the other side in the very same predicament only wanting to go west. But knowing that did little to soothe Tony's impatience. He wanted to be on his way.

Meanwhile, Cole finally reached the lake. Due to the same washout that had taken the railroad tracks, the main road alongside the tracks had become impassable. Cole had been forced to leave his horse behind and trudge the last few miles through the woods on foot. Having tested the ground near the washed-out area, he had found it to be too soft to dare risk the weight of his horse. It had almost not supported his own weight in places.

But Frank Gordon had not made the same decision. He felt in no mood to go tramping through the water-soaked woods on foot and carelessly coaxed his horse to follow the same path Cole had just taken. It had been a poor choice, for the animal quickly became buried to his belly in mud and Frank was almost unable to make it back to solid ground alive. By the time he had reached safety, Cole was long gone and Frank was thoroughly disgusted. Even though he had received a message during the night from William that had sounded extremely urgent, asking that he get the deed done as soon as possible, and even though he had sent a return message saying that he expected to get everything taken care of that very next day, he decided to wait and kill the sorry bastard some other time. Preferably later that afternoon when he returned from wherever it was he just went or else first thing in the morning. For now, he had to figure out some way to free his horse. That animal had cost him nearly a hundred dollars.

Having reached the lake safely, Cole noticed that the water was up even more than it had been the week before. He wasted no time in heading for the dam. When it first came into sight, he was horrified. The fog had finally lifted and he could easily see that the water was less than a foot from the dam's crest. He was also able to see all the work that was going on at both ends. Around thirty people, divided into two groups, labored frantically in the two different areas. When he realized one of the groups was struggling to free the iron fish grate that had been placed over the spillway years ago, he hurried over to help. When he reached the group, it was obvious that the grate was heavily clogged with debris, for almost no water flowed through the spillway. The grate had to go.

Standing chest high in the chilling water with at least a dozen other men, Cole worked frantically to pull the grate loose but it just wouldn't budge. It was being held in by the heavy build-up of debris and mud and a thick wedgework of cement. They didn't have enough collective strength to work it loose. They tried clearing away the thick layer of debris, but as soon as even a handful was removed, more came to take its place. It was a useless effort.

Spying a horse tied to a tree nearby, Cole had an idea.

"Does anyone have any rope?" he asked as he sloshed his way out of the swirling brown water and started to climb the wet, grassy slope toward the horse. One of the young men who had followed him out realized what he was going to try and ran off to find some rope. It was several minutes before he returned with a large coil of sturdy braided rope.

"Thanks, fella."

"James," the young man replied. "The name's James."

Cole nodded with a smile and immediately took the rope and jumped back into the water. The depth near the jammed-up spillway was now almost up to his neck and nearly reached the top of the grate, but Cole had already realized that the water would spill over the crest of the dam long before it would pour over the top of the grate. Taking a deep breath, he dove under and cleared a spot near the base of the grate so that he could push the rope through. A man on the other side grabbed the end as soon as he spotted it and worked it back into another area like he had been instructed while Cole surfaced for another breath. Plunging back

382

under, Cole quickly worked enough of the rope through the mass of debris tō enable him to tie it off. His lungs ached for air before he was finally through and able to surface again.

When he finally did surface, he tossed the other end of the rope back up to where James stood waiting on the bank. He watched anxiously while the young man struggled to secure it to the saddlehorn. Suddenly it started to rain again but no one took the time to look up and study the dark sky at the moment.

"Now when I say pull, back that animal up. The rest of you grab hold and pull too," Cole shouted up at them as he pushed his wet hair away from his eyes. Blinking against the heavy downpour of rain, he turned to grasp the rope himself and shouted, "Pull!"

He could feel the rope tighten in his grip and although the grate groaned several times, it did not give way.

"Pull!"

The horse whinnied and the men cursed as they gave it their all. Still the grate did not budge.

Climbing out of the water, Cole called to the rest of the men still trying to dig a trench on the other side of the dam. Once they had all joined them, there were over thirty men and a horse playing a frantic game of tug-of-war with the stubborn grate. They pulled until their boots were completely buried in the mud, but still the grate stood fast. It was no use. They just did not have the proper means to do the job. Cole realized now that even a dozen horses would not move that grate. It was embedded.

Abandoning the grate altogether, Cole and the others picked up shovels, picks, and whatever implements they could find that could dig or scoop and started back to work on the new trench. They desperately needed a spillway of some sort. The rain continued to come down hard, hampering their progress almost as much as the rocky terrain did. Water continuously filled the trench and made progress next to impossible. Despite their valiant efforts, they were losing the race to save the dam and they all knew it.

Cole saw that two leaks had already started to spurt along the face of the dam, shooting water out several feet. As he continued to work, the lake slowly rose to become level with the top of the dam and started to pour over where the mound sagged slightly in the middle. Even Captain Reid climbed down from his horse to help with the actual labor. Time was running out.

Catherine stayed in bed far longer than she normally would. She saw no real reason to get up. Just knowing Tony would be gone for several days had put her into a strange, melancholy mood that she could not seem to pull herself out of. She had gotten too used to seeing him and enjoying his company. And since she did not have to work that day anyway, she simply preferred to stay in bed and mope. She knew she should not feel that strongly about him, but despite everything, she did and there was nothing she could seem to do about it.

Glancing at the tiny Tampa clock on her bedside table, she realized it was almost eleven-thirty. Tony was barely gone from Johnstown an hour and she already missed him dreadfully. He had told her he would probably return as early as Monday, but that seemed so very far away. Her pout started to quiver.

It was then that Catherine realized she still cared for Tony too much. Covering her head with a pillow, she moaned softly. What was she going to do about Tony? How could she have let him come to mean so much to her? She knew better. Curse her traitorous heart.

A sharp rapping at her door brought her thoughts temporarily away from the misery that so thoroughly engulfed her. "Come in," she called out while she slipped the pillow back to where it belonged—under her head instead of over it.

Fully expecting her intruder to be Minnie, Catherine waited dutifully for her lecture on lazing away the morning while she watched the door open. But to her relief, her visitor turned out to be Jeanne.

"What are you still doing in bed?" Jeanne asked as she breezed into the room and came to sit on the edge of her sister's bed, causing it to sag slightly when she did. Pulling off the suede glove on her right hand, she reached out and felt of Catherine's cool forehead, then frowned. "You don't seem to be very sick to me."

"No, just lazy, I guess. I slept late. I had a hard time falling asleep last night for some reason and just didn't wake up when I should have. Nothing to concern yourself with," Catherine assured her. All of that was true to a certain extent. She had had a hard time falling asleep last night because she couldn't stop thinking about Tony and how he was going to be gone for three long days, maybe more, and how it bothered her that she would not be seeing him when it shouldn't bother her at all.

"Well, hurry up and get dressed. Minnie is downstairs preparing lunch for us and she's already pretty upset because you missed your breakfast," Jeanne warned her. "Father's a little concerned too. He remembers how cold and wet you were when you came home last night."

"Father? Is he still here?"

"Not exactly still here. He's back. He had to close down the brewery because of the flooding. After he had everyone clear off the ground floors and wax the machinery, there was little else that could be done, so he came on home. He'll be joining us for lunch," Jeanne explained as she watched Catherine ease out of bed and hurry over to her armoire to get dressed. "He seems to be in an extremely good mood for such a miserable day."

"How bad has it flooded this time?"

"They say most of the lower business district is already under a foot or so of water. As usual, the Little Conemaugh River is flooding the most. I heard that Stony Creek didn't start to flood until a little over an hour ago. And Father told me that the water in town had already gone beyond Main Street before he left the brewery to come home about an hour and a half ago. This just could be the worst flood yet."

"How awful," Catherine stated as she pulled her gown up over her head and quickly slipped into her chemise and underskirts. She gave her bedroom windows a quick glance, but could not see out. She had never bothered to pull the curtains back. "Is it still raining?"

"Yes, but not very hard at the moment."

"Well, that's good. I wonder if Cole went on up to the lake like he said he might?" Catherine questioned as she pulled on a lightweight blue and white gingham dress, which was one of her favorites, but because of the chill, she also wrapped her shoulders in a thick white crocheted shawl.

"Yes, he did. According to Patricia, he left just before daybreak," Jeanne told her, wondering how Patricia knew when he had left. Had he stopped off and wakened her just to tell her good-bye? Or had he . . . Jeanne pushed that thought aside. It was none of her business anyway.

"Then if there was trouble up at the dam, we would have heard by now," Catherine said with an obvious sigh of relief. "I'd hate to think of all that water up there coming down on us when we already have all this terrible flooding in the streets."

"Wouldn't that be a mess," Jeanne agreed. "I'd bet the water would swell all the way to here before it started to go back down. No telling what would happen to the buildings next to the river."

Another light rapping at Catherine's door cut the conversation short before it had a chance to become any more morbid than it already was. Minnie had come up to warn them that lunch would be ready in about ten minutes and that neither of them had better be late. She gave Catherine a quick once-over to be sure she was all right before heading back to the kitchen to keep an eye on the meal.

Not about to go against Minnie's staunch orders, the two went immediately downstairs and seated themselves in their usual places across from one another at the main dining table. Clayton came in minutes later and made himself comfortable in his chair at the head of the table, but before Minnie was able to bring the food out, there was a heavy pounding on the front door. Clayton quickly pushed his chair back and went to see who it might be and returned just minutes later with a solemn expression pressed hard into his features.

"Tell Minnie I'm not going to be able to have lunch after all," he said as he shrugged into his coat. "The water has already reached Market Street and is still rising. It's only a square away from the rooming house over on Locust and just two squares away from the one on Franklin. I need to get down there and make sure Kilburn has the evacuation of the ground floors under way. I especially want to see about the one over on Locust. After all, the furniture in that front parlor is brand-new. I sure hope Kilburn had the sense to get it upstairs."

Having said that, Clayton turned and walked out of the room only to return seconds later with an afterthought. "I want you girls to go on up into your mother's sewing room on the third floor and stay there this afternoon. There's no sense taking any risks. There's always a chance Cole might be right about that dam. And if it should go, I'd want you two safe and out of harm's way." He paused a moment, then added, "You would probably be safe enough on the second story, especially since this house is so solidly built up, but just the same, I want you to promise me you will go on up to the third floor. Do you promise?"

Catherine and Jeanne looked at each other then at their father. Neither was eager to spend the day in their mother's sewing room. Because it was usually kept shut, the room was very stuffy and musty-smelling. And it held too many memories of their mother.

Reluctantly, Catherine finally spoke up. "Yes, Father, we will go on up after we have eaten. I promise." But what she failed to promise was how long they would stay. She knew that would depend on how restless and bored they got while sitting in the confines of the tiny room. A game of hearts could only hold one's attention so long.

"Good, I should be back in a few hours," Clayton told them, then turned to leave again. After having taken only a few steps, he turned back again and said, "See that you keep your promise. I wouldn't want to lose my girls. I don't think I could stand it." Then he left.

Chapter Twenty-five

"Hello, missy, you are just in time for lunch. Katy and Jeanne are already in the dining room," Minnie said when she looked up from the stove to find Patricia entering the kitchen through the back door. "How does baked trout with shallot dressing sound to you?"

"Absolutely delicious," she said as she laid her umbrella aside and took a deep whiff of the rich aroma that filled the kitchen. "Smells delicious too. Are you sure there will be enough?"

"More than plenty. I was expecting your father to eat, but he has rushed off to see the flood. You just go in there and have yourself a seat. I'll be bringing the food directly."

Taking one last whiff, Patricia did exactly as told. She had hoped when she left the house that she would be in time for lunch. She was hungry but in no mood to prepare something just for herself—nor did she want to eat alone.

"Patricia, what a surprise," Catherine exclaimed when she noticed her oldest sister entering the dining room through the kitchen door. "Are you here for lunch?"

"And a little company. I was getting bored sitting at the house alone. Cole won't be back until sometime later this afternoon and I really don't have anything to do until then. What did I used to do with all my time before I started to work at the brewery?"

"You were married, remember? There's always plenty to do when you have a husband to care for," Jeanne reminded her. "Then before that, you were too busy trifling with all the boys to ever be bored."

"I didn't trifle with any boys," Patricia protested as she took her usual seat beside Catherine. Carefully, she placed the crisp white napkin over her tiered dress of pongee and brown velvet. She did not want to soil the skirt which was draped in large scallops and revealed a pretty white linen and lace underskirt. The dress had been selected especially with Cole in mind.

"Not much you didn't," Jeanne chuckled. "I used to wish I had your talent for batting an eye, but then I think green eyes were made for batting and mine were never really quite green."

"That's ridiculous," Patricia muttered, half-smiling. "If anyone had the reputation of having a wayward eye as a girl, it was you, green eyes or not."

"Let's not get into that old argument about which of you was the worst with a flirtation," Catherine admonished. "As I recall, you both were pretty silly when it came to your gentlemen callers."

Both Jeanne and Patricia opened their mouths to respond to that, but at that moment Minnie came through the door carrying a huge tray of steaming food and the aroma was so delicious that it took their full attention and caused them to drop the argument for the moment. They all eyed the plates being set before them and breathed deeply the tantalizing aroma, waiting until they had each been served so they could bite into Minnie's baked trout. No one could cook like Minnie did.

Once they had finished with what had been put on their plates, Patricia decided she was still hungry and rose to go see if there might be any more of that sumptuous dressing left when they heard someone knock at the front door.

"I'm already up," Patricia remarked sensibly as she laid her plate back down. "I'll get it."

When she hurried to open the door with intentions of quickly getting rid of whoever it was, she found Brandon Beam standing on the veranda, wet to the knees in his usual three-piece suit with the high-button frock coat.

390

"Is your father here?" Brandon wanted to know as he took off his derby out of politeness and looked eagerly past her into the house.

"No, he's gone down to the flood area for a while. I believe to check on his boardinghouses. Was there something important you wanted him for?"

"Not really, I guess. I just didn't see him standing about while I was down there. I knew that the brewery was already closed down and thought maybe he was here. I wanted to tell him how bad it is getting down there. I thought he might like to walk back with me after lunch and have a little look-see—too much chaos to be going down there in a buggy. But if he's already down there, I'll just have to make the walk back alone."

"And how bad is it getting?" Patricia asked, then remembering her manners, she stepped back and motioned for him to come inside.

"No, I better stay out here," he said politely, then looked down at his clinging trouser legs. "I managed to get a little wet while I was down there. I guess I should have waited to stop by here after I had gone home and lunched. Then I could have changed into dry clothes first. But I did want Clayton to know what-all was going on."

Patricia's curiosity got the best of her. "Just what is going on down there?"

"It's the worst flood ever," he answered readily, eager to tell some of what he had seen. "There's already been one fatality for certain and several people have gotten themselves pretty badly injured," he told her, then glancing beyond Patricia again, he nodded politely to Jeanne and Catherine. "Oh, hello, ladies."

"Hello, Mr. Beam, what was that you were saying about a fatality?" Jeanne asked, her hand pressed to her breastbone as she joined Patricia in the doorway with Catherine standing just behind her. All three of them were horrified that someone had actually been killed but curious about the details despite themselves. "I can't recall a death ever happening during any of the previous floods."

"Nor can I, but a man named Joseph Ross, who they say

was a driver for Cambria Iron, drowned when he accidentally stepped off into a cellar that had just been dug for a new building—one they were getting ready to go up over on Main Street. Seems he couldn't swim and there was no way for him to know the hole was there. The water's over two feet high around there now. It looks like a big lake has settled in on the whole lower part of town. A few men have taken to row boats in order to help some of the people that have gone and gotten themselves stranded. It's beyond me where they got those boats. The only time that river is really deep enough for any boating, the current is usually too swift to enjoy it, but those boats are sure coming in handy today."

"Is the water still rising?" Patricia wanted to know and hoped that the answer would be no.

"It appears to be," the man answered enthusiastically. "If it keeps up, there may be fishing in the park by this afternoon."

Patricia was appalled that the man found the situation so humorous, but kept any remarks that might relay her feelings to herself. After all, Mr. Beam was one of her father's best friends as well as his next-door neighbor and she should treat him with courtesy. But it became a hard task to manage when he started making light of the dam.

"And sure enough," he said with a half-grin. "They are a'claiming that the dam is absolutely bound to go this time—and say that if the river is up this high, the lake must surely be up as well."

"That makes sense," Jeanne put in, also annoyed with the man's frivolous attitude. "I heard that the lake is up and that surely has to be putting more strain on the dam."

"Even if it is, why should it mean the dam is going to actually break?" Brandon Beam asked with a disgusted shake of his head. His brow pulled together to express the absurdity of the idea. "It has stood the test of time. It's done its job for forty years. So why is it every time the river overflows its banks that someone invariably brings up that old hackneyed tale about the dam breaking?" Clearly, he was not worried over the prospect and had forgotten the girls ever had a part in circulating a petition. "Anyway, I'm going back down there after I eat a bite. Maybe I'll catch Clayton around there somewhere. Good-bye, ladies." With a quick tip of his derby, the man turned and strolled off toward the gate as if he hadn't a care in the world.

"I'm starting to really worry," Patricia said once she had closed the door. As she stood in the entryway a moment, staring at her two sisters, the true seriousness of the situation soaked in. "We already have more water in the streets than ever before. What if that dam was to break now? Just think of the danger that could cause. I think we should pack a bag each and get ourselves up to higher ground and stay there until this thing is over."

"That might be best," Catherine agreed hesitantly. "But where would we go?"

"Up to Green Hill. We could take Father's stanhope and stay up there until we see the water start to recede."

"I don't know. What if it should start raining again? We would surely get wet in that small buggy and catch our deaths in this chilly weather. I for one just got over a dreadful bout with a cold," Catherine reminded her. "And I'm reluctant to expose myself to another. Father says we should be safe enough right here on the third floor of the house even if the dam should break."

"She's right," Jeanne put in, not wanting to spend the afternoon and maybe even part of the night sitting in the lone seat of the stanhope and waiting out the flood in the woods somewhere, especially on such a cold and rainy day. "It would be best if we just stayed on the third floor. We would at least be warm, comfortable, and dry should the worst happen."

"Yes, but we need to keep in mind that we could be stuck up on the top floor for a few days," Catherine quickly pointed out before Patricia had a chance to respond to what Jeanne had said. "Maybe we should store some canned goods up there just in case."

"And it might be wise to go ahead and clear the cellar of anything that could ruin and prepare the bottom floor in case the water should actually come up to there. We all know the condition of that dam. I think it would be wise to take all the necessary precautions."

"Yes," Catherine added. "Better to be safe than sorry. Instead of running off, we should be preparing the house for several feet of water just in case."

Despite the reservations she still held, Patricia did see the logic in Catherine's suggestion and stayed to help her sisters and Minnie carry what furniture and carpets they could lift from the bottom floor on up to the second floor. Then they set about pinning all the curtains and drapes so that the hems would not be soiled by the muddy water should it rise that high. As soon as they had finished with the ground floor, they proceeded to clear the most important items out of the cellar and carried them up to the second floor too. Soon the second floor was so crowded they could hardly get around, but felt everything would at least be safe from ruin.

When they finally finished, they decided to walk down to Jeanne's house two blocks away and do the same thing there. Minnie asked to be allowed to go stay with her sister for the rest of the afternoon. Having helped with all the flood preparations had made her a little skittish. She wanted to be near her partially crippled sister in case such a terrible thing did occur. And she wanted to make sure any valuable furniture was stored safely away in the attic until the threat of flooding was over.

Once the three sisters had reached Jeanne's house, they proceeded to make the same sort of preparations there as they had at their father's house, but with Ruby's help this time. Working without rest, it took them just over an hour to prepare Jeanne's home for the possibility of flooding, but because their father had been so adamant about having them stay in the sewing room at his house, Catherine suggested they go on back and do just that. "It really is the most sensible place to be should the worst actually happen. Especially since the house is built up off the street the way it is. It'll be safer."

"And drier," Jeanne quickly agreed and left her house in Ruby's care, ordering her to stay up on the second or third floor as much as possible.

On the walk back, they realized that of all their houses,

Patricia's would be the first and most likely to be flooded. It was built in a much lower part of town. Having realized that, Catherine and Jeanne offered to walk with her over to her house and help prepare her bottom floor and tiny cellar but Patricia refused. "There's no need. If you think about it, there's not that much worth saving at my house, not since William paid his recent late-night visit. Besides, Cole and I will be able to clear what I do still have in no time. He should be getting back about now."

"Are you sure? We may be tired, but we are still willing to help you get some of your furniture and things up to the second floor," Jeanne offered again.

"No, it's after two o'clock now. Cole will be back any minute, that is if he isn't back already, and he can lift all the heavy things for me. Like I said, we'll have the bottom floor cleared in no time."

"I wonder how bad it's gotten by now?" Catherine said, and looked off in the direction she knew the Little Conemaugh River joined with Stony Creek. Even though she was unable to see the area from where she stood, her imagination and the description Mr. Beam had given them caused her to shiver and pull her cloak tighter around her shoulders.

"Maybe it has started to go down by now," Jeanne injected hopefully. "After all, it hasn't rained any since before noon and it was little more than a sprinkle then."

"We can always hope," Patricia said lightly, even though she did not feel very hopeful in her heart. Something inside her kept twisting at her, haunting her, as if it was trying to warn her. Looking skyward, she added with as much conviction as she could muster, "And I think the sky might be a shade lighter. Maybe the worst of it is over."

"Well, you'd better get on home so that you and Cole can get to work on your house just in case it isn't," Jeanne cautioned her. "I guess Catherine and I should go on up to the sewing room for a while. We can always carry a deck of playing cards with us and pass the afternoon playing hearts. Let us know when and if you hear that the water has started to go down. I don't want to spend any more time than I have to up there."

Patricia promised to do just that, knowing that Cole was probably out there in the midst of everything, helping where he could, and would be one of the first to realize when the water started to recede. Because of that, she felt certain she would also be one of the first to know.

On her way back to her house, Patricia passed Othell Shattels as he hurried away from downtown, his expression bent with concern. He stopped when he noticed her and told her in no uncertain terms to stay away from the flood area. "It's bad. Really bad. The river is flowing through the town like an angry shrew, knocking people down that venture out too deep and pulling them under when it can. The current is something terrible to behold. The Poplar Street and Cambria City bridges are down and other bridges are soon to follow."

"Have there been any more fatalities other than the Mr. Ross I've already been told about?" she asked, her eyes wide with the fear of what the answer might be to that. How she hated to think of anyone having to die such a violent death.

"Not that I know of, but if it keeps up, there will be. There are still some stubborn people refusing to leave their homes in the flats and the water's about to get too deep to even let them. When it does, they aren't going to be able to leave at all, even if they should finally decide they want to. Already, there's some who can't hope to get out at all except by boat, unless they have a hankering to try and swim the swift current. And that could prove to be dangerous. They never should have tried to stick it out inside their houses in the first place. They should have headed on up here to higher ground as soon as the river started to overflow but they think they need to stay and protect their homes. Such foolishness. What can they do? They should have gotten out while they could. And don't you go getting it in your head to go down there."

"I won't," she assured him. "I'm headed home."

"Well, don't you stay there too long. The best thing to do is pack up and get to higher ground. Most folks are making fun of me, saying I'm always expecting the worst to happen, but

396

you just mark my words. That river isn't through with us yet."

Patricia watched as the flushed little man hurried away in the direction she had just come before she finally turned and resumed her way along the sidewalk. Having heard the frantic quality in Mr. Shattles's voice, her feet now seemed to meet the walkway at a rapid pace. She was eager to get home and see what Cole had to say about the situation. He would know if they should head for higher ground or not. He would have seen the dam and known the danger if there was any.

When Patricia neared Mockingbird Street, she was surprised to find that the water had already reached her own yard. Even with the awful reports she had been hearing all day, she had never fully expected to find the water in her own yard. Never had a flood reached this level. Having to wade through several inches of water in order to get through the gate, Patricia hurried up the steps and unlocked the door. She was disappointed to find Cole was nowhere around and it looked as if he hadn't been there since morning. There was no note to tell her he had come and left nor was there anything else that would indicate that he or anyone else had been there.

Feeling more edgy than ever, she decided to keep busy while she waited for him. After changing her wet boots for a pair of dry ones, she immediately began to clear what she could of her meager furnishings along with some of her smaller area rugs from the first floor. Even with all the work to keep her occupied, she couldn't stop worrying about Cole and the dam, especially now that she knew he had never returned. What was keeping him up there? Was there trouble? She hurried in her effort to prepare her house for the worst. With the water already reaching her porch steps, it was inevitable that her house would be flooded should the dam actually break. It only had to rise another two feet to enter her front door.

As she worked, Patricia kept noticing the new wallpaper she'd had to get after William's escapade and hoped that Cole's predictions about just how much the water could swell if the dam should ever break would be proven wrong.

She remembered he had once told her that he felt the water could actually rise as much as ten or twelve feet when the first rush of water passed through. She wondered how long it would take for a lake that size to pass by. Sadly she shook her head and knew that her wallpaper would be doomed. It was only three feet from the floor where it met the lower wood paneling, which was highly polished and would withstand water far better. But then, maybe the water would just rise a few feet after all and her wallpaper would be safe. Better yet, maybe, just maybe the dam wouldn't break at all.

But the water at Lake Conemaugh was going over the top in thick heavy sheets and bits and pieces of the dam were falling away in chunks. The temporary ridges that had been thrown up had not lasted any time and there was very little hope left when the captain decided to send James Seale on horseback to the nearest telegraph station, in South Fork two miles away.

James rode like a crazed man and made the distance in about ten minutes, but because he was so new to the area and had stayed mainly at the lake, no one paid much attention to him or his warning. Nobody really knew who he was and did not credit him for having much sense. It was only after several minutes of arguments and desperate pleadings that the telegraph operator finally gave in and decided to pass his message along down the line and only then after James had paid her well. By the time he had returned to the dam, he could sense that the end was very near. He just hoped they had given the towns below enough warning.

"Did you get the message off?" Cole called out to him the moment he rode up.

"Yes, finally. But I had a hard time getting them to think enough of me to send it," he shouted back over the deafening roar of the water which was now crashing over the eroding dam in huge glassy sheets several feet thick.

"Maybe I should send someone else down there to reemphasize the danger here," Captain Reid said after he heard James's remark. "This dam is going to go. We will never get that trench dug in time to save it. Hey, Maguire," he called out to a man who had stopped his digging just long enough to wipe the grimy sweat from his brow. Ever since it had stopped raining, the humidity had been almost unbearable, despite the unseasonably cold temperature. "I want you to go down to South Fork and have them send another message down the line. This time tell them the dam is definitely going to go and to head for the hills."

"Yes, we need to be sure they get a warning," Cole agreed gravely as he looked back toward where the lake poured angrily over the weakening dam and cascaded down the steep mountainside. "And I want you to send a message to Mrs. Patricia Morgan on Mockingbird. Pay extra to have it dispatched directly to her." Reaching into his pocket, he dug out his wallet and handed it to the man. "Pay whatever they ask."

"Will do," the burly man replied as he shoved the wallet into his shirt pocket. "Mind if I borrow enough to have the same message sent to my wife? I'll pay you back. I promise."

"Sure, go ahead," Cole said quickly. "But hurry. Once this dam breaks there won't be any telegraph lines to send messages on. They are all too near the river."

"And stay there until you have actually witnessed the messages being sent. I want to be absolutely sure the towns down below get a warning," Captain Reid told him as he too dug into his pocket and pulled out a coin. "Here, this is for my message. Send it all the way to Pittsburgh."

"I can't believe they'd make you pay for passing along a message that is meant to warn the towns and save lives," Maguire grumbled as he hurriedly climbed onto the horse James had just ridden. Instantly, he spurred the animal into a steady lope and was headed back down the mountain toward South Fork to issue a final warning. Meanwhile, Cole and the captain picked up their shovels and returned to the narrow trench. Frantically, they continued to work at digging out the new spillway, even though everyone knew they would never be able to finish it in time.

It was three-thirty before Patricia finished putting everything she was able to carry up on the second floor and out of the way. The whole time she worked, she kept an anxious eye on her windows, watching for Cole. She did not know if she should be angry with him for not coming on back or be worried. But knowing Cole would never intentionally put her through such torment, she finally faced the fact that she should be worried, very worried.

From her bedroom windows on the second floor, she was able to see part of the business district in the distance where the water had already risen to the level of the lower windows of many of the buildings. It had also risen another foot in her own yard. She was glad that it had not rained again since before noon. She couldn't remember the water ever being this high or looking this menacing. She wondered if the dam might have already burst. Was that why the water was so high? How much higher would it get?

While leaning out of the window and staring morosely in the direction she felt certain Cole would come, she overheard someone talking. Looking down the street to her right, she found the source. A small boy was talking to an elderly man in front of her neighbor's house. She could hear them clearly. They were arguing about the dam. The young boy was trying to convince the man that the dam had already burst open and that the water was on its way, but the man did not believe a word of it.

"But, sir, it has burst. A message came through on the telegraph while I was right there—just minutes ago. It said for us not to waste time and to head for the hills. Everyone is to be told to get on out of town as quickly as possible."

"Hogwash," the old man muttered, shaking his head at such nonsense. "They always say that. I've been hearing that for as long as I can remember. If it was so, they would be ringing the firebells and calling the message out."

"All I know is what I saw and heard with my own two ears. I also heard someone say that the water was sure to reach Johnstown by at least six o'clock. That's not much time. That's only a couple of hours from now."

"Well, maybe I should just rush on back home then and get my fishing pole ready. If that dam has busted, I should be able to catch my supper right from my own back porch," the man chuckled, still shaking his head at such an outrageous thought. "And what a fine supper it could be. I hear tell that Lake Conemaugh is stocked with some of the finest fish around these parts." Then he burst out laughing and patted the boy on his head. "Those men at the telegraph office were shining you, boy. That dam ain't busted. They were just having themselves a little fun."

"No they weren't. I learned enough code to know that the message was about the dam," the boy replied. "You best listen to me and get yourself on up to the hills. I don't have time to stand here and argue with you none. I promised to spread the word just as quick as I could."

"You spread it, boy." The old man continued to chuckle. "You let the whole town know how gullible you are." Then he turned and walked slowly away along the edge of the water, still shaking his head and laughing softly.

The boy stood and frowned at the man a moment, then caught sight of Patricia.

"Ma'am," he shouted up at her and hurried to stand in front of her gate, shin deep in water. "You best be getting to the hills. The dam's done burst. The water's on its way. You only got a couple of hours."

Patricia was not about to argue with the boy. "Thank you, I will," she assured him and ducked back inside to hurriedly gather up her handbag and her umbrella. In case Cole should come by, she quickly wrote a short message on a piece of stationery and pinned it to the front door. She wanted Cole to know that she was going to stop by and get her sisters and then head for Green Hill. She'd wait for him at Johnson's bend.

After putting Duchess in the attic so that she would be safe from the water and carefully locking the door, Patricia lifted up her still damp pongee and brown velvet skirts and plowed right through the water. After she reached dry land almost a block away, she dropped her skirts and headed straight for her father's house. But to her dismay and extreme frustration, Catherine and Jeanne still refused to leave the house. Instead, they tried to convince Patricia to stay with them, since they already had food enough gathered on the third floor to last them a full week, even though they fully expected the water to have passed completely through and be out of their neighborhood long before morning. They had also decided to take a load of blankets, fresh clothing, water, and candles up there as well—just to be on the safe side. They felt they were fully prepared to last the duration no matter what that might be.

But Patricia still wanted to see if she could find Cole and decided not to stay with them. She realized time was running out when she hurried back to her house to see if he had come by in the short time she was gone. On her way there, she passed Orville McKinsey, a middle-aged man who lived just two doors the other side of Jeanne. He was carrying a box filled to overflowing with packages of dried food and canned goods.

"Quite a load you have there," Patricia called out as the two of them passed.

"Yes, I've been to town to stock up on supplies," he shouted over his shoulder. "I want to be prepared should the water actually reach up here and cause me to be housebound for very long." He stopped and turned. "You really should get on down there and stock up too. There are still a few stores uptown that are open for business. What if that flood should get up here and last for days? Better not to take risks." Before waiting for her response, he shifted his load from one arm to the other and headed on toward his house.

Patricia smiled. At least the man had enough sense to realize that the water could actually rise enough to flood even Walnut Street. He evidently believed in the warnings that the dam had burst. And even if he had his doubts, he was taking no chances.

As she continued along her way, she morbidly wondered if the danger could be even greater than even Orville McKinsey believed. Something in her sensed that it was as she hurried to find Cole so that they could leave Johnstown together.

First, she went to her own house, but a quick check let her see that the note was still there with no new additions. Next, she hurried over to his house. He was not there either and no one she asked had seen him all day. Finally, just after four o'clock, she gave up her search. Gazing off toward Green Hill, she decided to take her precautions without him.

Before she managed to get two blocks away, it started to rain again. Opening her umbrella and holding it close over her head, she felt a little annoyed that she was going to have to walk all the way to Green Hill in the rain and then climb the hillside in her slippery boots when Cole could have provided her with transportation had he gotten back early like he'd promised.

Several others had seen reason to take similar precautions and were worried enough to start loading wagons and buggies in order to move on to higher ground and assure their safety. A few carts and flatbeds loaded high with personal belongings and small children slowly made their way through the flooded streets toward the rain-drenched hills that surrounded Johnstown.

Chapter Twenty-six

Cole dug with all his might. His legs ached and his arms throbbed more and more with every stroke he made, but he and at least a dozen others continued to dig, continued to try, despite the futility of it all. They were still a good twenty feet from completing the emergency spillway at the side of the dam, and even if they finished it, they realized the trench would probably be too narrow to accommodate enough water to do much to save the dam anyway. Yet there was always the hope, the slight chance, that if they could finish it the force of the water as it rushed through would gradually chew away at the walls of the narrow channel until it did eventually grow large enough to do the job. It was the only chance they had.

By now, Cole had grown accustomed to the steady downpour of rain. He no longer noticed it pelt his back while he worked and had long since given up keeping his wet hair out of his face. He was cold and soaked to the bone, but paid little attention to his misery. His total concentration was on the work he and the others were doing and the time that was quickly passing. Even though they were all working as hard as they could, it seemed to him that they moved at a mere snail's pace.

He did what he could to ignore the persistent sharp pains that plagued his legs and the numbness that had started to settle in his arms and along his upper shoulders as he drove his shovel into the rock-hard earth again and again, hacking away what he could. The skies darkened and the rain came down harder still, but he never stopped trying. He refused to let go of his last shred of hope.

It was shortly after three when he first sensed a strange vibration beneath him and glanced up from his work in time to watch the water slice a huge notch out of the center of the dam. The large piece of earth collapsed and melted into nothing as it traveled with the rushing water downstream. Cole paused partially bent, frozen with his shovel—still full of mud—held in mid-air to stare with morbid fascination at how the water now centered itself at the deep gully and poured through in a large shooting spout. Then suddenly there came an awful rumbling roar from the ground and the rest of the dam slipped away right before his eyes.

When the huge mound of earth finally pulled itself completely free of the steep mountainsides that had anchored it in place for so many decades, it was with such a thunderlike sucking noise that it sounded as if the whole earth had split in two. Several men covered their ears and turned away, but Cole stood mesmerized.

They had failed.

Lake Conemaugh was on its way. Water tree-top high was crashing down the narrow valley toward South Fork, collecting huge boulders, logs, and ripping up whole trees as it went—stripping the earth clean. A farmhouse poised along the hillside on the very edge of its path was crushed and carried away as if made of nothing more than paper. The very ground on which Cole stood, frozen with horror, was slowly being eaten away by the tremendous force of water as it gushed past. Cole stood only a few feet from disaster— only moments away from his death.

At South Fork, a handsome young man in his mid-twenties paced restlessly in front of Stineman's store, so rain-soaked that he was now oblivious to the never-ending torrent that swept in on him. He watched, disgusted, as South Fork Creek continued to flood the lowlands. It was all this water that hampered the progress on the railroad repairs.

Impatiently, he had waited the past several hours for the Chicago Limited to be given the clearance to move ahead, wondering how much longer the repairs could possibly take. They claimed to have had a crew on it since before eleven. It was after three now. How much longer could it take?

Being outside, with nothing better to do than gaze about at the rain-drenched landscape, he was the first to notice the enormous, grinding wall of water on its way down the hillside, headed straight for them. At first it looked like a huge hill of some sort, rolling over and over, but he soon determined that it was a mountain of water. The mass was still possibly a mile away, but judging by the treetops disappearing around it, it was coming with such rapid force that it would be there almost immediately. Acting on instinct, he rushed to the nearest train, which he realized stood directly in the water's path and cried out his warning.

"Get out of the train. Everyone get out. Run for the hillside!" he shouted out frantically. "Run for your lives."

When no one came out, he hurriedly ran inside and woke the two men he knew were still asleep in one of the cars.

"Get up. You have to get out of here," he cried, without taking the time to fully explain the danger. "Run for your lives."

The panic in his voice was enough to set the two sleepy men in motion and the three of them barely made it to safety before the brawny assemblage of water struck the train and swept it into its angry maw.

A deep pain bore down in the very core of the young man's chest and seemed to crush the very breath out of him, rendering him weak all over, as he watched the fifty-foot-high mass of water surge forward around a bend where it hit the mountainside with a thunderous crash, then curled around to join the already swollen Little Conemaugh, and head toward Johnstown, driving before it a churning mass of debris that now included acres of felled trees, three small bridges, pieces of mangled houses, dead animals, most of a planing mill, railroad ties, rails, dozens of train cars, and its first four human victims.

Terrified, the young man's thoughts flew to his wife. She

was in Johnstown—directly in the water's path.

After having suffered so many setbacks, so many delays, he had finally been on his way to get her and take her back with him when there had come that final delay. Because of a washout somewhere down the line, he had unavoidably been detained there at South Fork. He should be with her by now. The man shuddered violently. Everything he held dear to his heart now lay in the path of that huge killing mass of water. Numbly, he watched while some twenty houses were demolished by the surging monstrosity right before his eyes. How many lives would it take before it was through? Would one be that of his beloved Kate?

On past South Fork, the water raged along the valley of the Little Conemaugh in the direction of Mineral Point—between the sharp, wooded bluffs that sent the riverbed swerving back and forth on its way toward Johnstown, which lay only fourteen miles downriver. The onslaught of water ripped up the tracks of the Pennsylvania Railroad as it raced along and stripped the valley of its lush, green vegetation. A mile down from South Fork, the valley narrowed abruptly. There the steep hillsides squeezed the great mass of water so that its front wall grew to seventy feet in height. Two miles farther down the valley, the water struck its first major obstacle, a huge stone viaduct that served as a bridge for the Pennsylvania Railroad. The huge edifice stood seventy-five feet high and bridged the narrow river gap with one single eighty-foot arch. The sandstone and mason structure was so large and impressive that the trains that crossed it always looked tiny in comparison.

Almost immediately, the massive collection of debris in the water jammed inside the huge arch and formed its own temporary dam. The bridge held momentarily and the water quickly heaped up behind the dam, surging back and forth, seething with yellow froth, mounting and growing, until it was nearly eighty-feet high and was able to lash out over the top of the bridge. Lake Conemaugh had formed again, held now by another dam, and when this second dam finally let go, it did so even more suddenly and with greater violence than the first one had. The stone bridge collapsed all at once and the water literally exploded into the valley with much more force than ever before.

Mineral Point was next. It was swept clean by the deadly forces of the water as it burst through the small village at a rate of forty miles per hour. Violently, it mauled and ravaged the small, peaceful borough with an angry, writhing force for more than forty minutes while it passed through and did not slow down until it hit a low area where the valley finally spread out. But the huge body of water immediately regained its momentum when the ravine narrowed again and became just as deadly as ever.

Because of the friction caused by the rough terrain of the rugged valley floor, the bottom of the monstrous mass of water moved at a much slower rate than the top, causing the top to continually slide over the front of the advancing wall, creating a violent downward smashing of water that literally crushed anything that got in its way. Very little survived the initial impact.

While it completely obliterated Mineral Point, the water sucked an even larger assortment of debris and human corpses into its breadth and charged on down the valley toward East Conemaugh where the railroad yards, two sections of the day express, a mail train, and several hundred passengers sat helplessly waiting.

Unaware of the danger, Tony stood on a small, covered platform just outside the Day Express, anxious to be on his way. He had given up the hope of staying dry and did not care that the rain gusted in on him at regular intervals, drenching him thoroughly.

"It's been nearly five hours now," he muttered to the elderly gentleman who had just stepped out for a breath of fresh air. Although the two had not formally introduced each other, Tony knew the gentleman was somehow associated with the stage company that was traveling on the same train. The company had just left Johnstown that morning after having put on the new hit comedy *A Night Off* at the Opera House there the night before.

"Yes, I know. I couldn't stay seated in the small confines of that train a moment longer," the older gentleman replied with an understanding nod. Tilting his head back, he breathed deeply the rain-dampened air and dodged a gust of water, for he was still dry and hoped to stay that way.

"I had to get out of there after only an hour," Tony admitted. "I've spent the last few hours milling about, but have since grown tired of even that. There's not that much to see around here." When he paused to let out a weary sigh, he thought he heard something out of the ordinary—something in the distance. "What was that?"

"What was what?" the man asked, looking around to see if he could spot anything unusual.

"That sound." He fell silent and they both listened.

Over the steady rhythm of the rain on the metal roof and the monotonous hum of conversation from the passengers still hemmed up inside the train, Tony was not sure at first what he heard blaring in the distance. It was like a mournful wail of some sort.

"That sounds like a train whistle," he finally concluded and fell silent again to listen. As the noise grew louder, Tony was certain it was a train. "Must be a warning of some sort. A good engineer never takes his whistle lightly."

The two of them turned to watch in the direction of the noise as it grew louder. Soon they could hear the rapid chugging of the engine.

When the train finally rounded the bend and came into view, Tony was surprised to see that it was traveling backward and at such a high speed. He recognized it was one of the work trains that had been sent out earlier. Glancing on past the train, he noticed that a rapid succession of treetops was disappearing in the distance. He had never seen anything like it and, not knowing what could cause such destruction, he stared at the movement a moment longer until he finally spotted the water through a tiny break in the trees. Instantly aware of the danger, he cried out for everyone to run for safety. The older man saw the reason for Tony's sudden alarm only an instant later and took up the cry.

A little more than half of the people aboard the train were

able to scramble to the safety of the nearby hillside. Tony was not one of them. As he leaped over the back railing of the train and ran along the side pounding and shouting, wanting to be sure everyone was warned, he noticed a young boy about four years old struggling to free the back of his britches leg from a piece of metal that protruded out from the side of the nearby mail train.

"Help me," the boy screamed in panic as he yanked furiously on the material. Tears streamed down his freckled face while the frightened people around him rushed by without even noticing him. "Somebody help me. Momma? Momma, where are you? Help me, Momma."

A grown man knocked the boy over in his own haste to get to safety and never bothered to look back.

Anger surged through Tony as he worked his way through the chaos of the rushing crowd, toward the child. Finally, he managed to get to the boy, and with a hard yank of his clothing, set the child free. Grabbing him into his arms, Tony explained as he ran, "We've got to get to the hillside."

Trustingly, the little boy clutched Tony's neck in silence while they hurried away from the train. Tony never took the time to glance back up the valley. His sights remained on the hillside before them. He was unaware of how close the water had come. There was a deafening roar, pain, then suddenly he was underwater, being swirled around in the murky depths until he was certain they both were going to drown. Then miraculously he felt himself being drawn into a large wooden freight car that somehow surfaced still intact, with him and the small boy inside. But as the air slowly gurgled out through the seams, the railcar rolled over on its side, trapping the two of them inside without much air left.

"Take a deep breath and hold it," Tony instructed the boy. Wasting no time, he tucked the child securely under his arm, then dove down and swam until he was able to surface in the open doorway. Carefully, he heaved the boy up and instructed him to climb out onto the railcar's side. Immediately he scrambled up to join the boy and the two of them hung on to the outside railing for dear life.

All around them, Tony saw that other people, barely

411

alive, also clung on to whatever they could, hoping to stay afloat, never knowing when the angry mass of water would suck their only handhold on life down into its dark depth or send them crashing forward over the front wall.

The water had collected even more debris and many more bodies now bobbed on its surface. A sixteen stall round-house had been crushed as if made of straw and the trains stationed there had been ripped apart as if mere toys. A few railcars burst into flames and burned alive the poor souls that clung to them before being sucked below and disappearing in a hiss of smoke.

All Tony could do was hang on to the freight car with one hand and the trembling boy with the other and hope that the car did not plunge them to their deaths while the water descended on the next town in its path: Woodvale. Tony watched helplessly as the tiny town with its prosperous woolen mill, its brick tannery, and the Gautier Wire Works, was wiped out in less than ten minutes.

By the time they had passed through, there was hardly anything left and Tony's attention was drawn to the huge pillows of steam that had bellowed from the wire works the moment the water had hit the huge boilers there. Instantly, that entire structure had been swept away and added to the mass of debris twisting in the wretched water around them. As his makeshift craft was being propelled onward toward Johnstown, Tony wondered where Catherine was. Closing his eyes, which were flooded with tears, he prayed for her safety.

Not quite an hour had passed after the dam had finally given way before the fifty-foot wall of water was first spotted approaching Johnstown. It was barely after four o'clock and the rain had just started to let up again. Most people were hopeful that the worst was finally over. Some even swore that the water was already going down in the streets. Very few had taken to heart that the dam had actually broken— such tomfoolery. That alarm had been sounded just one too many times.

But Patricia had believed.

She was only a few blocks away from Cole's house headed for Green Hill when the raging force of water finally reached the edge of Johnstown. She heard the tumid wall of water and debris barreling down on them before she turned to see it. It sounded like an angry locomotive, only much louder. And at first it looked like a great black ball of dust and smoke, much like the dust that always stirs before the cavalry, but this death mist did not bring aid behind it, only destruction.

Sounds of splintering crashes and thunderous explosions reached her as the water took the first houses of Johnstown. Fear gripped her, paralyzing her only a moment before she started to run for her life. Tossing her umbrella aside, she let her handbag dangle at her wrist while she lifted her skirts and ran as hard as she could, knowing she would never make it.

When the monstrosity overtook her, it felt as if a gigantic plank had swung and hit her squarely in the back. The pain was enough that she was momentarily stunned and even though she knew she was probably now under thirty or forty feet of water and her eyes were tightly closed, she saw odd visions of white light dancing in front of her. Her handbag was wrenched from her arm and her clothing tugged in every direction. She was well aware that the huge wall of water had descended over her and she realized the end was near. Holding on to her final breath for as long as she could, her next thoughts were of Cole. His image was so vivid before her that she tried to reach out to him; she wanted to touch him one last time.

Chapter Twenty=seven

Patricia struggled through the swirling mass of dark water and wreckage, unable to really determine which direction would carry her to the surface. As she fought her heavy skirts, something solid rammed sharply against her shoulder, shooting pain up through her neck. In a reflex action, she grabbed for it and held on with all her might. She had no idea what she held on to, but had an inner need to clutch something. Together, she and whatever it was she held on to, surfaced and plunged several feet into the air. Opening her eyes, she discovered what she held on to was a broken piece of a telegraph pole and tried her best to keep her hold on it, but found she was unable to. When she landed back in the water, she was several feet from where the pole landed. Frantically, she made a swim for it, but it disappeared below the surface again before she could reach it.

Floundering against the strong current of the water, she tried to find something else to hold on to before she could be dragged back under. She spied a large piece of broken roof only a yard or so away and wasted no time in swimming for it. Somehow she managed to grasp the edge with her right hand and held on with all her might. As soon as she had pushed her wet hair out of her face and started to put her other hand on the rough surface, she noticed a small, wet dog crouched only inches away from where she had almost placed her left hand. The dog was frightened and confused, and growled menacingly at where her one hand already clung to the edge.

"Nice doggie," she called to him only to hear his growl deepen. Slowly, she placed her other hand on the edge of the roof in order to hold on better for the swift undercurrents worked to pull her back under. The cowering animal snapped at her, causing her to jerk the left hand back and almost lose her grip with the other. Struggling to stay above the water's surface, she began to wonder what she should do about the situation but when something sharp struck her leg underwater and sent pain coursing through her thigh and hip, she realized that the dog was by far the lesser of the two evils. Quickly, she pulled herself up onto the structure, relieved when the animal did not attack right away. As she lay in a cold, wet heap beside the growling animal, coughing spasmodically from the filthy water she had swallowed, she hoped that the dog would soon come to accept her and that the makeshift craft would eventually carry them both to safety. At least, it should keep her from drowning.

Pushing her thick mat of wet hair out of her eyes again, she cautiously held her hand out for the dog to sniff and managed to speak in a calm, soothing voice. When the dog finally decided she was not there to hurt him, his growling slowly ceased and turned to gentle whining. Realizing the dog no longer meant her any harm, she uncurled herself and stretched out across the hard flat surface of the roof on her stomach and continued to grip the edge of the spinning craft with all her might. The trembling dog edged close to her and snuggled against her waist.

"Poor fellow," she said softly. "But at least you are alive." Sympathetically, she let go of the edge with one hand long enough to reach down and pet the shivering animal.

When she finally pulled her attention away from the terrified little dog and gazed around her at the chaos that surrounded them, Patricia was horrified by what she saw. Others like her were also hanging on to whatever happened to float by at the moment. Some of the frightened faces she recognized, others she didn't. Men and women alike cried out from sheer terror. Some reached out to her for help. People were struggling and dying everywhere. Suddenly a face was there, then gone. Dead bodies, both animal and human, floated around her like corks. A few of the bodies had been stripped of their clothing by the swift tides and others had even been stripped of their arms or legs. It was a gruesome sight.

Patricia watched helplessly as whole houses or just mangled parts came crashing into her section of roof, breaking off pieces while sending it shooting off in a new direction. She wondered how long her ever-decreasing link to survival would hold up. When was this piece of roof going to completely crumble and sink like she had seen so many do? Her arms ached from gripping the edge so hard. Darkness slowly descended, but she was not sure if it was due to the hour of day or because of her weakening state of consciousness. She realized she was injured somewhere on her head, for she constantly tasted blood and her jaw felt swollen, that side of her mouth out of proportion to the other, yet she didn't remember being struck on her face.

At first her craft propelled eastward toward Stony Creek until it caught the current there and was drawn southward, then westward toward where the creek normally entered the Conemaugh River. Swirling back and forth among the ruins in the water, she tried to focus on her nearest stable surroundings, but everything seemed to be moving. Petrified, she closed her eyes and waited for God's will to be done. The dog continued to huddle close at her side.

Catching a strange backlash current, the ever shrinking piece of roof she was on whipped around and swirled abruptly back into the main part of town, where the majority of the water now lay. She was unaware that the wreckage in the water had started to pile up at the Pennsylvania Railroad Bridge, forming another new dam, already hundreds of feet thick. The raging water with its heavy burden had lost some of its momentum at the huge bend in the riverbed just this side of the bridge and had been unable to break through the huge stone structure. A massive, swirling lake now formed over Johnstown.

In the distance, Patricia could see that Alma Hall, one of Johnstown's largest buildings, still stood and that there were several people hanging out of the second and third floor windows, trying to rescue anyone who came close enough. Concentrating with all her might, she manipulated her raft in that direction by stroking at the water with her one hand and leaning sharply to one side. The dog whimpered with concern over the tilting angle of the tiny craft.

"Here, catch," she heard a man's voice call out to her when she got close enough. Looking up, she saw that a rope was being thrown in her direction and she raised up on her knees and reached out for it, but in the process she lost her handhold on the roof and slid off into the cold water. To her amazement, the rope was in her hands and she gripped it securely while several men pulled her toward Alma Hall.

"Hang on," a man called to her from one of the second-story windows.

"I'm trying," she cried out, choking on the foul water as it splashed into her mouth. She kicked as best she could in her cumbersome boots in order to stay above water while they pulled her toward Alma Hall. When she drew closer, she recognized the man who had called to her. He was her father's lawyer, James Walters, and right beside him, pulling on the rope with all his might, was Andrew Edwards. She had never been so happy to see Andrew as she was at that moment.

Clayton had returned to the brewery just minutes before the water hit. He went back to gather up some important documents he realized he had forgotten to carry upstairs. Although the papers were inside a thick, metal safe, he was worried it might leak and everything would get water-soaked should the water actually get that high and the rate it had been rising all morning, he no longer dared to chance it.

He had just closed the safe door and had put the important stack of papers into a box with a few other things when he felt the entire brick structure shudder. He barely had time to look up before the building started to crumble in around him.

Reaching out for the bookcase beside him, Clayton closed

his eyes and steadied himself for the blow about to come, but before the ceiling could crash in on top of him, a huge gush of water burst through the wall, lifted him up, and carried him and the bookcase he clung to out of the way. Opening his eyes, he discovered himself at the forefront of a huge advancing lake. Terrified, he clung to an individual board that had once been a part of his massive bookcase. The churning force of the water itself seemed to be what was keeping him afloat. As he rode the mammoth wave, he realized that the dam had indeed burst and that this mass of water had to have come from Lake Conemaugh. Cole Gifford had been right all along. What an apology he owed that young man! How he wished he had listened.

Somehow Clayton worked his way backward away from the crashing front of the water. The single board he held on to no longer offered him much support. Letting go of it, he made a frantic swim for a sizable wooden structure floating nearby. Once he reached it, he realized it had once been the outer wall of a frame house. In the corner was a notch that must have at one time been part of a window. Hanging on the ragged edge, Clayton tried to pull himself up on top of it, but found it was an impossible task. The water kept pulling him back. He just didn't have the strength in his arms to fight the sucking current and lift himself on out of the water, so he simply hung on and tried to keep from being pulled below the surface.

After a whirling ride through the main part of town, the piece of wall he clung to was tossed into an area where the water was a little more settled and he was finally able to squirm up on top of it. A quick look around let him know that he was again headed for rapid water so he lay flat on his stomach and dug his nails into the wood in order to stay on. Soon he was caught in the swifter current, hurtled down Conemaugh toward the large stone Pennsylvania Railroad Bridge. He could see the massive structure just up ahead and wondered if he would pass right on through or be smashed against one of the large viaducts.

But as he neared the bridge, his craft gradually slowed down. By the time it hit the debris piling up against the side of the huge stone structure, he did not get the hard jolt he had expected. Briefly looking around to size up the situation, he noticed more huge pieces of debris were rolling in right behind him, headed his way. He pressed himself down and tried to hold on, but was knocked into the water by the tremendous force when a torn piece of flooring struck him hard. He tried to scramble back up to safety, but a piece of barbed wire had gotten tangled around his leg and held him down. Hurriedly, he tried to work his leg free but more debris quickly piled up on him, trapping both of his legs between a piece of roof and a broken floor. He tried, but was unable to free himself.

More wreckage heaped steadily behind him, ramming the pile again and again, tightening the hold it had on his legs until he could not bear the pain any longer and started to scream for help. It felt as if his right leg was about to be sheared right off. Spotting several people on the shore nearby, he shouted out to them, but soon realized by the pitiful way they kept throwing up their arms that they were unable to help him. Finally he fell silent and tried not to concentrate on the pain. He knew that if and when they could help him, they would.

"Clayton?" He heard a feminine voice call out and at first he seriously considered that it was the voice of an angel.

"Clayton, is that you?" No, it was too real to be an angel calling him.

"Yes, it's me. Who is out there?" he asked, straining his neck to see over the debris that had heaped up around him. She didn't sound like she could be very far away, maybe a hundred feet or so.

"It's Minnie. I'm trapped. My shoulder's caught. So is my hair. I can't get free. I can barely move."

"Hang on. Help will come. I'm sure of it," Clayton assured her, then started to call out for help again in an even louder voice. Minnie joined him in his cries as did hundreds of others who were also trapped or injured so badly in the wreckage that they could not move. Meanwhile, the debris continued to build up, pushing Clayton and Minnie higher up and pinning them in tighter. Clayton was still wet and felt muggy from a thin coating of oil on his skin. He shivered as much from his pain as from the cold. Darkness started to fall.

"Clayton?" Minnie called out to him again after a while. Her voice had grown decidedly weaker. "Clayton, do you smell smoke?"

"Now that you mention it I do," Clayton replied, more worried over the fact that Minnie's voice sounded so much weaker than it had before. Because of the piles of rubbish that completely surrounded him now, he was unable to see what-all was going on around him. A fire had broken out when the oil from one of the railroad cars caught in the wreckage had seeped down and made contact with a pot belly stove that still had live coals in it. Huge flames had instantly blared out of the debris only a few hundred yards away and were rapidly licking a path toward Clayton and Minnie.

"Mister, we going to die?"

They were the first words the boy had spoken since they had first been swept up by the water and it startled Tony from his worried thoughts.

"No, of course not," Tony assured him just as the railcar took a tiny dip and reminded him how very precarious their position really was. They just could be facing death, but there was no sense adding to the child's fears.

"Is my momma dead?" he wanted to know.

Tony's heart went out to the child and he pressed him closer to him. "No, I imagine your momma is still alive back at East Conemaugh and worried sick that she can't find you."

"Will you help me find her?"

Tony looked down into the hopeful eyes of the child and smiled. "Of course I'll help you find her. I'll see to it that you are back in the loving arms of your momma and your poppa before you know it."

"I ain't got no poppa. He ran off. Momma says he's dead, but my cousin told me different," the lad informed him and

Tony wanted to cry out at the injustice of what-all this child had had to endure. A child like this needed a father. Suddenly, he wished the boy was his own. He would never leave such a child as this. Having always loved the idea of being a father someday, he couldn't imagine a man being able to run off and leave his own flesh and blood behind. Bitterly, Tony hoped the boy's mother was right and the man was dead.

"Well, I'll see to it that you find your momma," Tony told him. "Just as soon as we get off this thing, we'll start looking for her together."

There was a tiny sob and he felt a tremor go through the boy before he heard him say, "Thanks, mister."

Tony wondered how he was going to keep that promise. How would he go about finding the woman? If she had been caught by the water too, she could be just about anywhere and he was well aware one of the possibilities was that she could be dead. He wondered what would happen to the boy if she was.

Looking around at the many dead bodies bobbing just below the surface of the turgid water or hanging on to floating debris, he again worried about finding the lad's mother. Whether the child's mother was dead or alive, it would be no easy task to locate her. But he felt he was worrying about that too soon. For now he needed only to worry about keeping the boy alive. They needed to get off the railcar and onto solid ground.

Suddenly, as fate would have it, a huge uprooted tree slammed into the wooden freight car and caused it to careen sideways where it became lodged in a fairly stationary pile of wreckage. The pile of debris had become so tightly packed that it was almost like a floating bridge.

"What's your name?" Tony asked the child as he studied the floating jam for possible weaknesses. There were a few questionable places, but the mangled structure was their only hope.

"Cyrus," the lad responded quickly. "Cyrus Graham."

"Well, Cyrus, I want you to do me a big favor. I want you to carefully crawl on your hands and knees over to the edge of the railcar with me. And when I tell you to, I want you to stand up and jump onto that pile of broken wood and trees over there. Think you can do that for me?"

The boy nodded and proceeded to do just as he had been asked. When they neared the edge, the corner of the railcar dipped into the water a few inches, but was still able to support their weight without turning over.

"Okay, jump over to the pile and then slowly work your way to shore." Aware that the floating pile of wood was being held in place by nothing more than a few broken limbs of a leafless tree still rooted to the ground, he added, "Be very careful, but do hurry." The mass could wiggle free at any moment and they would be out adrift once again.

Tony held his breath, ready to dive in and rescue the boy should he miss. But when the boy made his jump, he landed squarely on a piece of flooring securely lodged in the mass. Grinning, he turned to see if Tony had watched such a magnificent feat.

"That was a great jump. Now ease your way to land. I'll be right behind you," Tony promised.

The mass of floating rubbish creaked and moaned as Cyrus ran lightly over its surface and made an agile leap that put him on the shore. "It was easy," he called out to Tony in an excited voice. "Now it's your turn. You can do it."

When Tony stood to make a jump similar to the one the boy had just made, the railcar dipped further and broke loose from the mass. The water's current slowly started to pull it away.

"Mister, mister, don't leave me," Cyrus cried out, his voice shrill with fright.

Tony knew he would be breaking his promise to the trusting little boy if he didn't make the jump. Stepping back a few feet, he took a running start across the water-soaked surface of the railcar and made a desperate leap for the packed debris now several yards away. When he landed on the pile, it groaned from the impact and broke apart, causing Tony to fall into the chilling water. Clutching onto a large feather mattress that had been a part of the mass, he was immediately swept away then under. When he opened his eyes underwater, he looked toward the water's surface and thought he saw Catherine on a raft just overhead reaching down into the water for him. She was only a few feet away.

Pushing away from the mattress, Tony lifted his hand toward her and was certain their hands had made contact just moments before the wooden railcar he had been on earlier swirled back around and crushed him against the side of a drifting house. The pain was terrific and, as he tried to reach for Catherine's hand, again only inches from his reach, everything around him slowly faded to black.

Chapter Twenty-eight

Over two hundred and fifty people took refuge in the upper floors of Alma Hall that Friday night, and because there were so many stranded there, the men got together early in the evening, elected officials, and made several rules which were to be enforced on all floors. But because the rules were sensible ones, well thought out by those who had made them, they were thoroughly respected by everyone. No disputes resulted.

Due to the threat of a natural gas leak, no fires were allowed, not even candles. The only light they had came from the flickering glow of the huge fires that had broken out at the bridge across town and the smaller fires that would occasionally flare up in different locations around them. There was no source of heat. The only supplies that they managed to find in the various offices were confiscated and distributed to the most needy, usually the injured. Andrew Edwards was placed in charge of what little supplies they were able to assemble. He and the supplies were centrally located in one of the larger offices on the third floor.

Mostly, what they had managed to gather together consisted of extra clothing, handkerchiefs, and several cloth typewriter dustcovers, which could be torn and made into bandages. Someone had even managed to locate a few blankets and a couple of bottles of whiskey in one of the offices on the top floor. Curtains and drapes were pulled off every window to be used as blankets and bandages too. And in several offices they discovered snacks of some sort hidden away and those had been procured as well.

Of all the survivors taking refuge at Alma Hall, there was only one physician among them and he willingly set up a makeshift hospital in the same office with the supplies and, despite his own crushed ribs, went to work bandaging wounds and setting broken bones as best he could in such inappropriate surroundings. Patricia and two other women volunteered to help him in whatever capacity he might need them. They tried not to let the countless injuries and the multitude of suffering get to them as they worked.

At first, Patricia simply tore cloth for bandages and broke curtain rods into temporary splints while she followed Dr. Matthews around the room. Occasionally, she was asked to help hold down a leg or an arm, but she was not often asked to touch anyone. Then a young expectant mother was brought in and, although she was barely lucid, it was immediately evident that she had gone into labor. The doctor quickly examined her as best he could in the darkness that prevailed and asked Patricia to stay with her while he continued to tend to the others. "It'll be awhile yet. Call me when the time comes."

"But how will I know? I've never had a baby and I'm certainly not a nurse," Patricia said, panicky.

"The pains will get very close together and eventually you will be able to feel the crown of the head when she pushes. When you do, call, and I'll come a running."

Patricia nodded apprehensively. "I'll do my best."

"That's all I ask," Dr. Matthews responded and there was just enough amber light from the distant fires for her to see him smile reassuringly before he turned to leave.

Sitting on the wooden floor beside the young woman, Patricia made herself as comfortable as she could, then tore off a piece of her still wet underskirt and ran it across the woman's sweating brow. The woman responded by opening her eyes and gazing up at her. "Where's my husband?" she asked after a moment, blinking as if to clear her thoughts. "No one will tell me where my husband is. He should be here. I'm going to have the baby. It's not time yet, but I know I'm

426

going to have the baby."

"Not time yet?" Patricia questioned. "When are you supposed to have this baby?"

"In July. The doctor said it would be about the second week in July. But I know I'm having it now and I want my husband with me."

"What's your husband's name?" Patricia asked, aware that the two men who brought her into the room were the same ones who had brought in so many others. Neither had been her husband.

"Lowell. Lowell Edison. I'm his wife, Laura, and I need him here with me. Where is he?" she asked, trying to sit up so that she could look around. She grimaced when her body would not allow her to do what she wanted.

"Lie back down. You are supposed to keep still," Patricia cautioned her. "When did you last see your husband?"

"We were in the kitchen," she said, then frowned as she tried to remember. The sweat that had beaded along her forehead and cheeks rolled off her face and into her wet, tousled hair. "We were just about to have a cup of tea, when . . . when something dreadful happened. Our house . . . I think it exploded."

"Exploded?"

"I think. I'm not sure. I remember a splintering noise all around us. I remember the look on Lowell's face. But I can't quite remember what happened after that. Where am I now?"

Patricia explained about the flood and the fact that she had been rescued and was safe inside Alma Hall.

"But where is Lowell? He was rescued too, wasn't he?"

"Yes, I'm sure he was. He's probably on another floor is all. There are well over two hundred people crowded on these three floors. He's probably on one of them looking for you right now."

"Find him for me. I want him here with me," she sobbed weakly, her breathing shallow. "Please, find . . ." Her urgent plea was cut short by a sharp cry of pain as she drew up and doubled over on her side. "It hurts. Oh, how it hurts."

"Lay back," Patricia ordered her and reached out to hold

427

the woman's hand. Giving the hand a sharp squeeze, she continued to soothe, "It won't hurt long. The pain will pass."

And in a moment, it did pass, but Laura's desire to see her husband only grew stronger. Spotting Andrew standing watch over the supplies only a few yards away, Patricia called him over to them. "Andrew, this woman is about to have a baby and needs her husband. Can you please send someone around to all the floors to see if he is in the building somewhere, and if he is to have him brought here? His name is Lowell Edison."

"I'll go myself," Andrew offered quickly. "Just keep an eye on the supplies while I'm gone and try to get the doctor whatever he needs. I'll be right back."

Andrew was gone almost twenty minutes. Patricia continued to reassure the terrified young woman that her husband was safe and would probably be there at any moment, but when Andrew returned, she was able to detect the solemn look on his face and knew that the news he brought was not good.

"I checked in every room on every floor and no one answered to the name of Lowell Edison. Evidently, he's not in the building," he reported, his face rigid.

"H—he's dead?" The woman wailed and broke out in loud rasping sobs. "My Lowell is dead?"

"No, I didn't say that. He very well may be in some other building or he may have been able to swim to shore," he explained, kneeling quickly at her side. Pressing her limp hand between his, he tried to explain. "All I'm saying is that he's not in this particular building."

"Then he's still alive?"

"Yes, I'm sure of it," Andrew told her, even though he had no way of being sure of anything. Then he decided to get her mind off of the missing husband and on to the coming child. "And it looks to me like the next time he sees you, he will already be a father and not even know it. Won't that be a grand surprise? What does he want the baby to be? Boy or girl?"

"Boy. Lowell wants a son first," she told him, and smiled briefly, her eyes drifting shut from the effort. "But I don't care which it is, I just want . . ." Suddenly, she raised up in pain again and cried out through gritted teeth, digging her nails into the side of Andrew's hand. Looking pitifully up at Patricia she wailed, then pressed her eyes shut. "It hurts so bad. Is it supposed to hurt like this?"

"I don't know," Patricia admitted as she pressed the girl's shoulders back down to the cool floor and she finally relaxed. "I've never had a baby."

Opening her eyes again once the pain completely subsided, the woman glanced up at Andrew questioningly, seeking his reassurance.

"Well, don't look at me. I've never had a baby either."

He looked so sincere in that reply that the woman laughed weakly and some of her tension was temporarily relieved. Reaching out to gently caress her damp cheek, Andrew added tenderly, "But I'm sure the pain will all be worth it once you hold that little babe in your arms."

Again the woman smiled, then closed her eyes and slipped into a restless sleep, but was abruptly awakened by an even sharper pain, this one coming only minutes after the last. Patricia reached beneath the curtain that the doctor had draped over her. It was as much privacy as they could afford under the circumstances. Patricia slipped her fingers inside the woman as she had watched the doctor do. This time, she felt something spongy-wet but firm and was certain it was the baby's head.

"Doctor, Doctor, I think she's having the baby," she called out across the room, feeling a twinge of sudden panic. What would she do if the baby came out before the doctor could get over there? "Hurry. I think it is on its way."

The doctor finished tying the bandage he had just placed around a little boy's arm then hurried across the room. Kneeling, he reached beneath the curtain and felt around. Several women crowded around to watch.

Frowning, the doctor turned to Patricia and said through tight lips, "Get these people out of here. Get them out of here now." Looking up at Andrew who now stood just behind Patricia, he added, "Get me another curtain or a blanket or something and a few rags. And I'll need some scissors and some string of some kind if you can find it. And see if there is any of that whiskey left." Noticing that several of the women still had not left, he finally shouted directly at them, "Get out of here. Give me a little privacy here."

After Patricia finally convinced the women to move away and give the doctor the room he had asked for, she stood at a distance and watched. Then when the doctor motioned for her help, she gladly came to assist, taking the woman's hand and holding it reassuringly when she was not handing the doctor something he needed. The pains grew more severe and caused the woman to scream out again and again and Patricia could see the doctor's expression in the dim glow becoming more concerned with each pain that passed.

Andrew stood back near the woman's head, where he would not be able to see that which should be kept private, and held a curtain up in order to keep others in the room from watching. Every so often, his eyes would meet with Patricia's in the eerie radiance of firelight. Neither fully understood the doctor's mounting irritation, but they both were worried it meant trouble. And it did. Twenty minutes later, the doctor slumped protectively over the baby, tied the cord in two places, then cut the baby loose. He turned away from the woman with the tiny infant cradled in his arms. Grabbing it gently by the heels and holding it out away from him, he slapped the baby on the legs several times, but there was no response. Quickly, he cleared the baby's mouth with his smallest finger then blew tiny breaths into its mouth. Still no response. Sadly, he turned to Patricia and shrugged miserably. The baby was stillborn.

Patricia clutched the woman to her and held her as she cried hysterically over the loss of her son while Andrew went in search of something to place the baby's body in. The doctor stayed long enough to deliver the placenta and massage her abdomen in order to slow down the bleeding. While he worked, he instructed Patricia to have the woman drink some of the whiskey they had left and try to calm her somehow in order to keep the bleeding down. Then as soon as he could, he headed off to tend to the injured again.

Patricia held the woman a long time, sharing in her tears,

until Andrew finally returned with a wooden file box he had located in a nearby office. Gently, he lifted the tiny limp form into his arms and ever so gingerly wrapped it in a piece of torn cloth. As he gingerly laid the small, precious bundle into the cold darkness of the box, his emotions got the best of him and he collapsed forward over the box as he closed it and wept bitterly.

Patricia wanted to go to him, but couldn't. She still held the weeping mother in her arms. Silently, she watched Andrew's shoulders shake and joined him in his grief. They had seen too much death already. Why did this innocent little baby have to be a part of it? It seemed appropriate that it should start raining again at that moment.

For the rest of the night, Patricia sat on the floor with her back pressed against one of the inner walls, facing the window. Laura lay on the floor beside her with her head in Patricia's lap, while Patricia occasionally stroked her cheek for comfort. They both were wet, filthy, and shivering from the cold, but the whiskey and the emotional drain had taken its toll on Laura and the young woman fitfully slept. Patricia found she was unable to. Instead, she sat staring through the window at the amber glow of the fires outside that burned endlessly despite the rain.

Wearily, she listened to the faint moaning of the injured and the occasional outcry of hunger or pain from one of the children. Once she even thought she heard the pitiful howl of a dog and she wondered how the poor animal that had shared her tiny piece of roof had fared. She wondered whose dog it had been and if that person had lived to miss the animal. Such morbid thoughts plagued her continually, for she had seen a multitude of death floating in the water around her. She tried not to picture the bodies, but the images kept haunting her.

Away in the distance, every hour on the hour, through the entire night, the clock of the Lutheran church bonged a mournful sound as if tolling a sad farewell for those many dead. And almost as often a building could be heard breaking up somewhere in the night and crashing into the horrible morass of water that surrounded them. Almost always, screaming accompanied the cracking sound, for some poor souls had obviously taken refuge inside. Tilting her head back, she studied the wavering firelight as it played across the walls and ceiling, wondering why the water had not gone away. What was holding it back? Why didn't it all drain away? It didn't make sense. The water should have passed through, headed for lower land by now. Sadly, she wondered if morning would ever come and what they would find when it got there.

At one point during the night, the firelight in the room flared so brightly that she was suddenly able to see everyone around her in almost clear detail. Even though she could not get up and go look out the window for fear of disturbing Laura, she knew that some building close by had caught fire and the way she understood it there were not many buildings left. Immediately, several people flocked to the windows.

"It's St. John's," she heard someone exclaim. "It's the spire and the roof at St. John's."

Patricia looked around the room for Andrew and found him working his way through the crowd toward the window. When he got close enough to see, he froze and Patricia knew he thought of Faye. Would she have taken refuge there in the church's spire? Fresh tears filled her eyes at the thought of losing Faye. Closing her eyes tightly, she prayed that Cole's sister was all right. While she was at it, she prayed for Cole too, and Tony, and Catherine, and Jeanne, and Harrison, and her father, and Minnie. How she hoped that all those she held so dear to her heart had fared well. How desperately she prayed that they would all be found alive.

In the last chilled hour before light, the valley seemed to hang suspended in an unearthly stillness. Nothing moved, no sounds were heard other than the occasional gentle groan of the building as the water moved in and around it, making her wonder if Alma Hall was also in danger of collapsing.

There was something unsettling in the quiet. No more screams of terror shrilled the darkness, no more buildings were heard crumbling into the water. Just silence. It was then that Patricia realized for the first time that all the noises that had been so much a part of Johnstown had stopped—

absolutely every one of them. No more clanging of the mills in the distance, no clattering of wheels along the cobblestone streets, no coal trains rumbling past. No whistles, no birds, nothing. It was the most unnerving quiet Patricia had ever heard. She wanted to scream out just so she could break it, but she didn't. Instead, she seemed to be a part of the hush, as if she was contributing to it somehow.

Slowly, her tiny view of the sky through the nearest window began to lighten yet still nothing stirred. Finally, she balled up her underskirt, which she had taken off during the night to use as cover, and slipped it beneath Laura's head while she carefully eased out from under her. Her legs had grown numb from the cold and her lack of movement and she found she could barely walk. As she made her way around the injured lying across the floor in a scattered patchwork of bodies, she found Andrew sitting near one of the windows holding a small child in his arms. Although the child was sleeping, Andrew was not. Instead, he sat staring absently, entranced, at the coming of day.

Patricia decided to leave him to his thoughts and stepped over to one of the windows and looked out. It was her first look at the vast destruction below and the impact of what she saw pierced her stomach like a sharp, fiery blade. The first dim shapes of morning had begun to emerge through the thin mist, and although very little stood out in detail, for there were no shadows, no clear edges to anything yet, what she saw was hideous enough to take her breath from her.

The valley looked smothered in a smoky gray shroud. Everything seemed to be the drab color of pewter. Odd patches of the valley and the distant hills were lost to low-hanging ribbons of mist while spread out below them was a vile-looking lake that should not be, crusted over with a grinding pack of wreckage and human flesh. Johnstown was a vast sea of muck, rubble, and filthy water, and there was a peculiar stench in the chilled air like nothing she had ever smelled before.

Nearly all of Johnstown had been destroyed. From Locust Street over to the Little Conemaugh was a flat, open space of nothing. It had been so thoroughly swept that there was

433

absolutely no indication that houses and building had ever stood there. It was now an empty tract of mud, rock, water, and scattered debris not yet determinable in nature. The only buildings Patricia could see from this window were close by along Main Street. They had been so badly ravaged and gutted that they were for the most part useless, but they still stood. And off at the corner of where Jackson and Locust once met, was part of the St. John's Catholic Church with its blackened rafters still smoldering and wreckage dumped against it as high as the building was tall. The top had burned down level with where the water line must have once stood. But now a strip of unburned building several feet deep was visible above the water. That meant that the water was indeed going down, ever so slowly, but it was going down.

Turning her back on the massive destruction of the town she loved so dearly, Patricia tried not to wonder what horrors lay ahead as she quickly left the window and made her way back to Laura's side. Wearily, she sat down and closed her eyes. She did not intend to seek out other windows in order to see what the rest of Johnstown might look like. She had already seen enough.

Chapter Twenty-nine

As the water slowly but steadily withdrew from along the outer edges of town, the thousands that had somehow escaped the flood and had taken refuge on the surrounding hillsides gradually returned. Individually or in small groups, the weary survivors made their way back down the steep slopes with hopes of helping in some way; not really sure of what they could do, but knowing they should do something. Most were ragged, wet, and a great many of them were injured in some way. All were exhausted. Except for a fortunate few, they had been forced to spend the long night in a cold rain with nothing more to shelter them than the trees. But their thoughts were no longer on their own miseries. They were centered on the macabre scene of death and devastation that surrounded them. They were concerned about their families, their friends.

Very few buildings remained and none of those had held against the mighty torrent without having sustained some sort of damage. And as they got closer they could see that most of the buildings were nothing more than outer shells; the windows and the inner walls had been washed away by the force of the water. The hazy mist had lifted and everything had started to come into sharper focus. The true magnitude of what now lay before them became dismally clear. Johnstown was a ravaged wasteland.

The litter of thousands of lives—an entire city—was strewn everywhere. Splintered furniture, twisted tools, and shattered toys had mixed together with books, dishes, chamber pots, bicycle wheels, trunks, candlesticks, telephone poles, chunks of machinery, shredded trees, animal corpses, nail kegs, bed quilts, utensils, clothing, and all manner of building materials thrown up in grotesque heaps ten, twenty, and even thirty feet high, or lay gently shifting back and forth in the huge pools of murky water that still covered so much of the valley floor.

People soon began to step out of the few buildings that still stood. Alma Hall, the Franklin Street Methodist Church, and the Union Street School were the largest of the buildings left and bore steady streams of those who had somehow survived the night. Rescue efforts began right away to get the marooned down from rooftops and out of the few mangled trees that still stood. Small bands began to search the rubble for signs of life, of which there were few, while others struck out on their own in search of their families and loved ones.

Many buildings still crumbled and fell with horrific suddenness, crushing anyone who might have sought shelter inside. Large piles of debris shifted and collapsed for no apparent reason, making the rescue efforts treacherous work. The going was necessarily slow but those who searched for their friends and family were undaunted by the danger and death that lay everywhere.

At the enormous stone bridge, squads of men and boys, many of whom had remained there all night, continued to work hard to free the people who were captured and still alive inside the flaming pile of wreckage. For many, a rescue had been impossible and they had met a cruel and tragic fate within the burning clutches of the twisted heap. Men, women, and children fought the flames off as long as they could but eventually had burned to death right before everyone's eyes. Many a strong-hearted man broke down and wept at the horrendous sounds of the screaming victims who suffered such horrible deaths. But to some, death had become oddly second nature. It no longer affected them. They had numbed their hearts to the atrocity of it all. They refused to let themselves care anymore.

An hour after daybreak, Patricia was back at work, ignoring her own pain while following Dr. Matthews around the room with what few pieces of cloth they had left. Now that there was light to work with, the doctor was re-examining everyone he had cared for the night before. The injuries looked far worse by the early light of day and Patricia felt her stomach coil at the sight of so much blood oozing from thin, raggedy bandages that were lifted to reveal huge gaping wounds. She felt extremely lightheaded on occasion, but managed to stay on her feet and do whatever was asked of her. She was determined to be strong. She was determined to help.

It was far into the morning before Patricia was finally able to sit down on the floor again and when she did, she slumped forward and ran her hand over her tired face, hoping to revive herself somehow. That's when she noticed her own injury for the first time. Up next to her hairline, just inches above her right eye, was a tender, swollen area about an inch wide. When she searched for the center of it with her fingertip, the pressure of her own touch sent pain coursing right through her right eye and into her jaw.

Carefully, she continued to prod the area until she finally discovered something hard and sharp in the core of it. A jagged edge protruded through her skin when she gently pressed on the wound. Rather than bother the doctor with her injury, knowing he had to be very near exhaustion by now, Patricia gritted her teeth against the pain and worked with it until she finally was able to pull a narrow piece of broken glass out.

Blood poured instantly from the wound and down her forehead. Having already used all the cloth they had gathered for bandages, she had nothing to press against it except the palm of her bare hand. While she held the cut with her hand and waited for the bleeding to stop, she leaned back against the wall and closed her eyes. For the first time since the horrible disaster had occurred, sleep almost overtook her. Her hand lessened its pressure on the cut and the bleeding continued.

"There you are," a familiar voice said and brought her

back out of her dazed state. Opening her left eye, she saw James Walters standing over her with something in his hands. Quickly wiping the blood away from her other eye with the back of her hand, she opened it too in order to get a better focus on the strange brown mass that was in the lawyer's hands. To her amazement, it was the same dog that had shared her raft during the flood.

"Where'd you find him?" she wanted to know as she wiped her bloodstained hands on her skirt and smiled up into the sad face of the shaggy animal who had yet to look down and notice her.

"So he is yours? I thought so," James said and bent over to set the dog on the floor beside her. When the animal looked up and noticed Patricia for the first time, it crouched low and began to wiggle its way toward her, wimpering and patting its tail as it went as if it wasn't sure what sort of reception to expect from her.

James smiled with satisfaction when Patricia reached out and began to lovingly stroke the animal's matted fur, then he started to explain. "Right after we rescued you and Reverend Edwards had already left to bring you up here, John Williams, who was in the window next to mine, managed to catch hold of that little chunk of roof you were on before it could float away with your dog still on it. Between the two of us, we were finally able to talk your dog into coming close enough to the edge so that we could grab him and lift him off. I would have brought him to you sooner, but I was put in charge of the fourth floor and have been too busy with that to go looking for you before now."

"I appreciate your trouble, but he's not my dog," she said with a tired shrug. Pushing her tangled hair away from her face with her fingers, she looked back down at the cowering animal. "But leave him with me. I'll take care of him until it is safe to let him go in search of his real owner. They say dogs have a strong natural sense of where home lies."

"So I've heard," James said, then reached down to rub the small dog's scraggly head. "So long, old fellow. I leave you in able hands. Take care." Then he gave the animal a final pat and left.

For the rest of the day, the dog lay on the floor right where James Walters left him. Although he never once moved from the spot, he continually kept his eyes open and trained on Patricia. Whenever she neared a door, he tensed and rose to his haunches, but he never once tried to approach her. He seemed content just knowing she was in the room.

That afternoon, while Andrew and Dr. Matthews went out to see if there was anything of a hospital facility being set up anywhere, Patricia volunteered to stay in the building on the third floor and care for the people too injured to leave on their own accord. There were almost a hundred of them. Some were already in the state of unconsciousness, but so far the only fatality at Alma Hall was that of Laura Edison's baby.

Andrew promised Patricia that just as soon as they could locate a decent place to put them all—still afraid Alma Hall could collapse yet—that he and the doctor would be back to get them and relieve her. But it was late afternoon before either of them returned. Dr. Matthews came back first, having found out that there was a makeshift hospital being set up in one of the only two school buildings left. He had brought four able-bodied men with a door and a huge piece of planking to carry people down the stairs on.

"The other school is being used for a temporary morgue," the doctor went on to explain. "When Andrew gets here, tell him he should carry that poor little baby on over there," Dr. Matthews told her, his expression grim. "Then tell him to try to find me at the hospital. That's where I'm going to be from now on."

"But what about all these people?" Patricia asked, waving a hand to indicate all those still in the room.

"I was hoping you could stay on a little longer," he admitted sheepishly. "I'm more needed there. I've already done all I can for these people without having the proper equipment and supplies, but they will still need someone here to help take care of them."

"How much longer do I need to stay?" she asked and tried to hide the disappointment from her voice. She was eager to get out and find Cole.

"That's hard to say. Right now I only have one small wagon to transport all these people in. It's only large enough to carry a very few to the hospital at a time. How long you have to stay really depends on whether or not I can find someone else with a wagon that is willing to help get these people moved. But I warn you, there are very few wagons left. I almost didn't find one at all. I had to go all the way up to Prospect Hill and rent this one from a man who lives up there."

"In other words, I'll probably be here through the night," she surmised. "And possibly into the morning."

"Unless I can find someone to relieve you, I'm afraid so. I'd let Reverend Edwards take your place, but I'll need him to help get the injured into the wagon and then on to the hospital. I won't be able to oversee that operation much longer."

"That's all right. I'll stay as long as I'm needed," she told him as she watched the four men carefully lift a man who had been unconscious for several hours and gently place him on the small door. Next they lifted another man who had lost most of his face and was barely lucid and placed him on the huge piece of planking they had brought with them. Then they quickly carried the two injured men out.

"Try to see that those with the most serious injuries get carried out of here first. And as soon as everyone is gone, you are free to leave." With an appreciative smile, the doctor reached out and gave her shoulder a gentle squeeze. "You are a good woman, Patricia. I hope the saints take notice." Then with his arm pressed against his side to steady his own broken ribs, he followed the men through the door.

Patricia spent a second night in Alma Hall. When she was not busy rendering what aid she could to the wounded or offering comfort to the sick, she sat on the floor beside Laura and, whenever she found the young woman was awake, tried to keep her company. Patricia did what she could to cheer her new friend but found the deed almost impossible to do and understandably so.

Once when Patricia returned to find Laura on the floor asleep, she sat down and laid her own head back against the

440

inner office wall in order to rest, only this time she was able to sleep. When Andrew returned late into the night to help with the ongoing evacuation of Alma Hall, he found her still sleeping soundly and did not bother to disturb her. Quietly, he helped the others carry three more of the badly injured right through the door beside her and downstairs to the waiting wagon. He was glad to see she was finally resting. He had worried about her, especially after having lost so much blood through that cut on her head. He was tired of all this death. He couldn't bear to lose one more friend to the flood. He was almost to an emotional breaking point as it was.

At her own insistence, Laura Edison was one of the last to be transported out of Alma Hall. She had hoped her husband might realize where she was and come looking for her. But her hopes proved futile. Another endless night passed and her Lowell did not come for her. She grew more and more depressed.

It was well into morning before Laura and one other last patient were finally transported out of Alma Hall. Although Patricia was very anxious to go in search of her own loved ones and find out if her own house still stood, she stayed by Laura's side until she was finally carried down the two flights of stairs and placed in the back of an open wagon.

"I'm going to ride back to the hospital with Laura," Andy told Patricia as two men eased Laura onto the flat bed of the wagon. "I promised her I'd do what I could to help locate her husband for her once I had her settled in over there and back under a doctor's care."

"I hope you find him," Patricia responded quickly as she glanced over at the wagon where Laura lay, her eyes barely open and staring unseeing up into the gray sky. "She has lost a lot of blood and has gotten very weak and pale since the loss of that baby. She needs her husband. He would give her a reason to try to get better sooner."

"I agree," Andrew said with a slight nod. Then looking at Patricia, he noticed how pale and gaunt she looked and he was also aware of how much blood was caked in her wild array of matted hair. "Why don't you climb into the wagon too and ride over to the hospital with us. You need to have that cut looked at. It's gotten very red and swollen. It looks infected. It shouldn't take very long."

Patricia reached up and touched the affected area and realized that it had become even more tender to the touch, but she did not want to take the time to have it looked at. Besides there were hundreds, maybe thousands of people with worse injuries than hers that needed a doctor's attention far more. "No, I think I'll wait before having it looked at. I'm eager to see if I can find Cole. Have you seen him or heard anything?"

"No," he answered simply, then upon seeing her brow furrow with worry, he added, "but I've been too busy getting the injured to the hospital to be asking anyone much of anything. I did get the chance to ask a nun I came across if she knew what had become of Faye—Sister Mary—but she had no idea. And I hear Harrison's at the hospital somewhere, although I haven't actually seen him."

He paused a moment while he climbed up into the buckboard and sat down beside the driver. "In all honesty, no one really knows much of anything just yet. They are just now getting organized in their rescue efforts. Oh, there are still a few out there looking on their own for some loved one or another, but most have gotten themselves organized into teams and are working in shifts. And I also found out that they are trying to get together a list of the living as well as a list of the dead. So, maybe soon we will be able to know something more about what happened to everyone. By the way, I've already gone by and reported you as being alive."

Having to be reported alive seemed a little absurd, but Patricia did not yet know the extent of the damage and death the flood had actually caused. She had just now stepped outside for the first time. Eager to be in search of Cole, her sisters, her father, Tony, Harrison, and Minnie, she thanked Andrew then bid him good-bye and turned her back to the wagon even before they had pulled away. As she looked around her, she noticed that the flooded area was getting smaller. Only lower Johnstown, down near the point, was still actually under water. But as she looked around her, she thought that the entire valley looked like a hideous sea made of muck and rubble.

Now that she was outside among the ruin and closer to the wretched bayou of destruction, she found that the damage was far worse than she had at first thought. The magnitude of damage that lay around her was appalling. The putrid stench of mud and death was far worse on the ground and things she had not been able to make out from the third-floor window were now clear to her. Drifts of mire and refuse were everywhere, sometimes piled higher than her head, and now that she was outside, she could see that human corpses made up a substantial part of the huge heaps of debris that cluttered the area. Just a few feet from where she stood at that very moment, a human hand protruded out from the base of a small pile of broken wood and wadded clothing. It looked as if it still reached out for the help that never came.

Pulling her eyes from the morbid sight, she shuddered then quickly scanned the area in every direction. Although the huge piles of clutter blocked her view in several places, she was able to see that a narrow patch of buildings on the far edge of the town, close to Green Hill, did not appear badly affected. Nor did any of the houses on the hillsides themselves. The area where her own house had once stood was leveled. Nothing was left but a huge, littered void.

Looking next to see if she could find her father's house, Patricia noticed that only two houses were left standing in that area. With the exception of those two houses and a bent tree, the entire neighborhood around Walnut Street was swept away. As she narrowed her eyes to focus better, she noticed that one of the two houses looked like it might be Jeanne and Harrison's and her insides churned with excitement. But the other house was too far away to be her father's. It was too far the other side of the Methodist church. Too far beyond where the park had once stood.

Staring over the piles of rubble, at where she judged her father's house to have been, she realized that there was not a trace to be seen of the large three-storied structure that had once been her home—nor any other of the stately homes that had stood on that block. Fear pierced her heart as she stared at the empty place where the house had once stood. Her

443

sisters had been in that house the very last time she had seen them. What had become of them? Were they all right? Or had they been swept away with the house?

Her heart pounded wildly in her chest, pushing a tight throbbing pain up to her throat as she started to run straight for Jeanne's house. Tears stung her eyes and the cold air burned the surfaces, but she was afraid to blink, afraid the house might disappear from her sight. With all her might, she prayed that her sisters had gone back to Jeanne's house for some reason before the water actually hit. Maybe they had forgotten to put something away that Jeanne had thought of later that afternoon. Something Jeanne would want saved. For if they had returned to Jeanne's in time, the two of them might still be alive. Desperately, she clung to that hope as she held her ragged skirt high and ran the five blocks with all the strength she still possessed. She rejected any thought that they might be dead. No, they had to still be alive. They had to.

Tunneling her vision on the house itself, Patricia refused to notice the grisly view of destruction and death that surrounded her. Even when she found herself wading through the thick mud and mire, she refused to look down for fear of what she might see. She kept her sights on the house. Whenever the view was temporarily blocked by the huge piles of mangled lumber, brick, furniture, and bodies, she kept her eyes pinpointed on where she had last seen the house.

The stench was almost unbearable, weakening her as she went, but determination drove her on toward the house. As she neared what used to be her sister's well-manicured lawn—green with early summer delights—she noticed that not one bush or tree still stood and only part of the brick fence remained, though cracked and broken all along its length. An ungodly stack of refuse was piled up against the far corner of the fence twice the fence's height, almost as tall as the house itself. And all over the yard were thick layers of mud and waste.

When she turned her attention to the house itself, Patricia noticed that all the windows on the bottom floor were gone, completely dashed out, as well as several on the second floor. A small high-backed chair stood lodged in one of the front windows in seemingly perfect repair. When she headed forward, she noticed that the front door was also missing.

"Jeanne? Catherine? Is anyone here?" she called out and stepped closer to the house. She paused long enough to listen for a reply. There was none. As she walked through the doorway, she called out their names again, louder. Still there was no response. There was no sign of anyone having been inside the house since the flood waters had retreated. She saw no footprints on the floor where almost a foot of sandy mud and muck mixed with splintered pieces of wood, metal, glass, and dented utensils lined the floor in heavy drifts.

As she peered through the house, she noticed that the wallpaper in every room she could see had been stripped right off the walls, and the banister had been swept clean from the staircase, but oddly, the fireplace mantel stood just as it always had, completely unharmed.

"Jeanne? Catherine?" she called out once more even though she no longer expected an answer and none came. "Where are you?" Her voice dropped to a bare whisper as her throat became choked with emotion. "Please be alive somewhere. Please don't be dead."

When she turned to leave in order to continue her search elsewhere, her eye caught sight of the small candelabra that usually sat on the mantel. Carefully, she picked it up out of the mud and wiped it as clean as she could get it with her ragged skirt then gently returned it to its proper place as if it somehow mattered. Then she hurriedly walked out of the house.

Her next thought was the hospital. Andrew had said that Harrison was supposed to be there. Catherine also might be there, working, trying to help with all the injured. She was a hospital aide and would want to help in any way she could. And Jeanne might be there too, if for no other reason than to be near Harrison. Even if neither sister was there, Harrison might know where she could find them. And he might also know where Cole was. How desperately she wanted to find Cole. To be held in his strong arms and tenderly comforted.

She needed his strength.

With that thought foremost in her mind, Patricia rushed out of the barren yard and down a path where Walnut Street had once lain. Remembering where Andrew had told her the hospital had been set up, she hurried eastward through the wrecked streets toward the Fourth Ward school building.

Unprepared for the horrors she might find there, Patricia rushed headlong through the front door only to be stopped cold by the sights that met her after she was but a few feet inside. The room was filled with battered, bleeding people who sat in agonizing pain on narrow school benches or directly on the floor, waiting for a doctor or a nurse to help them. Those who had already been tended to lay side by side on the floor beyond the room, all down the halls, and in some of the outlying rooms, crying and moaning in excruciating pain, for there was as of yet no medication of any kind to help lessen their pain.

Patricia's heart felt as if it were being wrenched right out of her as she passed among the maimed and wounded. People without arms. People without large portions of their faces. It was like a grotesque nightmare—only she knew there was no waking up from this.

When she finally found Harrison inside one of the school rooms near the back of the building that had been set up for examinations, he was busily trying to tend to a young woman who stubbornly demanded that he leave her alone. She claimed that she was not the one in need of his help. Wildly, she gestured toward her child and demanded he do something for the boy. The child would not wake up.

Patricia felt her strength draining out of her and she reached for the door frame for support because clutched tightly against the young woman's breast was a small boy about a year in age who had already gone pale and stiff from death. The small child was dressed in a blue and white sailor suit left dingy from the dirty waters. Patricia realized the little boy must have drowned for there was no sign of injury on his sweet face. His peaceful expression truly did look as if he was simply asleep.

"But Doctor, listen to me, it's my baby that needs your

help. Not me. I'm fine," the woman tried to explain, then began to shriek hysterically when Harrison again insisted on examining the large gaping wound on her face instead of checking her son. "Damn it, Doctor. Leave my face alone. Do something for Johnny!"

Tears quickly blurred Patricia's vision and she clutched the door frame tighter when she noticed the tormented look on Harrison's worn, unshaven face. He realized he had to try to get it across to the woman that her son was already dead.

"I'm sorry, but Johnny is beyond my help," he began as he laid a gentle hand on her shoulder. His voice was so choked with emotion that it did not sound like Harrison at all. "There's nothing I can do for him. But I can help you. You are hurt. I need to take a good look at that cut along your cheek there. It needs to be cleaned and bandaged."

His words only served to make the woman more hysterical. Shaking with the outrage she felt, she pierced the air with her pathetic screams and struck out at Harrison again and again, hitting him across his back and shoulder with a tightly clenched fist until he finally had to call out for assistance. Someone had to help restrain the woman so that he could get a look at the wound that had started to bleed again.

"Liar!" she screamed at the top of her voice, oblivious to the thick trail of blood that now coursed down her cheek and neck. "Liar! He's not dead. You just don't want to help him. What kind of doctor are you?"

An older woman, who Patricia recognized to be Mrs. Demlow, one of the richest and most aristocratic women in Johnstown, and one Patricia never would have expected to be helping out at the hospital, rushed over and took the trembling woman and her dead son into her arms and held them close, oblivious to the blood that was quickly soaking into the shoulder of her dress.

"There there, now," Mrs. Demlow said in a soothing voice, trying to calm the hysterical woman before she hurt someone. "There's nothing we can do about your son. It's simply too late. Johnny is no longer with us. He's playing in heaven now. We will miss him, but at least he doesn't suffer

447

like so many others here."

Eventually, the woman's loud screams of protest melted into quaking sobs and she wept quietly against Mrs. Demlow's warm shoulder. With tears in her own eyes, Mrs. Demlow sagged to the floor with the sobbing woman still in her arms and pressed her head closer to her and began to rock back and forth, continuing to comfort the woman as best she could. Harrison looked away from the heartbreaking scene, his face rigid with emotion, and after a moment, spotted Patricia standing in the doorway and staring, mortified by what she had just witnessed. He hurried across the room to her.

"Are you all right?" he asked as he came to stand in front of her, passing a hand in front of her to see if he could distract her.

"I—I'm fine," she lied, then looked away from the two women. Her legs felt very weak and she had become extremely lightheaded in the last few moments. Harrison's voice seemed to fade in and out as he spoke to her.

"You look pale," he said, concerned, as he pushed her tangled hair out of the way with his thumb so that he could get a good look at the reddened wound on her forehead. Then he proceeded to examine a swollen place along her jaw and the deep blue bruises on the arm exposed to his sight, where her sleeve had been torn off at the shoulder. "And that cut on your forehead needs to be looked after. We don't have any medication yet, but we have been hearing rumors all morning that some is on its way from Pittsburgh. Until it arrives, I can clean it with cooled boiled water and bandage it with a clean cloth."

"No, not now. Maybe later. Go on and tend to the others. I just wanted to see if you knew where Cole or Jeanne or maybe even Catherine might be. I've been to your house, but no one was there."

"I'm afraid I haven't seen any of them. I've asked around but I've had absolutely no word of Jeanne, or any of the others for that matter." He paused and seemed to look right through her. "I can only pray that she is all right."

Patricia understood how he must feel. Hot tears of

disappointment stung her eyes and caused her throat to constrict until she could barely swallow. Her legs weakened in response and felt too wobbly to bear her weight, but she managed to remain standing. How desperately she had hoped to get news of Cole. She needed to be with him and be assured he was all right. And she also needed to know that the rest of her family and friends were still alive. "Have you seen or heard from Father?"

Harrison merely shook his head as he took her into his arms and held her close, as much for his own comfort as hers. "I'm sorry," he said in a tight voice. "I wish I could say that I've seen them all. But I can't."

Patricia leaned against him for a long moment, trembling in her efforts to keep from crying, before Harrison spoke again.

"Patricia, I want you to go to one of the refugee centers that are being set up around town and get some rest. You need it. And then when the medication does finally get here, I want you to come right on back here and let me treat that nasty cut over your right eye. It could get very serious if it isn't looked after very soon. I'm afraid infection has already started to set in."

"I don't need any rest," she protested and pulled her head back and looked him in the eye. "I'll come back and let you tend that cut, but I don't need any rest yet."

"Oh, yes you do. I've already heard about how long you helped at Alma Hall. This morning, Dr. Matthews told me all about everything that went on there just before he succumbed to his massive chest injuries."

"He did? Where is he now?"

"Resting, I hope."

"It's a wonder he's still alive. I could tell he was in terrible pain, but he refused to admit it. Andrew and I both tried to get him to slow down and at least rest a little, but he wouldn't listen to us. There were too many injured and he felt duty bound to take care of them. He simply would not rest."

"Why should he listen to you two when you wouldn't take the same advice from him? And speaking of Andrew," he said as he slowly let go of her and stepped back. "Here he

449

comes now."

Patricia turned around just in time to see Andrew and another man about five years younger heading straight for them.

"Guess who I have here," Andrew said with a broad smile stretched across his lightly stubbled face as he indicated the man walking beside him with a slight tilt of his head.

"Don't tell me. This is Lowell Edison," Patricia guessed eagerly and cried out with joy when Andrew nodded that it was indeed. It renewed her hope to know that someone had been found in all the mayhem outside. "Does Laura know he's here?"

"That's where we are headed," Andrew explained with a happy lift of his brow. "This ought to raise her spirits some." Reaching out and pulling his newfound prize by the shirt-sleeve, he chirped, "Come on, let's go see your wife." Looking toward Patricia, he asked, "Want to come?"

"No, I was just about to leave. I'm still trying to find Cole and my sisters. You haven't heard anything about them yet, have you?"

Andrew's bright smile faded. "No, I'm afraid I haven't, but I have started to ask around. It's only a matter of time. Check back with me now and again and I'll let you know when I've found out anything."

"There—" Harrison broke into her thoughts after Andrew had rounded a corner and was out of sight. "Andrew is going to search for Cole for you. You can get some rest after all."

"No, I can't. I still plan to look too," she said adamantly. "I have to know what has happened to him. And to my sisters. To everyone. I couldn't possibly rest until I know."

Harrison paused a long moment. He understood how she felt. "Have you tried the morgue yet?"

Patricia stiffened. "No, I haven't."

"If you're going to insist on looking, I wish you would try there first. It's over in the Adam Street schoolhouse. I understand they are keeping a list of everyone who is brought in, but they are not actually burying them until they are positively identified. All the unidentified are left lying, open to public inspection, until someone comes along that

450

can identify them. If Jeanne or Catherine are there among the dead, I would rather they go ahead and be buried and their bodies no longer subject to public display." Harrison paused. His eyes reddened as tears filled them and spilled out onto his unshaven cheek. "I need to know, even if it turns out she is dead. I would be able to concentrate better on my work if I knew for certain Jeanne's fate. If you really insist on looking, please, look there first."

An unbearable pain twisted inside Patricia's chest, making it almost impossible to speak. "I will, Harrison. I'll go there first."

Then without another word, she left the building and headed straight for Adam Street, her heart filled with the dread of what she might find there.

Chapter Thirty

The closer to the Adam Street schoolhouse Patricia got, the stronger the vile odor of death grew. Just before she reached the solid brick building that had somehow withstood the torrential onslaught with relatively little damage, she paused, her insides turbulent with black emotions. Pulling in deep breaths through her clamped teeth, she sought the strength it would take for her to go inside. It would take far more from her than she had realized. While she worked to steady her nerves and calm her churning insides, she pulled her gaze from the many people sitting on the grassy slope of a nearby hill, where they carefully watched the comings and goings of the morgue, and glanced toward the opened doubled doors in front of the light-bricked building where she knew she would eventually have to enter, willing herself to move forward and get it over with.

As she forcefully gathered her courage, her eyes were drawn to the steady movement near the front of the building and she was aghast at the way bodies were being hastily tossed off carts or wagons and hauled inside like so much cargo. Still unaware of the magnitude of the disaster, she wondered how anyone could possibly treat the bodies with such a lack of respect. Anger welled inside her, but she pushed it aside as she made her way to the door. Her goal was not to fight with these calloused helpers, it was to see if Jeanne or Catherine were among the dead.

"Can you help me?" she asked a man sitting at a small desk near the wide entrance. When he did not look up in response to her question, she asked again a little louder. "Sir, can you help me?"

Busily logging in the descriptions of the bodies being hauled past him while an associate pinned small white cards to them that would help with identifying them later, the man looked up at her only briefly. "What is it?"

"I am looking for my sisters. I—I thought that . . . well, that . . ." She just couldn't bring herself to say it.

"Over there," the man said abruptly and pointed to another man at another desk just inside the door. "Give Mr. Ewan your sisters' names." Then he dismissed her by turning his back to her and glancing over at the next body waiting to be carried inside.

"Thank you," she muttered, then turned to look at the man she had been directed to. Reluctantly, she stepped inside the building, careful not to touch anything, and walked up to the desk. She choked on the sickening stench that hung heavily in the humid air as she opened her mouth to speak. "Sir, I was told you could help me."

"Name of who you are looking for," he said in an abrupt, monotone voice as he reached for his list. When she did not immediately respond, he looked up and his expression softened into a sympathetic smile. "Please, madam, give me the name of whoever it is you are looking for."

Patricia had to take several sharp breaths before she was able to steady her voice enough to force her sisters' names off her tongue. "Carol Jeanne Rutledge and Catherine Marie Mackey."

"Rutledge . . . Rutledge . . ." the man repeated as he looked down the first page of the list, then lifted it and began studying a second page.

"How many names do you have?" she asked in a trembling voice.

"A couple of hundred on my personal list and another couple of hundred on these other lists that have been sent over from the other temporary morgues in the area." Looking up at her shocked expression, he explained. "There may be thousands before we are through. They are finding more bodies with each pile of rubbish they search. We have a steady stream coming in."

"Thousands? I had no idea it was that bad."

"It is and I'm afraid it's our job to try to get them all identified. We've got what's considered the main morgue here, and because of that we are constantly being updated on all the names. Even if your sisters were brought in elsewhere and sent on to be buried from there, I'd have their names on this list pretty quick. And if they go unidentified in one of those places for very long then they get brought here. It's an effort to try to centralize everything."

"And do you find either of my sister's names on your list?"

"Haven't yet," he said with a shake of his head, then proceeded to glance over the long list. "No, no Rutledge on here at all. Now let me check for the Mackeys."

Patricia watched the man's face closely. And when he glanced over the last page of names with no mention of having spotted Catherine's name, she felt her relief slowly wash over her.

"No, there's no Mackey on here either," he told her as he leaned back in his chair, obviously relieved himself. "Anyone else?"

"Would you mind looking for Faye Gifford, or she might be listed as Sister Mary? And Minnie Hess?" She was certain Cole's name would not be there. In her heart, she refused to believe he would allow any harm to come to himself.

After another glance over his list, he smiled and said, "Neither of those either. But now you need to go in through those double doors over there and talk to someone in the assembly room. There's still a chance your sisters or friends have been brought in but never identified."

Moving ahead slowly, Patricia was not sure if she had the stamina to carry this out after all. When she stepped inside and got her first glimpse of the many rows and rows of dead lying tightly knit on the schoolroom floor, she was so horrorstruck that she reached for the wall just inside the door and fought for her breath. She had not expected to see so many bodies and laid out in neat rows like so much

455

merchandise. When she glanced at those closest to her, it was obvious that the bodies had been washed and straightened as best they could. She wondered why some of them were draped with pieces of cloth or paper and some were not. There seemed to be no order to what was being done.

"Have you come to view the dead?" a grave little man asked as he approached.

Patricia merely nodded.

"Do you need someone with you?"

She noticed that others in the room seemed to be viewing the bodies in pairs or trios. "No, I don't need any help."

"If you're sure, then go ahead. But if you find that you would like someone to go around with you, just call. We have men willing to assist you in any way. And if you happen to recognize anyone, anyone at all, please let me know."

"I will," she said grimly and turned to look back out across the crowded floor. Remembering that Catherine was wearing a blue gingham dress, Patricia glanced around for sight of such clothing but quickly realized that although the bodies had been washed down, most of the clothing was so stained that the coloring was dulled. From a distance, everyone appeared to be wearing some shade of brown or gray.

Starting down the nearest aisle, Patricia felt her legs quake beneath her weight and her knees grow rapidly weak, but she willed herself not to faint. She had to see this through.

As she edged her way down that first aisle being careful not to let the ragged hem of her skirt brush any of the dead, she suddenly realized why some of the bodies were partially draped while others were not. They had no clothing on. Their clothes had been torn away by the raging waters. Then she noticed that the faces of some of the corpses were also covered but soon found the reason for that. It was to protect the weak at heart from having to view the mutilation. A few of the bodies had even been decapitated.

Forced to lift the soiled drapes from the faces of the women corpses that had no clothing to distinguish them from the rest, Patricia found herself growing rapidly ill. But still, she was determined to continue. She had to know.

Finally she reached the last row and started to feel the first flutterings of hope. She was nearly through and had not happened across her sisters yet, nor her father, nor Minnie, nor anyone else. As she started down the final aisle, she felt some of her strength returning and her breathing eased until she got about halfway through and her gaze fell on Catherine.

Horrified, her hands folded over her mouth and attempted to keep the scream from bursting past her lips but failed, for the sound vibrated through the room in blood curdling volume. Never had she felt such a soul-crushing pain. It bore through to the very core of her, grinding and twisting as it did. Everything inside her crumpled and withered, until she finally collapsed from the force and sagged to the floor.

"No! Dearest God, please, no!" But there was no mistaking Catherine's sweet face.

Unable to take her eyes from her sister, Patricia clutched at her retching stomach and started to take in deep rasping gulps of air. The pain tightened its excruciating hold on her and she felt certain she was going to faint.

One of the aides who had been standing by and had witnessed her collapse hurried to her side, but Patricia refused to be coddled by a stranger and pushed the man away. "Leave me be," she wailed, still bent over with the gorging pain of having found her youngest sister among the dead. "Just leave me be a moment."

The man stood back and waited while Patricia continued to stare at the pale features of her sister, devastated by the ache that centered itself in her heart. Patricia's stricken face became a ghastly shade of white as her grief continued to grow to overwhelming proportions and she began to sway, but somehow she remained conscious.

"Not Catherine. No, not Catherine," she repeated over and over as she gazed, transfixed, at her dear sister. It felt as if her very heart had been wrenched out of her as she reached out a hand to touch her sister's cold, lifeless form.

To Patricia, Catherine looked as if she might simply be resting. As if at any moment she might open her pretty blue eyes and offer a mischievous smile. There were no noticeable injuries marring Catherine's face in any way—only a small bruise on the left side of her neck. Someone had caringly combed her curly brown hair and had straightened her tattered clothing around her. She looked so peaceful, so serene. There was nothing in her features to indicate that she was truly dead other than the ghostly white pallor of her skin and the faded blue tint of her lips.

As Patricia's eyes slowly swept over Catherine, knowing it would be her last glimpse of her dear sister, she became aware of a withered card pinned to one of Catherine's ragged sleeves. On the card the number 317 had been scrawled and nothing more. The oddity of that caused her to fall quiet and stare.

"One of your sisters?"

Sitting back on her ankles and looking up through her tears, she saw that the tiny man she had talked to when she had first entered the room had joined the other man and they both stood beside her, waiting patiently.

"Yes, that's . . . Catherine."

"Then this is for you," he said, and promptly produced a large water-stained envelope that also had the number 317 scrawled across it and held it out to her.

As soon as she had taken the envelope from him, he searched his list for the same number and promptly wrote in the name: Catherine Marie Mackey. "May I also have your name for my records?" he asked, then wrote Patricia's name down as next of kin as soon as she had told it to him.

"What's in here?" Patricia asked as she sat staring at the lightly blotched packet she held in her trembling hands. It looked as if it had been carelessly stored out in the rain.

"Your sister's effects. We have had to start removing any jewelry or money from the bodies and place those items in envelopes for safe keeping. As morbid as it may sound, we've had a lot of body looting going on. Rings were disappearing right out from under our noses."

Patricia was overwhelmed with a sickening disgust. What sort of person would rob the dead? Only the lowest, vilest of creatures could do such a thing.

"Can you stand? You would be much more comfortable viewing the contents of the envelope over on one of the benches next to the wall," the man said, offering her his hand.

Rising to her knees, then forcing herself up by her own accord, Patricia chose to continue her search. She still had not found Jeanne, nor her father. "Thank you, but I need to make certain my other sister is not . . ." She paused. She simply could not say it.

"I understand," the man said sympathetically. "Let me go along with you."

The man made no attempt to touch her or speak to her again, for which Patricia was grateful. He simply followed a few paces behind her in order to be close in case she should need him again. Hurriedly, she examined the last of the bodies. To her relief, Jeanne was not among them nor was her father. Nor was Cole, even though she had truly not expected to find him there. She was certain Cole was all right. After all, he had been up at the lake and would have seen the danger in time. He would have kept himself safe. No, she felt that he was probably out helping rescue the marooned and the injured at that very moment.

As had been suggested, Patricia walked over to sit on one of the tiny benches with the envelope clutched tightly in her hands. When she sat down and glanced up at the man who continued to follow her, the pained expression in her eyes was enough to let him know that what she needed most from him right now was her privacy. Nodding, he walked back across the room to the door where a pair of men had just entered, staring in wide-eyed disbelief at the number of corpses that lined the floor.

As soon as she was alone again, Patricia gingerly began to open the sealed envelope, wondering what could be inside. Catherine wore no jewelry that she knew of nor did she usually carry money on her person and surely would not have had her purse with her at the time of the flood. Carefully, she bent the flap back and poured the contents into her palm. Inside was a small enameled comb that had been in Catherine's hair and a large golden locket and chain.

459

At first, Patricia felt there had to be some sort of mistake. Although she thought the hair comb looked familiar enough, she was certain she had never once seen the locket. Curiously, she opened the casing to examine it further, hoping to find a clue as to who it might actually belong to. Inside, she found a small wedding band and a photograph so water-soaked that it no longer held an image. Further examination led her to notice that right across from the photograph was the surprising inscription: "To my wife, Kate, with all my love."

Patricia stared at the inscription in wonder and realized for the first time that Catherine must have actually been married and without anyone knowing a thing about it, but there was just too much plaguing her thoughts at the moment for the significance of that to really soak in. Placing the ring back inside the locket, she gently snapped it shut and slipped it into a small pocket at her waist, then rose from the bench and started toward the door—her thoughts half on the fact that Catherine had secretly been married and half on what to do about a burial.

"Sir?" she called to the man who now stood watching the two men as they picked their way through the many aisles of dead.

"Yes? May I help you?" he asked, already headed in her direction.

"What should I do about Catherine?"

"There's nothing you can do. Now that she has been identified, she will immediately be buried up on Prospect Hill. Her grave will be clearly marked so that you can later put up a proper headstone if you wish, but there will be no immediate services. There are just too many dead for that. You understand. We have to dispense with them as quickly and efficiently as possible."

"Of course," she rasped, choking on tears again as she turned away. There would be no flowers, no parting hymn. Catherine would have no proper funeral.

"Oh, and if you don't locate that other sister soon, you might come back because as you can well see, bodies are being brought in here all the time." While he spoke, two more were being hauled in and inserted into the empty spaces where other bodies had just been removed for burial. It seemed to be a never-ending process.

Praying fervently that she would find Jeanne and everyone else she sought and not have to return to this place, Patricia hurried on out the door. Once she stepped outside, she paused long enough to gulp down several breaths of fresh air. While she stood clutching her middle, she noticed another open cart loaded high with bodies pull up and stop only a few feet from her. Unable to take any more misery, Patricia looked away, but not before catching sight of a small boy in a dingy blue-and-white sailor's suit piled in among the dead.

Despite Andrew's earlier claim that the rescue efforts were now organized, there seemed to be no order to what went on around her as she made her way back through the devastated city toward the hospital. People milled about everywhere—some in groups, some alone—scavenging the ruins, still searching for the living as well as the dead. They appeared to be no better than walking dead themselves, for there was no food or drinkable water and very little shelter to be found. Everyone was cold, dirty, and hollow-eyed from lack of sleep. But still they searched.

Fires burned in a dozen different places across town. There was no electricity or gas, and no one knew when a broken gas main might leak out near one of the fires and cause an explosion, but they needed some source of heat in order to fend off the unseasonal cold.

The town needed help from the outside but there was no way to ask for it. Every telegraph and telephone line was down. Bridges were gone, roads impassable. The railroad, for all intents and purposes, no longer existed. And with all the dead lying about everywhere, some of them already bloated and black, plus the hundreds of carcasses of drowned horses, cows, pigs, dogs, cats, birds, rats, the threat of a violent epidemic was very real and extremely serious.

Patricia wondered when and if this horrid nightmare

461

would ever end. She wanted things to start getting back to normal. How could she ever find anyone in all this confusion? She had tried the Registry Bureau to see if anyone she sought might already be listed among the living, but even there she failed.

"Jeanne, where are you?" she cried out softly to herself as she glanced around her morbid surroundings. She felt such utter hopelessness. Where was Cole? Why wasn't he with her, helping her through this? If he truly loved her, wouldn't he want to be with her, see that she was all right?

Although the sky had started to clear, and for the first time in days there was no sign of a threatening raincloud, everything around her continued to look dreary, draped in a drab and doleful gray. The bright and bustling city she had loved so dearly was now dressed in its own death shroud and, other than the scraping of wood and brick as the wreckage was moved around, the air was mournfully silent. Pillars of smoke stained the somber blue sky while the heap of rubbish at the stone bridge continued to smolder and flame where the water gradually lowered, exposing more that would burn. Patricia could never remember having witnessed a more heartbreaking sight than the Johnstown that lay before her now.

A splintering crash sounded in the distance behind her and Patricia reeled around in time to watch one of the few remaining churches crumble slowly to the ground. It was Todd Street Methodist, the same church that had ostracized Andrew just last month. The blood-chilling screams that ensued made her skin crawl and she realized that many poor, unfortunate souls had sought their safety inside and had just met their death. Could one of them have been Cole?

Although her heart pounded with fear from the mere thought, logic told her that Cole would not have been inside. He would never be sitting around, seeking his comfort, when there was so much to be done. He would be out helping in some way. But could Jeanne have been in there? Or her father? Or Minnie? She felt faint as she thought of her loved ones being crushed to death like that and leaned heavily against a large pile of debris for enough support to keep her

462

from falling, only to be brought back to her senses when her hands met with the slimy mire that coated the mass. Determined as ever, she wiped her hand on her already filthy skirt and continued on her way to the hospital.

As soon as Harrison spotted Patricia entering the room, he went to her to hear the news. He was saddened to learn that Patricia had found Catherine's body, but relieved to the point of tears that Jeanne was not yet listed among the dead.

"At least now I can honestly have hope. And I no longer have to worry that her body is lying neglected at one of the morgues. Thank you, Patricia. Thank you so much."

"And I'm not through looking. I am still determined to find her. And, Cole. I just wish I knew where to look next."

"I don't know where Cole could be, but I've been thinking about it and I believe that if Jeanne is still alive and able that eventually she will see the house and go to it looking for me. But if she's injured, I feel certain she will be found and brought here. Why don't you go to the house and wait there for a while just in case she does decide to check it."

"That makes sense. I know I went there the moment I spotted it," Patricia agreed. "I'll do that. But if you hear from her or Cole, you will find some way to get word to me, won't you?"

"I promise. Andrew is in and out of here all the time. I'll send him if either Cole or Jeanne is brought in," he assured her. "And if she does come there, don't you waste any time in bringing her to me."

Even though nothing had really changed in the past few minutes, Patricia felt a little lighter in her heart as she walked back toward Harrison's house. They were working together to find Jeanne and Cole and had a logical plan. Suddenly the sky looked a shade bluer to her and the cold did not grip her with the same bone-chilling intensity. And for the first time she became aware of the faint sounds rustling behind her. When she turned to investigate, she discovered she was being followed.

"Well, hello there," she said in surprise as she knelt to pet the bedraggled little animal. "Have you been following me all day?"

Her thoughts had been so intensely centered on finding some trace of Cole or her sisters that she had completely forgotten about the dog. "Don't you know where your home is?"

When the shaggy little dog continued to peer up at her through the mud-caked hair that surrounded its eyes, she felt something inside her soften. There was a good chance his home did not even exist anymore. This little animal needed her. "Well, come on then. You can stay with me until we find some way to reunite you with your owner."

Wagging his tail in appreciation, the dog followed her the rest of the way to Harrison's house, though he no longer kept a safe distance behind her. Instead he stayed right at her heels. Patricia laughed at the noticeable excitement that showed in his shining black eyes and wiggling tail whenever she happened to look down at him. It was the first time she had laughed since the terrible ordeal had begun two days ago. It felt good.

When Patricia finally reached the house, she found that she was too keyed up to sit and idly wait for Jeanne. She needed to keep busy. Despite her exhausted state, she began the massive clean-up, starting with Jeanne's kitchen.

Using a sturdy flat piece of metal that she had found in the pile of rubble outside, she got down on her knees and started to shovel the mud and muck from the floor. Then, using a thick pine branch that the same pile of rubble produced, she swept the floor as clean as she was able to get it under the circumstances.

The cellar was still two feet deep in flood water, but the water had settled enough that she was able to put the clear top water to use cleaning the household items that had somehow remained inside the house, starting with the ground floor. Scooping the water into a dented laundry tub that she had found pressed up against the side of the house outside, she carried the water upstairs to the kitchen where the air was fresher and worked hard to clean everything in sight, putting the washed items wherever she thought they belonged when she was through.

By the end of the day, she had several rooms fairly clean. They could still use a good washing in soap and the furniture and floors a generous coating of beeswax, but at least they were no longer covered with mud, slime, and broken debris. She had even managed to drag most of the few pieces of furniture that were still on the bottom floor out into the backyard and scrubbed them as best she could with plain water. Then after the pieces were nearly dried, she pulled them back inside and placed them in whatever room they were supposed to be in. But there was one piece of furniture that baffled her, a small side table. As she washed it, she knew she did not recognize the design and wondered if it was even Jeanne's or had it been washed in with the tide. There was no way to really know until Jeanne finally returned.

Next Patricia went upstairs to take a look at the damage up there. She was delighted to discover so much of the furniture and belongings that they had stored upstairs was still there. Most of it was pressed up against the west wall, but somehow a lot of Jeanne's things had remained in the house. It wasn't because the flood had not tried because the water marks on the walls showed that the muddy water had risen a full ten inches above the level of the second-story windowsills. And it had been forceful enough to have broken out several of the second-story windows.

With less than an hour of daylight left, she started to sort through the scattered mixture of Jeanne's belongings, deciding what should be taken downstairs and washed first. When she went back downstairs, she carried down the first armload so she would have them ready to start cleaning early the following morning. She continued to work until it was too dark to see. She desperately wanted to keep her thoughts off the coming night and how she would be spending it all alone.

But she was not totally alone. The whole time she had worked, the dog had remained at her side. He never let her get fully out of his sight. Whenever she went down to the cellar for more water, he was right behind her and when she had gone upstairs to look around, he had run up ahead as if to assure himself no one was up there that might harm her. He was turning out to be far better company than she had realized he would be.

Just as darkness settled in, Patricia rewarded him by using a bit of the water still in the laundry tub to wash the matted dirt out of his hair. Once most of the dirt was gone, she ran her fingers through its length in order to get the tangles out and make him more comfortable. Once she was through, she rubbed some of the moisture from his thick coat with the hem of her own skirt.

When it became too dark to do anything else, Patricia went into the living room and made herself as comfortable as possible on the still damp sofa. As she expected, the dog promptly followed and curled up at her feet.

"Good dog. Get lots of rest. We have a long day ahead of us. There's still so much to do," she told him with a melancholy sigh as she pulled her wet boots off and placed her feet up beside her, tucking them under the driest section of her ragged hem in hopes of helping keep them warm. Once she was settled in, her thoughts turned to Cole and how his loving embrace would drive the clinging chill from her bones. Just the memory of his passion-filled kisses brought her heart a moment's warmth, but the warmth quickly passed, for he was not there and she had no idea where he might be.

She was extremely disappointed that Andrew had not come by during the day with any news of him. All afternoon, she had kept a constant watch for him, but Andrew never came, nor did Cole himself. And now that it was dark and the frigid night air was slowly creeping through the paneless windows, she wanted Cole more than ever. Tears of frustration spilled down her cheeks as she sat huddled in the corner of the sofa, staring off toward the Pennsylvania Railroad bridge where the smoldering fire still turned the night sky a ghostly shade of amber. The homeless pup lifted his head to look up at her then whimpered quietly as if he understood and shared her sorrow.

Laying her head against the back of the sofa, she stared into the darkness of the ceiling above her and wondered

466

again where Cole could be. He had to be out there somewhere. She felt sure he was alive. So why couldn't he take the time to let someone know of his whereabouts? Didn't he know about the hospital? Didn't he know Harrison would be there? Hadn't he noticed that Jeanne's house still stood? If he truly loved her, why didn't he come home?

Chapter Thirty-one

Patricia was finally able to block out the occasional cries of anguish and hunger that drifted in through the darkness and the eerie feeling that had come from having to spend the night alone in a desolate valley filled with unburied dead because at some point during the early morning hours she eventually fell into a deep, dreamless sleep. When she opened her eyes again, several hours had passed. Slowly, she roused herself to face another dark and dreary day. Another day of not knowing if the other people she loved had met fates similar to Catherine's. Poor Catherine, how she was going to miss her sweet little sister. Poor Tony, how hard it was going to be on him when he returned from New York to discover what had happened.

Easing her feet to the floor, Patricia became aware of the sharp, shooting pains in her legs and back. Pushing her sad thoughts aside, she leaned forward and rose from the sofa to stretch. More muscles than she had at first realized were sore, extremely sore. The cramped, aching pain left no part of her untouched. She realized she had spent too many hours lying huddled in the cold without moving. And she had abused her body by pushing it past its limits yesterday and knew she would probably try to do the same today. She needed to work and work hard. She had to keep herself too busy to worry, too exhausted to think, too numb to care.

When she walked across the damp wooden floor to the nearest window, she noticed that the peculiar stench that was now a part of Johnstown was more prevalent than ever. Through the paneless opening, she looked skyward and saw that more heavy clouds had rolled in during the night and that the weather once again looked like rain. The thought of more rain in the already drenched valley made her extremely apprehensive. It was the last thing they needed, especially now.

Her spirits plummeted further when she let her gaze drift down from the menacing clouds overhead to the ravaged city. Barely a dent had been made toward getting the mire and wreckage cleaned up, and in this neighborhood they had just begun to do anything at all. A few clean-up piles of rubble and debris burned where the work was going the strongest. Eventually, everything that had been rendered useless would be burned and nothing would be left of Johnstown but a vast wasteland jutted only by a very few buildings and even fewer trees. Only the youngest plant life had survived. The tall sturdy trees that had shaded the peaceful city and graced the lovely park had been pulled up by the roots or had snapped at the base as if they had been mere matchsticks.

Further scanning her bleak surroundings, she wondered just how many of the buildings could be safely left standing. That's when she noticed that much of the thick, heavy billows of smoke that rose and filled the mournful sky still came from where nature had cast its own funeral pyre at the railroad bridge. Here it was, Monday morning, three days later, and that wretched fire continued to burn. When would they ever get the flames out? Cheerlessly, she hoped that if it had to rain again, the moisture would at least help them finally get that fire under control, but then it would also make it next to impossible to burn the putrid rubbish that needed to be gotten rid of as quickly as possible.

Stiffly, Patricia pushed herself away from the window and the morbid sights. She glanced at the pile of filthy, grimy articles she had brought down the night before and placed beside the laundry tub but decided to put off any further cleaning until she had visited Harrison again. Some news might have come in during the night while there was no one available to run a message to her.

Eager to find out if there was any news about anyone yet, Patricia hurriedly washed her face and arms in the frigid water and rinsed the dried blood from her hair, finding the water's temperature extremely unpleasant but invigorating to a degree. When she ran the cold, wet cloth past her lips, she wished for the dozenth time that the water was drinkable. Her thirst was unbearable. It took all the willpower she had not to scoop up a handful and drink it down, but she knew better.

Trying not to dwell on her parched throat and swollen tongue, she forced aside thoughts of the water, keeping in mind how many had died and bled in it, and headed for the hospital. As she walked, she became aware of how extremely stiff and sore she really was. She suffered pain in far more places than she ever had before. There was hardly a place on her that didn't hurt when she moved. Wishing she could simply ignore the discomfort, she tried to convince herself that the exercise she was getting would eventually help work some of the soreness out of her tired, aching muscles. She was certain she would feel much better soon.

But by the time she reached her destination, she was not only as sore as ever before; the whole upper right side of her head had started to throb. The dull, pulsating pain centered itself just above her right eye, where the swollen cut had become much worse. Soon the pain worsened and ran hot trails down the side of her neck all the way to her shoulder.

At first, when she walked into the hospital in search of Harrison, she fully intended to tell him about the pain and hear what he had to say about it. Maybe there was something that could be done despite the lack of medication. But when she finally located him, he looked so haggard and hollow-eyed that she feared for his own health and decided not to bother him with her minor problems. She could bear the pain awhile longer. He had enough to worry about. There were too many people far more seriously injured than she was.

"You need to take a rest," she told him when he stopped working long enough to talk with her. "You won't be any good to anyone if you drop to the floor in a heap of exhaustion."

"I'm fine," he lied, then rubbed his hands over his pale, stubbled face as if trying to get the blood in his cheeks and around his eyes to circulate better. It did serve to give his sunken features a moment of color. "I look a lot worse than I feel because I haven't had a chance to shave yet." He frowned as he thought about that. "I don't even think I know where to find a shaving razor even if I was to manage to find the time, so you will just have to be understanding and forgive my appearance for now."

"It's more than the three days' growth of beard that worries me," she continued, undaunted. "You should see your eyes. They are all drawn in and you have dark circles an inch wide beneath them. Frankly, Harrison, you look terrible."

"Thanks," he muttered as he attempted to straighten his torn collar and adjust his blood-splattered coat. "I may not look my best today and I appreciate the concern, but have you looked in a mirror lately? You are not exactly in top form yourself. You look like you've hardly slept. And that cut of yours is getting worse. Let me have a look at it."

"Not unless you are willing to do it sitting down," she stated firmly and crossed her arms defiantly, stepping back when he made an attempt to move closer.

"Okay, okay. Let's go over to that bench over there," he said and indicated a small child's bench that sat against a nearby wall.

Although still adamant that he was not as tired as he looked, he moaned out a sigh of deep appreciation when he sagged down onto the bench beside her. But he paused only a moment before he leaned toward her, blinking his eyes as if he was having a hard time focusing. "Now, let me have a look at that cut."

Patricia sat perfectly still while Harrison lifted several strings of hair away from her forehead in order to see the cut, but she jerked her head sharply back when he gently prodded the red surface with his fingertip and sent sharp pain coursing through her.

"This needs to be tended to right now. It can't wait any longer," he told her. Then without giving her a chance to protest, he stood and hurried over to a huge wooden box that sat on a table near where he had been working and pulled out a large brown jug with a cork in it and a small piece of folded cloth.

"Although we still haven't received that shipment of medication we keep hearing is on its way, Alan Cross, an elderly man that lives somewhere up on Prospect Hill, brought us several jugs of his best homemade whiskey to use—elixir he calls it," he explained with a tired smile as he doused the cloth with a little of the jug's contents. Sitting back down beside her he warned, "Now, this is going to burn, but it will help wash out some of that infection. Be still."

Patricia gritted her teeth and clutched her fists so tightly that her nails began to dig tiny trenches into her palms as he firmly pulled the gap of the swollen cut open and applied the whiskey to the inside, washing the wound out as best he could. She had never felt such pain. Every muscle in her drew tight until she began to tremble from the intensity.

"There now, that's better," he said when he finally leaned away from her. "Take this cloth and hold it firmly over the wound. It'll bleed like that for another minute or so, but that's good for it. And even though I've cleaned it once, I still want you to come back when those supplies get here so I can clean it again properly and dress it."

"When do you think the supplies are going to finally get here?" she asked, swaying slightly as her body slowly relaxed and the pain subsided.

"I hear that one of the tracks has already been replaced between here and Pittsburgh. They supposedly have had around-the-clock crews working on it since Saturday morning. I understand that a relief train reached the depot sometime this morning, but that might simply be a rumor. I certainly haven't seen any signs of those medications or supplies yet. But if it's true, they could get here at any moment. It could be that they are having a time sorting through everything and getting it to wherever it should go. I hear the train also brought clothing, food, and drinking water among other things. They are calling it the survival train and it's rumored that the people who came with it plan to dispense all the extra food and supplies they brought directly to the public right there at the depot."

While Harrison told her more about what he had heard concerning the survival train bringing with it a crew of undertakers and possibly a few doctors, a soft, gentle voice interrupted him. "Sir? Dr. Rutledge?"

They both looked up and saw a young woman, about twenty years of age in a worn and muddy hospital's aide uniform, carrying a tray with a small stoneware pitcher of weak tea, a tall mug, and half a loaf of wheat bread. Patricia realized it was the same uniform Catherine always wore to work and felt a deep thrust of sorrow. Gravely, she blinked away the tears that had sprung to her eyes.

"Doctor, you need to keep your strength up," the woman went on to say as she set the tray on the bench beside him. Smiling apologetically, she added, "This is still the best we can do until the supplies from the train get here."

"Looks like a feast fit for a king to this hungry man," Harrison assured her with a smile. "Thank you, Bethal."

As soon as the young woman had left, he moved the tray over between them and tore the bread in half. "Here, Patricia, eat," he told her firmly. "And no arguments."

Having had nothing to eat or drink for nearly three days, Patricia was not about to refuse. Gratefully, she accepted the mug filled with tea and began to gulp it down.

"Slowly," Harrison warned with a frown and reached up to pull the mug away from her lips. "Take it in little sips."

Obeying his orders, Patricia began to take tiny sips, savoring the way the almost tasteless lukewarm liquid felt going down her dry throat. Next, she accepted her part of the bread and broke off a tiny piece and placed it in her mouth. Never had bread tasted so heavenly to her and she chewed it slowly to enjoy it to its fullest; but when it came time to swallow, she found that she couldn't. Her tongue was too swollen. "I don't think my stomach will accept food just yet," she finally said and sadly held the rest of the bread out to him. "I can't seem to swallow it."

"Nonsense, you have to eat," he told her, then poured more tea into her mug. "Here, try washing it down with this."

To her amazement, it worked. By following each tiny bite with a small sip of tea, she finally got the entire piece of bread down.

"Thank you for sharing with me," she said in earnest. "I do feel much better now. I knew I was thirsty, but I had no idea how hungry I was."

"Quite all right. I've already had two such meals," he assured her as he tore off a piece of his own bread and placed it in his mouth. "And there's more bread available if I want it. A Mrs. Clifton, Nell Clifton, who lives up on Prospect Hill is providing it for us. Her house is high enough that it was not affected by the flood and that saintly woman brings us all the bread we want. She also brought us water from her well to use in making the tea." Reaching a hand out, he asked, "Mind if I borrow the mug back?"

Patricia sat and quietly watched while Harrison ate his meager meal. As soon as he was through and had placed the tray out of their way, she asked the question that was foremost on her mind. "Have you heard any news at all concerning Jeanne or Cole?"

Shaking his head dismally, he replied, "Not a word. No one has seen either of them. Have you been back to the morgue to check there?"

"Not yet," she admitted. "But I plan to go by there next. I wanted to check with you first."

"I wish you didn't have to go back. I hear there are more unidentified bodies than ever, hundreds in fact." A faraway look was in his eyes as if he was trying to keep his thoughts distant from what he was saying. "And there are hundreds yet to be found. Despite this unseasonably cold weather helping to slow down the decomposing process, we still have a true fear of pestilence. The clean-up is taking too long. I hear they have barely made a dent in the wreckage, and although the flames are finally out at the bridge, the charred mass is still too hot in places to let them fully explore it yet. I fear they will find evidence of many more dead once they start prying that mass apart."

"At least the flood waters are still going down," Patricia put in, hoping to lift his downtrodden spirits with the only good news she could think of.

"Yes, the water is still going down—giving up more and more of its dead as it goes. Did you know that the death toll is now estimated to reach two or three thousand? Maybe even more."

A cold shiver ran down Patricia's spine at the thought of such a high number of deaths. Even after she had seen so many bodies at the morgue yesterday and had seen parts of bodies sticking out of almost every pile of rubble, she had never expected the death toll to be nearly so bad. Her eyes misted as she wondered if any of them would prove to be Jeanne. Or her father. Or Minnie. Or Faye. But she refused to consider Cole among the dead. She was still determined as ever to believe that he was alive. He was too strong and too smart to let himself be killed and she would never allow her nagging doubts to have full rein.

True to her word, Patricia went straight to the central morgue after she left the hospital. Although the pain at her temple was not nearly as severe now, she still had an annoying throb that bothered her whenever she made a rapid movement of any kind. Trying to keep her head as level as possible, which kept the pain at a minimum, she went inside to make her search.

When she first entered, she noticed that there were more undertakers on the job, preparing a huge backlog of bodies for burial. Pine boxes that had not been there the day before were now stacked as high as the ceiling and half filling the room. Patricia wondered where they had all come from and decided the rumor about the train must be true and that they had brought supplies for the dead as well as the living. A tear spilled from her eye as she wondered if Catherine had been buried in a box, or had she simply been dropped in the ground as she was. Blinking hard, she turned her attention to the task at hand.

As Patricia entered the main room where the unidentified were still being laid out in tightly packed rows for public

476

viewing, the stench became so overwhelming that she had to press her only sleeve against her face in order to breathe while she passed among the rapidly decaying bodies in search of Jeanne, her father, or Minnie. When she finished with the final row, she was so relieved to discover that no more of her family was found in among the dead that she started to cry with huge open sobs. Her knees almost buckled from the force of her relief.

Upon seeing her shaky tears, the man in charge rushed over to her with his list in hand, thinking she had spotted a loved one among the corpses.

"No, I'm not crying because I found anyone," she explained and stopped to sniff. "I'm crying because I didn't. Don't you see? There's still hope that my sister and my father are alive somewhere out there. And Minnie. And Faye. They must still be alive too." Patricia refused to even consider Cole or mention his name. That would be admitting her fear. No, she needed to believe he was still alive.

"I understand. And I hate to do anything to tarnish that new hope of yours, but there is still a chance one of them could be brought in at any time. You need to continue to check back with us at least once a day until everyone is accounted for. Because of the conditions here, we can no longer keep bodies for identification more than forty-eight hours. After that we will be forced to place them in unmarked graves with nothing more to help identify them than a description of what they looked like and what they had on, if anything. It's sad that they have to be buried with no name like that, but we have no choice. To keep them any longer would be risking the spread of disease. We certainly don't need that."

Patricia did not want to hear anymore. Holding her hand out to stop his constant chatter, she quickly promised to return the next day if she did not find her loved ones, then fled from the building, again overwhelmed by tears. Only now the tears she shed had nothing to do with the joy she had felt. Her hope had been so badly battered by what-all the man had said that she was again frantic with worry.

When Patricia returned to the hospital to tell Harrison

that she had not found Jeanne at the morgue, she immediately sensed something was not right with him. He had not sighed out with relief like he had the last time. And although he had already been pale enough when she had left, now he looked white as a sheet and the news she had just brought him did not help bring color back to his cheeks like she had hoped it would.

"What's wrong?" she wanted to know. "Is it Jeanne? Have you heard something about Jeanne?"

Harrison shook his head gravely. "No, it's not Jeanne." He took his gaze from hers and tried to blink away the misery that scalded his eyes. His voice broke from the emotional strain when he spoke again. "It's Cole."

"What?" she asked. Tears sprang to her eyes and her heart began to thud frantically against her breast. "What's happened? Where is he?"

Reaching out and taking her into his arms, he sobbed his anguish for a long moment before managing to talk in a barely audible whisper. "He's dead."

"No!" She shrieked and tried to pull herself free of his embrace, but he held her clasped tightly to him. "No! It isn't true. I don't believe you. Where is he? Take me to him."

Again Harrison had to struggle a long moment before he was able to explain. "I can't. I don't know where he is. A man, a Mr. McGuire, was brought in while you were gone to the morgue. He was up at the lake with Cole when the dam gave way. He told me how three men had been swept into the mass of water there right after the dam broke. Cole was one of them. The three were dashed to their deaths right before the man's very eyes."

"Then you haven't actually seen Cole?"

"No, but if he was swept into that mass of water and dashed against the valley floor, then there can be no hope."

"Oh, yes there can. Cole's not dead. I know he isn't. There's been a mistake. Maybe it was just a man that looked like Cole."

"Patricia, I wish I could agree with you and continue to give you hope. But the man saw Cole being swept into the water with his own eyes. There's no way he could

478

have survived."

"Yes, there is. Cole would find a way. He wouldn't die. He just wouldn't do that to me," she said quietly. "He wouldn't let himself get killed like that. He's alive. You'll see."

Harrison grabbed her by the shoulders and held her at arm's length. He stared curiously down into the calm depths of her green eyes. He had been fully prepared to deal with hysteria and tears, but had no idea how to cope with such strong denial. "Patricia, I don't think you understand. He is dead. A man actually saw it happen. He saw Cole do gown." His voice became low and constricted. "Cole died while making a final attempt to save the dam. He gave his life trying to save ours."

"You really believe he's dead, don't you?"

"It's the truth," he replied in earnest. Tears ran in steady streams down his drawn face as he thought of the crooked smile he would never lay eyes on again.

"I have to go," she said quickly and pulled herself free of his grasp. "I still have a lot of work to do to your house. I don't want it to be in such a terrible state when Jeanne returns. It would break her heart for her to see it the way it is. I think I'll go by the depot on my way and see if that relief train brought any soap with it. I can't get anything really clean until I can get hold of some soap."

Harrison watched with a heavy heart as Patricia turned and calmly walked away. He knew that eventually she would come to understand that Cole was indeed dead. And when that happened, it was going to be a devastating blow. He just wished he could be there to comfort her in some way when she finally did come to accept Cole's death. She did not need to be alone at such a time. She would need someone to help see her through it. But he was needed here. There was nothing he could do for her now.

After waiting in line for almost an hour, Patricia was finally given the box of soap she wanted. She was also handed a day's ration of food and drinking water wrapped neatly in brown paper and tied with cord. Before she left, she

479

was told that there would be clothing available later that afternoon should she or someone she knew need it.

Clutching her new possessions to her breast, Patricia left the depot. She was beyond being appalled by the dead bodies still entangled in piles of debris or by the clusters of people that had come to Johnstown to look upon the horrors. It was easy to pick out the sightseers from out of town by their clean clothes and neat hair. But it was gratifying to know that along with the morbidly curious sightseers had come helpers.

The supply train had been full of people interested in the flood for one reason or another. Some had come to assist in distributing the food and supplies fairly while some came to aid in the clean-up. Many came in search of loved ones. And some came because of their jobs. Artists were there to sketch the aftermath for the newspapers and more reporters poured in to get their stories. Even a few photographers had arrived and had set about taking their ghastly pictures. But far too many had come just to witness the death and devastation. Although the thought of that was repulsive, it no longer turned Patricia's stomach. She was too numb inside to be affected any longer.

Since the train was stationed at the Pennsylvania Railroad Station, Patricia had to pass fairly close to the bridge both coming and going. Water was still twenty feet high there. Acres of crushed houses, uprooted and broken trees, mangled railroad ties, rails, and all manner of unrecognizable refuse had been solidly hurled against the wide, stone bridge. The top layer of the jam was charcoal black and still smoldering in more places than not. Men worked constantly with picks, crowbars, axes, saws, and spades to break pieces loose and pull the charred remains of bodies from the blackened mass. Again it was a morbid sight, but strangely it did not affect Patricia in the least as she stared blankly at the gruesome sight.

While returning to Jeanne's house, the rain came again and with it rose a mournful wail from those who had grown tired of the torments God had heaped upon them. The intermittent crackles of thunder now seemed almost like sardonic chuckles of the demons who surely must rule the sky. Many had totally lost their faith in their God. They no longer considered him just, while others bonded together and made their faith stronger. Patricia wasn't sure what she believed anymore.

Turning her face away from the rain, she looked downward as she continued along her way. She watched with little interest as the huge drops of water splattered against the already wet earth and formed instant puddles. As she neared the place where Walnut Street had once lain, she thought she saw her own handbag lying half buried in the mud. Because the odds of finding it were so great, she stepped over and knelt beside it. She stared at it a long moment before she finally shifted her load to one arm and used the other to pull the handbag out of the mire. Untying the drawstring, she looked inside and found that her comb and a broken piece of a pencil was still inside. Everything else was gone. Reaching in, she pulled the comb out and quickly wiped away the dirt. Then while she still knelt, holding her belongings in one arm, she began to try to run the comb through her matted strands of hair.

That's when her roving eye spotted a masculine hand protruding out from under a door only a few feet away. On the hand was a familiar emerald ring. Hesitantly, she leaned over, lifted the door, and peeked beneath it. There, lying face up and staring at her with unseeing eyes was William. He had his valise clutched to his heart in a viselike grasp and his mouth was open in a soundless scream. Horrified, Patricia shrieked and dropped the door back over him. Clutching her load to her breast, she picked up her ragged skirts with her free hand and ran as fast as she could toward Jeanne's house, her heart hammering wildly against her chest.

When she finally reached what was left of her sister's yard, she dropped to her knees, faced the dark skies, and let the water pelt her skin, cleansing her. Ripping open the box of soap, she grabbed up a handful and roughly scoured herself with a demonic obsession until her skin was red and raw in places. But still she did not cry out her anguish. She had not shed a tear since her visit to the morgue. As she picked up a slime-covered bookend and carried it inside to wash it clean with the soap, she wondered if she was finally cried out, but had a feeling her tearless state was only temporary.

Eventually, the rain stopped again and the sun began to peep out of the lessening clouds late that afternoon. The air became warmer and more humid, but despite the rising temperature, Patricia continued to work herself to a frazzle, trying to keep one step ahead of her emotions. She didn't want to think of Catherine or William or the little boy in the dingy sailor suit, and she especially did not want to think of Cole. It was not until she dropped to the floor, exhausted, that she finally succumbed to the tears she was so desperately trying to hold back. These particular tears and the huge rasping sobs that nearly took her breath from her were for Cole. For the marriage she now knew would never be. For the children they would never have. For the love and laughter they would never again share.

Lying face forward with her cheek pressed against the cold floor near a broken-out window in what once had been the main salon, her senses were assailed by the sickening stink of the damp wood and mildew but there was nothing she could do about it. She was unable to find the strength to get up. Her muscles refused to respond. A shadow fell over her as she lay there wondering how long until her strength would return, and at first she assumed she was on the verge of passing out, but she soon realized that the shadow that had come over her was from someone standing just outside the window, looking in at her.

Fear tore through her limp body and her insides quivered as she realized what was about to happen. There had been many reports of violence and looting throughout the city. Reportedly, people thought dead but in fact still alive had had their fingers cut off just so a looter could obtain a valuable ring. Others had been beaten senseless simply for the food they possessed. Thieves preyed on the weak and injured and Patricia realized he had already spotted her as an easy target.

But even her fear did not give her the strength to get up or even speak. She wanted to tell him to take what he wanted and leave her alone; but the words did not form. She was defenseless and stared in weak horror as the tattered man climbed right through the window to get to her. She heard Scruffles growl when the man stepped inside and she felt her heart cringe with fear. Giving one last desperate effort to get up and run, a pain grasped her and before she was able to get to her knees, she buckled back to the floor. Sadly, she made no further attempt to get up. She realized it didn't matter what the stranger had in mind for her. Life was not worth living with Cole gone. Slowly, she slipped into unconsciousness before she was able to discover her fate or even get a good look at the man's features. He was never more than a blurry shadow that loomed over her.

Chapter Thirty-two

"Patricia? Patricia, speak to me." Cole kneeled on the wooden floor beside her and quickly rolled her over into his arms. He was shocked to see how pale and drawn her face was. The brown hair that fell down around her face looked stark in comparison. Drawing her head into his lap, he tried to revive her by patting her cheek with his palm. When she did not respond at all to his touch, his heart began to hammer sharply against his chest and his voice became frantic. "Patricia? Please, speak to me."

Having just made his way to Johnstown from eighteen miles down the Conemaugh River, Cole had no idea where to turn in order to get help. From what he had seen of the city, he was not too sure help was even available. But he had to do something. He had to at least get her off the cold hard floor and make her comfortable and warm.

Lifting her into his arms, he was instantly aware of how much lighter she felt and wondered how she could have lost so much weight in such a short time. She felt practically weightless to him. After discovering that the only place to lay her on the lower floor was a small, cramped sofa, Cole carried her on upstairs in hopes of putting her to bed. But when he discovered the beds were so mildewed that they made his eyes water, he searched out somewhere else to lay her. Finally, he found a large leather couch that had fared well and gently placed her on it. Again he attempted to wake her but failed. Panic filled him. What was wrong with her?

Why couldn't she wake up?

Fighting his tears, he pushed her hair back away from her face in order to place a delicate kiss on her temple and noticed for the first time the large swollen wound on her forehead. Fear wrenched his heart as he realized his beloved Patricia had been badly injured—so badly injured in fact that it had rendered her unconscious. Kneeling on the floor beside the couch, he bent over her pale limp form and held her close. He had no idea what to do for her other than comfort her and keep her warm. He hoped that all she needed was rest and time. Time to fight the infection. Time to heal.

Patricia grew steadily worse as the night drew on. Cole never left her side throughout it all. He continued to take care of her, cooling her hot cheeks with a damp cloth during her fevered fits and calming her with a soothing voice when she cried out in her dreams. As the night passed, he grew curious about the dog that also remained at her side, never more than a few feet away. Although he sensed the dog was still extremely wary of his presence, the animal seemed to accept the fact that he meant Patricia no harm and had stopped his incessant growling. For the last few hours, the animal had simply lain nearby with his eyes trained on Patricia, waiting.

By morning, Patricia's fever was worse than ever. Her cheeks had become bright red against her pale skin and Cole's concern over the intensity of her fits finally caused him to leave her side in order to seek help.

"I want you to watch her and keep anyone from coming up here and harming her," he said to the dog as he rose to his feet. "I'll be back with help as soon as I can." He knew the dog would protect her. The animal had already shown his protective instincts where she was concerned. He just wished he could order the animal to make sure she did not try to get off that couch and roam around in her fevered state. Taking off his tattered work shirt, made of heavy flannel, he placed it over Patricia's exposed feet. "Take care of her. And don't let anybody near her."

The dog must have sensed what Cole had said for he

486

wiggled closer to Patricia's side and began to growl again.

"Good dog," Cole said and reached down to pat him. At first the animal cowered away as if expecting a blow, but when he discovered Cole's hand was friendly, he offered his head for more. Cole smiled at the animal's acceptance.

"Now remember, you are in charge until I can get back," Cole said before he left the room and headed toward the stairway.

When he stepped outside and felt the brisk damp air on his bare skin, he looked around and wondered which way to go. He wanted to find Harrison if he could. As he started toward where the most buildings still stood, he offered a quick prayer that if and when he did find Harrison, his friend would still be alive.

After questioning several people, Cole learned about the hospital that had been set up in the schoolhouse. He felt certain that if Harrison was still alive he would be there helping. As soon as he reached the door, he asked the first person he saw who looked like a doctor if he would be able to find Harrison somewhere inside.

"You might have had he not succumbed to exhaustion during the night," the man told him. "Even after all these doctors from Philadelphia and Pittsburgh arrived, Harrison continued to help out with the injured and the multitude of sick. On top of all the ones that were hurt in the flood, hundreds are now coming down with pneumonia. Harrison, being as stubborn as ever, refused to rest as long as he felt he was needed and worked on and on until finally he dropped. We refused to let him work at all after that."

"Where is he now?" Cole wanted to know, looking on past the man in his eagerness to find Harrison. Even if he couldn't go with him to Patricia, maybe he could tell him what to do for her. Maybe what she had was pneumonia. If he could just get Harrison to get him the medicine, he would give it to her exactly as he was instructed.

"We had him taken over to Dr. Pyle's house over on Locust to be cared for by Laurence's wife. For some reason, Dr. Pyle's house received very little damage and Laurence is letting certain people stay there and be cared for away from this crowded environment. I understand Dr. Matthews is there too. I'd tell you to go on over there to visit Harrison, but he really needs his rest right now. In his weakened condition, he just might come down with pneumonia too."

Morosely, Cole realized that Harrison could be no help after all and he certainly couldn't expect any of these doctors to drop what they were doing to go with him in order to see what was wrong with Patricia. He could bring her here, but as he surveyed the crowded conditions of the hospital, he wondered if that might not do more harm than good.

When he returned to Patricia's side, he was still undecided as to what to do. She was a strong woman, but would she be strong enough to fight whatever was wrong with her without proper medication and care? And as weak as she was, did he dare carry her into that den of sickness and death?

Lost deep in thought, he knelt beside her and took her hand in his again and pressed it to his cheek. In doing so, he discovered that her fever had climbed higher still. He simply could not risk her health any longer. Pulling his shirt up higher over her, he lifted her into his arms and carried her out of the house. Anxiously, he turned toward Locust Street and plowed right over the huge piles of refuse that stood in his way. As he stumbled over the debris in his haste, he prayed that the doctor's wife would have a kind enough heart to take Patricia in too.

When Cole reached Locust Street, he was surprised to discover that Dr. Pyle's house not only stood with no noticeable structural damage, it still had glass in most of its windows and even a front door. It was a curious sight to see it standing upright in among all the ruin that surrounded it. It was as if the water had parted and gone around in order to preserve this house.

With Patricia pressed securely against his chest, Cole went directly to the door and tapped it with his foot as a way of knocking. Eventually, the door opened and a tall black man wearing an unmarred jacket and clean shoes greeted him.

"May I help you?" he asked, eyeing the small, limp form in Cole's arms.

"I need to speak with Dr. Pyle's wife," Cole responded

firmly and stepped on inside. He was not going to be turned away.

"Come in," the man said and with a sympathetic smile moved back so that Cole could step further inside. "But the dog has to stay outside until he has had a proper bath," he said and gestured to the little animal at Cole's heels. Closing the door before the dog could get inside, he went on to say, "Mrs. Pyle is busy right now, but you can go ahead and put the young woman down on the sitting-room couch." He gestured toward a door to the right then added, "I'll go ahead and tell her you are here. Who shall I say is calling?"

Knowing she would not know his name, he said, "Just tell her that I'm a friend of Harrison Rutledge's in need of help."

The thin man nodded and promptly left the room. Moments later, Harrison himself entered.

"Cole, what the devil are you doing here?" he asked with openmouthed amazement. "We thought you were dead."

"I came close a couple of times, but I'm not here for me. I'm here for Patricia," he said as he gestured to the couch.

"What happened?" Harrison asked as he hurried to Patricia's side.

"I don't know for sure. I went by your house and found her lying on the floor. She was already like this. But when I first saw her, I thought her eyes were open and I even thought I detected movement, but I must have been wrong. It was dark. I tried to rouse her, but couldn't so I made her as comfortable as I could. At first, she slept calmly, but sometime in the night she began running this high fever and talking out of her head. I got scared, Harrison. I didn't know what to do for her."

"You brought her to the right place," Harrison commented as he pulled Patricia's eyelids back with the edge of his thumbs and examined her pupils. "Bring her on upstairs. She can have my bed."

Remembering what the doctor at the hospital had told him, Cole knew he should argue that Harrison needed the bed for his own rest, but Cole was too concerned for Patricia. "I'll follow you" was all he said.

As they made their way up the stairs Harrison began to

explain their neat, orderly surroundings. "Laurence's house has been turned into a kind of hospital in itself. Dozens of his friends and family have been brought here for special care, away from the crowded conditions at the main hospital and away from the problems those crowded conditions are causing."

"So I was told when I went to the hospital looking for you."

"Then you also heard how I nearly passed out. Odd feeling. But I've already started to recover. Once I got a hardy cup of chowder in me and a few hours' rest, I felt much better. I've started helping Mrs. Pyle with her patients. I guess I could go on back to the hospital, but since all those other doctors have arrived, I'm not as needed there as I feel I am here. Laurence is having to divide his time between this place and the hospital and I'm afraid the hospital is getting most of it."

"If you'll just show me what to do, I'll help in any way I can."

Harrison stopped just outside an open door, turned toward Cole, and smiled broadly. "Now, how did I know you were going to say that?" Then gesturing toward the doorway, he said, "In there. I'll be right back. I need to get something to clean and dress that wound. I'll also see if I can get her a clean gown to wear."

Moments later, Harrison returned with a small woman at his side. In her tiny hands was a large pitcher of warm water, a towel, and a fresh white gown.

"If you gentlemen would kindly step outside, I'll do what I can to make this poor girl more comfortable," she said without waiting for introductions. "Harrison, you can come back in once I have the gown on her and tend to her, but right now you are needed down in Bradford Kayeby's room. He just tried to get out of bed and tore his stitches apart in the process. He's bleeding again."

"That was Dr. Pyle's wife," Harrison explained once they had been hurriedly ushered out of the room by the tiny woman. "She is no nonsense all the way. I think she'd make a damn good doctor herself. Too bad she's a woman. Wait here while I go tend to Bradford. It shouldn't take too long. Then I'll see what I can do about getting you a shirt and maybe even a bath."

The thirty minutes Cole had to wait for Harrison's return seemed like hours. Then when Mrs. Pyle refused to let him enter Patricia's room with Harrison until he had indeed had a good bath, Cole started to become frustrated. He wanted to be with Patricia, but realizing the little woman meant business, he followed her directions to the bathing room downstairs where he would be provided enough warm water and soap to bathe thoroughly. While he was bathing, the black man who had answered the door entered with not only a clean shirt, but clean trousers, underwear, and stockings as well.

"Missus Pyle said I was to bring you these clothes. She said it was the closest thing we had that might fit you," the man told him as he laid the clothing on a stool.

"Thank you . . ." Cole paused and waited for him to fill in his name.

"I answer to most anything, but my name's Abraham," he said with a smile as he gathered up Cole's dirty clothes from the floor.

"Thank you, Abraham. And tell Mrs. Pyle thank you too. She is being far too courteous considering the circumstances."

"I'll tell her," he said. "Will you need anything else?" When Cole assured him there was nothing else, Abraham smiled once again and left.

When Cole took the folded pair of dark gray trousers from the stool and slipped them on, he discovered that the legs were inches too short, and the blue and gray shirt was extremely tight across his shoulders with sleeves that hit his arms just above his wrists, but knew the clothes would do until his own could be washed and dried. Despite the odd fit, it felt good to be bathed and in fresh clothing again.

After he returned to Patricia's room, he discovered that everyone was already gone. She was alone in the room and resting peacefully. The clean white bandage on her forehead let him know that Harrison had already been there and had

491

tended to her wound. A grateful smile spread across his unshaven face and he knew he should do something for Harrison but wondered what. The first thought to cross his mind was to go back to his house a little later and secure it from looters.

Quietly, he entered the room and knelt by Patricia's side. In a loving gesture, he brushed her cheek with his fingertips. She now wore a soft white gown and lay on crisp, clean sheets. Her freshly washed hair was combed back and away from her face. If it wasn't for the deep flush of her cheeks and the dark gray semicircles that curved down from her eyes, she would look like she was simply sleeping and would wake up at any moment. There was no longer evidence of pain in her features.

"She's been given something to help bring down the fever and ease her pain," Harrison explained from the doorway.

Cole jumped, startled at the sudden appearance of his friend. "Is she going to be all right?"

"That's hard to say," Harrison said honestly. "She's in very, very bad shape and I've already done all I can for now. About all we can do now is see that she gets lots of rest. I'll know more in a few hours." He paused a moment and he gazed sadly down at her peaceful expression, then turned and started for the door. "You need to get some rest too if you are to be any help to anyone. We still have a few cots not in use yet. Pretty sturdy ones at that. I'll send one in. You can set it up right in here if you want and get yourself some sleep, but I'll have to have it back if any more patients get brought in here. The cots were sent to us for use as hospital beds."

"I don't need . . ." Cole started to say but realized his words came too late. Harrison had already left the room.

Moments later, Abraham appeared at the door carrying a large bundle of canvas and wood. "Where do you want this set up?" he asked, his eyes scanning the small room for a likely spot.

"Just lay it down. I'll put it up myself," Cole told him and did just that as soon as Abraham had left the room. Knowing Harrison's request was a sound one, he lay down on the cot and tried to get some sleep so that he would be in better

492

shape to help. But despite the fact that he hadn't rested in over four days, he was unable to fall asleep. The harder he tried the more he worried about Patricia and the more restless he became. Finally he got up and went in search of Harrison to see if there was anything he could do to help, to keep busy.

When Harrison refused to find something for him to do and ordered him back into Patricia's room to get some sleep, Cole decided to go on back to Harrison's house and board up the windows and doors. It would give him something constructive to do with his time and hopefully help keep him from constantly worrying about Patricia.

By the time he reached Harrison's house again, the sun had already vanished behind the hill and nightfall rapidly approached. Having secured a pocketful of nails from a work crew, he went straight to work searching out the sturdiest boards from the debris in the yard and a large rock to use as a hammer. As soon as he figured he had gathered enough planks and pieces of flat wood, he picked up an armload and carried them inside, ready to get to work.

As he entered the room where he had found Patricia earlier and bent over to drop his load in front of one of the windows, he noticed a woman and a small child crouched on the small sofa in the far corner. It was too dark to make out their identity so he stepped closer and greeted them with a simple "hello."

There was no response. He stepped closer still and saw that the two were either asleep or dead and his heart began to pound furiously in his chest when he realized that the woman was Jeanne. He had no idea who the young girl held so tightly in her arms might be, but the woman was definitely Jeanne.

His stomach coiled into a tight knot when he reached out to touch her and discovered she had already gone cold. She was dead. He closed his eyes with overwhelming despair and sank to his knees. Why couldn't he have come earlier like he'd planned? Maybe it would have made the difference. Tears scalded his eyes as he choked out her name. Every teasing word he had ever said to her came immediately back to haunt him. "Jeanne, Jeanne, I'm so sorry."

To his amazement, she stirred. "Jeanne? Jeanne? Can you hear me?"

Slowly, her eyes opened and she offered him a weak smile. Next the child stirred in her arms and Jeanne gently nudged her. "Wake up, Amy."

Overwhelmed with relief, Cole pulled them both into his arms and held them close. His voice trembled with emotion. "I thought for a minute you were dead."

"Who, me?" she asked in a shaky voice. "Never. Amy and I are very good at taking care of each other."

"Amy?" he questioned.

"Yes, meet my new friend, Amy Clifton. Her father works at Cambria Iron's company store and plays baseball for the Quicksteps. They got separated during the flood. I promised to help her find her parents and her baby sister. Amy? This is one of the friends I told you about. This is Cole Gifford."

The girl looked at him through wide blue eyes. "Me and Mrs. Rutledge were washed all the way down to Sang Hollow. On top of a house."

Cole smiled at the lively animation in her face. "I know what that must have been like. I was carried all the way past Nineveh on a tree trunk."

"We met one man who said he had gone further than that. He told us he had been washed clear to New Florence," the little girl told him with a solemn shake of her head. "I guess we were pretty lucky that a man at Sang Hollow threw us that rope like he did. I wonder how far down the river my parents got washed."

"We'll have to ask them when we find them," Jeanne put in, wanting to keep the little girl's hopes up.

"That's a good idea," Cole said quickly. "For now, though we need to get you out of here and over to Dr. Pyle's house so that Mrs. Rutledge's husband can see that she is all right. He's been worried sick about her."

Jeanne's eyes lit up. "Harrison's alive? I was worried sick about him. We went by where the hospital used to be and I saw how all that was left was a small abutment that had once been part of the front steps."

494

"Yes, he's alive. Come on, I'll take you to him. Can you walk?"

With renewed strength, Jeanne stood and reached out a hand to the little girl. "I'm fine. Come on, Amy. I want you to meet my husband. He's a doctor and can see to that cut you have on your shoulder."

The little girl frowned suddenly. "Will he give me a shot?"

"Probably not," Cole assured her with a chuckle and scooped her quickly into his arms. "There's nothing to be afraid of. Dr. Rutledge is a good doctor."

The little girl looked skeptical, but finally nodded her agreement.

"Cole, it's wonderful to see you. I was so worried when I got back to Johnstown and saw how much destruction there was. I was afraid everyone might be dead. Is Harrison really all right? How about everyone else?" she asked eagerly as they made their way through the dark toward Locust Street.

"Yes, Harrison is fine. He's working himself too hard, but other than that he's doing just fine. Maybe you will be able to convince him to rest a little. No one else can seem to."

"That sounds just like Harrison. He's stubborn as a mule when it comes to his work. I'll see what I can do," Jeanne said, relieved. "And what of everyone else? Do you know what has become of anybody else? What about Patricia? Have you see Patricia? Was she with you when the flood hit?"

"No, I was still at the lake when the dam gave way, but I have seen Patricia." He paused, wondering if he should tell Jeanne how sick her sister was or wait and let her judge for herself. There was a chance Patricia had improved, was finally awake, and he might have worried Jeanne for nothing.

"Where is she?"

"She's with Harrison. I'm afraid she's been injured and is under his care right now."

"How bad is it?"

"That's hard to say. I only got to talk to Harrison for a moment. He's very busy."

"Have you seen Catherine?"

"No," he replied simply. He did not want to be the one to tell her.

"How about Father? Or Minnie? Have you seen either of them?"

"No, I haven't. I didn't get back to Johnstown until late yesterday afternoon and I'll admit I spent all my time looking for Patricia. I haven't had much of a chance to try to locate anyone else. I came across you purely by accident."

"Well, I'm going to start looking for them first thing tomorrow," Jeanne said adamantly as they stepped up onto the narrow walkway in front of the Pyles' house. Just before they reached the door, she ran her hand down over her tattered dress then reached up to touch her tangled mass of hair and asked worriedly, "How do I look?"

"To Harrison, you are going to look like a dream come true."

Chapter Thirty-three

"How is Jeanne?" Cole asked the moment Harrison had stepped back out into the hallway where he had been forced to wait for nearly half an hour.

"I had to sedate her," Harrison said, concerned. "Maybe I shouldn't have told her about Catherine yet. For some reason, she blames herself for her sister's death. She claims she is the reason they stayed in town instead of heading on up to Green Hill." Shaking his head, he rubbed his tired, stubbled face with his hands. "I know I should have kept my mouth shut, but she just wouldn't quit pestering me for information. She could tell I knew something. And I never have been able to get a lie past that woman."

"At least now that she's sedated she'll get the rest she needs," Cole said in an effort to console his friend. "How's the little girl?"

"She's asleep in a cot right next to Jeanne's. Other than a nasty little cut on her left shoulder, the girl's fine, just tired. Came through the whole ordeal like a little trooper."

"And Patricia? How's she doing?" he asked, almost afraid to hear the answer. He had caught a glimpse of her when he had carried Jeanne into the room, but had been run out of there in such a hurry by Mrs. Pyle, that he did not manage to get a very close look but knew that Patricia was still unconscious.

"No change. She still has a high fever and is comatose. But if you look at it on the up side, she's no worse either. You can go in and sit with her if you like. Jeanne's decent now. Just be quiet."

"What about you?" Cole asked as he looked down into the hollow eyes of his friend. "When are you going to get some rest?"

"I'll be back in a little while. I've got to make one final round then I'll come back here and stay with Jeanne for the rest of the night. I'll probably catch some sleep then."

Jeanne slept through the night, morning, and late into the following afternoon. When she finally awoke from her drugged stupor, she found it hard to focus on anything around her. Groggily, she stared at the ceiling until she was able to make out the intricate pattern of the plaster inlays. The ceiling did not look familiar to her. She wondered where she was.

Feeling something solid and warm beside her, she rolled her head to the left and looked down to see what it could be. She found Amy snuggled close to her side. Only inches away from them was an empty cot—evidently Amy's. Slowly, she started to remember until she again knew where she was. Blotting out the fact that she had learned of her sister's death, Jeanne smiled at Amy's sweet face, resposed in sleep, dreaming a child's innocent dream. It pleased her that Amy had been provided a bath and her pretty golden hair had been washed and brushed until it shone with sparkling highlights. Her ragged dress was gone and a soft white sleeping gown was in its place. To Jeanne, it looked like she had a precious little angel lying fast asleep in her arms.

When her gaze finally drifted up from the child's sweet face, she noticed Patricia lying in a nearby bed, also sound asleep. Her heart jumped with quiet joy at the sight of her older sister. When her gaze deflected to a slight movement in the far corner of the room, she discovered Cole nodding off in a large, upholstered chair with his feet propped up on the edge of Patricia's bed. He looked terrible. His dark hair fell loosely forward across his forehead and he had not shaved in days. And although his clothing was clean, his trouser legs were torn and frayed at the hem and his shirt had a gaping hole near the front pocket, exposing part of his lightly haired chest beneath. Jeanne quickly drew her sight to his boots on the floor at his side. They were also scuffed and torn. She realized Cole had somehow been caught in the flood too, then slowly she remembered his telling them how he had been washed as far as Nineveh and had been forced to walk back to Johnstown like she and Amy had, which was no easy task as muddy and rain-soaked as the countryside was.

A slight movement near his boots caught her eye and she was startled to see a small, long-haired dog lying beneath Cole's chair with his big brown eyes trained on her. When the dog realized she was looking at him, he lifted his head and began to wag his tail.

"Good morning," she said softly, and brought Cole to with a start.

"You mean good afternoon," he responded and blinked his eyes in an effort to bring himself back fully awake.

"Afternoon? How long have I been asleep?" she asked, the dog temporarily forgotten.

"Oh, I'd say about eighteen hours now."

"Eighteen hours?" she said more in a surprised response than as a question. "I had no idea I'd been asleep for so long. How's Patricia?"

"Still hasn't come to," he replied and glanced over to his beloved's sleeping form. "But her fever is finally coming down and her coloring is much better."

"Have you been here all this time?"

"Except for a few hours this morning. You may as well know, I've put myself in charge of all three of you. I'm totally at your beck and call. Your every wish is my command," he said obediently as he put his feet back on the floor and bowed forward, causing the chair to tilt and the dog to duck his head. "By the way, it's about time for you and Amy to take your medicine."

"What medicine?"

Reaching behind him for a large brown bottle that stood on the dresser, he told her, "This medicine. Harrison is afraid you might catch pneumonia, especially after having been out in the cold damp air as long as you two were. It's mostly a precaution. Can't have the doctor's wife getting sick. It just wouldn't look right."

"I'm not sick. That medicine should be given to the ones who are really sick."

"Don't worry. There's plenty of it to go around now. Several relief trains have come in and brought more than enough medicine. Clara Barton has arrived with her Red Cross crew and brought more medicine and medical supplies than Johnstown will ever need. And there's also enough food now. People from all around the country have generously been sending us relief supplies of all kinds. In fact, as soon as you've had your medicine, I'm going to go down and see if I can't get you a bowl of hot soup and some fresh-baked bread. Some for Amy too."

Amy stirred a moment, but did not wake up. Instead, she snuggled closer to Jeanne, then was still again.

"Maybe you should wait until she's finished sleeping," Jeanne told him. "I hate the thought of wakening her."

"You're probably right. She does need her sleep. But I'll go on down and get you something. How about a good hot cup of tea to go with it? With sugar and cream?"

"Sounds good, I guess." She paused a moment and frowned as her thoughts took in more of what had happened the evening before. "Why didn't you tell me about Catherine?"

Cole glanced toward the window a moment, then looked back into her accusing gaze. "I started to, but I just couldn't do it. I know how you loved your sister. I didn't want to be the one to tell you."

Staring him directly in the eye, she asked straight out, "Is there anyone else dead I should know about? If so, tell me now."

"There are thousands dead, I'm afraid, but no more of your family that I'm aware of. I have not heard a single word either way about your father or Minnie, nor of your housekeeper, Ruby. But, I did see Andrew Edwards this morning, when I went out to check on Amy's parents. He's doing just fine and told me that he got Tony on that train

500

on time, so he's probably still safe in New York. I asked about your father and Minnie as well as my sister, Faye, but he hadn't seen or heard from any of them. He did direct me to a place where they are keeping a list of the living so I could check to see if Amy's parents might be listed there. I'm afraid they weren't. And before you ask, yes I did think to look for everyone else, but other than a few co-workers of mine, I didn't recognize many of the names listed. I don't think the list is really working effectively. Too many people don't know about it."

Jeanne frowned. "They actually have a list for the living?"

"Yes, they are trying to simplify the searches everyone is doing, looking for lost loved ones, trying to find out what became of friends and family. As soon as I left there, I went to the central morgue just down the street."

"And?" she asked nervously.

"Is Amy still asleep?"

Jeanne bent over and stared at the child a long moment, then nodded. "Sound asleep."

"I did find her parents listed there. They are both dead. No baby sister was listed though. But I don't hold much hope that the baby can still be alive if the mother is dead."

Staring down at the child with tears glistening in her eyes, Jeanne sobbed. "How tragic. Poor Amy. How did you find out her parents' names?"

"She was awake for a little while this morning and eager to talk about her family."

"Poor thing. How am I ever going to tell her?"

"I wouldn't right away. I think you should wait awhile. Give her time to get her strength back. The flood took its toll on her too, not quite like it did on us older folks, but it did just the same. Besides, by waiting, we might be able to locate some of her relatives or someone else she knows really well. Maybe having someone she knows and loves with her when you tell her will help soften the blow. Do you know if she has any relatives?"

"Yes, she has an uncle and aunt right here in Johnstown. Her aunt's name is Stella Duncan and her husband is associated with the street car company, but I can't remember

501

what she said his name was. I agree. It might be best to wait and tell her after we have located the whereabouts of these relatives."

"I think it would."

Still misty-eyed, Jeanne pulled the child closer and held her firmly against her. Her maternal instincts surfaced. Suddenly, she found herself wishing she could have Amy to raise as her own. She would see that the girl was raised right. If it turned out that the child's aunt and uncle were also dead or for some reason unable to take her, she intended to talk Harrison into adopting the girl. More tears brimmed her eyes as she wondered if it might be possible. Would Harrison go along with the decision? He had often mentioned wanting children, but he had meant children of his own—children she had as of yet been unable to give him. If Amy turned out to be a true orphan, would he agree to taking her into their home?

"Where's Harrison?" she asked as she sniffed back her tears. Quickly she put her emotions in order. She wanted to talk with Harrison about Amy's fate as soon as possible.

"He went to the hospital to get more medication about an hour ago," he told her, but failed to mention that Harrison also planned to stop back at the morgue to see if her father's body had been brought in during the seven hours that had passed since Cole had been there. "He should be back any time now. Do you want me to see if I can find him for you?"

"Yes, tell him that I need to talk to him."

At that moment, the door opened and Harrison stepped inside.

"Like I said, your wish is my command," Cole said with a large grin as he indicated Harrison's arrival.

Jeanne's eyes went lovingly to her husband. Despite the fact that he had finally found the time to shave, his face was haggard and worn. He looked exhausted, but as he walked over to greet his wife, a loving smile slowly lifted his features.

"Guess what?" he said as he bent down and kissed her lightly on her cheek. "Minnie's alive."

"She is?" Jeanne asked eagerly. "How do you know?"

"Saw her myself. She was brought into the main hospital

502

early this morning. She was very ill and her scalp had to be stitched back into place, but she's alive and doing as well as can be expected. She's been lucid ever since the operation. In fact, I'm afraid she talks as much as she ever did." He chuckled, hoping Jeanne would join him, but she didn't.

"Her scalp had to be stitched back into place?" Jeanne asked, horrified as she reached up to touch her own hair.

"Yes, seems she was trapped in all that junk that jammed up at the bridge. Her shoulder was pinned in by a board or something and her hair was caught by something else. She never knew exactly what had her. When the fire broke out, it was very near where she was trapped and the men that rescued her realized they did not have time to try to pry her loose. She was too deep into the mass. They had to jerk her on out of there right then if they wanted to save her life. In the process, though, they tore her scalp loose. But don't worry, Christopher English did a fine job of stitching it back. She's going to be as good as new in a few days and her scar will hardly be noticeable."

Jeanne closed her eyes and sighed aloud. "At least she's alive." When she raised her lids again, her eyes were moist with joy. "Did you have any luck finding out about anyone else. Had Father been admitted?"

Harrison's eyes cut away from hers and sought Cole's for a brief moment then darted over to Patricia's restful face. The smile faded from his face and deep grooves furrowed his pale brow. Finally, he spoke. "No, your father had not been admitted to the hospital."

Jeanne eyed him for a long moment. "You're not telling me everything. You know something about my father, don't you?"

"Yes, I'm afraid I do." He knew better than try to lie to Jeanne.

"What about Father?" she asked, her voice quivering with an overpowering apprehension.

Harrison's face tightened, his eyes barely meeting hers.

"He's dead?"

Harrison nodded as he sank to the floor beside her. "He was also trapped in that treacherous pile of wreckage over

503

at the bridge. Only they were unable to pull him out in time. He was buried too deep and there was just not enough time to pry the boards and tree limbs holding him. He had a chance to be rescued first. Minnie told me how the rescuers had actually reached him before they even knew about her, but that your father had demanded they find Minnie and save her first. It took several minutes to pull Minnie free. There was not enough time left to save your father too. He died in the flames."

Jeanne pressed her eyes closed and bit hard into her lower lip. Clenching her fists beside her until her knuckles turned deathly white, she prayed that the pain piercing her heart would hurry and pass. Losing both her sister and her father was almost too much for her to bear. Quickly, Harrison bent forward and held her close until her tears finally rushed out.

"And, Cole, I might as well tell you now, there's more. I discovered that Tony is dead too. The day express never made it beyond East Conemaugh. I came across his body while looking for Clayton and Faye. I identified him so that he could be buried right away. I asked that he be buried near Catherine, but they said that was most likely impossible, but would see what they could do." Harrison watched with heartfelt sympathy while Cole turned his face away from them and bowed his head. He could tell by the tightening of his friend's neck muscles that he was struggling hard with his emotions so Harrison politely averted his gaze and pressed his cheek against Jeanne's forehead. Silently they wept together while, absently, he reached one of his hands down and gently stroked Amy's golden hair. So much hurt, so much grief, so much death. Would there ever be an end to it?

Early the following morning, Cole was called on by a committee of townsmen that had been picked to survey the huge pile up at the bridge. The men who came to see him were some of the same ones that at one time had shunned him for his radical ideas concerning the dam, only now they openly sang his praises for his amazing foresight. Cole felt their songs of praise came a little late and had almost refused

504

to see them.

When he did finally go downstairs to see exactly what it was they wanted with him, he was told they sought his opinion concerning the problem at the dammed bridge. They wanted his advice as a professional engineer to help them decide exactly what should be done to break up the tightly packed, almost solid structure made of the twisted wreckage from the flood. Days prior, the men had been put in charge of cleaning up the dam as quickly as possible and had already tried steam-powered cranes and heavy duty levers, but the going was too slow for that. The threat of disease was getting to be too great. The water seeping through the mass was so contaminated that people and livestock as far away as Pittsburgh were getting sick just bathing with it. They had to loosen the pack and dispose of the decaying bodies as quickly as possible. They found they needed expert advice on how they should go about doing it, having already rejected the idea of simply burning it down to the ground. Too many still hoped to find traces of loved ones inside. And just that morning a small child had miraculously been pulled out of the depths still alive.

Cole went with them immediately to look over the massive heap that stretched for acres and as soon as he saw how tightly woven the wreckage was, he quickly agreed with another man's suggestion. Dynamite was the only solution. If placed well away from the bridge and in the tightest packed areas where it would be hardly likely anyone could have survived anyway, they could loosen up the mass and not risk any structural damage to the bridge at all. Once loosened, they should be able to pry the rest of the jam free with relative ease.

Helping to choose just the right spots to blast and the amounts of dynamite to use at each place, Cole stayed on to help until nearly nightfall. The dynamite worked. The cranes were now able to remove huge pieces of debris with little problem and the discoveries beneath the wreckage were gruesome. As soon as he felt he was no longer needed, he made his excuses and left. He did not think he could stomach much more; besides, he was too worried about Patricia to

505

stay away any longer.

That afternoon, Harrison had been forced to return to the hospital once more to see if he could get a hold of more bandages. Not having anticipated the number of patients that would end up at the Pyles' house, he had badly underestimated how much he would need. When he went to the small room that was being used to store the incoming supplies, he came across Andrew huddled to the floor. He was bent forward with his knees drawn up under his chin. His face was completely covered by his broad hands.

Without a word, Harrison walked over to him and slid to the floor beside his friend. Not knowing what else to do, he reached an arm around Andrew's shoulder and quietly comforted him. He did not need to ask. He was becoming very adept at detecting grief. He realized Andrew had learned of some loved one's death, possibly Tony's. Or maybe the enormity of it all had finally worn him down. Whatever the cause of his tears, Harrison wanted to comfort him.

After a long moment of silent weeping, Andrew lifted his face away from his open hands and stared at Harrison. His eyelids were swollen and tinted red as if he had been crying for quite some time.

"Faye just died."

"Faye?" Harrison felt his heart constrict and his own eyes started to water as he conjured up a vivid picture of her always ready smile.

Andrew nodded. "She was brought in here unconscious late yesterday afternoon. I was here when they brought her in. This morning, even though she had not come to, it had started to look as if she was getting better. But then she died." His voice broke with another loud rasping sob, then he again gasped for control of his emotions. "She never woke up. I had so much I wanted to tell her, but she never woke up. I loved her. Did you know that? Did you know that I loved her? I did, you know. I loved her dearly."

"We all did," Harrison said quietly as he raised a hand to

506

dash away a tear. Briefly, his thoughts went to Patricia. She too was unconscious, appearing to get better. Would she share Faye's fate as well? Fervently, he hoped not.

"No, Harrison, I *loved* her. As a man loves a woman. As you love Jeanne. I loved her with all my heart. I never had the courage to tell her because she, she . . ."

"Because she was a nun," Harrison surmised and shook his head sadly.

"Yes. Because of her vows to God. I knew she could never love me back. She already belonged to another. It was reflected in everything she did or said, even in the poetry she wrote. But I wanted her to know how I felt. I wanted to tell her. If she had woken up, I planned to tell her everything. I wanted her to know how I felt."

Harrison bent his head forward a long moment, then raised it and stared up at the ceiling, trying to focus on anything but the pain he felt. He was straining against the overpowering urge to break into bitter weeping. "I'm sure she knew. A woman has ways of knowing those things."

"But I wanted to tell her myself. I wanted to find out how she felt about me. Maybe I had no right, but I stayed by her side all morning waiting for her to wake up so I could tell her just how I felt and how I needed for her to get well. But she never woke up. She died. Damn it, she died."

Harrison did not have the words to satisfy his friend. He simply held Andrew close and let him pour out his heart and soul. His own emotions broke free and he began to sob uncontrollably along with his friend. Tears spilled unrestrained down his cheeks. Then he thought about Cole. How was he ever going to tell Cole of his sister's death?

Chapter Thirty-four

The putrid odor of death clung to everything, so strong in some places that the search crews had to tie handkerchiefs doused in whiskey around their faces in order to continue their work. Others simply doused themselves and remained in a drunken stupor for days on end, but even so, they continued to work.

As Cole made his way back toward the Pyles' house, he had to cover his nose with his hand just to keep his stomach from retching. The stench got so strong near the huge pile of bricks, slate, and books where the library had collapsed that his eyes watered and lungs refused to accept the air. Choking, he hurried past until he was able to breathe again though still through his cupped hand.

When he entered the Pyles' house, he quickly shut the door and leaned against it as if hoping to keep the horrid smells and the grotesque images of all he had seen that day on the other side. After a moment of holding his breath, he finally dared to take another lungful of air. The pungent odor of medicine and the imploring aroma of a baking ham filled his nostrils as he stepped away from the door.

"Harrison," he called out, having spotted him on his way down the stairs, bent slightly while he talked with Mrs. Pyle.

Harrison looked up and lifted a finger as if to ask him to wait one moment as he continued to talk with Mrs. Pyle. When he finished, Mrs. Pyle turned and headed back up the stairs while Harrison walked toward Cole. The solemn expression on his face made Cole's heart plummet to depths unknown.

"What's wrong? Is it Patricia?"

Harrison stared at him a long moment as if he had not fully understood what Cole had asked. His gaze was centered somewhere over Cole's left shoulder.

"What's happened? Is she all right?" Cole grabbed Harrison by the sides of his face and turned him so that he had to look at him. "Is Patricia all right?"

Harrison blinked with noticeable confusion, then his eyes turned to Cole's and he looked at him as if he had just noticed him for the first time. "I'm sorry. I have so much on my mind right now that I can't seem to keep my thoughts straight."

"You look exhausted," Cole commented, his brow drawn with worry. "You can't keep this up. What I wanted to know is how Patricia is."

"I'm afraid there's been no change."

"Shouldn't she be coming around by now? The fever's been down for quite some time. Why doesn't she wake up?"

Harrison shrugged. He was not sure she would ever wake up. Just moments ago another patient who had been unconscious for nearly two days had died. That was six he had lost since he had come to the Pyles' house. "I don't know. I'm doing all I can for her. I swear it."

Cole saw such deep agony reflected in Harrison's eyes that he felt his heart go out to his friend. "I know you are. I just wish there was something else we could do. I wish there was something I could do. I feel so helpless."

"So do I," Harrison said and his gaze drifted off into the distance again. "So do I." With his head tilting slightly to one side, he walked off toward the kitchen.

Cole wished there was some way to make Harrison rest. In the past six days, Harrison had only slept twice that Cole knew of. Once had been right after he had nearly passed out Monday from working too hard at the hospital and had been forcefully brought here and put to bed. The only other sleep he could remember Harrison getting was the following

Tuesday night, and only for a few hours then. Something had to be done to stop Harrison from gradually killing himself.

As he slowly climbed the stairs and headed down the hall toward the last door, Cole's thoughts shifted from Harrison's self-destructive conduct to Patricia's lack of improvement. His heart felt heavy, made of lead, as he reached for the door handle. He hated to think of her dying, but knew it was a distinct possibility. He wondered if he would be able to bear the heartache. He paused just outside her room in order to wipe away all evidence of the tears that had just sprung to his eyes.

It took all the strength Patricia had to try to open her eyes. It felt as if someone was pressing down on her lids, holding them shut, forcing her to remain in the dark.

She was able to hear voices in the distance. Soft voices. Whispering voices. She wanted to see who it was. She wanted to find out where she was. Finally, she managed to lift her lids enough to see her first rays of light. So unaccustomed to its brightness, she squinted her eyes shut again, then slowly tried it again. Turning her head toward the sound, she tried to focus on whoever was talking but found that her surroundings were too hazy. She blinked a few times, in an attempt to clear her vision, but everything continued to look as if she was peering through a thin veil of tears. Her eyes fought to close again and she let them.

For several more minutes, she lay there listening to the voices until she felt she had to try one more time to see who was there. She felt too weak to call out to them. Slowly, she opened her eyes again and this time her vision was clear. She could finally see Jeanne sitting on a cot on the far side of the room bent over and playing with a little girl. They were both looking down at a small rag doll the girl held cradled in her arms. Patricia felt so overwhelmed with relief at seeing her sister still alive that she tried to call to her, but nothing came out. Why was she so weak?

Letting her gaze drift away from Jeanne for a moment, she began to wonder where she was and how she got there. Drawing her brow together in an attempt to remember, she felt a sharp stab of pain. Relaxing her face, she remembered the wound on her forehead and the sliver of glass she had pulled from it. She also remembered being at Jeanne's and working frantically to get the awful mess cleaned up. Why had she been so adamant about cleaning that house? She remembered working as hard as she could, pushing herself beyond her own limits. Working until she had literally dropped.

She pressed her eyes closed. She remembered. Cole was dead. She had been trying to keep from facing the fact. And Catherine was dead. Patricia felt herself start to tremble as her grief bit deeply into her heart. Who else had been killed? She couldn't remember. Opening her eyes again, she discovered her vision had again blurred. At least Jeanne was still alive. And Harrison. And Andrew. But she wondered if she was very glad to still be alive. What was life without Cole?

"You're awake!" she heard Jeanne exclaim with glee. "Patricia, you're awake."

Patricia tried to focus on her sister, but couldn't for the rush of tears that still spilled from her eyes. Still unable to find her voice, she simply nodded.

"I was so worried," Jeanne sobbed as she gently set Amy aside. Hurrying over to where Patricia lay weak, Jeanne slipped her arms around her and lifted her sister into her embrace. "I was so afraid you might die."

Emotion knotted in Patricia's throat, but eventually she was able to speak. Closing her eyes tight, she found the strength to hug her sister closer to her and cried softly, "I thought you were already dead. I looked everywhere for you." Biting into her lower lip, she tried to hold back her sobs, but found she was unable to. Weeping uncontrollably, she clutched her sister to her breast. "Hold me, Jeanne. Hold me as close as you can."

"I will," Jeanne promised in a high, strained voice. "I will."

Lost in their intense need for each other, neither sister noticed the door slowly open or even that Cole had stepped inside and stood staring at them in joyous disbelief. When Patricia finally opened her eyes again, her gaze was drawn to his wide-eyed form standing just a few feet away. Her breath caught in her throat. She was afraid to move, afraid to even blink, for fear his image would disappear. She knew her blurred vision was playing tricks on her. He wasn't really there. He couldn't be. But she was willing to go along with the cruel deception for as long as she could. For one last precious moment, she could believe Cole was still with her.

"Patricia," he said as a smile slowly stretched across his face and he bounded toward her.

"Cole?" she asked, her head starting to swim. Had her vision actually spoken to her?

Jeanne pulled away about the time Cole reached the bed. "Cole! You're alive!"

"And you are finally awake," he exclaimed as he sank to the bed beside her and pulled her into his arms and clasped her to him.

"Am I? Am I really awake? Are you really here?" she asked as she pulled back enough to search the silvery depths of his glittering blue eyes. Quickly, she reached up and felt of his rough, unshaven cheeks, then let her fingertips curl toward his lips and feel the warmth there. Trailing her touch along the soft contours of his mouth, she started to tremble. "I thought you were dead too. Someone told Harrison they actually saw the water sweep you away at the dam. They told him you had been plunged to your death. Harrison said if that was so then there was no way . . . you had to be dead, you had to be."

"And miss our wedding?" he asked as if insulted by such a thought. Then in spite of their small audience, he gently lowered his lips to hers in a long, lingering kiss, drawing her as tightly to him as he could. The sweet torrent of their love stirred vibrantly between them. "Not a chance. It would take much more than what I've been through to keep me from marrying you. Much more. Even a mountain of water is no match for a man in love."

"Nor a woman in love," she murmured and drew him to her for yet another kiss.

"Just promise you will love me forever," he said softly as his lips played gently against hers.

"Forever. If not longer."

Epilogue

"I don't care what Harrison says, I feel fine and I'm going to the cemetery with you," Patricia protested. "Just because I'm going to have a baby in a few months doesn't mean I have to be pampered so. I'm tired of being ordered to stay inside all the time."

"But most women don't go out after they get as"—Cole paused as he tried to find a delicate word to describe Patricia's greatly swollen middle—"as round as you are. They prefer to stay inside and out of sight. And they enjoy being pampered."

"Maybe that's so. But I'm not most women." She folded her arms over her protruding stomach and narrowed her green eyes. "And I want to go with the three of you to visit the Grandview Cemetery today. I want to visit Catherine's and Father's graves and I want to be there when the new governor dedicates that special monument to the hundreds of unknown dead."

Cole gave up. Even though he was not so sure it was proper for Patricia to continue to be seen in public as far into her pregnancy as she was, he refused to argue with her about it. If it didn't matter to her, why should it matter to him? Besides, whenever she was this set on doing something, there was not much he could do to stop her. She was far too independent for that.

"What could happen anyway?" she went on, sensing that his resistance had already weakened. "I'll have my doctor right there with me the whole time."

"All right, all right. You can go. But we are not going to stay very long. We will visit the graves, hear a few of the speeches, and leave."

"As long as I get to go," she concluded. "I don't want to miss today's ceremonies."

Exactly three years had passed since the terrible disaster had swept through the valley, and in that time Johnstown had managed to rebuild much of what the flood had washed away. Even so, there were huge scars that would never be erased. There were thousands of people who were sorely missed. And even though James Seale and several others had testified during the official inquiries that had followed the disaster, the fishing and hunting club had never been brought to justice.

As Cole and Patricia rode the short distance to Harrison and Jeanne's new home over on Maple Street, they passed the spot where Patricia's father's house had once stood. A three-story graystone house now stood proudly in place of the red brick that had once been Patricia's home. Two small children played idly in the yard. Usually, Patricia tried not to think about how dreadfully she missed her father and her sister, but today was a day to reflect back. To try to remember Johnstown the way it had been. To remember those who had died. To miss and mourn the many who had meant so much.

Almost everyone in Johnstown had a reason to visit the cemetery that day, the third anniversary of the flood—not just because of the scheduled dedication of the new monument. Almost everyone had lost someone to the flood. Thousands of people, dressed in their funeral best, milled about. They filled every section of the vast rolling cemetery—visiting the many gravesites, fighting tears, and clutching loved ones.

As early in the day as it was, more than half of the graves were already decorated with a colorful assortment of flowers and as soon as Cole had pulled up along the narrow lane leading into Grandview, Patricia and Jeanne gathered up

516

their own bundles of flowers and hurried straight to the graves of their dear sister and father. Despite the fact that Clayton's body had never officially been located, Patricia and Jeanne chose to have a memorial stone with his name placed next to Catherine's grave when they had had her body moved from Prospect Hill shortly after the flood.

None of them was particularly surprised to see the elaborate array of flowers that was already on Catherine's grave. Just like what had happened the two previous years, someone had gotten there before them and had placed the lovely mat of pink and white flowers over the grave. And just like in previous years, whoever had brought the flowers was already gone, leaving them no clue as to who he was.

After Jeanne carefully arranged two bundles of the flowers they had brought with them at the bases of both Catherine and their father's stones, they all paid their teary respects then went to place what flowers they had left on the nearby graves of Tony and Faye. They had even brought a small bouquet for William's grave even though one of the fake copies of the petition that Cole had been keeping at his house had been found inside the valise he had been found still clutching to his breast even in death, as well as a note from Frank Gordon insinuating he would fullfill whatever plans William had for Cole as soon as he could. The note had been dated the day before the disaster, but because Frank Gordon had also died in the flood, they were never quite sure just what these plans might have been.

After quietly having placed the flowers they had brought for Tony at the base of his headstone, and the ones for William at his, they next approached the site of Faye's final resting place. Andrew Edwards was already there, sitting on a small granite bench, staring absently at her headstone. He had already placed a large bouquet of mountain laurel on her grave, knowing they had been one of her favorites.

The moment Cole spotted him, he walked over and laid a sympathetic hand on his shoulder.

"How are you, Andrew?" he asked quietly, turning to look at his sister's elaborately ornate gravestone. He fought the initial pang of remorse as he read the inscription for what had to be the hundredth time. It was taken from one of Faye's own poems as Andrew had remembered it:

> Miss me,
> Yes.
> Remember me.
> Yes.
> But do not mourn for me,
> Yea, cease.
> For in my final rest,
> I have eternal peace.

"I'm fine," Andrew responded softly to Cole's inquiry then broke his gaze and looked up at his friend. "And you?"

"Nervous as any expecting father should be." He smiled and nodded toward Patricia who was overseeing how Jeanne arranged the flowers around those Andrew had already laid at the base of Faye's headstone.

Andrew smiled. "She's looking well."

"Even though she refuses to stay inside and rest like she is supposed to. She's being very stubborn about that."

"I can imagine." Andrew nodded and laughed gently. "Patricia is not one to cut herself off from the rest of the world. If she is still refusing to stay inside come next Sunday, bring her to the Franklin Street Methodist Church to hear me speak. Maybe I'll choose the topic of obedience." He laughed again and looked back up at Cole. "Although I haven't quite decided whether or not to accept the ministry there, I have agreed to offer several sermons. Sort of a trial run I guess you'd say."

"I'm glad to hear it. I hope you take the ministry there. I know you've had several other offers, but I think your work can be best done in a larger church."

"I'll admit I am leaning more and more toward the idea every day." He let his gaze drop back down to the gravestone and his warm smile faded. "I do miss her. I miss her dreadfully."

"I know. I do too," Cole said and gave Andrew's shoulder an understanding squeeze. "She was one of a kind—special. Even when we were children she had a heart of pure gold."

"I would have loved to have known her back then," Andrew said and a half-smile lifted his face as his gaze returned to the headstone.

"We are headed over to the far side of the cemetery for the dedication, which is due to begin at any minute. Why don't you walk over with us?" Cole invited.

"No, I think I'll sit here awhile longer with my thoughts," Andrew told him. "For some reason I feel closer to my memories here. But you four had better hurry on. It sounds to me as if the ceremonies have already started."

Cole took Patricia by the arm and Harrison did likewise with Jeanne as they left Andrew. In mutual silence, they crossed the long sweep of green grass and walked beneath the darker green of the sparsely set trees. On the way to where the crowd had gathered for the special ceremonies, they passed near where Laura and Lowell Edison were placing a small bouquet of flowers on the tiny grave of their stillborn baby With them was a pudgy little boy with a perpetual grin who Patricia recognized as the flood orphan Laura and Lowell had decided to adopt shortly after both his parents had been identified among the dead.

"Hello," Patricia called out to them as they drew closer.

"Oh, hello," Laura greeted just before her eyes dipped down to take in Patricia's well-rounded form. Then gazing down at her own protruding middle, she giggled. "I wonder which of us will be first?"

"Maybe it'll be a tie," Patricia replied warmly, but wanted to turn to Cole and say, "See I'm not the only one who refuses to stay hidden away." Managing to restrain herself though, she visited with Laura a moment. Since Laura and Lowell had decided to move to Altoona shortly after the flood, the two women rarely saw each other, but because of all they had shared during the after crisis of the flood, they had promised to never forget one another and wrote occasionally.

519

After a few minutes of their catching up on all that had happened since last they had exchanged letters, a loud round of applause was heard coming from the crowd that had gathered at the far side of the cemetery and Cole felt inclined to give his wife a polite nudge. "We are about to miss the dedication entirely, dear."

"Okay, okay, I'm coming," she said as she gave Laura a look of both apology and exasperation. "Do write when you get the chance." Then she was gently pulled away.

As they approached at the rear of the crowd, they could hear the governor, Robert Pattison, speaking through a megaphone, and judging by the teary eyes of many of those around them, his speech had already touched many hearts. Leaning gently against Cole, Patricia cocked an ear toward the raised platform where she could barely see the man's head and listened carefully to his final words: "We who have to do with the concentrated forces of nature, the powers of air, electricity, water, steam, by careful forethought must leave nothing undone for the preservation and protection of the lives of our brother men."

Again everyone broke out with applause and an unseen choir raised their voices and sang "God Moves in a Mysterious Way." The large granite monument was then unveiled and many stood and stared at it, strangely motionless for several minutes, before turning away and slowly making their way back down the winding road that led to town.

Patricia and Jeanne remained silent, inwardly reflective, until they reached Cole and Patricia's house. The only words spoken during the short ride back to the city had come from Cole and Harrison and had mostly dealt with the weather. It was not until the women had changed from their mourning clothes and into their usual dress that their moods eventually lifted. While they worked together to get supper ready for their two families, since Minnie had been given the day to share with her sister, they were finally able to discuss openly what they were feeling.

"I took the locket with me again to the cemetery today,"

520

Patricia told Jeanne as she gently dropped a mound of chopped carrots into a large iron pot.

"In hopes of giving it to whoever leaves those flowers on Catherine's grave?" Jeanne asked without looking up from the large stoneware bowl of cake batter she was adding ingredients to.

"Yes, I honestly believe he is the one who should have it. After all, he must be the one who gave it to her. He was her husband."

"I wish we had gotten there early enough to meet him this time. I'd like to know what Catherine's actual last name was at her death. I think her gravestone should be changed to include that name. It would be the proper thing to do. Catherine would have wanted it," Jeanne said, pausing in her task as she thought about her sister. She blinked back the moisture in her eyes as her heart wondered what it would be like to have her there with them at that very moment.

"Next year I am determined to get to the cemetery in time to meet him," Patricia said, determined. "Even if it means getting there at the crack of dawn and waiting for him to appear. I had hoped to get an earlier start today, but Cole wouldn't hear of it. Not in my present condition."

"You still believe it is Franklin Hitt, don't you?"

"Yes, I do. And I want to meet him. I want to tell him how touched I am by his strong loyalty to Catherine's memory. I want to get to know him. There's a part of our sister we never knew that only he can provide for us."

Jeanne thought about that. It was true. Catherine had had a side neither of them had ever known about. She had been a married woman. She had loved enough to keep that marriage a secret even from them, knowing that if her father had found out, he would have sought the man out and done what he could to destroy that marriage. How hard that must have been for her.

"Momma?" Amy's voice cut through the room and jolted both women from their melancholy thoughts.

"Yes, dear?" Jeanne responded and turned to watch her daughter bound into the kitchen, her shiny blond curls

521

bouncing gaily behind her.

"When is supper going to be ready? I'm hungry," she complained as her sparkling blue eyes scanned the table for signs of what they might be having.

"It will be a couple of hours yet," Jeanne told her, then spatted the child's hand when she tried to stick her finger into the cake batter. "You go on outside and play. I'll call you when it's time to wash up."

"Yes, ma'am," Amy replied with a pout and reluctantly turned away.

"Amy? Why don't you go see if you can find Scruffles? He has a new playmate you might be interested in," Patricia told the girl, hoping to find something her niece might be interested in. "Remember, I told you how he had fathered a fine litter of pups with a dog down the street? Well, we were given the pick of the litter. We now have a little Scruffles."

"Does the puppy have a name?" Amy paused at the door to ask.

"Not yet. Why don't you go out there and play with him awhile and see what you would name him? If you like him, maybe your mother will let you take him home as your very own." Patricia offered as she looked over to take in Jeanne's raised eyebrow.

"Thanks," Jeanne muttered.

"She needs a dog," Patricia defended herself. "Look at how much fun she always has playing with Scruffles. Besides, if the pup is anything like his father, he will make a wonderful watch dog."

"Maybe," Jeanne said, refusing to commit herself until she had spoken with Harrison on the matter.

Before Patricia could offer more arguments in favor of Amy having her own puppy, Cole and Harrison entered the kitchen through the back door. Already they both had come out of their coats and ties and had rolled up their shirt-sleeves in an attempt to get comfortable.

"Was that little whirlwind that just passed us Amy?" Cole asked as he walked over to give Patricia a gentle kiss on her cheek.

"Yes it was," Patricia replied and smiled at her husband's tender show of affection.

"How long until we eat?" he wanted to know as he stepped over to the stove and peered under the lids of the different pots and pans to see what delights awaited them. Harrison was right behind him, peeking over his shoulder and commenting over his favorites.

"It will be a couple of hours yet," Patricia said with an exasperated sigh as she watched Harrison lean over the edge of the table and try to sneak a taste of the cake batter with his finger.

"Ouch!" he complained when he received a sharp rap on his hand from his frowning wife.

"You should know better. We just shooed Amy out of here for trying that exact same thing," Jeanne scolded him, trying not to grin at the boyish pout of her husband's face.

"Yes, Harrison, you should know better," Cole berated him while he edged sideways toward the door with his hands obscurely hidden behind his back. "You should have more willpower than that. What's a couple of hours anyway?"

Patricia skirted the work table she had been standing behind and hurried to the door to stop him before he could pass through. "Give them to me," she said as she held out her hand. "Those are for after supper."

"Whatever do you mean?" Cole replied, his eyes wide with false innocence.

"Hand over those cookies." Without giving him a chance to argue his cause, she reached around him and confiscated the cookies then ordered him out of the kitchen. "Just because you now hold a position of some authority at Cambria Iron does not mean you can come in here and do as you please or take what you want. The kitchen is my domain. Vice president or no vice president, you are not going to fill up on cookies or the like before supper."

"But you know what a sweet tooth I have," he insisted but realized she was not weakening in the least. Finally, he sighed. "Very well, I'll go, but can I at least have some little something for my sweet tooth?"

523

"No."

"Not even a little kiss?"

Giving in to a delighted laugh, she agreed. "I guess a little kiss isn't going to do you any harm."

"In that case, I'll have half a dozen," he said with a throaty growl and gently pulled her into his arms.

"Take all you like," she murmured as she lifted her hands to his neck and met his loving kisses halfway.

Each month you'll receive 4 brand new Zebra Historical Romance novels as soon as they are published. Look them over *Free* for 10 days. If you're not delighted simply return them and owe nothing. But if you enjoy them as much as we think you will, you'll pay *only* $3.50 each and save 45¢ over the cover price. (You save a total of $1.80 each month.) *There is no shipping and handling charge or other hidden charges.*

—————— Fill Out the Coupon ——————

Start your subscription now and start saving. Fill out the coupon and mail it *today*. You'll get your FREE book along with your first month's books to preview.

CAPTIVATING ROMANCE
by Penelope Neri

CRIMSON ANGEL (1783, $3.95)

No man had any right to fluster lovely Heather simply because he was so impossibly handsome! But before she could slap the arrogant captain for his impudence, she was a captive of his powerful embrace, his one and only *Crimson Angel*.

PASSION'S BETRAYAL (1568, $3.95)

Sensuous Promise O'Rourke had two choices: to spend her life behind bars—or endure one night in the prison of her captor's embrace. She soon found herself fettered by the chains of love, forever a victim of *Passion's Betrayal*.

HEARTS ENCHANTED (1432, $3.75)

Lord Brian Fitzwarren vowed that somehow he would claim the irresistible beauty as his own. Maegan instinctively knew that from that moment their paths would forever be entwined, their lives entangled, their *Hearts Enchanted*.

BELOVED SCOUNDREL (1799, $3.95)

Instead of a street urchin, the enraged captain found curvaceous Christianne in his arms. The golden-haired beauty fought off her captor with all her strength—until her blows become caresses, her struggles an embrace, and her muttered oaths moans of pleasure.